My Swordhand is Singing

'a scary, satisfying read . . . Sedgwick has taken early vampire legends and masterfully crafted them into this dark tale. His story is like a journey into a beautiful gothic painting.' *Daily Telegraph*

'this masterly, well-crafted vampire story breathes new life into the tale of the living dead . . . a well-written book with wide appeal.'
The Bookseller

'Vampire legends brought vividly to life in a finely written, bone-chilling gothic tale . . . Expertly researched and rich in detail, the slow, creeping sense of menace and myriad horrors of the deep woods will transfix readers.' *Publishing News*

'a beautifully written, atmospheric, gothic fantasy . . . Sedgwick maintains tension, pace and mystery throughout the book.' *Inis*

The Kiss of Death

'With his formidable skill, Marcus Sedgwick renders Venice the most perfect backdrop for this intensely gripping vampire action.' *The Bookseller*

'gripping . . . What makes Sedgwick such an interesting author is not just his imagination, which has a consistently unpredictable and original cast to it ... but his voice . . . The pared-down Sedgwick style is . . . both dramatic and effective' Amanda Craig, *The Times*

'he is superb ... at creating atmosphere . . . Sedgwick is also tremendous at that worst form of horror, when a trusted person turns out to have gone over to the dark side . . . the book is a class act.' *Guardian*

Marcus Sedgwick

THE SWORDHAND
OMNIBUS

Includes

My Swordhand is Singing

and

The Kiss of Death

Orion
Children's Books

This omnibus edition first published in Great Britain in 2011
by Orion Children's Books
a division of the Orion Publishing Group Ltd
Orion House
5 Upper St Martin's Lane
London WC2H 9EA
An Hachette UK Company

1 3 5 7 9 10 8 6 4 2

Originally published as two separate volumes:
My Swordhand is Singing
First published in Great Britain 2006
by Orion Children's Books
The Kiss of Death
First published in Great Britain 20068
by Orion Children's Books

The Orion Publishing Group's policy is to use papers that are
natural, renewable and recyclable products and made from wood
grown in sustainable forests. The logging and manufacturing
processes are expected to conform to the environmental
regulations of the country of origin.

A catalogue record for this book is available
from the British Library

Printed in Great Britain by Clays Ltd, St Ives plc

ISBN 978 1 4440 0276 8

www.orionbooks.co.uk

Contents

MY SWORDHAND
is SINGING

Marcus Sedgwick

For my father

Acknowledgments

I would like to thank various kind people for their help. Thanks once again to Fiona Kennedy at Orion for her usual insightful comments throughout the writing of the thing, and to Elizabeth Roy for her continued support. And thanks also to Matt Whyman, who reminded me about Joseph Campbell just when I needed reminding.

This is my seventh novel from Orion and it seems an opportune time to express my deep gratitude not only to the Orion Children's Books team, but also the Orion sales team, all of whom continue to do a wonderful job on all of my books. Thank you everyone.

"Once, they were as plentiful as the blades of grass in the meadow..."

Contents

Eastern Europe
– early 17th century

The Land Beyond the Forests

The Song

*T*here is a land beyond the forests. A land so beautiful that as you stand at the edge of the trees and gaze across the pastures to the snow-brushed mountains, you know that heaven is surely but a step away. From this land comes a song, and from the song comes a story. A story of murder.

Down from the mountains one day came three shepherds. They had been in the high pastures for weeks with their flocks and were glad to be heading home, but in the minds of two of the shepherds, there was death.

The third shepherd, the youngest of the three, and maybe the richest and maybe the most handsome, knew nothing of this, until one of his lambs, the smallest lamb, that he had saved from dying in a late Spring snow, came to him and warned him of the plot to kill him.

Now the shepherd looked sadly at his lamb, and said:

'If this is true, then I am doomed to die. But, my faithful creature, do this for me. When they have killed me, tell them to lie my bones somewhere close by, and bury my pipes with me, so that when the wind blows, it will play a tune and my sheep may come near, and my dogs too.

'Tell them not that I am dead, but instead that I went to

1

marry a princess from a distant land. Tell them how a star fell at my wedding, tell them how the sun and moon came down to hold my bride's crown, tell them how the trees were my guests, and the mountains my priests. How birds were my fiddlers, and stars my torchlight.

'But if one day you meet a white-haired woman; my mother, my old mother, tell her simply that I went to marry a princess, there on heaven's doorstep.'

And so it all came to be.

Deep in the Woods

When he fell for the fifth time, when his face plunged into the deep snow, when his hands burnt from the cold but he didn't care, Radu the woodcutter knew he was going to die. Somewhere behind him in the darknesses of the forest he could hear the man who had attacked him. He was scared now, almost too scared to move, almost too cold to run anymore, but still he knew something was wrong. Something that should not be.

He got up and stumbled on desperately, sending snow flying in little spurts. Even here among the thickness of the trees it lay heavily on the ground, whisked and funnelled by the east wind into strange hills and troughs, like white beasts lurking at the foot of the birches.

Radu looked behind him, but could see nothing. Nothing but the vast unfathomable forest. It was said you could ride from Poland to Turkey and never leave the trees behind, but he knew that wasn't true. Nothing could be that big! Not even the Mother Forest.

He stopped for a moment, listening hard, but all he could hear was his own panting as he sucked air into his painful chest. He no longer knew where he was, though the forest had been his home all his life. His hut and his village were far away. He looked around, straining to recognise anything, but all he saw was a hundred thousand silver birch trees.

A branch cracked, and with horror Radu's eyes snapped back to his pursuer. Now Radu saw him again, he knew what was wrong.

'In the name of Jesus and the Forest . . .'

The words fell dead in the softness of the snow, but even as they did Radu turned and began to run, lurching wildly from tree to tree. His right hand left a smear of blood on the paper bark of a birch, but that wound was irrelevant now. It was such a short while since he'd been cutting wood with his axe. The axe that lay somewhere in the snow, its blade stained with blood, already frozen. *His* blood.

He hit another two trees, but barely noticed, and suddenly he realised where he was. Close to Chust, where his fellow woodcutter Tomas lived in a hut outside the village.

For a fleeting moment a flame of hope ignited in his heart. He had run fast, the village was only a short way through the trees, and he could no longer hear his attacker behind him.

But then Radu rounded a tree and ran straight into him.

The man was not tall, but he was fat. Bloated. His skin was as white as the trees around them. There was dried blood at the corners of his shrivelled mouth. It had taken Radu all this time to recognise him.

Radu took a step backwards, his fur boots brushing through the snow. He tripped over an unseen root, but kept his feet. He lifted a hand and pointed at the man.

'But Willem. You're dead!'

The man lunged forward and shoved his hand like a knife into Radu's chest, feeling for his heart.

'Not any more,' he said.

And now it was Radu who fell dead in the softness of the snow.

Slivovitz and Snow

*P*eter trudged behind his father towards Chust, shivering as he went. Their hut lay a little way behind them, outside the village itself. St Andrew's Eve was still a few days off, and the snow was strong already. It would be a brutal winter. Through the cold Peter could smell his father; even the biting wind could not rid him of the constant reek of slivovitz and beer.

'Did you know Radu well, Father?' Peter said, simply so there was something to say. His father didn't reply and Peter knew the answer anyway. They didn't know anyone well – until they had come to Chust they had never stayed in one place long enough to know anyone at all. But Peter was aware that his father had helped Radu, the woodcutter from Koroceni, once or twice in the last year. Sometimes even the most solitary of woodcutters needed help felling a large tree.

The edge of the village was in front of them.

'Hurry,' said Tomas. 'They won't wait for us.'

'They can't be starting,' said Peter. 'I can't hear the church bell.'

His father spat into the snow, but didn't look round.

'There won't be bells at a suicide's funeral.'

7

He walked into the village, through a small gate in the rickety birch paling that marked the boundary. The fence, no more than knee high, and capped by a ragged thatch, was designed to stop chickens from wandering too far. It ran right around the settlement, marking its perimeter; apart from a few fields, everything beyond it was forest. In places along its length, as here, were gates with porches.

Peter hesitated at this gateway, nervous. It wasn't just that they weren't liked in the village; there was more to it than that.

'Suicide?'

Peter ran after his father, and caught up quickly. The ground was a mess of frozen mud and slush, and his father was unsteady on his feet, as usual.

'Be quiet,' Tomas said, glaring at his son. He nodded at the huts, and Peter understood he should not have spoken. That was all right. Peter was used to silence, used to keeping his own company; thanks to his taciturn father, most conversations Peter had took place in his own head.

Two sour-faced old women stood in the shadow of a low doorway. They spoke under their breath to each other and stared at Tomas and his son, a heavy man who looked older than he probably was, and his strong, young boy.

Peter knew they were not liked, and the village had little to offer. There was something bleak and unsettling about the place, almost menacing, though Peter could not have put it into words, and yet for all that Tomas seemed content to stay. And in truth, Peter was happy to stay too. They finally seemed to have put down some roots after years and years of moving, and besides, there was Agnes.

They hurried on, down the slight hill that led to the area laughingly called the square, as if this was some great city in the south and not a Godforsaken village in the middle of nowhere. Chust was home to no more than two hundred people, but here in the centre there were houses in place of huts; a few of them had two storeys. As they went Peter kept an eye out for Agnes, but it was not a day to be abroad unless you had business to attend to. They passed the end of the street where she lived with her mother, still in mourning after her husband's death. Briefly Peter slowed his pace, hoping for some sign of Agnes, but there was none.

Slipping from the far corner of the square, a small track squeezed between two of the larger houses in the village; the priest's house and the feldsar's house. That way led to the church, which lay on a rise beyond. Peter could see its sagging wood-tiled roof with the onion-dome tower on its back, halfway along, like a boy riding a pig, but was surprised when his father strode away towards the other side of the square.

He paused, and then understood. He should have known better. Radu was a suicide; there would be no bells, and there would be no holy ground for him either. Peter hurried on.

His father was nearly at the far side of the village.

'They think he killed himself?'

Tomas said nothing.

'Father?'

Tomas stopped for a moment and looked, not at his son, but somewhere away over his shoulder.

'He was found hanging from a tree by a rope round his neck. So he killed himself. Wouldn't be the first lonely woodcutter to have done that.'

Something occurred to Peter.

'Why isn't he going to be buried in his own village?'

His father grunted.

'That type of death. They wanted nothing to do with him. Said he died on Chust land so we could deal with him.'

'And we agreed?' asked Peter.

'Who is "we"? There is no "we" here,' Tomas said, abruptly. Then he sighed. 'There was no choice. It was that, or leave him to the wolves. And anyway, the Elders commanded it.'

They were out of the village now, and through the trees they could see a few people gathered in a small clearing.

Peter thought about Radu, about how he might have died. His father told him he was a dreamer, but Peter couldn't dream what might have happened to Radu. It was not the stuff of dreams, it was the stuff of nightmares.

'But Father,' Peter whispered. 'You said Radu's chest was burst, that his heart was pierced.'

'What of it?'

'Well, he can't have done that to himself and then hung himself from a tree.'

'So it must have happened afterwards.'

'You mean someone else did it to him after he was dead? Who would do that? Why?'

Tomas shrugged.

'The wolves . . . ?'

Peter was about to reply, but could tell his father was being deliberately obtuse.

10

'Listen, Peter. If a man is hanging from a tree by a rope, he killed himself. If Anna told them that's what happened then that's what happened. Let it lie!'

Peter was not satisfied, but said no more. There was something troubling his father, he knew.

They made their way towards the meagre funeral party. There was Daniel, the priest, and Teodor, the feldsar; half doctor, half sorcerer. Radu might only have been a wood-cutter, and not even from the village, but still two of its most important inhabitants had come to bury him. Peter wondered why. Why were both of them here? He knew they didn't always get on. People were as likely to visit Teodor with spiritual needs as Daniel, and just as likely to pray for their health with Daniel as visit the doctor. Each man knew he had to tolerate the other. An uneasy alliance.

A little way away stood the village sexton, an old man with strong arms but few teeth. It was clear he wanted nothing to do with the affair, and having struggled to dig a shallow hole in the frozen ground, he leant on the top of his tall spade, sucking his gums, peering out from under a black wide-brimmed felt hat.

Snow continued to trickle down round and about as Tomas nodded greetings to the others.

Outsiders were never welcome, even if this father and son had taken to their work well enough. They were a strange pair. The father was a drunk, everyone knew that, but there was an air about him. Something in the way he held himself. He was fat from drink, his face flushed and his eyes milky, but he still had a head of strong black hair.

The son was a young man, really, new to the game. He

11

had even darker, thicker hair, and his skin was smooth and brown, as if he was from somewhere in the south. His eyes were rich and dark brown, like Turkish coffee, but he was nervous, for all his young strength, and there was something more refined about him than his father. Few of the villagers had ever wondered what might have happened to the boy's mother, though it must have been from her that this refinement came.

Peter was absorbed in his own thoughts. Wolves couldn't have done that to Radu's chest after he hung himself from the tree. It didn't make sense. Someone must have stabbed him through the heart with great force, and then hung his body in the tree afterwards.

But why? Most murderers tried to conceal their victims' bodies. Why display it instead?

To Peter, it seemed like a warning; a warning that death was walking in the woods.

And Peter was right.

The Suicide's Burial

*I*t wasn't until Peter saw a low-slung hay cart approaching that he realised Radu's body had not yet arrived. But here it came, uncovered on the back of Florin's cart, pulled by an ox rather than a horse. Peter had seen this in other villages, the locals believing that the horse was too pompous an animal to be trusted at funerals, and was flighty too, inclined to kick and bridle, disturbing the dead person's soul.

No one wanted that.

Besides, oxen were dependable, and noble in their own way.

Florin was a farmer, but there was little farming to be done in the winter and he had been told to fetch Radu's body. This didn't please him, but Anna had instructed him and he could not refuse. She was the most fearsome of the Kmetovi, the village elders, a terrifying lady of unknown age who commanded total obedience. She had assumed control of the village when her husband had died, and no one had dared to dispute this state of affairs. And her husband might have been a ruthless man, but even so he was just a shadow of Anna. So Florin had made his way to the woodshed behind the church where Radu had been put, though Anna herself was having nothing to do with the burial.

Another thing that did not impress the villagers was that Radu's body had lain unguarded in the shed since he had been found. Anything could have happened to it. A cat might have jumped across it, and everyone knew what that could mean. But then Radu was already a suicide, so maybe there was no hope for him now anyway. His future was already in great danger.

Florin walked on one side of the head of his ox, and Magda, his old wife, walked on the other. Peter was surprised she had come, but not surprised to hear her singing. She sang the song that was always sung whenever anyone died, or was married or indeed, when anything important happened at all. Peter had heard it many times, in all the other places they had lived. It was called the Miorita. *The Lamb*.

By a rolling hill, at Heaven's doorsill,
Where the trail descends to the meadow and ends,
Here three shepherds keep their flocks of sheep.

Hearing the song again, Peter's mind began to drift. As a child he had been fascinated by the song's story; the little lamb that talks to his faithful master, the murderous shepherds, the princess. The mother, who will wait in vain for her son to return. Peter had never known his mother, but though he tried very hard to feel something of a life that never happened to him, nothing came. Later, as he grew up, he thought about the story in more detail, and came to think it baffling and stupid.

Peter's dreams were shaken from him by a snort from the ox.

Radu had arrived.

There was little ceremony. Father helped Florin lift the body from the cart, Daniel mumbled some words from the Bible, and the sexton glared from underneath his hat. Peter watched, disturbed by the brevity of it all. Was there really so little to celebrate in a life that would soon be forgotten for ever? He gazed at Radu's face. He had seen dead bodies before, everyone had, but the look that was literally frozen on Radu's face shook him. It was a mix of shock and horror, and incomprehension. Peter shuddered, and wished that he and his father were back in their hut by the stove.

There was no coffin. The men lowered the body into the hole, but then something strange happened. Now in the grave, Radu was turned over, so he lay face down. This wasn't something Peter had seen before.

Florin had wheeled his ox around and he and Magda began to trundle away, both riding in the cart. Peter turned to see Teodor step forward. He untied a cloth bundle that he had been holding all the while and a clutch of twigs fell into the snow. Just before the sexton started to pile clods of soil over Radu, Teodor placed the twigs on and around his body. They were short, but stout, thick with long sharp thorns. Peter knew they were hawthorn, and glanced at his father for some explanation, but Tomas' lips were tightly drawn.

The funeral was over, and each party went their own way back to the village.

In the square, Tomas clutched his son's arm. It was only midway through the afternoon and already the light was failing. Peter's mind was full of questions, about the funeral, about why they had attended it at all. He was astonished when his father had said they would go, but maybe it was the right thing to do. It was just that it was a long time since Tomas had done the right thing.

Tomas shook his shoulder.

'I'm tired. Let's go home, son.'

Peter smiled.

'Lean on me, father.'

Tomas draped his arm around his son.

'I think there's some slivovitz left.'

The smile slipped from Peter's face, but as they made their way, he dutifully supported his father's weight.

'Why did they turn him face down?'

Tomas said nothing.

'What were the thorns for?'

'They're not for anything,' Tomas snapped, pulling away from his son. 'They're simple, superstitious people here. Don't take any notice of their foolishness.'

'But . . .'

'But nothing, Peter. We have wood to cut. And plum brandy to drink.'

And Peter knew, as so often, which of them would be cutting wood and which of them drinking brandy.

The Goose

*D*usk fell with the snowflakes as father and son made their way home. Peter was as tall as his father now, and certainly as strong. Maybe Tomas had once been a powerful man, but Peter could not remember that time. He did less and less work, and relied more and more on Peter to keep them fed. As far back as Peter could recall Tomas had drunk. Once upon a time it must have been different. Peter's mother had died giving birth to him. Tomas had found a wet nurse, but had brought Peter up himself ever since the child could walk and talk. Maybe he couldn't afford the nurse any more, but it seemed he had wanted the woman out of their lives as soon as possible. Since then it had just been the two of them.

On Peter's fifth birthday Tomas had given him a folding clasp knife. Not a toy, but a well-made and useful tool.

'Time you learned to use one,' Tomas said.

Peter had watched, entranced, as his father took an off-cut of a branch and quickly carved a small bird for Peter. A goose.

'It's a good one,' Tomas said. 'Sharp.'

'Yes, it's a good one,' his little son had echoed, laughing,

though it was not the knife he meant, but the slender little goose, the very image of the birds that he loved to gaze at as they flew overhead.

Later, Tomas taught him to read, and that wasn't the action of a drunkard, nor even a soldier, but once Tomas had belonged to a very different kind of family. Now the drink seemed to possess him, like nothing else, and it cost Peter a lot of effort chopping logs to buy a bottle of slivovitz or rakia.

As they came in sight of the hut, Peter could see the birch smoke trailing up from the chimney, gently twisting into ghostly shapes in the dusk, drifting away and spreading like mist through the tree tops.

Peter smiled. The fire was still alight; the hut would be warm.

The hut stood in a strange position. The river Chust, from which the village took its name forked in two here, as it snaked through the woods. With deep banks, the river had spent ten thousand years eating its way gently down into the thick soft dark forest soil. Its verges were moss-laden blankets that dripped leaf mould into the slow brown water. But at a certain point, in its ancient history, the river had met some solid rock hidden in the soil, and had split in two. It was in the head of this fork that the hut stood.

Just over a year ago, in the late autumn, Tomas and Peter had been travelling again when they'd heard there was the need for a woodcutter in Chust. They'd been moving from village to village, always heading as far from civilisation as it seemed possible to go, and ever deeper into the vast forest.

Tomas was pleased, and they took the job. There was a perfectly good, and large hut on the edge of the village, but Tomas had insisted they build a new one of their own. Peter was used to such eccentricities, and he merely bent his back to the axe to cut the trees to make the planks for their new home.

They laid a rough bridge of two halved tree trunks to cross to the middle of the fork, and began to build. Winter was coming on by the time the hut was finished, with a stable on one side and a tool shed on another, and though Peter started to cut wood to earn their keep, Tomas got his spade out.

'What's that for, Father?' Peter asked, but his father, as so often, only replied with actions.

He surveyed the hut from the very tip of the river-fork. Then he strode around the sides of its single storey, inspecting it from every angle.

Peter leant on his axe and watched his father from across the river where they had decided to make their timber yard. Tomas stood at a point twenty paces from the front of the hut, in the exact centre between the two arms of the river.

He swung his spade from his shoulder, thrust it into the spongy soil, and began to dig. Peter shook his head and went back to work. They had promised the Kmetovi deliveries of chopped birch a week ago, and they had already aroused suspicion by deciding to live outside the village. Father had tried to explain that it made more sense for them to live closer to their work, but that sort of logical explanation impressed no one in Chust.

After an hour, Peter straightened his back and looked

across to his father. Tomas had by now dug a deep but narrow pit. Peter sat down and pulled his knife from his pocket, the same one he'd been given on his fifth birthday. From another pocket he pulled a piece of plum wood he'd been working on, and began to shave curls of wood from the back of the little sheep he was carving.

Tomas was already up to his waist in the soil, when Peter suddenly looked up to see his father's eyes on him.

'Get on with your work,' he called. 'I've got enough to do here.'

Peter muttered to himself, but did as he was told. His father was in a mood. A mood that told Peter to keep himself to himself. It seemed to Peter it had always been like that, living in the same single room, but like leaves that fall from the same tree, always spinning ever further apart.

Peter muttered again. There was always something.

Always something to do. Somewhere to go.

Something he was told to do. Something he was told not to do.

Something like the box his father owned, that he was never allowed to open.

After two days' digging, Tomas' hole had become a trench, and Peter began to have an inkling of what his father was doing. Two more days and the trench was four feet wide and stretched from very nearly one arm of the river to the other. Only a small gap of maybe three feet lay between the hole and the gurgling water at each end.

'Careful,' Peter said, unable to keep quiet. 'If you dig any closer the bank will give way.'

Even as he said it he finally saw that that was just what his father wanted.

Tomas laughed, and swung his spade into the top of the last plug of earth. Water gushed into the trench, filling it more quickly than Peter would have believed possible. Tomas ran to the other arm of the river, and breached the soil there too. He had dug the channel on a slight slant, so that water was already flowing in from the arm of the river nearest to the village, through the channel, and away along to the other arm.

'I always wanted to live on an island!' Tomas called to his son, suddenly full of joy, laughing like a young boy. He climbed out of the water, soaked to the chest, and went inside to dry his clothes by the stove.

That night he got drunk on rakia, while outside the flowing water did a good job of cleaning and widening the trench, removing the last clods of soil from its two mouths. As he sat by the fire, his arms ached from the work, and through his tiredness something stirred within him. His muscles remembered working that hard. Years ago, he had swung his arms, but not with a spade.

Not with a spade.

Now, Peter and his father made their way over the same bridge of trunks they had laid a year ago and onto their little triangular island.

Their horse, Sultan, whinnied softly as their footfalls sounded on the bridge. He pulled at his tether, a simple rope from his bridle to a tree stump.

'Put him in, Peter,' Tomas said.

Peter nodded.

He patted Sultan's flank and led him into the tiny stable.

'Hay again, Sultan,' he whispered. 'One day I'll bring you some beet. You'd like that. One day soon, I promise.'

Sultan flicked his head towards Peter, but it was a gentle gesture.

By the time Peter got inside, Tomas had already poured himself a mug of rakia.

'Have some?' he asked.

Peter shook his head.

'For God's sake!' his father shouted, without warning. 'For God's sake have a drink with me for once!'

Peter stood, shaking a little, trying to stay calm and be friendly, as he always did at these moments, though inside his heart felt as if it was in a vice.

'I will, Father, I will.'

He went over to sit by the stove with Tomas. The lamp glowed; a lone moth flitting about against the smoky glass. His father fumbled for another mug and poured a thick finger of rakia into it.

Peter forced the firewater down, trying not to shudder as it burnt its way into his belly. He knew that would irritate Tomas further. But his father seemed placated, and began to hum tunelessly. Peter looked at him, opened his mouth to speak and closed it again. He could see his father's eyes had glazed, his mind elsewhere, miles away. Years away, maybe. Peter tried to think of something to say, something that would reach out to his father, despite the drink, make a small bridge across to his island.

But it was Tomas who spoke first, breaking the silence.

'We haven't heard that tune for a while, have we?'

Peter shook his head.

'I never understood it, anyway,' he said. 'Why does the shepherd let himself be murdered? Without trying to fight, or to argue? It's stupid.'

'Ah,' Tomas said. 'Ah.'

He began to sing, his eyes shut and his face turned to the roof beam.

'By a rolling hill at Heaven's doorsill.'

The moth tumbled onto the table, exhausted by its efforts to fly into the light. It lay on its back, struggling.

'Where the trail descends to the plain and ends.'

'Why does everyone sing it anyway?' Peter asked suddenly. 'The Miorita?'

Tomas stopped and turned his gaze momentarily on his son, but he was distracted by the moth, which suddenly flipped over onto its legs. From the strange milky skull-shape on its back they could see it was a death's head moth.

'It makes no sense, but people sing it all the time.'

Tomas slammed his hand down on the table and left it there. The moth had no chance of escaping. Peter winced, and looked away as his father lifted the squashed corpse from his palm, opened the door of the stove, and threw it in.

There was something wrong with killing even such a small thing for the sake of it. There was no point saying so, Peter knew that, unless he wanted a lecture about what ten years in the King's army did to your opinion on killing. Ten years in the army and four in jail. Enough to make any man violent.

Peter stood up and got the pot from the cupboard, to make soup.

'The song, the Miorita, makes sense to some people,' Tomas said, cantankerously, but Peter had turned his back on his father, as he chopped vegetables, and couldn't tell what his father thought of it himself. Presumably he ranked it alongside all the other superstitious nonsense people spouted. His mood was thick and dour, now. The death of the moth seemed to have put a sudden end to his drunken good humour, and he sat by the open door of the stove for the rest of the evening, staring into the flames, until the bottle was empty and he staggered to his cot, ignoring the soup that Peter set in front of him.

Peter finished his own meal, then sat by the fire, carving a miniature fir tree. Something about that appealed to Peter; it was almost like giving back to the forest, rather than just taking wood to sell and to burn all the time. Turning one small piece of wood back into a tree again was an offering to the Mother Forest, and Peter believed that was very important. It would never do to anger the great power that lurked all around them, every day of their lives. Peter finished the carving and put it on the shelf above his bed, along with all the others.

He sighed. He had never had his father's skill with his hands and the tree was clumsy. But it was his.

The snowy night hung thickly over the village, and the two arms of the river, and the trees. The forest stretched away in almost every direction for five hundred miles, unbroken except for the faint huddle of a village here and there.

25

The hut crouched on the island Tomas had made, as if waiting, a dim light shining weakly from the gaps in its two tiny shutters.

Away, across one of the river's arms, something watched the hut. It stirred. The figure of shadow moved slowly from cover and then sped like daybreak into the trees.

St Andrew's Eve

A few days after Radu's funeral Peter went into Chust. They were owed money by various people for deliveries of logs, and Peter knew it was better that he collected it than his father, who might have spent half, or worse, in the inn before he got home.

It was a bright day, but the snow still lay defiant on the ground, with promise of more hanging like a grey blanket in the sky. Peter was passing the wooden well at the northern end of the village when he saw the first plumes of smoke curling up into the air. He was puzzled at first, but then remembered that it was St Andrew's Eve.

As he rounded a corner there was the first bonfire. Slung over a fire pit, a huge iron cauldron was spewing coils of steam into the cold morning. Around the fire stood a paltry crowd of people, each waiting patiently with a wooden bucket in hand. They took no notice of Peter as he passed, on his way to his first call, Daniel, at the priest's house.

In the square was another bonfire, with an even larger cauldron, and even more people waiting, with their buckets. By the cauldron stood Teodor, the feldsar, and a fat man whose name Peter didn't know. Teodor seemed to be in charge of the fat man, who filled each bucket from the cauldron as it was presented to him. Occasionally Teodor would wave the man away and stand by the cauldron, muttering something over its steaming mouth. Whether it was bad temper at a job badly done, or magic, Peter didn't know. If it was magic, Peter wondered what the priest would have to say about it. After a while, Teodor stood back and nodded for the work to begin again.

It was a messy, smelly job, and now Peter could see what he knew was in the cauldron, for there were thick black patches that had been spilled here and there in the snow-packed square. Tar.

All across Chust, and Peter knew, probably all across the country, people would be doing the same thing. The priest's house lay on the far side of the square, by the narrow alley that led to the church, and Peter could already see Daniel, outside his house, brush in hand. He dipped the fat, short, round hog's-hair brush into the tar, trying to be quick before it set again. He was working laboriously, painting the tar onto the windowsills of his house. Others worked on their houses around the square, some slowly and methodically, others fast, but all around the village, every window frame was being coated with the thick black tar. It was tiring work; the tar cooled rapidly and got harder to use, and the clumsy hog brushes came apart all too easily.

Peter stood right behind Daniel, but the priest was so intent on what he was doing that he didn't notice. He had moved to his door now and after he had covered the frame with a good layer of the stuff he scraped the last from the sides of his bucket and daubed a large untidy cross on the door itself. He stood back to inspect his work. He would have liked to have had a better looking cross; he would have to get some more tar.

'Does the protection of the Lord need the help of tar, Father?' said Peter.

The priest jumped and turned to see Peter.

He scowled, dropping his empty bucket to the ground. His hands were sticky, and he tried to wipe them on his robes, but it was no use. He was a tall man, balding, with a sharply-pointed beard that mimicked the sharpness of his nose.

'St Andrew's Eve, Peter,' he said, as if that was an answer. 'You and your father would be wise to take the same precautions. It's a long journey from here to St George's Eve. And it can be an evil journey.'

Peter agreed with that at least, against his better judgement. He thought of the Miorita; it was when the shepherds had come down from the hills for the winter that the murder had happened. Tomorrow would be the first day of December. The whole dark winter lay before them, and the winter was a dangerous place to be. It was just that Peter didn't have much faith in tar getting them through the long winter months. By the spring, by St George's Eve, flowers and holy sweet basil would be growing in the pastures, showing that God's power was increasing again.

In the towns they'd lived in no man of religion would have abided such superstitious practices. But here, in the depths of the forest, it was different. Somewhere among the trees the path that led directly to God had gone astray. It had got lost among the folktales and superstitions and the

29

hushed talk of the fireside.

Don't get involved, was what his father would have said, Peter knew that. He decided to take his father's advice for once.

'Father Daniel. I've come to collect money. We brought you two loads last week.'

'You did bring me two loads, but then there was a funeral to pay for.'

'What has that to do with us?'

'The woodcutter was your friend. Since there was no one else to pay for the funeral, I'm going to take it from what I owe you. I will pay you for one load of wood only.'

'He was no more our friend than he was yours!' Peter said angrily. 'Someone from Koroceni ought to pay.'

'Well you go and find someone from Koroceni and I'll happily take their money for the funeral.'

'That was no funeral anyway,' Peter said, knowing he was speaking rashly.

Daniel opened his door, then turned, pointing a long finger at Peter.

'Be careful what you say. He was lucky he got buried at all. We did our best for him. You should pray that it is enough!'

He made to go inside and was shutting the door when Peter stepped forward and stopped it from closing with one strong hand.

'Father,' he said, as firmly as he could. 'Our money.'

Daniel glared at him.

'One load only.'

Peter nodded. He could see he was not going to get any more from the crooked priest.

'Wait there,' Daniel said, and Peter obeyed, but kept one foot inside the door. He and his father had been cheated too often for him to be careless about things like that.

The priest returned and grudgingly placed the few coins in Peter's hand.

'Take my bucket back to Teodor,' he said. 'Tell him I need a little more. Tell him we all need more tar.'

Peter stepped back from the door, and picked up the bucket from the snow. He shoved it into Daniel's hands.

'Tell him yourself. I have money to collect.'

The Dulcimer's Melody

*P*eter stalked away across the square, immediately regretting his confrontation with the bad-tempered priest. It was the sort of thing that had kept them on the move all his life. Never settling anywhere, never belonging with others. Peter might not have liked Tomas' odd choice of a permanent home, but he was simply glad they had finally come to rest. What they needed now was to avoid trouble.

Peter heard them before he saw them. Their music drifted ahead of their caravans. Gypsies.

Three caravans and an open wagon rolled into the square and people stopped what they were doing to watch. The caravans were brightly painted in yellows and reds – the canvas of their rounded roofs covered in strange, foreign swirls of colour. Against the dull grey-brown walls of the houses the gypsies looked even more striking, and the villagers were entranced.

The first caravan was pulled by a bay mare, and driven by a tall strong man, with long black hair that he wore in a pony tail. On top of his head was a tiny round hat, and on his lips a smile, not a broad one, but one that looked as if he knew things.

The music came from the back of the open wagon, where four musicians played. There were two fiddlers and a man with a shallow drum. Next to the drummer sat a man with a dulcimer, which he played with miniature metal hammers. That was what Peter had heard first, an unearthly sound that spoke of other places and other times.

The four musicians sat in the four corners, but there was a fifth person in the wagon. She stood up as she began to sing, and her voice lifted gently above the music and floated round the square. Up to this moment, Peter had not recognised the tune, so exotic was the sound of the dulcimer and the drum, with the fiddles wavering on top. But there was no mistaking it as the girl's voice picked out the familiar melody of the Miorita.

Tell not a breath of how I met my death,
Say I could not tarry; I have gone to marry
A princess - my bride is the whole world's pride.

A princess. Peter was transfixed. The girl was maybe just a few years older, but Peter knew she was very different from him. Even at this distance he could see her pride, her confidence. She stood tall, easily countering the rocking of the wagon with the sway of her hips, where she rested her hands, fingers splayed. Her head was up, her raven hair falling in ringlets across her shoulders.

Once again Peter struggled with the song. It made no sense to him. He still couldn't understand why the shepherd behaved the way he did. He hears he's going to be killed by the other shepherds, maybe jealous of his youth, or his handsome looks. So much, so easy. But then he does nothing. He doesn't run away, or hide. He doesn't fight. He accepts his death, and concocts that story for the lamb to tell his mother. That he married a princess from some distant land. Peter, who had never known his mother, could nonetheless understand wanting to protect a loved one from the painful truth. But he couldn't understand anyone accepting their murder so readily. Unless maybe it was the only way to such great beauty.

Such beauty as the cosmic princess from the song . . .

Suddenly Peter was aware that the gypsy girl was looking straight at him, fixing him with a stare that was powerful yet at the same time utterly devoid of emotion. He was unable to look away, and now the caravans and wagon pulled to a halt in the centre of the square, and the musicians struck up a different, livelier tune, that leapt to the beat of the drum. It was an instrumental, and the girl sat down in the wagon, no longer looking at Peter, though he could do nothing but look at her.

'I hope you don't think she's more beautiful than me?' said a voice behind him.

He turned to see Agnes looking up at him, smiling.

Even as he spoke he knew she had only been joking, yet some foolishness inside answered for him.

'No, no,' he said quickly. 'Of course not. I was just admiring the song, that's all.'

Agnes stopped smiling.

'It was the song you were admiring, was it?'

Peter shuffled awkwardly. He looked down at Agnes, her short brown hair framing that pretty round face, those grey eyes and that little nose.

'How are you, Agnes? How's your mother? I haven't seen you for a while.'

'That's because you come to the village only when it suits you.'

'Agnes, I'd come more often,' Peter stammered. 'I'd come to see . . .'

He stopped, he didn't have the courage to say it.

'I know,' Agnes said, and with a jolt in his heart Peter thought she had guessed what he was about to say. But she hadn't. 'You'd come more often if only you weren't so busy, if only your father let you, if only you had the money.'

'Don't Agnes,' Peter said. 'That's not fair. You don't know what it's like.'

He'd said the wrong thing.

'Don't I?' she cried, her voice high and uneven. 'Father died less than a month ago, Mother's stayed in her bed ever since. I have all the work to do and look after her too, and you think *I* don't know what it's like?'

She turned and hurried away.

'Agnes,' Peter called. 'Wait! Please?'

People were staring; he ran after her for a few steps, then faltered.

'Agnes,' he said quietly, but she had gone. He could tell the air what he wanted to say, but what was the point?

He turned and looked at the gypsies again. A crowd had gathered round and some were even throwing a little money into a hat that a child was taking round. The colours of the gypsy caravans and clothes sat in bold contrast to the drab huts and houses of the village.

Peter smiled bitterly. It would not be too strong to say he was unsettled by the gypsies, but he felt some empathy with them. Here were the villagers, happy to listen to their music, happy even to pay for it, yet there was a contradiction. Peter knew that they would not be allowed to stay in the village overnight, and would have to pitch somewhere outside it when darkness fell. They were tolerated, not trusted.

He understood how that felt. And more, besides. Something about the gypsies spoke directly to Peter's heart, though what it was, was hidden to him.

Night was falling as he trudged home through the snow. His pockets jingled with the money he had collected as he walked. Now all he had to do was keep Tomas from drinking it all, as well as explain why the priest had only paid for half his wood.

Should he tell his father there were gypsies in the village? He thought better of it. He could see his father's look of disinterest already, and besides, he felt something for them. If his father poured scorn on them the way he poured scorn on everything else, it would be one more thing to have happy dreams about that Peter would have lost. One more thing to push them apart.

Like the box. It was one of Peter's earliest memories, and it was a painful one. His father had a long wooden box, that had always been with them, but Peter had never seen inside it. Wherever they had been, wherever they had lived, the box had always come with them. Tomas always tucked it away out of sight under his mattress, and though Peter couldn't remember, he knew Tomas must once have told him never to open it.

As Peter had grown, so had his curiosity. One day it got the better of him. He'd been about to open the box when his father came into the room. Tomas thrashed Peter so hard he woke from the pain every night for weeks. But Tomas had done something worse.

On the shelf by Peter's bed sat the wooden goose Tomas had carved the day he gave his son his knife. He snatched the carving from the shelf, and threw it on the floor, crushing it with his boot. Then he threw the pieces into the fire.

To this day, Peter resented it. What could be so important that Tomas had to keep it from him? The box was like his life, as far as Peter could see; something he had no control over, something shut away, not to be talked about, full of secrets and riches he must not explore.

Shutters barred every window as Peter walked out of Chust, but he could hear the sound of singing from every home he passed. Another form of protection, for everyone knew you should sing on St Andrew's Eve to keep evil away.

Peter shrugged. It was the first night of the year when evil was loosed on the world, and all the villagers had to protect themselves was tar and singing.

Above his head he suddenly heard the beat of wings and then the honking of geese. He looked up to see the birds streaming their way across the sky like a living arrow head.

'Very late,' Peter whispered to them, 'very late to be heading south.'

But at least the geese could leave; late or not, they could take flight away from the cold heart of winter.

For everyone else, it was a long journey indeed to the safety of the spring.

7

Sheep and Wolves

For the next few days Peter worked hard, chopping and delivering as much wood as he could before the snows really bit deep. On about half the days he managed to get his father to help him. The rest of the time Tomas sat by the stove in the hut, drinking his way through a small barrel of slivovitz that he'd bought with the money Peter brought back from his last trip to Chust.

Late one morning, as they were chopping logs from the lumber pile, Tomas dropped his axe. Not for the first time Peter noticed his father's hands shaking. Tomas bent to pick the axe up from the snow but dropped it twice more before he began to swing it again.

'Get on with your work, Peter,' he said, gruffly, seeing his son staring at him.

Peter didn't move.

'It's cold out here, isn't it?' Tomas said, pausing. 'Can't keep my damn hands still.'

'Yes, Father,' Peter said. 'The wind's cruel today.'

But later, back in the warmth of the hut, Tomas' hands were still shaking.

Peter and Sultan made a dozen trips around the village, their battered cart laden and creaking through the snow. Most people had good stores of seasoned logs already, but no one would refuse another delivery; you could never be sure how hard the winter might be. The difficult thing was getting people to pay for the wood straight away, but nevertheless, Peter came home most days with coins to put in the tin under the loose stone in the corner of the hut.

One day, Peter came home with more than money. Stories were flying around the village, and Peter brought some of them with him too. He led Sultan over the bridge onto their island and hurriedly fed him. While the horse ate, he threw two blankets across the beast's back. He dragged a bucket through the channel that joined the two arms of the river, and poured water into Sultan's trough.

'Drink it before it freezes, boy,' Peter said, shutting the stable door. He felt strange calling the horse 'boy'. Sultan was older than him, and somehow, Peter knew, much wiser, but that was what Tomas often called him and it had become a habit.

'One day, I really will get you some beet.'

Peter found his father inside, as usual. For once, though, there was no drink in sight, and there was a pot bubbling on the top of the stove.

'There's all sorts of commotion in the village,' Peter said, before he had even closed out the cold.

'What?' Tomas asked, looking up from stirring the pot.

'Sheep have been attacked. In their sheds. Cattle in the pasture, too.'

'So the wolves are getting hungry,' Tomas said. 'What of it?'

'It's not wolves. Well, that's what they're saying in Chust.'

'So what is it then?' Tomas asked.

'I think you know what they're saying,' Peter said.

'Pah!' Tomas spat on the floor. 'Idiots! And you're an idiot too for listening.'

'I'm just telling you what I heard,' said Peter. 'That's all. You know the miller who died last month? Willem? His widow says he visits her in the night.'

Tomas said nothing, and turned his attention back to the pot on the stove.

Peter kept going, for once seeing the chance to actually get his father to talk.

'She says he's been visiting her for a week now. She's very ill. Pale and won't eat.'

'So what? She wouldn't be the first silly old woman to say that! That snooty girl of yours. Agnes.'

'Yes,' said Peter, angrily. 'What about her?'

'They told me in the inn yesterday that her mother's been saying the same thing about her husband.'

Peter looked at his father.

'They said what?'

'You heard,' Tomas said.

'And you didn't tell me?'

Tomas whirled round, sending the pot of stew flying to the floor, but oblivious to this he stormed over to Peter, who flinched, convinced his father was going to strike him.

40

'No,' Tomas shouted right into his face, 'I didn't tell you, because it's all nonsense!'

Peter stood, breathing heavily, trembling. The stew was spreading across the floor. He looked back at his father, determined to hold his gaze.

'I'm going to see Agnes,' he said quietly. 'I'm taking Sultan. I'll be back late.'

Peter strode out of the hut and with a silent apology to Sultan put the horse's saddle and bridle on again. He galloped into Chust, fuming with his father as he rode, happy to let him have to clear up the spilled stew.

In the hut, Tomas stared at the mess he'd made.

He got on his hands and knees and tried to scrape what he could back into the pot, but all he managed to do was fill it with a muddy slop. He took the pot outside and threw its contents into the river, then swilled it out and went back indoors. He threw sawdust over what was left on the floor.

He stood, breathing in quick gulps of air. His eyes fixed on the barrel of slivovitz, but he forced them to move on, and found himself staring at his bed.

He glanced at the door, but knew Peter was way into the village by now. Nonetheless, he threw the bolt and went and knelt by his low cot, as if he was about to pray.

Instead, he rummaged with both hands under the mattress and pulled out a long, flat wooden case.

He let the mattress fall onto the bed again, and placed the box on top. He waited for a moment or two, catching his breath, as if scared of what he was about to do.

The case had a simple catch and no lock, and was rather

41

plain, made of a dark coloured wood, so unlike the pine and birch of the Mother Forest. Tomas looked behind him once more, at the door, hesitating still. Then he took a deep breath and raised the lid, and from inside he lifted a strange and beautiful object up into the flickering orange lamplight.

It was a sword, and it was as frightening as it was beautiful, and as foreign as the sun in winter.

Its slim but lethal blade curved back halfway along from the hilt, widened out for its last third, before tapering to a fearsome point. The hilt itself was sheathed in horn; glossy, grey and mottled, and the crosspiece was an elegant brass creation.

The blade's surface was completely smooth, apart from by the hilt, where a strange device was engraved in the steel. Two triangles interlocked forming a six-pointed star, between each arm of which was a small circle. In the middle of the star was a seventh circle, and around the outside ran two concentric circles, keeping everything in order.

Tomas held the sword not by the hilt, but with its blade resting gently on his palms. He seemed hypnotized by it; even his breathing appeared to have stopped.

The only things that moved in the whole hut were the flames dancing in the stove and the tear that fell from Tomas' cheek onto the blade.

Memories flooded his brain, unbidden and uncaring. Suddenly he snapped from the reverie, roughly put the sword away in its case and rammed the case under the bed, as if it were of no worth, though nothing could have been further from the truth.

He grabbed a mug from the table, filled it to the brim with slivovitz, and began to drink, trying to wash the memories away.

Outside, there was a noise. Footsteps sounded on the log bridge to the island.

'Peter?' Tomas called, unsettled by something he could not place.

But Peter was by then knocking on the door of Agnes' house.

The Shadow Queen

'*G*o away, Peter!'

Agnes leant from the upstairs window, looking down at where he stood in the street, holding Sultan loosely by his reins. Dusk had fallen across the village. Agnes' father had been a well-to-do merchant, a draper, and the house was one of the very few with two floors.

'Let me in, Agnes,' Peter called up to her, as quietly as he could. Here and there people came and went down the long street, and Peter was wary of them, wanting to avoid prying eyes. In truth, however, they were all hurrying home, eager to be out of the coming night. As so often, the streets of Chust seemed filled with a subtle menace that Peter could not have named.

'I will not,' Agnes said, for the fourth time. 'I told you. We have barricaded the doors. And the windows downstairs.'

'Well open them again,' Peter said, exasperated now.

'No, Peter. Are you mad? It's getting dark. Go home.'

As if in agreement, Sultan whinnied gently beside him. Peter put his hand out and patted Sultan's neck to reassure him. There was little he could do. He had ridden to see

44

Agnes, and now she wouldn't even let him in.

'Agnes,' he tried again. 'Agnes, you must tell me that you are all right. I've heard a story, Agnes, that your . . . '

He stopped, waiting for an old man to hobble slowly by and out of earshot. In that little space of time Peter pondered what Tomas had told him. He didn't know that he believed what he'd heard, but he wasn't entirely sure that he didn't.

'What, Peter?'

'I heard that your mother said . . . That your . . . father. Your father has been back to visit her.'

He whispered as loud as he dared, glancing up and down the street as he did so. Agnes' reply was quiet, almost inaudible.

'What of it?'

'So it's true?'

Agnes said nothing. She glared down at Peter, who was getting cross as well as cold. Why couldn't she give him a straight answer? He couldn't believe she seemed so calm about it, but then an awful thought crossed his mind.

'Have you seen him, Agnes?'

For a moment, her face softened. She looked away across the rooftops, towards, Peter thought, the church.

'No, I haven't,' she said, quietly. Almost sadly. 'I haven't seen him. And I don't know if Mother has, or if she's just . . . '

She trailed off.

'Agnes, I'm sorry. I want to help you. Won't you let me in? Let me check everything is all right. Can I bring you anything?'

'No, Peter. What could you do anyway? I can manage, I've blocked all the doors. I've protected the windows. We'll be all right. You should go away. It's not safe out there. In the dark. You know what people are saying, don't you?'

Her voice dropped to a whisper, so that Peter had to strain on tiptoes to catch the gentle words as they fell down to him.

'It's the Shadow Queen. People are saying she's back, that she's coming to make Chust her own. Some people even say they've seen her!'

With that Agnes seemed to have scared herself, and with a wave of her hand, indicated that the interview was over.

The Shadow Queen.

Peter knew what his father would say about that. All nonsense and tittle-tattle. Nevertheless he suddenly felt very exposed in the lonely village street, with no one but Sultan for company.

He swung his leg over Sultan's back, and began wearily to head for home again.

The Eternal Return

'Come on, Sultan.'

Peter bent over Sultan's neck and whispered in his ear. 'I'm tired too, but we should get back to Father.'

That was true, but it was also true that despite himself, Peter had been unsettled by Agnes.

Locking herself and her mother away every night seemed a desperate measure, and her talk of the Shadow Queen may just have been village gossip, but as Peter rode through the deserted streets, the darkness began to eat at him.

He steadied himself, and rode on, but it was not long before he caught himself peering into the shadows that curled at the street corners. Then he'd snatch his eyes away again, like a frightened child. The darkness suddenly seemed to press in on him from all sides, ominously. What if it were true? What if the Shadow Queen were true, and was coming to take them all?

Peter and his father may not ever have seen her, but they had met plenty of people on their travels who said they had.

Was it last year? Or the year before? Peter couldn't remember, but once, he and his father had been passing through a district away to the south east, nestled up against the Karpat mountains. They had stopped in a village for the night. All evening, as they sat in the inn, there was talk of only one thing. The Shadow Queen. The locals spoke in hushed whispers, as if she was standing at the window of the inn, intent on catching anyone maligning her.

'She's a thousand years old!' someone said.

'Rubbish! She was born at the beginning of time. She has no age.'

'Yes,' someone else agreed. 'And she's ten feet tall and has a hundred teeth! She can devour five children at once!'

'Ah!'

The audience grew fat on these morsels, while more beer was drunk and songs were sung. Peter found himself glancing over his shoulder, and after a while, moved closer to the fire.

The following day was a Sunday, and as it turned out, Palm Sunday, but Peter and Tomas were surprised to hear the locals call it Shadow Day. They were even more surprised when they learned that they would be seeing the Shadow Queen herself later that day. After all the talk the previous night, it seemed absurd to hear the villagers discussing her imminent arrival.

Tomas announced that it was time to leave, but Peter was by now intrigued, and eventually persuaded his father to stay for an hour more.

'Very well,' Tomas said abruptly. 'Maybe then you'll see what sort of superstitious buffoonery we are talking about.'

They found a heavy oak, climbed into one of its massive lower branches, and watched.

They didn't have long to wait before the Shadow Queen arrived. All morning, the villagers had been busy. Everyone had something to do or somewhere to be, but finally, just after noon, they made their way outside the village to a large field that led down to a wide, fast-flowing river. Here, on the grass, a large bonfire had been built, of birch logs on willow branches, kindled by hay from the village barns. Some people milled about, while others had much to do, and finally, there was a sudden lull in all the hustle and bustle and a hush spread across the pasture.

Then, so quiet, that first Peter wondered if it was just the wind, came the voices of the village.

'The Shadow Queen! The Shadow Queen!'

Not a cry, but a thousand awed whispers that spread through the crowd. Now even Tomas sat up and shifted his position to get a better view. All eyes turned to the edge of the village, where a cart slowly trundled out to the field. It was pulled by a single white horse, driven by a young woman. And in the back of the cart sat what could only be the Shadow Queen.

Tomas began to laugh.

The Shadow Queen was made of straw. A simple effigy, dressed, strangely for a queen, in a man's clothes. She was a life-size figure, though, which lolled about as the cart rolled awkwardly out into the field.

'The Shadow Queen!' Tomas said, mockingly, but Peter threw a twig at him and glared. It was never a good idea to make fun of strangers, they knew that well enough.

The cart reached the margin of the field, near the bonfire and the river. Tomas and Peter got down from their tree and went to watch the rest of the ceremony.

Solemnly, the Shadow Queen was sawn in half, and the two halves thrown onto the blazing bonfire, which snapped and cracked, sending blackened stalks of straw high into the warm spring air. Eventually the fire burned through, but there was one last ritual to observe. The ashes were gathered and cast into the river, where they sped away south, never to be seen again.

Peter tried to ask the villagers about it, but the answers he got only confused him more. Was that really the Shadow Queen he had seen? Who had been burnt? Was it just a straw dummy? Everyone he asked gave him a different answer, but it seemed that the locals knew it was just a straw figure, but somehow, at the same time, it *was* the real Shadow Queen too. In burning her, here, at the start of spring, they had sent her away, sent her underground for the spring, the summer and autumn, so that she would plague them no more. At least, until St Andrew's Eve, and the start of winter. Then, as the long cold nights spread across the land, she would return, bringing illness, plague and pestilence with her once more. Evil would wash before her in a wave of malevolence.

Peter was unable to understand how the villagers made sense of it – the frightening figure of hideous power described in the inn the previous night was such a far cry from the laughable doll that had been sawn and burnt in the field.

As Peter got talking to more locals, there were those who claimed to have really seen her, up in the mountains, or in the depths of the forest, or lurking in the graveyard.

As he was being told that the clothes the figure wore were those of the most recent widow's husband, intended to keep him from 'coming back', he noticed that Tomas was rolling out of the village on their own cart, having decided to waste no more time.

'Stop him from coming back?' Peter asked the man. 'What do you mean? Coming back?'

Refusal

*P*eter's thoughts had drifted to a sunny field, a long time ago, which might have done something to keep the power of the night at bay. In fact, it had done nothing to make him less scared as he rode home through the murk. There was a little starlight, but he knew he wouldn't be able to gallop Sultan once they were in the forest. Still, there was nothing to stop him from hurrying up the last street to the edge of the village.

He kicked Sultan on, suddenly feeling more terrified by the admission of his own fear, but just as they picked up speed, something rushed into their path.

At first Peter didn't clearly see what had happened, but Sultan, usually so sure-footed, shied and reared. There was a scream. Peter fought for a moment to stay on Sultan's back, but lost the fight and hit the ground hard. In a moment's confusion, it seemed that Sultan was going to fall and crush him, but then he rolled beside Peter, struggled to his feet, and limped away, frightened.

Peter spun off his back and onto his front, worried that Sultan was going to bolt for home. Then he remembered the scream just before he fell.

'You nearly killed me!'

All Peter could see at first was hair, lots of it, coiling like small black snakes.

The figure moved into a sitting position, and began to smooth her long skirts into place, checking that nothing was broken. Now he knew who it was. The gypsy girl, the singer.

'You ride very badly!' she said, pointing a finger right at him.

'Me?' Peter spluttered. 'It was your fault! What in heaven's name were you doing? Running in front of a horse like that!'

She ignored Peter's anger entirely, but with it, her own rage seemed to have vanished.

She smiled at him, and tried to stand, but immediately shrieked.

'My back!' she cried, sinking to the ground. 'Oh! I think it is broken!'

Peter doubted that very much, but nonetheless she appeared to be in pain.

'You must help me!' she declared. 'You nearly killed me! So get me out of this road.'

Peter stood up slowly. He hurt too, but there was no point in protesting.

'Carry me. Over there.'

She nodded at the side of the road, to a low bank of grass.

Peter sighed and bent over her. For a moment he considered how best to pick her up, then slid an arm under her legs and the other under her shoulders. She was light enough for him – he was used to carrying logs all day. But logs didn't wriggle, or complain, or hiss in pain, and he was glad when he had taken her the short distance and placed her on the soft grass, the start of a narrow strip that kept the forest away from the village.

They were just beyond the ragged edge of the huts here, with just the odd one or two dotted about, the street turning into nothing more than a snow-covered track that wound away into the trees. The puny thatched fence that marked the end of the village was defence against nothing, and yet being beyond it was disturbing. The Shadow Queen had already settled in the back of Peter's mind.

'Your back isn't broken,' he said, looking down at the girl. 'You couldn't move your legs if it were.'

'My name's Sofia,' she said. 'What's yours?'

He sighed, looking round to see that Sultan was still close by.

'Peter,' he said.

'I think my head is maybe hurt,' Sofia announced.

Peter opened his mouth then shut it again. She might sing beautifully, but he was finding her enormously irritating. Still, as he had carried her, he hadn't stopped himself from noticing that her legs were long, and that her dress was cut very low. Nor had he stopped himself from looking at her brown skin, so different from everyone else in the village, and more like his own.

'My head hurts,' Sofia said again. 'Here. You must feel it. Come here!'

Peter stood where he was.

'Come!' she demanded, and reluctantly, he knelt down beside her. She grabbed his hand nimbly and pushed it into her thick hair.

'There's a bump. Yes? No?'

Peter gingerly moved his fingers through the girl's hair, but could feel nothing.

'I think you're fine,' he said, pulling his hand away.

As he did, Sofia took his hand in hers and didn't let go.

'I think I'm lucky you didn't kill me,' she said, but gently this time.

Awkwardly, Peter sat next to her. Still she didn't let go of his hand.

'What were you doing, anyway? Out here, in the night? You shouldn't even be in the village after dark.'

'Because of who we are?' Sofia said haughtily.

'Yes,' Peter said. Then added, 'But I don't make the rules around here.'

The girl laughed.

'No, I am sure of that.'

Peter felt offended, at the same time wondering why Sofia was still clutching his hand. He realised that he didn't want her to let go.

'What do you want?' he said. 'It's dangerous out here.'

'Let me tell you,' she whispered, so quietly that despite himself Peter leant closer to her.

Peter was aware of the warmth from her body, and could smell her long raven locks. In that split second he wouldn't have cared if the Shadow Queen was right behind him.

'I want you to stay with me a while,' Sofia said.

Then she pulled his hand quickly, catching him off balance. He half fell on top of Sofia, who lifted herself high enough to plant a kiss on Peter's lips.

Peter yelped as if he had been bitten by a dog and jumped to his feet.

She laughed.

'Peter!' she said, smiling.

He backed away and ran to Sultan.

'Peter!' Sofia called, this time more urgently. 'Stay with me! My back hurts! I can't walk!'

But Peter wasn't fooled by Sofia's tricks anymore, his thoughts full of Father and the hut, and Agnes. What would she say if she knew what the girl had done?

Sultan seemed sound enough after his fall, and Peter plunged into the forest, heedless of the danger of galloping over difficult ground in the dark. Behind him Sofia's cries grew fainter.

'Come back! Come back and help me. Peter!'

He rode.

Visitors

As Peter rode he saw neither trees nor snow, but instead a glorious vision of Sofia. The girl was arrogant for sure, but all he could see was the rich tresses of her hair, her welcoming brown eyes and dark skin. With a wrench he shook himself, and tried to push Agnes back into Sofia's place. He found Sofia floating into his mind again, and started to work on the image, lightening and shortening the hair, turning the brown eyes grey. Finally he watched as the brown skin grew paler, paler, paler. There, that was Agnes.

But no! He watched in horror, transfixed as Agnes' skin took on an evil whiteness, the whiteness of death, and became impossibly wrinkled and old. Her lips shrivelled, her nose became pointed and thin, her hair grew lank and noisome. Her eyes flattened and widened, darkening and disappearing in shadow.

Shadow.

'No!' Peter cried into the air, then snatched himself away from the grotesque vision.

He let Sultan slow to a walk once Sofia was out of earshot.

They followed the bank of the river Chust out to the hut, but Sultan was uneasy. He sensed something up ahead and now stopped completely.

For a while Peter urged him to walk on, and managed a few more steps. Then once again Sultan stopped, this time for good.

'What's wrong, boy?' Peter whispered, his attention divided between the horse and whatever might be up ahead that was bothering him.

Sultan made no noise, but merely stood as still as any horse can.

'Well, you'll have to stay here.'

Knowing what Tomas would say about leaving their most expensive possession alone in the forest in the night, he reluctantly tied Sultan's reins to a sturdy birch.

Peter turned round and all there was to see were the shadows of the night forest. Trees stretched off into the distance in every direction, becoming grey ghosts and then no more than suggestions of ghosts. In the gloom the river chugged softly somewhere away to his right, but there was just enough starlight to make his way, so he started off towards the hut.

As he went, Sultan gave one final snort, then was silent.

Peter knew Sultan well, he was trustworthy, not the sort of horse that spooked easily. So he knew Sultan's refusal to go any closer to the hut was a sign that something was wrong. He slowed his walk to a crawl as he stepped as gently as he could along the river bank, and was glad at least for the sound of the water rushing, hiding his quiet footfall.

There was the hut in front of him, across the log bridge.

At first sight nothing seemed to be amiss, but Peter's heart froze as he made out the shapes of not one, but two horses on the bank, just beyond the bridge. The horses were tethered, and alone.

He stared through the pricking darkness at the hut, but could see nothing, could hear nothing but the water. There was light coming from inside, flickering slightly, as if people were moving around.

Something was wrong. No one ever came to see them, certainly not late at night. He put a foot on the bridge, eyeing the horses as he did so. He didn't recognise them, but noticed that strangely they bore no saddles. He turned his attention back to crossing the bridge without making a sound. He succeeded and stole a few hurried paces across the island to the hut, but instead of opening the door and walking straight in as he usually would, he slid close to the wall, crouching nervously beneath the shuttered window.

He could hear voices.

He raised himself on his knees, bringing his ear as close to the window as he dared. He knew that he could not be seen from inside, but still something made him desperate to keep hidden.

Now he could make out words.

'. . . you have no choice . . . '

A muffled reply; Peter knew it was his father's voice but the words were not clear.

'Once, you would have spoken differently.'

'You cannot refuse. There is no choice. The Shadow Queen has taken your choice away.'

The Shadow Queen. Who was his father talking to in

there? Now several voices all spoke at once, urgently.

'. . . the Shadow Queen is coming . . .'

'. . . more hostages.'

'. . . where is it, Tomas?'

'I don't have it.'

'You will agree. You have to understand that.'

'No!'

His father again, shouting this time.

There was silence for a short time, then quieter voices, indistinct but insistent nonetheless.

Peter was about to risk moving closer, when the door flew open on the far side of the hut. He dropped to the ground, and crawled to the corner by Sultan's stable. Between the cracks in the planks of the stable, he saw four figures leaving, and crossing the bridge.

The light from the open door shone across the island and the bridge. Its glow was weak, but enough for Peter to see the identity of the visitors.

From their colourful cloaks, Peter knew them to be the gypsies who had sung with Sofia in the village.

Closer

Agnes closed the door to her mother's room, and leant against the door frame for a moment, her eyes shut, running her hand through her hair. She had lost count of how many times she had been in to check on her through the day, and now the evening was thickening and the long night lay ahead. She had been trying all day to make some sense of her late father's business; people had come to collect orders that she knew nothing about; there had been arguments. She was exhausted.

She was still furious with Peter, but deep down she knew that was unfair. He had been trying to help. But he was tactless and certainly not as bold as she would have liked him to be. As she would have liked her future husband to be.

She blushed as she considered what she had told no one else, not even Peter himself. And he was poor too; she would never have dared tell her father of her desires. A draper's daughter does not marry a woodcutter's son.

Father, however, was gone. Though that was not what her mother said.

Agnes tried to push that thought away as she busied herself for bed. She slipped out of her clothes and into a nightdress, and began to brush her hair, but her fears would not stay away. Her hands began to tremble, and she dropped the hairbrush clumsily down on a table by the window, backing away from it uneasily. She knew the window was protected, but it didn't quell her fear.

What if Father had been coming back? To Mother, in the night? She did not doubt for a second that it was possible; everyone knew it. Cattle and sheep had been attacked in recent days, too. And it was true that her mother did seem to be getting weaker with every night that passed. Weaker, and paler.

But he would not come in the house tonight, no one and nothing would; she had taken further precautions. There was still tar from St Andrew's Eve on each window and door, and earlier in the day she had crushed five whole bulbs of garlic and smeared the paste on every window frame and doorsill.

There was no way in now. Or so she hoped.

She climbed into her own little bed and listened to the noises of the night.

In the street, outside Agnes' house, beneath her window, a large and bloated figure wavered, trying to come nearer. The figure, dressed in muddy, slightly torn clothes, sniffed the night air, laden with reeking garlic fumes.

And Closer

*A*gain he sniffed the air. Now he cursed and moved down the street, shambling slightly. Something pushed him away from that house, the house he remembered, but he sensed there would be others.

It was to be even easier than that, however.

Two streets away, a young man called Stefan made a fatal mistake. In fact he had made several, each worse than the last. First he had decided to spend the evening in the inn, where he had got very drunk with his friends. Secondly, he had played cards all night, and for some reason lost every hand, and almost a week's wages; all the money he had in the world. Then he decided to stay in the inn when his friends left together, and drink until his credit ran out.

Eventually the innkeeper had thrown him out. It was a cold night, but not snowing, and the ground was a mess of old snow and mud and footprints. He had been shuffling home, too drunk still to be miserable about his evening, when he saw someone in front of him, no more than arm's length away.

Stefan puzzled for a moment to place who it was.

'Crista!' he announced, pleased he had remembered.

It was the draper, the one with the pretty daughter. What was her name? He couldn't remember at first, then it came to him.

'And how is little Agnes?'

The draper said nothing, and then slowly, very slowly, it occurred to Stefan that there was something strange about seeing Constantin Crista here. If only he could remember what . . .

Faster than a cat could blink, Stefan flew back against the wall. Crista leant in, pressing him back, holding his head away to one side with one hand, while his other arm held the young man fast. He leant his head in closer, his mouth nearing Stefan's neck.

His lips, now just a finger's breadth away, parted, and then Crista stuck his tongue out, straight through the skin, right into the artery.

Stefan struggled for a moment to realise he was dying.

Creeping

*D*aylight crept slowly over the mountains, and through the trees, and finally limped along the twisting streets of Chust. It was snowing, but softly. Agnes awoke, her heart feeling lighter than it had done for some time. When she went in to see her mother, she smiled and even said she was feeling a little better. Agnes went back to her own room and dressed, then went downstairs to light a fire and make some porridge, picking her way past bolts of cloth stored at random in the hall.

Then she heard shouts from outside, and a scream.

She dropped the pot she was holding and frantically began to pull the barricade of chairs and tables away from the door.

The Waters of Chust

Deep in the forest, by the river, Sultan stood patiently. He snorted from time to time, blowing great clouds of steam into the frozen morning air. Nearby, the only other sound to be heard was Tomas slowly sawing his way through a tree trunk that lay prone on the forest floor.

His mouth was a tight line, as he tried to close his mind to everything except the saw and the tree. That was all he wanted to think about, but despite his hangover, and the exertion of sawing, images jostled in his head. He had been made to think about things he had sworn to forget. Himself, twenty years ago. He paused in his work, exhausted, and glanced at Sultan. It was enough to make him remember another horse he had once owned. A huge stallion called Prince. How they had ridden! And how people had fled at the very sight of them! In his mind's eye now, Tomas could look to his right, and there was the king himself.

Mighty. How mighty.

For no more than a second, Tomas remembered glory, then saw the glory turn sour, as it had always done. Peter's face rose before him and with it, their argument from the night before. Then he remembered what he had done.

He bent to the saw again and worked until he collapsed over the carcass of the tree, fighting for breath, sobbing.

Sultan stamped his hooves in the snow.

Agnes

*P*eter woke late to find his father had already left the hut. Pulling his boots and coat on, he stamped out into the snowy morning and looked around. The river flowed slowly by as usual; there was no sign of anything strange. No sign even of the hoof prints of the other horses from the previous night. He looked into the stable and saw that Sultan was gone too.

After watching the gypsies leave, Peter had waited a while, shivering in the stable. Then he'd gone back to find Sultan, who seemed perfectly happy now to come home. He had stabled the horse, and gone in.

That was when the trouble began.

More arguments, more drink.

It seemed reasonable enough to Peter to ask why they, or rather why Tomas, had received a visit from gypsies they had never met before. And what it was they wanted, so late at night.

Tomas, however, was saying nothing.

He flung himself around the hut, jar of drink in hand, spilling most of it, drinking some, and saying absolutely nothing. Peter had never seen him this bad, but for once he was not afraid of his father. He could see something was wrong, really wrong. Tomas was agitated as well as drunk, and Peter wanted to know why. He demanded to know.

That was when Tomas hit him.

There had been no more after that. Peter went to bed.

Now he stood in the morning air, wondering where his father was. He felt the side of his head, where Tomas had struck him, but it didn't occur to him to feel sorry for himself, just as it didn't occur to him to be angry with his father.

Finally he thought to check the toolbox in the hut, and found that Tomas' axe and the best saw were missing. So he had gone to work, that was something, though Peter knew his father was still likely to be drunk from the night before. Well, the cold and the work would sober him up soon enough.

There were sudden footsteps on the bridge, light and fast.

'Peter! Peter!'

Agnes.

She ran to him, and right into his arms without saying another word.

'Agnes!' Peter said. 'What is it? What's wrong?'

Agnes said nothing, but trembled against him, her arms clutching him tightly.

'Have you run all the way from Chust?'

At last, she lifted her head from his chest and stared up into his eyes. Her face was full of fright.

'There's . . . '

She broke off and began to sob, hard and loud.

'What?' cried Peter, infected by her fear.

'Another death. Last night.' Agnes wailed.

Peter grabbed her shoulders and held her away, needing to see her face, to see her speak, in order to understand, to believe.

'Another death?'

'Stefan,' she cried. 'You know Stefan? The miller's son? They found him in the street this morning. I saw . . . Oh, Peter.'

She stopped again and began to cry, burying her face in Peter's jacket.

'That's terrible,' Peter said. It was all he could think of to say. Poor Stefan, but at least . . .

At least what? He was thinking of a girl, and not the one who stood in front of him now. He forced himself to think clearly, to try to help Agnes.

She seemed to be mumbling now, almost incoherently, and Peter only caught two words.

'The blood!'

He steadied himself, knowing he needed to calm her down, though he felt far from calm.

'It's all right,' he said. 'You're safe. You're all right. It's terrible about Stefan, but you're safe. And I'll make sure it stays that way. I'll come to your house and stay through the night. Nothing will hurt you.'

'No, Peter, no!'

Agnes pushed herself from him, almost screaming.

'You don't understand.'

'What? What is it?'

'Stefan wasn't married.'

'So?' asked Peter.

'Stefan wasn't married. There's to be a Wedding of the Dead.'

'I know,' said Peter. 'I know, but that's normal . . . '

'But Peter,' she cried, 'I'm to be the bride!'

The Wedding of the Dead

Nunta Mortului. The Wedding of the Dead.

Stefan, the young man found in the street with his blood all around him, had not been married. So that he did not have to suffer the fate of going into the ground as a bachelor, he would be married at his open grave side to a girl from the village.

That girl was to be Agnes. She was the oldest unmarried girl, and so had been chosen. It had been agreed by Anna and the other Elders, and that was that. There was no possibility to decline, or refuse.

And after the wedding service had been performed at the grave, Stefan would be buried, while Agnes, in order to serve the period of mourning, would be sent to a small hut at the edge of the forest, where she would see no other living soul for forty days.

Peter had done his best to console her, but what could he say? All he could do was assure her that he would see that her mother was all right, make sure she was looked after, that there was enough food in the house. As for the wedding, nothing could take away either her fear of going through with it, or of the forty days isolation she must endure.

Forty days in a tiny hut, with all contact forbidden. Just within sight of the village, but outside it nonetheless, with the whole mass of the Mother Forest lurking at its back.

This was the second funeral Peter had attended in the village, but it was so unlike that of Radu the woodcutter. Most of the village turned out, and besides, there was the added attraction of the wedding. There had not been a Nunta Mortului for several years, and the bride this time was particularly pretty, which moved the hearts of even the most cynical.

The bride was ready. She had been dressed not by her mother, who was too ill to stand, but by two women chosen by the Elders. She had arrived in the cemetery, wearing a long, stiff wedding dress that had been found for her. The dress however, was a sinister parody of its usual form, having been dyed black; it served as wedding and mourning dress in one. It was completed by a high headdress and heavy beaded veil, also black, which hid the bride's face totally. Peter could only guess that it was Agnes from her height and figure. He could see she was having trouble walking; her dress rustled like dead leaves with every uncertain step; she held her hands clasped tightly in front of her. Maybe it was the weight of the clothes, maybe it was because she couldn't see, but in his heart Peter knew the real reason. She was scared stiff.

The groom had arrived too. He had been made ready at his home, where he had been dressed in his best clothes, suitable for church. A wedding. Or a funeral. His body had been rubbed with lovage. Protection. His coffin lay uncovered on trestles beside his grave.

The sexton had worked hard on this grave, harder than on Radu's, but then this was a proper burial, in the graveyard, overlooked by the sow-backed church with its wooden tiled roof and sharply pointed onion dome. People crowded around, leaning on the fences, hemmed in between other graves, each with a wooden grave marker. Most were brightly painted wooden crosses, set under small wooden roofs to shelter them from the worst of the weather. These little houses were painted too, and most bore inscriptions concerning the occupant. A very few of the graves in the yard were stone, the resting places of the richest citizens of Chust.

Around the coffin stood the mourners, around them lay the graveyard, and outside the graveyard lay the village. Beyond all of this stood the endless silent forest, watching the wedding of the dead, seeing all, saying nothing.

Peter wrestled to get as close to Agnes as he could, but he was still far from her. Even so he felt Agnes' loneliness from where he stood. It was as if her forty days' segregation had begun already.

As Daniel intoned the opening words of the wedding service Peter saw that Agnes was trembling. At various points in the service, she had to make responses, but though Peter stood on tip-toe and craned his neck forward, he couldn't hear what she said. Maybe he was too far away, maybe her voice was too small. He could only guess at what she was having to say, agreeing to marry a dead man. As for the groom, he was excused from having to make his responses, being in no state to do so.

As well as Agnes and Daniel there was the familiar figure of Teodor, the feldsar, who stood nearby but took no part in the ceremony. Old Anna stood next to him, her cruel, aged face glowering at anyone who dared look in her direction.

The wedding was soon over, and the burial began. As Stefan's coffin lid was lowered onto the box, Peter saw Teodor step forward. Daniel reached out and put a hand on his arm, as if trying to stop him approaching the coffin. Though he couldn't hear what they said, Peter could tell there was some argument between them. People began to grow agitated, and shifted uneasily. There was some muttering, and then at last Daniel appeared to relent. Teodor stepped forward, placing various items inside the coffin, along with the body. A net, some whitethorn, and some small figures, like a child's dolls. Then the lid was hammered into place and the whole thing put in the ground. As it went, the mourners began to sing, spontaneously, of one accord. They sang the Miorita.

At first, their singing was quiet, but as the verses told of the shepherd's fanciful version of events, of his marriage to the princess of the stars, their voices grew louder, and more rousing, until Peter found that despite his scepticism, there were tears in his eyes.

At my wedding, tell how a bright star fell,
Sun and moon came down to hold my bridal crown.

As the singing reached its climax, a single image was left in Peter's mind. The princess from the stars. The young shepherd had found his magical bride, even in death.

Peter woke from his dream of the princess. The burial was over and, determined to try to get across to Agnes, he began to push through the crowd. He was cursed for his lack of manners, and pressed in on all sides by the crowds swarming through the graveyard. Looking to see where Agnes was, he saw with alarm that she was being led away by Anna and the other Elders.

'Agnes!' he called, but it was no use. She was too far away, and the Elders were taking her straight to the hut. There she would begin her mourning. Impotent, Peter watched her disappear, imagining her dread at the terrible prospect of the isolation to come. It was said that she should speak to no one while she was in mourning for her husband. In this way, after forty days, it would be understood that she had mourned her husband for a lifetime, and could adopt the position of a young, unwed maiden once more.

Desperately Peter made one last effort to push through the crowd, and managed to fight his way to within a few feet of Agnes, but here his way was barred. The Elders formed a procession around and behind Agnes, a cortege to guide her way to the hut. Angry faces turned on him as he tried to force his way through.

'Agnes!' he called, and at last she heard. He saw her turn, and begin to pull at her veil, desperate to see him.

'Get away from her, boy!' someone shouted sternly at his side.

'But she's my . . . '

'She's nothing to you anymore. Not now! She's married someone else!'

Peter wrestled, trying to protest, but a fist struck him in

the back, and then another in his kidneys.

He collapsed, gasping for air. As he fell he caught a single glimpse of Agnes. She had succeeded in wrenching the headdress and veil from her face, a face that was now wreathed in horror alone.

18

At the Threshold

*P*eter limped wearily home from the wedding. He had decided that Sultan needed a rest, and had walked all the way, along the forest path that led home. The trees crowded in on him, silent but strong, and once again Peter had the sense of being watched. He shook his head free from the feeling; he had more pressing things to worry about. His side and back still hurt from the blows he'd taken.

He staggered across the bridge, and let Sultan find his own way to his stable.

As soon as he crossed the threshold he knew things were wrong. Tomas lay on the floor of the hut, his eyes open, but unable to move.

'Father!'

Peter rushed to him.

'What happened?'

Almost as soon as he asked the question, he smelt the drink that clung to his father's clothes, to his breath. As if to confirm it, Peter saw a smashed stone jar of slivovitz lying nearby, its dregs oozing into the earthen floor.

'I can't move my arm,' Tomas said, 'or my leg.'

He nodded his head at his left side, on which he was lying. His eyes looked at Peter wildly, like a frightened dog.

Peter was scared, and what scared him the most was that he had never seen his father frightened before. It was not something he had thought possible.

'Help me up.'

His father was very heavy, and being a dead weight, unable to move two of his limbs, made it hard to lift him properly. Peter did his best, but despite his strength, it was all he could manage to drag his father to his bed and haul him onto it.

At last it was done.

'The drink,' Peter said as gently as he could, though he felt angry inside. 'The drink did that to you.'

'Nonsense,' Tomas spluttered out, 'I had a fall.'

Peter said nothing. This was Tomas before him. Tomas did not have falls. But then, his hands never used to shake either.

He didn't believe his father, but he didn't want to fight him either. He needed to keep things simple. Practical.

'Are you in pain?' he asked.

'A little,' Tomas said. 'Nothing serious. Just can't move my damn arm.'

Peter pulled the covers from under his father, and put them over him. Then he went and stoked the stove, and made some soup. By the time he had done that, Tomas seemed slightly better.

'I think I can move my fingers,' he said. 'Yes? Are they moving?'

Peter wondered why he couldn't tell for himself. He

didn't want to think about what it meant. He looked at his father's hands, but could see no movement at all.

'Yes, Father,' he said, 'I think they are moving.'

With that, Tomas had exhausted himself, and fell asleep, but even in his sleep he tried to move his fingers, as if to close them around something, something like the hilt of a sword.

Dreams rode like wild horses through Tomas' sleep, dreams in which he himself was riding, and riding hard.

Riding out for a reason, for a cause.

A good cause.

Turnings

*T*he days passed.

Tomas recovered, slowly at first, then more rapidly. He had taken soup from Peter after he had woken from the accident, and had seemed more lucid. Peter was surprised that though he had refused to attend the Nunta Mortului, he had asked about the wedding, and even how Agnes was.

On the third day, Tomas got out of bed for an hour or so, moving his arm and leg freely once more. He even went out to talk to Sultan for a while.

Peter was worn out. It fell to him to do all the work he could, as well as nurse his father, and make two trips into Chust to deliver logs, collect money, and buy food. In the village he tried to enquire after Agnes, but no one would even meet his eye, let alone talk to him. But then, what was there to say? Apart from a basket of food that was left silently on the windowsill of the hut once every morning no one went near her. No one had spoken to her, and no one was willing to talk about her. No one was allowed close.

There was an ominous mood in Chust, that much Peter did notice. Something had changed, and a place that was dour at the best of times had become even more cold and unwelcoming. Peter knew what it was; fear. More cattle had been attacked; two were found with dried blood caked to their forequarters, and a couple of ewes had been killed, seemingly drained of blood. It was not the work of wolves, but no one would say more than that.

When he went to talk to Agnes' neighbours to see how her mother was, they refused to speak to him at all, merely indicating that they would look after everything. Peter felt the village excluding him, felt barriers that he couldn't break. One shrewish old woman bluntly told him they weren't wanted. He and Tomas had always been outsiders, Peter knew that. Now that darkness had descended on the village, anything strange, anyone foreign was a target for hostility.

Had Agnes' mother received more visits in the night from her father? That, he didn't know, and again, no one would tell him.

Time wore on, and Peter grew anxious and restless. Tomas got better, and needed his son's help less and less, so Peter was free to worry about other things.

Agnes had been shut up in the hut for six days. The hut lay beyond the little thatched fence, beyond the threshold, beyond the safety of the village, and was no place for a young woman, even in normal times. These were not normal times. Something evil was happening around Chust. Maybe it was something called the Shadow Queen, and maybe not, but Peter knew it was bad. Tomas dismissed all talk of the Shadow Queen as nonsense, but the villagers believed in her, and whether or not she was real, the result was the same; fear and suspicion had crept into Chust like an outbreak of plague. Soon, everyone would be infected, and Tomas and Peter would have to leave, move on again, back to their old nomadic life. Running, always running, though Peter still didn't know what it was they were running from.

By the time Tomas swung an axe again, Peter had made his mind up.

He couldn't go near the hut in daylight – it could just be seen through the trees from the edge of the village, and he knew he couldn't take that risk. If he got caught, the very least that would happen would be that Agnes would have to start her mourning all over again. But he *was* going to visit Agnes.

All day he worked with Tomas, but reserved his energy as much as he could. Tomas didn't seem to notice. Peter had sensed a change in his father, in which he seemed to have retreated into himself. He was quieter than usual, and even drinking a little less. Peter wondered how much, if anything, it had to do with the accident, or with the visit from the gypsies, but Tomas wasn't telling.

That evening, Tomas drank and Peter ate stew, and they both stared into the fire in the pot-bellied stove, thinking their own fire-side thoughts. Then they went to bed, and while Tomas was soon snoring heavily, Peter lay awake, thinking, and waiting.

When he was sure Tomas was sound asleep, he swung his legs out of bed, and by the faint glow coming from the stove, slipped his boots on and left the hut. Outside, he pulled the door to again, and waited for a moment, listening, but he need not have worried; his father was still snoring just as loudly as before.

Once again, he left Sultan where he was; the noise of getting the horse from the stable might be enough to wake Tomas.

The bridge lay picked out by faint starlight, and Peter cautiously slipped across the planks, the pure water gurgling past underneath.

It took him a while to reach the village, but he wasn't going in tonight. Instead, he chose a path that ran along the eastern edge of Chust, and set off around it. As the boundary fence curved here and there, so did the path, and Peter didn't hesitate. It wouldn't do to hesitate. If he stopped to think who or what might be out in the night forest, he would never have left the safety of the hut. In the last few days there had been two murders, and wolves were the least terrifying of the possible culprits. Peter hurried on, and pushed thoughts of anything and anyone else to the back of his mind.

Another few minutes and he saw the shape of the church hunkered in the darkness. He went on past it, and then slowed. Somewhere soon, he knew, he would meet another, smaller path running out from the village and up to the hut where Agnes had been left.

As his pace dropped, he began to wonder if there was something wrong with his eyes, because suddenly it seemed he could see much less than before in the dark. He lifted his face to the sky, trying to see what light there was, and felt snow flakes brush his face. Snow clouds had moved in, taking almost all the light away.

Just as he began to doubt he would be able to find the path, he heard the crunch of grit and pebbles underfoot.

He turned to the left and hurried up the path, which rose steeply with the ground, towards the edge of the trees. There, a stone's throw back inside the forest, was the hut.

20

Hands in the Dark

'*A*gnes,' Peter called, as loudly as he dared.

Nothing.

Peter stood at the door of the hut, and wondered if he should try to open it and go in. But maybe better not, he thought, it might startle her.

'Agnes,' he tried again, a fraction louder this time.

'Peter? Is that you?'

She was awake.

'Agnes, it's me, Peter,' he said, feeling stupid. 'Can I come in?'

He heard movement inside and felt the door shift slightly as Agnes leant against it on the other side.

'I can't let you in, Peter,' she said. She sounded miserable. 'You know I have to stay here by myself. And anyway, the door's locked. They locked me in.'

Ignoring her protests, Peter tried the door, but it was indeed shut tight.

'Come round to the window, Peter, we can talk there.'

Peter crept around the side of the hut, feeling his way by running his hand along the rough wall. He heard the creak of a wooden hinge as Agnes opened the shutter and suddenly her voice was right above him.

'Peter. Here!'

The window was small, and quite high up, about head height. It had a wide window sill, where Agnes' baskets of food were left. With an effort, she could have climbed out of the window and escaped, but the Elders knew what they were doing. Locking the door was merely symbolic; they knew she could not escape even if it stood wide open – she had nowhere to go, and would not be allowed to return to village life until she had completed her mourning properly.

'Peter!' Agnes said again, sounding a little calmer. 'Can you feel my hand?'

Sure enough, Peter felt around in the darkness, and there was her arm. He slipped his fingers along her sleeve until he felt her hand.

'Agnes. Let me in. I can't stand the thought of you alone in there. It's not safe.'

'No, Peter,' Agnes said, but her voice wavered. 'You know what will happen if we're caught. And I'll have to begin all over again.'

'But Agnes, it's not fair. Why did *you* have to marry Stefan? Why not someone else?'

'Because Anna chose me. When you've lived here a bit longer you'll understand that that's how it is.'

Peter said nothing. He had lived in Chust long enough to understand that the old woman's word was as good as law.

'At least you feel a little warmer tonight,' Agnes said.

Peter froze.

'What did you say?'

'Your hand,' Agnes said, innocently. 'It feels warmer than last night.'

Peter suddenly let Agnes' hand drop from his, as if it were something dangerous. She tensed, sensing something was wrong.

'Peter, what is it?'

Peter hesitated, then spoke quickly, his words catching in his throat.

'Are you saying I came here to see you, last night?'

'Yes, you did. You asked me to . . . Oh Peter! It wasn't you . . . ?'

Suddenly Peter felt the huge darkness of the forest behind his back, in which myriad horrors might be tracking him. It surrounded him with almost unbearable menace, a vast world which ruled and ran his life, seeing everything that passed beneath its branches, yet giving away no secrets.

'Agnes. You have to let me in.'

He spoke with a quiet strength, but mingled with fear, and it scared Agnes into agreement.

'Yes,' she said, 'oh God! Yes. It wasn't you? Yes. But the door, the door!'

'Never mind. Stand away from the window.'

He reached up and groped around with his hands, swinging the shutter open and gauging how wide the window was. Small, but he could make it. Putting a foot against the irregular log wall of the hut he found a decent enough foothold and half jumped, half pulled himself though the gap. Then, he wriggled and pulled and fell head first into the hut, spraining his hand as he landed.

'Oh!' cried Agnes. 'Are you all right?'

'Don't you have any light?' said Peter, standing up. He rubbed his hand, but it wasn't a bad injury.

'No. I'm not allowed. Tell me you're joking, Peter. That you just said that to get in here with me.'

But when Peter said nothing in reply, Agnes knew the truth.

'Who was it?' she whispered in horror. 'He said he was you! He asked to come in.'

'You didn't . . . ?'

'No!' Agnes said, quickly. 'I wouldn't let you . . . him . . . in.'

'Thank God for that, Agnes.'

'But who is it?'

Peter shook his head in the dark.

'I don't know.'

He went back to the window. He could sense from the stillness outside that it was still snowing, though he couldn't actually see it. The shutter was banging against the outside of the hut. Somewhere there was an iron handle to pull it shut. The last thing in the world he wanted to do was put his hand back out into the night, but he had no choice. Expecting his wrist to be grabbed at any moment, he felt out through the window, found the handle and pulled the shutter inwards, swinging the bolt into place. He turned to Agnes.

'I don't know,' he repeated, 'but something is wrong around here. Tell me exactly what happened.'

'I told you. You . . . someone came to the window last night. He asked to come in and I said no. He asked again and I said no again and . . . '

Agnes stopped.

'Oh!' she said.

'What, Agnes?'

Peter felt for her in the dark and put his arms round her. 'What?'

'When I wouldn't let him in, he asked for a kiss.'

'You didn't do it?'

'Peter, I thought it was you. I've been so scared. Anyway I said no, but I let you . . . him kiss my hand.'

Peter swore.

'I thought it was you.'

'I know. I know.'

Peter felt Agnes suddenly tense in his arms. Her head jerked up towards his in the blackness.

'Oh God and the Forest!'

'Agnes? Agnes?'

'He said he'd come back again tonight.'

Threads

For a long time neither of them moved, as if expecting to hear a voice at the window at any time. When they were finally convinced they could hear nothing, they began to breathe again.

'Sit down,' Agnes said, guiding Peter to the small bunk where she had been sleeping. They sat on the edge of the bed, neither willing to voice their fears.

Peter cursed himself for being so naïve. He could have brought his axe with him. He had tried to believe Tomas, that this was all village superstition, but deep down he had known something evil was afoot.

'Have you been all right here?' he asked.

'Yes,' said Agnes simply. 'But I'm worried about Mother. I've been thinking about her. And about Father.'

'Your mother's fine,' Peter said quickly. 'I saw her yesterday. I spoke to widow Caterina next door. She was very reassuring.'

It was all lies, but Agnes didn't need more to worry about, and as far as he knew, her mother was all right.

'But what have you been doing? Six days!'

'Spinning,' Agnes said. She laughed. 'If you could see the

floor of this place. There's enough wool to dry up the river in here. They said I may as well make myself useful. And I started after a couple of days. I was too angry at first. But then I began to get bored and I was grateful for something to do. I must have spun a mile of it by now!'

'And someone brings you food every day?'

'Yes, one of the Elders I think, but they don't speak. I just hear the basket being left on the window sill. It's such a small window. I can only see a few branches and a little bit of sky. But at night, I can see the stars in the heavens . . . '

She sighed.

'I'm going to find out what's going on, Agnes. Trust me. I've got an idea.'

'But what about . . . him? If he comes again. He said he would.'

'That's my idea. We'll find out what's happening. How much wool have you spun? Really?'

Agnes and Peter waited. Peter had explained to Agnes what he wanted her to do. She wasn't happy, though eventually she had agreed. They waited, and though Peter had often longed to be alone with Agnes, now that it was happening he didn't know what to say or do. Surely there were a thousand things he wanted to ask her? Surely she wanted to talk and talk to him, to hold him and maybe kiss him? But somehow they sat next to each other, as mute as stone. Peter wondered if it was because they were both scared out of their wits, but he began to suspect there was another reason. A reason that shocked him at first, but once he had picked it up and looked at it and turned it over in his mind, a reason that he calmly accepted as something approaching the truth.

The truth. That maybe he didn't love her.

For much of the time they sat in silence on the bed, in reach of each other, but miles apart. After a while Peter found his mind playing tricks on him. He saw tiny pin pricks of light but decided it was his imagination. Nevertheless he felt he could have been anywhere; his enforced blindness seemed to remove the walls from the hut, and even the presence of the forest itself receded until he felt utterly alone.

Hours passed, and Peter was just about to ask Agnes if she had any food, when he heard a noise outside. It was clear from the way Agnes suddenly shifted next to him that she had heard it too.

Silence, for a moment, then: 'Agnes? Agnes? Are you there, pretty one?'

Peter's heart pounded. He reached across and nudged Agnes, wordlessly urging her to answer.

'Yes,' called Agnes up to the window. 'Yes, I'm here.'

Her voice was frail and nervous, and Peter thought it was too obvious, but whoever was outside didn't seem to have noticed.

'Let me in, pretty Agnes!' came the voice.

'Who is it?' Agnes replied.

'It's me,' the voice said. 'Peter.'

Agnes sat dumbly next to Peter, the sheer terror of the moment paralysing her, but Peter nudged her again, willing her to go over to the window. He strained to see in the blackness, all his senses going wild but telling him nothing.

Still she refused to move, but he pushed her to her feet, shoving the end of the wool into her hand as she went. He squeezed her hand.

'I can't let you in, Peter. You know that.'

'Let me in, pretty one. I'm so cold!'

'I can't let you in, Peter.'

'I'm so cold. Feel my hand. Open the shutter and feel my hand.'

There was silence and Peter could imagine Agnes, rooted to the spot from fear. In his mind he tried to force her to move, to stick to his plan.

'Open the shutter, Agnes, pretty one. You felt my hand last night.'

After a long, long pause, Peter heard Agnes move up to the window and unbolt the shutter.

'Here,' she said, bravely.

'See how cold I am?' said the voice. Peter marvelled at it. It didn't sound like him, but it was so quiet that he couldn't have said that it wasn't his own voice either.

'Touch me,' said the voice. Let me in.'

'I won't let you in, Peter.'

'Then kiss me.'

There was another terrible pause, as Agnes steeled herself, trying to be calm enough to go through with what she and Peter had agreed.

'Very well,' she said finally, in a tiny voice. 'I will kiss you. Wait a moment.'

Agnes moved and found the small stool she sat on to work. She pulled it to the window.

Peter waited in an agony of fear, paralysed by inaction. All he could do was pray to the forest to protect her, if that was who he should be praying to.

He heard Agnes climb onto the stool. Then she leant through the window. He heard the faint noise of the thread starting to slip out from the huge winding of wool on the floor, and silently prayed that his idea would work.

There was a moment of total silence, and Peter tried not to think of what was happening. He couldn't hear the kiss.

Then Agnes shrieked.

'You're so cold!'

'Come here!' said the voice, suddenly loud, angry and vicious. 'Let me in, pretty bitch!'

There was the sound of a struggle and thuds fell against the wall outside. Agnes screamed and fell back into the hut. Peter now dared to stand and pull the shutter back into place.

'I'll be back,' said the voice, shrieking in rage. 'I'll be back tomorrow night!'

Silence.

Calling

For a long time, neither Agnes nor Peter dared move. Eventually Peter crawled over and found her huddled on the floor. He held her gently and then realised he could hear something.

The wool was being pulled out slowly from the winding.

'You did it!' Peter cried. 'Well done!'

Agnes was silent.

'You did it.'

Peter went over to the shutter, and felt the wool paying out through the gap between the shutter and frame. It was not moving fast, or even that steadily, but it was moving.

Being careful not to snag the wool, he opened the shutter again, and saw that the snow had stopped. The sky had cleared and there was enough starlight to see the outlines of the trees. He spent a long time looking for the terrible visitor, but could see no sign.

Faint light was spilling onto the floor of the hut now and he checked the pile of wool. Agnes had been busy; there was enough wool to stretch to Turkey as far as he could tell. Making sure it could move freely from the skein that Agnes had coiled from her spinning, he turned to her.

'Agnes. It's time for me to go. Stay here. I'll be back soon.'

He lifted Agnes up and placed her on the bed again, pulling the blanket up to her neck.

She turned to face him.

'Don't go,' she said, her voice small and still.

'I have to. This is what we agreed. You've done your part. Now I must do mine.'

He took her chin in his hands, and tilted her face up to his.

Agnes shivered.

'I kissed him, Peter.'

'You did what you had to. You fixed the wool. That's all that matters.'

'He was so . . . cold. So . . . '

But she couldn't explain what she had felt.

'Stay here,' Peter said, and leant down, kissing her forehead. 'It'll be light soon. That will make you feel better. Close the shutter when I've gone.'

He got up and without another word, set the stool upright by the window once more and climbed out, slightly more easily than when he had entered, earlier in the night.

Once outside, it was easy to tell that dawn was still far off, and it was hard to see clearly. But Peter smiled to himself. He didn't need to see, he just had to follow. Agnes had done her job well. The distaff that she had been spinning with had a metal clip on it. They'd broken the clip off and tied the wool to it. In that awful moment as she leant out of the window, she had fixed the clip onto the back of the jacket of her nocturnal visitor.

Now all Peter had to do was follow the wool, and he

would find the culprit. He tried to tell himself it was probably just some young fool from the village who had a desire for Agnes, but nonetheless, he wished he had his axe with him.

Peter followed the wool, threading his way through the trees.

Agnes lay on the bed in the hut, unable to move. Overwhelmed by fear she blinked in the gloom for a long time, powerless to get up and close the shutter as Peter had told her to. Her mind was occupied with a single thought; she had kissed the thing at the window. She could still taste something on her lips, something foul. At last she made a small movement and wiped her lips with the back of her hand. It felt no better, so she did it again. And again, and again, and then frantically began to scratch at her face, desperate to rid herself of whatever revolting coldness it was that clung to her.

She rolled onto the floor and crawled to find her jug of water, wasting it all trying to wash the taste from her lips. Then she heard a noise at the window.

She lifted her head as she knelt on all fours, like a dog getting a scent.

'Peter?' she called. And then panicked. It *had* to be Peter. Who else could it be?

'Peter! Come in and help me! Come in!'

Things to Cover our Dead

Peter stopped, to check the wool. It lay slack. So. Whoever it was, was back home, and Peter knew that every step he took was a step nearer the mysterious visitor.

He checked the sky. If only dawn were closer. It struck at his heart. He longed to see the sun, for what evil can occur by daylight?

Nonetheless, by starlight he could see the village in front of him, and now he could even see the wool stretching away towards the village. His breath quickened. It would be soon.

Picking up the pace once again, he hurried on, letting the wool run freely through his hand now.

He came to the first houses and saw that the wool ran away up a small alley that he had never noticed before. He must never have made a delivery there, but it didn't matter. He didn't need to know where he was going, he just needed to follow the wool. Once again he praised himself for his quick thinking in the hut, and thought of Agnes. At least she would be safe for the time being. Her assailant was somewhere out there ahead of him, presumably climbing angrily back into bed. Well, he would be angrier still when Peter had finished with him.

He followed the wool up the alley, moving more slowly than before, taking care not to make a sound. He was in luck. The snow that had been falling through the night had been gentle, but persistent, and enough had fallen to re-carpet the streets with a blanket that hid any noise he might have made. Something bothered him as he padded through the snow, but he couldn't place it. A few more steps and he turned round. Behind him he could see his footsteps in the fresh snow. He looked forward again, and there was the wool running in front of him.

So why couldn't he see any footsteps from the man who he was following?

The wool turned a corner into a wider street that he knew well. He'd been convinced that it was going to lead to one of the houses he'd already passed, but they were behind him and the trail showed no sign of ending. Ahead lay the back of the priest's house, but the wool ran on beyond that, and round another corner.

He hurried up the street, glancing at the tarred windows of Daniel's house as he did so, then turned the corner.

He stopped dead.

The wool led away. There were no houses left. There was only the church before him, but that was not where the wool was taking him.

In the half light he could now see the greyish line snake out across the purer whiteness of the snow. The wool caught on a stone here, and on a fence there, but it was unbroken as it led the way, surely and utterly, straight into the graveyard.

Now, moving as if in a nightmare, Peter's feet stepped unwillingly forward. The wool felt like wire in his hands. Maybe it was just that it had been frozen in the snow, but it seemed to cut into his skin like metal.

He came to the gate of the graveyard. There could be no doubt. The wool ran over the fence next to the gate, as if his quarry had sailed clean over it. Dumbly, he gripped it, as if it were a lifeline, leading him to safety, when in reality, it was leading him towards death itself.

The wool wound its way between this grave and that, snagged on crosses, trailing on the ground, and now, his eyes wide open in horror, Peter saw its destination.

There, no more than five feet away, was Stefan's grave. The wool went not only right up to the grave, but then disappeared into the soil itself. Then Peter saw that though there was snow all over the graveyard, and on the other graves, Stefan's was, for some reason, free of it.

An awful self-destructive curiosity pulled Peter closer. Unable to stop himself, he got down on hands and knees and crawled the final few inches towards the grave. As he approached, something else caught his attention. There was a hole in the soil, at the head of the grave, near the cross. The hole was about the size of a small fist, and perfectly circular, like a rat hole in a river bank.

Peter leant over it.

He looked in.

There was just enough light to see inside the hole.

At the bottom he saw an eye.

It was open, seemingly lifeless, though looking straight at him.

Then it blinked.

Peter screamed and ran as if the devil himself were chasing him.

The Hut

*A*t first he ran blind, not thinking where he was going. Not thinking at all. He blundered out of the graveyard to the edge of the village once more, and then he knew where he had to go.

Only once did he stop and look behind, but he couldn't see anything, and neither could he hear anything; and that was some comfort. But what comfort could there be for what he had seen at the bottom of the dreadful hole? That cold, dead eye.

Was that Stefan in there? Dead? Or, even worse maybe, alive?

Agnes! He had to get to Agnes and warn her. Get her to leave the hut.

It didn't take long for him to stumble through the trees, retracing his steps around the edge of the forest and to the hut.

He ran straight to the window.

Silly girl, he thought, seeing the shutter hanging open. But then a worse thought pushed into his mind.

He jumped up at the window, once again landing uncomfortably halfway over the sill.

105

'Agnes! Agnes!'

But already he knew she had gone.

'No!' he shouted. 'Agnes, where are you?'

He dropped inside the hut, frantic, praying that she lay horror-struck in a corner, but she was not there.

Overwhelmed by fear, and tired, he suddenly felt utterly powerless. He forced himself to stay calm. He had to find her. She had gone. Or maybe she had been taken . . .

Whatever, he had to find her.

Yet again, he made to climb from the window of the hut, and then he saw something that froze his blood.

No more than twenty feet from the hut, and heading straight towards it, was the figure of someone he knew to be dead. Radu, the woodcutter. So it was not just Stefan who was out there. How many were there?

Peter gasped, and dropped back into the hut, terrified.

There were noises on the roof. It took him a moment to realise the thumps were footsteps. There was another of them on the roof, too!

He looked to the shutter. Getting to his feet, he waded clear of his terror and made it to the window. He saw Radu nearly at the hut, when suddenly a face appeared, upside down, in front of him.

'Help me!'

It was a face he was glad to see.

He put his arms out and pulled Sofia by her shoulders, dragging her through the window. They collapsed in a heap.

'Quick,' Peter shouted, 'the shutter!'

'Wait,' Sofia cried, and before Peter could do anything, she snatched something from a bag around her waist and flung it out of the window. Only then did she tug the shutter closed and bolt it tight.

'All right,' she said. 'I hope.'

Once again it was dark in the hut, and Peter had no idea what she was talking about, or even what she was doing here.

'I made a circle of it. Right around the hut.'

'Of what?' said Peter, at a loss.

'Millet seeds,' said Sofia simply. 'We'll be safe for a while. Just pray the sun gets here soon.'

'It's at least two hours till sunrise,' Peter said, 'and I don't see that millet will save us from anyone.'

'Really?' Sofia said. 'So have a look for yourself.'

Peter didn't move.

'Go on, have a look!'

Peter crept to the window and peered through a crack in the shutters. Whether it was starlight, or the moon showing at last, he didn't know, but there was enough of a silver grey light outside to cast an appalling scene. There, on the snow-covered ground, he could see thousands of millet seeds, forming a circle around the hut, just as she had said.

Sofia talked to him as he peered through the crack.

'One of them's been in here once already tonight, I think. That's why I used the seed.'

'But what are you doing here?'

'Looking after you,' Sofia said.

'What?'

'I saw you coming up from the village, and then I saw *him*.'

She nodded through the wall.

107

'I climbed a tree, dropped onto the roof and got as much of the stuff around the hut while I could, before he got here.'

Through his spy hole, Peter watched, wide-eyed in horror, as Radu knelt in the snow, picking the seeds up, one by one, placing them in his pockets. Every now and then he glanced up in Peter's direction, and although Peter knew Radu probably couldn't see him, the look of malevolence on his pale face terrified Peter even more.

Sofia, in contrast, seemed calm.

'He can't come in till he's picked them all up.'

'And what if he does?'

She didn't reply.

'And what if he does?' Peter cried, turning away from the crack.

Radu was out of sight somewhere, randomly working his way round the hut. It was even more frightening to Peter to know he was out there, but not be able to see him, and he could bear it no more.

'He's dead, Sofia! That man is dead. I went to his funeral!'

'I know,' she said, frankly, but gently.

'That's no answer! I don't understand. How can he be out there when he's dead?'

'I don't know either. But he is. We call people like him 'hostages'. He is dead and he is out there. And he is trying to get in here.'

'But it's not possible.'

'Did you not see him with your own eyes?'

'Yes, but . . . '

'Then Peter, you must understand that it is possible.'

Peter turned back to the window, to the crack.

Radu was in sight again, still slowly working his way through the seed. His fingers were swollen, and clumsy, and he was making heavy going of it. His skin was blue, in places almost black.

'And if the sun comes up before he finishes, then we're safe?'

'Yes,' said Sofia, 'for the time being.'

Peter wheeled round on his heels like a trapped animal looking for an escape, but there was none.

'And you? What do you mean you're looking after me? I don't understand.'

'Be still, Peter. We must be calm.'

'Calm? How can you be calm?'

Sofia put her arms out wide, a gesture of submission.

'Peter, you think this is easy for me? You think I am not scared enough to drop dead right here? Because I am. I am. But I have something you do not. I have knowledge. I have done this before, many times. But trust me, you will need all your wits about you. You will need to be calm, in order to live. Do you understand me?'

Peter shook his head, in disbelief, but he understood.

'But what about Agnes?' he said. 'I must find her.'

'I think it is probably too late for your friend.'

'How can you say that?' Peter cried. 'What do you know?'

'I know that she has been taken from here. Given what you have seen you should understand. We can do nothing. For the moment we are trapped. If we can get out then that is a start. That might be of some help.'

It was almost too much for Peter.

'What do you mean?'

'If we can get out of this, so good. But there is a greater evil at work. There are bigger battles to be fought.'

Something clicked inside Peter.

'You mean the Shadow Queen, don't you. But I don't understand.'

'No,' said Sofia. 'I know. Your father has spent your whole life stopping you from understanding.'

'What do you know of my father?'

Sofia paused.

'More than you do, I suspect.'

The Winter King

*I*t was strange. Even as it was happening, Peter knew it was strange. It was like sitting in the centre of a hurricane. Outside, a man whom he had seen buried was prowling around, intent on doing them harm, and only prevented from doing so by millet seeds. Inside the hut, in relative safety, he sat quietly, though not peacefully, with a girl he barely knew, as she told him the story of his father.

'Have you heard of the Winter King, Peter?' Sofia asked.

'Yes,' he answered. 'It's a story. The King who'll save us all from every evil. He was supposed to have saved the land from the Turks. Everyone knows that story. But it's just a story that the peasants tell each other.'

'The peasants? That's not you talking. That's your father. It's more than a story. Your father could tell you that the Winter King is real. Or was. Your father fought with him.'

Peter laughed.

'Don't be foolish. My father fought with King Michael. They fought the Turks.'

'That's right, Peter. King Michael *was* the Winter King. That was thirty years ago, no more. But memories are short when lives are short. Already the King has become a legend.

'The Turks were greater in number, but the forest in winter is a treacherous place for the unwary. They were overcome by King Michael's men. Massacred. Some escaped and slipped away in to the depths of the trees, never to be heard of again. The Mother Forest dealt with them. When her anger is aroused she takes no prisoners, but it wouldn't have happened without the Winter King.'

Peter nodded his head. He understood what she meant about the forest, and thought about why he made his little carvings, to give something back. It would never do to betray the forest's generosity; Peter believed that those who thought the forest was simply a gathering of trees were foolish, unwise, and that there was something else that gathered *among* those trees.

'The Winter King,' Sofia said, 'who will save us from all evil. Now he must save us from the Shadow Queen. His greatest battle ever.'

'But he's dead. King Michael is dead.'

'Yes. He died and the new king was weak. He let the country crumble into factions, no longer unified. In the chaos that followed many bad things happened. Fighting between men who had been allies. And your father was put in jail.'

'How do you know this?'

'I know because your father fought with my father.'

'A gypsy? Fought with King Michael.'

'A gypsy, yes, Peter,' Sofia glared at him. 'What is so wrong with that? There is more to some of us than there might seem.'

'And your father is here now? He spoke to my father that night when . . . '

112

Peter stopped.

'My father is dead. He died in jail when I was just three years old. My uncle leads us. My uncle, Milosh. And yes, he went to speak to your father that night, when we met on the road.'

Peter remembered it all too clearly. He hated himself, with Agnes missing, but he couldn't help remembering what had happened. What he had felt. Blood rushed to his face as he remembered how he had carried Sofia, cradled her arms and long slender legs, and how she had held his hand.

'I'm sorry about your father,' Peter said, but Sofia merely held his gaze, a sorrowful look on her face.

'That night,' Peter said, quietly.

'What of it?'

'That night, when you . . . '

Sofia interrupted him.

'Don't think anything,' she said, flatly. 'I was sent to delay you from returning home, so my uncle could speak to your father alone. I did what I had to do. My uncle has been following your father for years and he didn't want anyone to get in his way.'

Now Peter was angry. With himself, with Sofia. Too angry even to ask why her uncle had been hunting Tomas. Was that why they'd always lived on the move? Always keeping to the edges of the civilised world? He was not surprised at what she said, and yet, he knew he was disappointed too. An image of Agnes flickered into his mind and though he tried to push her away, he could not do so entirely.

Frustrated, he turned back to the crack in the shutter.

Still Radu crawled around. Peter tried to work out if more than half the seed was left on the ground, but Radu's feet had turned the snow to mush, making it hard to see anything clearly. He wondered if it was his imagination, but it seemed to him that Radu was moving faster than before.

He turned back to Sofia.

'And now?'

'What do you mean?'

'So the Shadow Queen is coming. Making dead people walk again. To make us like them? But the Winter King is dead. How can he save us now?'

'King Michael is dead. But the Winter King lives. In us. In your father. In us, the gypsies. Even in you, Peter. We all belong to each other, to the ancestors, and we can fight. We have fought for as long as I can remember. Moving, travelling, fighting. We live the life of gypsies, but we fight the fight of the Winter King.'

She stopped.

Peter shook his head, sighing. It was too much. He didn't want to be here, didn't want to believe what he was hearing – a story coming to life.

'Peter. You must join the Winter King. We need you. We need your father.'

'Why?'

'Because your father was the finest warrior in King Michael's army. He was famed for it. And he had something else. A sword. A Turkish sword. He found it on a campaign far into Turkish territory in the summer before that final battle in the winter forest.'

'A sword? What sword?'

114

'A fine sword, Peter. One that is perfectly balanced. It is as light as the wind, yet as hard as the winter. But there is more to it than that. It stops them.'

'What do you mean?' Peter asked, still confused by everything Sofia was revealing to him.

'People like him. Outside. The woodcutter. The sword stops them. Returns them to the soil, for good. It was forged in a land often plagued by such people. There they call them vrykolakoi. Here we call them nosferatu, or moroii. It is all the same. They are all hostages. And once, it is said, they were as common as the blades of grass in the meadow, or berries in a pail. In every land they have a thousand names. It doesn't matter; it is up to us to stop them.'

'Us?'

'Us,' said Sofia. 'The ancestors. All across the land there are groups of us. Some are gypsies, some are soldiers, some are common people, some are priests. It doesn't matter. Those who fight the hostages are all ancestors; my uncle, my father, your father. Even you, Peter.'

Peter shook his head, incredulous.

'We need your father's sword.'

'My father was no warrior. My father has no sword,' said Peter. 'I would have seen it.'

But even as he said the words, he thought of the box his father had kept from him all these years. Was it possible? Was there really a sword inside?

'Perhaps,' said Sofia. 'But wherever it is, we must find it.'

'My father is no hero,' Peter said bitterly, still refusing to believe. 'He fought with Michael, that is true, but he is not a great soldier. My father is a drunkard.'

Sofia stared at him, but Peter could not fathom what she was thinking.

Now something else struck him. Saying nothing, he moved yet again to the crack in the shutter.

He stepped back, as if he had been stung.

'Sofia,' he said. 'Look.'

She came and pressed her face to the hole, and gasped.

Outside, Radu was busy picking up the seeds, but Peter's fears had proved true. Radu was moving more quickly. His hands flew through the snow, sending small flurries all around him.

It was not possible, but it seemed that he grew faster with every passing minute, until he whirled around the hut, like a dervish, faster and faster.

The remaining seeds grew fewer, and fewer. Very soon, there would be none left at all.

Escape

'What are we going to do?' Peter cried.

'I don't know,' Sofia said quietly. 'I'm thinking.'

'There's no sign of dawn. He'll be finished long before!'

'Listen to me. How far is it from here to your hut?'

'Not far,' said Peter, 'but far enough. Why?'

'I've got a little of the millet left. If we throw it behind us as we run, he'll have to stop and collect it.'

'This is madness!'

'Can you break the door down?'

Peter looked at the door and nodded.

'I think so. How much seed do you have left?'

Sofia showed him the scraps left in the bottom of the little sack-cloth bag. He didn't like what he saw.

'Very well,' he said. 'I'll break the door down as soon as he's on the far side. I'll lead the way, you throw the seed. And I warn you I am a fast runner.'

'So am I,' said Sofia, tipping her chin up. 'A kiss for luck?'

But Peter was in no mood to play her games.

Sofia moved to the shuttered window, her hand raised, waiting till she saw Radu move away.

'Oh!' she whispered. 'He's finished!'

'Then it's time to go!'

Peter ran at the door and jumped, landing with both boots square on near the lock. The wood was in fact quite thin, splinters flew in all directions, and the door smashed open with a loud crack.

Peter landed in the snow and the wreckage of the door, and scrambled to his feet. He heard footsteps immediately behind him and for a second thought it was Radu, but Sofia passed him in an instant, flinging a few grains of millet as she went.

'Come!' was all she had time to yell, and Peter followed.

Within a few strides he had caught her, and grabbed her hand, pulling her on. He threw a glance behind. What he saw made his limbs want to seize and stop, but he forced himself to run. Hardly more than a breath behind them, Radu followed, lurching through the snow.

Sofia flung another handful of grain which struck Radu in the face, and he howled, hurling himself to the ground, scrabbling to pick it all up.

Now at last they put some distance between themselves and their pursuer. They did not dare slow down, and sickeningly, as Peter looked back once more, he could see Radu closing on them again with shocking speed. If he could run that fast, Peter thought, what in the name of God was his strength like?

Fleetingly, he wondered how they would be any safer in his father's hut than the one they had left, but they were running too hard to gasp a single word to each other, and Peter decided that if they could get to the hut, he could perhaps get to one of their axes before Radu got to them. And his father? Maybe he could help them. Was there really a sword in that box? If what Sofia said about him was true . . .

Even as he ran, Peter knew that was ludicrous. His father was a drunkard, who must have malingered his way through his years under King Michael. He was no use.

Sofia shouted at him.

Stop shouting, Peter thought, just run! He bounded a few more paces through the trees, before realising what she had said.

'It's all gone!'

They were on their own now, with only their legs to keep them from harm. Radu groped in the snow, then stood. He had all the seeds.

Sofia shrieked and, for a few steps, overtook Peter.

'There!' he shouted. 'The hut!'

Had he turned he would have seen Radu close behind, his hands clawing out towards them, inches away.

A dozen more paces would see them over the bridge. But Radu was on them. Seeing that Sofia was the easier target, Radu flung himself at her. Sensing the attack, She dodged to the side, but she had misjudged her distance from the river itself, and the bank gave way under her foot.

She slipped and tumbled into the water with an almighty splash.

Peter stopped, only feet from the bridge. He hesitated, seeing Radu standing on the bank, looking at Sofia in the water. Then he spun around and saw Peter, and made for him.

'Go!' shouted Sofia, from the water. The current was taking her the wrong way, away from the hut and the island on which it stood, but she seemed to be swimming.

Peter didn't need telling twice.

He ran over the bridge, screaming.

'Father! Father! Wake up!'

Peter made the hut, not daring once to look back, desperate to find his axe, but as he burst through the door, it suddenly occurred to him that he had heard no footsteps on the bridge behind him.

He turned in the doorway, and saw Radu on the far side of the bridge, shaking his fists at him, but making no effort to cross. Peter watched, confused and relieved in equal measure, as Sofia reached the island.

'Help me out!' she called to Peter, angrily.

He ran over to her and wrapping his hands around her wrists, pulled her in one long motion from the water and up the steep bank.

'What in the devil is going on?'

Tomas staggered from the hut, a lamp in his hand, pushing the hair back from his eyes with the other. He had been dragged from a bottomless sleep, and was not amused.

'Father!' Peter cried. 'It was after us! Look there!'

But when Peter pointed to where Radu had stood at the edge of the bridge, there was nothing but the rustle of bare branches in the half-light.

He had gone.

The Island

Peter stood, panting heavily. He began to shake and for a while was unaware of his father shouting.

Sofia was wet through with icy river water. She moved to Peter who acknowledged her with a lifeless smile.

'What in God's name?' Tomas said. He grabbed Peter by the scruff of his neck. 'What are you playing at? Who's that?'

Sofia stepped right up to Tomas, ignoring his rage.

'You know me, Tomas!' she declared. 'I am Sofia, Caspar's daughter.'

For a moment Peter thought he saw a glimmer in his father's eyes, but it was gone.

'I don't know what you're talking about,' Tomas said, deliberately. 'I don't know anyone called Caspar.'

Sofia fell back suddenly, as though he had struck her.

'Liar,' she said.

Tomas lifted his hand in fury, but Peter stepped between them.

Tomas tried to push him aside, but Peter stood firm, though his legs shook.

'Father,' he said. 'Why are you angry? If this girl is nothing to you? Or do you know her?'

Tomas spun away.

'Get her off here!' he spat.

Peter pulled Tomas back and was surprised by how easy it was. He looked at his father's face as if for the first time. His face was ruddy and swollen from drinking, his nose pockmarked, his cheeks veined and broken. He stank of drink. He was old.

As they stood facing one another, Peter became aware that daybreak had come. A few low streaks of sunlight pushed weakly through the trees, gules dappling the roof of the hut here and there.

'Father,' he said again, more quietly this time. 'Sofia says you knew her father, that you fought with him, for King Michael. Is that true?'

Tomas stared at his son.

'She says you were put in jail after the war. With her father. And she says that you have a sword. A sword that stops these people who have come back from their graves.'

Tomas blinked, and walked away, still mute.

Peter wouldn't give up.

'What is it? What are these people, who won't stay dead? Father?'

'Nonsense,' Tomas said over his shoulder. He moved towards the door. 'All nonsense, and gypsy tales.'

'No!' Sofia cried, 'No. Look at me! I am soaked to the skin. We were chased by a dead man. He chased us here!'

'Nonsense,' Tomas said again.

'No!'

Sofia stepped towards Tomas, seething, but now Peter

stopped her, grabbing her soaking sleeve firmly at the elbow.

'Sofia,' he said gently. 'Don't.'

'What, Peter? You too? Do you think this is a gypsy tale? Your father knows it's true. Ask him! Ask him why he built a house on an island if it's all nonsense!'

Peter's hand dropped from her arm.

'What do you mean?'

'Do you need to ask? You saw the dead woodcutter stop at the water. You saw it with your own eyes. They cannot cross running water, which is why your father put himself on an island in a river! Ask him!'

Peter was cold and tired, shaking violently now, and yet his heart had just been chilled still further.

'Is that why you did it, Father?' he said. 'Is that why you dug the channel?'

Nothing.

Then Tomas turned back from the doorway.

'Get her off here,' he said, almost too quietly to hear.

'Father, we can't do that. She's wet to the . . . '

'Get her away! Go!'

Thrown into a rage, Tomas spat the words, his eyes wild. Just as suddenly tears welled in the old man's eyes, as he stood in the doorway, defeated.

Peter looked at his father and his shame was almost too much to endure.

He turned to Sofia.

'It's all right,' she said, before he could speak. 'I'll go.'

'You can't,' Peter said, but she was already crossing the bridge.

'It's not safe.'

Peter lifted his hand to Sofia, but in friendship.

'It's safe enough,' she said. 'The sun is almost here. There can be no evil by daylight. I must go back to my people.'

'Wait!' Peter said. 'You'll freeze before you get there.'

He was weighing something up in his mind.

'Take Sultan,' he said, at last. 'He'll give you some warmth and you'll be home quickly. I'll come for him later.'

Sofia nodded.

'Thank you. You must not worry. I'll look after him.'

Peter smiled.

'When Father finds out . . . '

Sofia returned the smile.

They fetched Sultan from his stall. He seemed pleased to see Peter. He snorted steam into the cold morning air.

Sofia swung herself easily into the saddle.

'What will you do?' she asked.

'I'm going to look for Agnes. I must.'

'Peter, you should know . . . '

'Don't say it,' Peter said, interrupting her. 'I must try to find her. She . . . I . . . '

He hesitated. He couldn't say what he was thinking, and anyway, he didn't even know if it was true. Had there ever been anything between them?

'I understand,' Sofia said. 'But be careful.' She leant down in the saddle, and taking Peter by surprise, kissed his cheek.

'For luck,' she explained, kicking Sultan into life. She laughed. 'You should have let me do it before – we might have had an easier time of it!'

Peter watched her go, and then heard her begin to sing.

She sang the Miorita, of course, and Peter smiled in spite of himself.

> Let it just be said I have gone to wed
> A princess so great; at Heaven's gate.

Peter watched her go, and without even meaning to, raised a hand to his cheek, feeling the wetness of her lips with his fingertips.

As soon as she was out of sight Peter suddenly realised how bitterly cold he was. He went into the hut, and saw his father poking the fire, trying to coax it into life after its quiet slumber through the long night.

'Father,' Peter said.

Tomas lifted his head.

'Has she gone?' he asked, still shaking from his outburst, but Peter didn't answer. Through his mind ran a series of pictures, each more evil than the last, culminating with the awful sight of Stefan's eye staring from inside his grave.

'Son?'

Exhausted, freezing, and scared, Peter's body gave up, and the world faded as he collapsed onto the floor.

The Dream of the Queen

*I*n the dreamworld through which Peter struggled, everything was shadow. As he lay unconscious, he knew nothing, saw nothing, yet somewhere nearby a presence closed in on him.

Out of the darkness, a white spectre floated towards him. As it came closer he saw a pale face, disembodied and deathly. It was the face of an ancient but powerful woman, with strong nose and eyebrows, and vicious eyes. Now the face pressed right against his own, and he saw that though the face was ghost-white, there was a shadow across it, from eyes to lips, a strange five-sided shadow, like an inverted pentagon hanging from the brow and pointing at the lips.

The face drifted away, and fortunately for Peter, when he woke, he remembered nothing of his nightmare.

Ancestors and Hostages

*W*hen Peter woke, it was to the sound of singing. Someone was singing the Miorita, but as he opened his eyes he realised that it was him. Had he been singing in his sleep?

> *Tell my murderers*
> *To let my bones lie somewhere close by,*
> *By the sheepfold here so my flocks are near,*
> *On the open ground, so I'll hear my hound.*
>
> *Tell not a breath of how I met my death,*
> *Say I could not tarry; I have gone to marry*
> *A princess - my bride is the whole world's pride.*

That stupid song! It was even in his dreams now.

Peter opened his eyes and found he was lying in bed. He swung his legs to the floor and sat up, rubbing his head.

Suddenly he knew what it was about that song that annoyed him so much. It was the weakness of it. The meekness. The way the shepherd gives in, without even trying to fight his murderers. Peter couldn't understand it, giving in to fate, to death, without even trying to stop it. Surely you had to be stronger than that, to survive? To live?

Tomas was nowhere in sight. The shutter was open and Peter saw bright, burning daylight beyond, though he had no idea what time it might be. Daylight. How he had longed for it! How he wished it would never grow dark again. What had Sofia said?

'There can be no evil by daylight.'

He stood up, unsteadily at first, unable to get the Miorita out of his head. He thought about the end of the song, where the shepherd marries the princess from the stars. That's the story he tells his lamb to pass on to his mother. To stop her from grieving, from being hurt. Peter understood that. If only he hadn't hurt his own mother. It had been his first act in the world. His birth, her death. If only he could have saved her from harm! And though he knew he was guiltless, the guilt still came.

The full meaning of the ending was lost to him; a cloud he could not penetrate. Nonetheless, there was something about the story that was pulling him in. The princess. A wedding to the cosmos. A place and a purpose in life, even in death.

No.

He killed his thoughts, tired of it all.

Peter put his hand above the stove. Still warm. Gradually everything that had happened came back to him, right up to the moment when he had collapsed. Someone, presumably Father, had put him into bed, but how long had he slept? His belly ached with hunger, so maybe it had been a long time.

He felt awful. He was hungry, his head hurt, his legs ached, but he had to ignore all that, because there was something he had to do. The something was Agnes, and now he remembered the shock of finding her prison hut empty when he had returned from the graveyard.

'By the Forest!' Peter said, aloud. 'What is happening here?'

He needed his father. He checked the tool box and found that his father's axe was missing. Had he actually gone to work? Without Sultan?

He was useless as a source of physical help, but Peter instinctively knew that what Sofia had told him about Tomas was all true. If only Tomas would admit it, then maybe he could help Peter to understand the things he'd seen. In the hut, in the graveyard, in the forest . . .

All he really wanted to do was harness Sultan to their cart, put Tomas and everything they owned onto it, and ride far, far away. Peter had once heard there was a country to the west by the sea, a warm country where grapes as large as apples hung from endless vines. Maybe they could just ride and ride until they found it.

But Tomas was out somewhere, he had lent Sultan to the gypsy girl, and there was Agnes to find. If anything had happened to her . . .

He closed that thought because the end of it puzzled him, and was not what he wanted to feel.

Then he remembered something else.

The sword.

Sofia had talked about a sword and now after all these

years, Peter knew what was in his father's box without even opening it. He looked around the room until his eyes fell on his father's mattress. That was where it was.

He took a step towards the bed, then hesitated, thinking about a small wooden goose, and the tears he had shed when Tomas had destroyed it.

But no.

There should be no more secrets.

Guiltily, he stepped forward and lifted the mattress, feeling out with his other hand for the box.

There was nothing there.

The Elders

*P*eter walked to Chust. As he went he chewed on some rye bread he'd found in the jar, trying to quell his aching belly and find some strength. By the time he reached the village, the bread was all gone, but his hunger remained.

'That will have to do,' he said.

He had no plan, but as he walked down the main street he suddenly thought that maybe he should start at the hut. That was where he had last seen Agnes. Maybe daylight would give some clue as to where she had gone. Maybe some tracks.

The thought of daylight made him look to the sky. The earlier morning sun had vanished behind a high and thick bank of cloud. But, it seemed light enough, and he had no choice. He would go back to the hut.

He retraced his steps back up the main street. As he went his thoughts were invaded by the events of the night. He had seen things that were not possible, or rather that his father had told him were not possible. All his life Tomas had told him to ignore the stories they heard, as they moved from one town to the next. Now, in the smallest, God-forgotten place they had ever lived, it had all come true. It had all come to life, just like Radu and Stefan seemed to have done.

He was passing underneath a high window, when his attention was caught by raised voices.

He might have walked on, were it not for two words.

' . . . Shadow Queen . . . '

He paused, but could make out no more, because of the babble of voices. Deciding he was wasting time, he hurried on towards the hut.

It looked so different by daylight. What had been a place of living terror a few hours before was now simply lifeless; cold and empty. By day, though still not welcoming, it held none of the horrors of the night.

Peter hunted around, but found nothing. There had been enough snowfall in the night to obscure even the frantic marks Radu had made scrabbling for the millet. The wood from the shattered door lay cast around, almost hidden but for one or two spikes of timber.

And in the freshly fallen snow there was not the slightest sign of a footprint, or anything else that might have given Peter a clue.

Inside, his search was just as useless. There was nothing there, but the bed, the stool, and piles of unspun wool.

The only thing he learned from his visit was that it had been real. Everything he had thought he had seen, all the awfulness, had really happened.

He sat on the stool, wondering what to do. In truth, he knew there was only one answer, but he didn't like it. He must walk back to Chust, find an Elder, tell them what had happened, and ask for help looking for Agnes.

The Elders. Old Anna, taciturn but fearsome. He certainly didn't want to face them. And then he realised – those voices floating down to him from the window had come from Anna's house.

An irrational anger seized him, and he stormed back into Chust.

31

Village Talk

*H*e didn't even knock.

As he thundered towards Anna's house, it occurred to him that it was all her fault. She was the one who ran things in the village, she had ordered that Agnes should be the bride at the Nunta Mortului. She must know by now that Agnes was missing, that the door of her prison lay splintered in the snow. She should have organised a search party.

He burst into Anna's house and followed his instincts up a low flight of stairs. There. He could hear the voices again, and flung open a door, striding into the room, all sorts of accusations on his lips.

What he saw took the words away.

'How dare you!' Anna was the first to recover from the shock of Peter's entrance.

She was surrounded by a motley group. Other Elders, as well as Daniel, the priest, and Teodor, the feldsar, stood arranged on one side of Anna. On the other Peter was amazed to see a party of the gypsies. Sofia was not there, but Peter recognised Milosh, her uncle, at their head.

Peter suddenly doubted himself. Feeling like a small and

stupid boy he wanted to run from the room, but he forced himself to speak.

'Agnes!' he blurted out.

'What?'

Anna barked the word at him, and even that was enough to unsettle him. She was an alarming figure. Very tall for an old woman, her face was sharp and her nose sharper. She had eyebrows like a man's that seemed fixed perpetually in a scowl. It was no wonder she ordered everyone else around, controlling this wretched little kingdom with ease.

Peter tried again, desperately trying to make some sense.

'Agnes! You put her in the hut, but she's been taken! By those things!'

Anna took several steps towards him, and despite himself, Peter retreated slightly.

'People are coming back from the grave!' he yelled. 'You know it. I heard you talking about the Shadow Queen. And they know it!'

He pointed at the gypsies.

'They've come to try to stop it, but Agnes is missing! You have to do something! Help me find her.'

Peter stopped. The silence in the room that followed was even more terrifying than Anna herself.

'This is not your place, boy,' Anna said, when she was sure he had finished. 'You do not belong in this village. You and your useless father! I have tolerated you. Now I find out there is more to you than at first appeared.'

Almost imperceptibly she glanced towards the gypsies. They must have told her about Tomas. The sword.

'You should understand this, boy. Chust is my concern.

Do not trespass on my patience. I am aware of everything, not just in Chust, but all around it. I have been discussing the threat posed by the Shadow Queen with those assembled here. These people, from the village and outside it, who are wise enough and powerful enough to act. And yet you dare to break in here and insult us all!'

She stopped for effect, and Peter took the opportunity.

'But Agnes,' he gasped. 'You've as good as killed her! She was taken. Why don't you . . . '

'Be quiet!' Anna shrieked, with such intent that the room seemed to darken. 'You know nothing. Yes. Agnes is no longer where she should be. In the hut. But she was not taken. She left herself. You helped her! She has disgraced us all by breaking her honour in this way.'

'No,' said Peter. 'That's not true. She's missing.'

'Enough!' Anna declared. 'Remove him. We have no time.'

The men closed around Peter, and though he struggled, they forced him from the room easily, and dragged him back down the stairs.

In a moment he found himself sitting in the street in the snow.

'But Agnes!' he cried. 'We must find her and help her.'

One of the Elders paused and considered Peter.

'You are a foolish boy. Agnes is at home. With her mother. She has disgraced herself, and you helped her do it. Count yourself fortunate we don't punish you and your father for the shame of it all.'

'At home?' Peter could scarcely believe what the man had said. 'At home?'

'Go and see for yourself.'

The man spat at Peter's feet, and shut the door.

Peter stood up, and looked down the street that led to Agnes' house.

He ran all the way there, skidding in the snow and ice.

He didn't even have to get as far as her house.

There she was, up ahead of him, looking just as she always did, though Peter saw with a shiver that she was still dressed in her mourning weeds. Why hadn't she changed to her own clothes? The forty days had been broken after all; was there still a need to dress for them?

She was crossing the street, towards her front door.

'Agnes!' he called, breaking into a run again as he saw her unlock the door.

He saw her turn and look at him, but the relief he felt rapidly turned to confusion, as she saw him, then deliberately looked away.

She opened the door and while Peter was still yards away, slid inside.

Peter was in time to hear the door being bolted from inside.

'Agnes!' he called through the door.

No answer. He tried again, this time slamming the palm of his hand against the wood.

'Agnes! What is it? What's wrong?'

'Go away, Peter.'

Her voice came through the wood, muffled and faint.

'What?' Peter cried. 'What do you mean? Are you all right? I've been looking for you since . . . What happened to you?'

138

'Go away, Peter.'

Once again, her voice dull and flat.

'Why are you being like this, Agnes? What's wrong?'

Peter strained to hear her, pressing his ear to the door to catch her words.

'Go away. I left the hut and now I'm in disgrace. My whole family. Hah! What's left of it. Go away, Peter. I want nothing to do with you. I never did want you. You were never good enough for me. Now you are less than useless.'

'Agnes!'

'I'm well, Peter. Does that make you happy? Now go away.'

Peter stepped back from the door, looking stupidly at the wood, trying but failing to understand.

Agnes was right.

What was he good for?

He walked away.

As he went he passed again by Anna's house, but this time could hear nothing.

Neither did he see Old Anna looking down at him, as a wide smile slowly spread across her face.

'The sword.'

She mouthed the words silently.

'The sword!'

Stillness

*P*eter brooded. Tomas drank. For days neither of them stirred from their own little island.

Something had changed.

For a year or so, Tomas and his son had enjoyed a period of relative comfort and simplicity. They had stopped running and found a place to live, with plenty of work to be done, and for some of that time Tomas had even been sober enough to do some of that work.

Not any more. Everything was closing in around them, like snow clouds sometimes enveloped the mountains and the forest. The flakes that fell from them were the purest white, but the clouds from which they fell were darker than confusion, darker than death.

Tomas had only spoken once. He'd been staring out into the forest from the door of the hut, when without warning he said, 'We may have to move on, Peter.'

That was all, and he would say no more, despite Peter's questions and pleading. Peter was left running over everything that had happened in his mind, again and again, struggling for the answers he desperately craved.

The day after Peter had been thrown from Anna's house, the day he had seen Agnes, they had a visitor.

Peter was stirred from his mood by the sound of hoof beats on the bridge.

He went outside to find Sofia leading Sultan home.

'You didn't come for him,' Sofia said.

Peter shrugged.

'I had things to do,' he said.

'There,' she said, smiling. 'I looked after him. As I promised.'

Peter took Sultan's reins willingly enough, but didn't speak.

Sofia watched him stable the horse and come back to the front of the hut. She tried again.

'It was kind of you. To lend him to me,' she said. She hesitated. 'It was good of you to . . . trust me.'

Peter turned to her.

'I did trust you, Sofia,' he said. 'But then I found your uncle telling the village Elders all about my father. My father just wants to be left alone. You had no right to do that.'

'I am not responsible for what my uncle does,' Sofia snapped. 'But that is not the point. It is hardly important what anyone knows about you and your father. They went to talk to the Elders about the threat from the Shadow Queen. They went to offer their services in the name of the Winter King. You can't hide on your little island forever, Peter.'

Peter waited for her to finish, then went back inside.

'Thank you for returning Sultan to us,' he said quietly as he entered the hut.

Through the door he heard Sofia.

'The Miorita, Peter. You should understand it.'

He heard her gentle footsteps retreat across the bridge, the bridge to their *little island*.

Damn her! Peter thought. What did she mean by that? The Miorita? What had that to do with anything? And yet, it was not only the gypsy girl who had got under his skin. That song had too.

'*You should understand it.*'

What did it mean?

After that brief encounter, Peter had spent the hours lying on his bed, ignoring Tomas as he opened jar after jar of rakia, thinking about Agnes, about the forest, and Radu and Stefan. About Sofia.

And yes, about the Miorita, too.

After three days, Peter's body rebelled. His mind might have been drifting rudderless like a raft on the open sea, but his body was used to hard work and he was restless. Finally, on the third morning, he practically threw himself out of bed and pulled his boots on so violently that even Tomas raised an eyebrow.

'What are you doing?' Tomas asked.

'Going to work,' Peter said. 'It's all I know.'

He grabbed his axe, put Sultan into the harness of the cart and they lurched off into the depths of the snowy forest.

Peter didn't particularly care where they went, but at the back of his mind was a tree that he and Tomas had been going to fell some weeks before. It was a huge old birch and

143

it would take days to saw and chop it all, but Peter just wanted to see it fall, and smash to the ground. His body cried out for it. And he wanted this wood to fall, not to carve, but to burn.

After an hour or so they found the tree. They were far into the depths of the forest, but it was a sunny morning, and for a short while it was possible to believe that mid-winter was more than a few weeks away. Peter tethered Sultan to a tree some way from the birch, more from habit than necessity. His horse was by some way the most reliable thing in his life. That, and possibly the forest, though recent events had made him begin to doubt that the forest was always benign.

Peter sized the tree. Even from the ground it looked vast, and he had learned in his career as a woodcutter that no matter how big a tree looked in the air, it would be twice as big when it was on the ground. He tried to circle its girth with his arms, and could only just brush his fingertips against each other.

He stood back, made a silent prayer of thanks to the forest, and then swung his axe as if his life depended on it.

Woodchips rained around him, and around Peter's feet the snow was rapidly covered with the spoil from his axe.

Something possessed him as the axe flew through the air faster and faster with each stroke. He formed a perfect undercut in less than twenty strokes, and freed the opposite side of the tree from its sheath of bark. Then he began the real work, making the cut that would bring the monster to the ground, exactly where he wanted it.

Still the blows from the axe fell, and nothing could have

stood in its way, not twenty men, and least of all a tree, even one that would keep a family warm for a whole winter. A vision of his father thirty years ago came into his mind, in King Michael's army, fighting the Turks. And maybe other, more deadly enemies.

Peter's axe fell. Tomas' sword swung.

Both cut their foe to the ground, blow after blow after blow.

Suddenly Peter stopped. He had been so hypnotised by the swing of his axe, that he had barely noticed how far he had cut. The trunk where he'd been chopping gave a deafening crack, as if lightning had struck nearby. The tree moved. It had begun to go.

Peter stood back, knowing he had done enough. How slowly it moved at first, barely perceptible, as it inched its way from the sky. There was another crack as the timber split under its own weight, and then the tree came with a rush, leaning into the air, finding nothing to support it, and accelerating downwards till it hammered into the snowy floor of the forest.

The ground shook.

Sultan whinnied and Peter looked over at him.

'That's all for today,' he said. On any other day he would have begun the process of sawing logs short enough for Sultan to drag home. The cart was empty and waiting, but Peter wanted to do no more work. He had escaped from the torpor of the hut, and felt his body come alive once more. More than that, he had been in control, and it felt good.

Peter never knew how it happened, but suddenly he saw something glinting in the snow. Looking closer, he saw it was an axe and immediately, instinctively, he knew whose it was. It had belonged to Radu.

Suddenly he was filled with dread, seeing the axe as an omen.

His exhilaration at felling the tree evaporated, for he was certain, as certain as he had ever been of anything, that his father was in trouble. At that very moment.

Even as his blows had struck the tree.

He wasted no time, but freed Sultan from the harness, and leaving the cart and the fallen tree where they were, galloped back home.

Tomas

As soon as Peter saw the hut, he knew he was right. Whatever it was that had told him of the danger to his father had not lied.

Peter rode Sultan straight over the bridge, and threw himself from the horse's back, then froze. The place had been turned upside down.

There had obviously been a fight; the saw donkey lay on its side, the stable door was swinging open, the log pile by the hut had collapsed.

Then Peter saw blood in the snow. An irregular, smeary trail of it leading across the small triangle that was their island, to the ditch that Tomas had dug. With bile rising in his throat, he followed the trail, dreading what he might find. He looked over the lip of the bank and saw a body face down in the water, snagged by a tree root.

Peter recognised the clothes. It was one of the gypsies. He turned and ran to the hut.

'Father! Father?'

There was Tomas, lying beside his bed as if he'd been trying to get there before collapsing on the floor. Peter crouched beside him.

'I thought you were . . . ' Peter began, but couldn't bring himself to say it.

Tomas smiled, but he was obviously weak. Next to him on the floor was his axe. Peter saw blood on the blade, and he knew whose it was.

'Are you hurt?'

Tomas shook his head.

'Fit as a flea. Help me up, will you?'

Peter tried to lift his father onto the bed, but couldn't manage it. He was so heavy, now, it was hard to believe.

With a grunt Tomas sank back to the floor, and Peter knew he had been lying about being hurt.

'What did they do?'

'Nothing,' Tomas smiled. 'I wouldn't let them.'

'Wait,' Peter said, and dragged the covers from the bed. 'Lie on these instead, till you're ready to get up.'

'Get me a drink, would you?' Tomas said, wincing as he rolled onto the makeshift bed.

Peter didn't know what to say, but that in itself was enough to irritate Tomas.

'I've just been attacked by four men. I've killed one of them. I need a damn drink, Peter!'

Peter nodded.

'Sorry. Yes, yes.'

He fumbled around with a bottle, trying to find a mug.

'Give me that.'

Tomas snatched it from Peter and drank deeply. Slivovitz dribbled down his chin, and dripped onto his shirt.

Peter knelt by his father again.

'What did they want with you, Father? Why did they do this?'

Tomas took another drink, then looked into Peter's face.

'I'm sorry, Peter,' he said. 'I've lied to you.'

Peter shook his head, putting his hand onto his father's shoulder.

'Listen to me. I've lied to you. About so many things.'

'I don't care,' Peter said gently, 'I don't care about that. Why did they do this? What did they want with you?'

'It's not me they want. Well, not any more. Not now I'm like this.'

Peter wasn't sure whether he meant hurt, or something more, that he was a useless drunk.

'It's not me they want. It's that.'

Tomas nodded up, behind Peter.

'There,' he said, pointing. 'Up in the eaves, behind the beam.'

Peter followed Tomas' shaking hand to the top of the wall. He stood on a stool, and felt around, and there, tucked into the crook between the joists and the roof, was the box.

'Take it down, Peter. Take it down.'

Peter had seen the box before, but now, even before he opened it, he knew what was inside. And if the sword were true, then it was all true.

His father, a hero.

'The sword?' Peter asked.

Tomas nodded.

'Have a look if you like.'

Peter's hands trembled as he lifted the lid and gazed upon the blade inside. He didn't dare touch it.

'But why?' he asked, shaking his head. 'It's just a sword.'

Tomas laughed, then winced again.

'Sit down, Peter. Listen to me. I've lied to you. That thing you see there. It's so much more than a sword. It has power over those who return. Return from the grave. You understand?'

'Sofia told me. What I don't understand is why you've denied them all these years. Why?'

Tomas took another drink, then a deep breath. He looked across the room to the fire.

'Thirty years ago, I fought with the King. They call him the Winter King now, but then he was just King Michael. The Turks had fought their way far from home, right up as far as Poland. For years we'd been powerless to stop them, the noble Voivods who ruled each region too busy arguing with each other to unite. Michael changed all that, and got each Voivod to swear allegiance to him. In that way he formed a mighty army that pushed the Turks back as far as the Danube. The river ran red! And then we pushed even further. I was with him as we headed far into Turkish territory. It was there that I found the sword.

'And there that I learnt of something worse than the Turks. I had heard of the vrykolakoi before, in fireside tales. Everyone has. But in that strange land I found myself fighting them as well as the Turk. The sword was made in a land where these terrors were common, and it has the power to destroy them for good, with a single stroke.'

Peter nodded, but it still didn't make sense.

'But why are the gypsies fighting you for it? Why have you never told me about any of this?'

'Wait. A story has its purpose and its path. It must be told correctly for it to be understood. Remember that, Peter.

'Well. The wars ended, but not before the king died. Not from the sword, but from some disease that found him on our forays onto foreign soil. It ate him from inside and it was terrible to see. It was then, in the disbanded armies that were making their way home, that I met Caspar. Sofia's father.

'From him I learned all about the ways of those who return from death. They are to be found in every land, he said, and I found out how true that was. He had heard about my fighting, about my sword, and we spent the years that followed hunting them down, and putting them back to eternal rest.

'For they are like a disease, too, Peter. They infect the living and make us like them. Once an outbreak starts, it is like an epidemic. It can be hard to stop. Sometimes a great many people die before it is brought to an end.'

'And the Shadow Queen?'

Tomas shook his head.

'That I do not know. I thought she was no more than a story. But if she is real, I don't know how she is involved in all this.'

Tomas paused, staring at the floor, breathing heavily.

'Sofia said you were put in jail after the wars, because of the chaos when King Michael died. Is that not true?'

Tomas shook his head.

'No. It was Caspar's fault.'

'But he died in jail too! Or is that a lie, as well?'

'No, that much is true. After years of hunting the dead, I had had enough. Things were getting more dangerous for us, simply because we were living in a time of peace. Think about it. Think of what we used to do. We would prowl around at night, hunting through graveyards, digging up graves. Why? To stop them, send them back. Kill them, if you like. During a time of war and strife, no one gives much care to their dead. They are lucky if they get to bury them at all. But in times of peace, men who desecrate graves are not well-liked. I wanted to stop. He had married and had a baby girl; I wanted to do the same.'

A baby girl, Peter thought. Sofia.

'But Caspar convinced me to continue; he said it was too important. Soon we were arrested, but I had hidden the sword. We were tried and both ended up in jail, for desecrating the grave of a nobleman. A nobleman who was returning from the soil every night to attack young girls. It didn't matter. The local Voivod locked us away for life and I would have stayed there for ever had he himself not been deposed. That came too late for Caspar, and I vowed that when I got out I would have no more to do with any of it.

'That was years ago. I met your mother a year later. She died giving birth . . . to you, Peter. And I renewed my vow to fight no more, to look after you. I just haven't done a very good job, that's all.'

'No, father. That's not true. I didn't understand things, about the box, about why we had to keep moving all the time. But I understand one thing. You think it was my fault that my mother died —'

'No!' Tomas cried, sitting up, grimacing with pain. 'No. I never thought that.'

'Didn't you?' Peter said, quietly, 'Didn't you?'

They fell silent.

Peter thought about his father's old life. He had fought with the King, and the King had died. He had fought with his friend to protect people from the hostages, and instead of reward, they had been jailed. His friend had died there. Turning his back on this warrior life, he had found a wife, and seen her die giving birth to his only son. He should have been proud of his son. But he had turned away from him. Was it simply too much, to see a reminder of his wife's death every day?

So finally, as soon as Peter was old enough to fend for himself, Tomas had turned to the one thing in life that had never let him down. Drink.

Peter looked again at the sword.

'To stop me seeing this, you broke my toy,' he thought. 'My little wooden goose.'

But he said nothing.

Though his heart had been damaged by his father's story, there was one small seed of hope. Tomas had finally told him everything. There were no more secrets between them, secrets that had kept them apart all Peter's life.

They could act.

'Tomas. My father,' Peter said. 'Why did they do this to you? You were on the same side, once.'

'There are no sides here. I vowed not to fight anymore, and I will not. Look at me! One scrap and I'm all but done for. Another one would kill me.'

'So you refused to join them? And they wanted the sword instead? So why not just give it to them? Give it to them and let's get out of here. Go far away.'

153

'And go where? We've been running all our lives. The hostages, those who return, are everywhere. The ancestors, those that fight them, are everywhere too. But the sword is mine and I will not give it up. They'll be back soon, and I suppose next time they'll send more than four weaklings to get it. I cannot help that.'

'No, but it doesn't have to be this way. If you won't help them, then just give them the sword. It makes no sense to keep it. Then they can try to stop this epidemic.'

Tomas grew suddenly angry.

'I told you! It's not my fight anymore! It's not our business. We're just simple woodcutters. I want to live quietly on this island. Bother no one, and be bothered by no one!'

Peter stood and stared at his father.

'How can you be so selfish!' he shouted. 'Help them! Give them the sword at least. They need you. I need you!'

'Everything was fine until they arrived.'

'If that's true then why do you drink? It's killing you, and yet you will not stop! And why would you need to drink but to stop yourself from seeing, from thinking?'

In answer, Tomas kicked out and knocked a chair flying across the room.

Peter jumped back and watched, horrified, as Tomas lifted the bottle of slivovitz to his lips.

By the time Peter had closed the door of the hut behind him, Tomas had still not stopped drinking.

The Camp

*P*eter had not been to the gypsy camp before, but he knew it was somewhere away to the west of Chust. He'd heard they'd settled in a clearing in the trees. Sultan moved easily through the great forest, still willing to do his master's bidding, despite their fruitless logging trip.

Peter's mood was grim, and though rage boiled inside him, his face was nothing but a mask of determination. As he rode he kept one hand on the reins, the other on the shaft of his axe. The world had gone crazy, turned itself upside down. His father had killed someone, and he was riding to confront the victim's family. He might just need his horse and axe to make it out alive.

And if he didn't make it out again? At that moment, he didn't much care. Wasn't that what the Miorita was telling him? To accept your fate, meekly, with no resistance, no struggle. If that was the case then he would go to the gypsy camp without fear, and get them to leave Tomas alone, to fight their own battles.

And as for Sofia . . .

He kicked Sultan in the ribs unnecessarily hard. The old horse broke into a canter, but shook his head to show he wasn't happy.

The clearing was ahead, and even at this distance, through the trees, he could see the yellows and reds of their caravans, and wood smoke twisting up into the sky.

He pulled Sultan to a halt, and tethered him to a tree.

'Wait here,' he said. 'I'll be back soon.'

Peter wished he was as confident of that as he sounded, but sliding the axe from Sultan's saddle, he knew he had no choice but to go through with it. The gypsies would regroup, and be back for the sword.

At first he walked boldy, upright, making no attempt to hide himself as he neared the clearing. He could see the camp clearly now. There were five caravans, and two open carts. The caravans were arranged in a circle with their doorways facing a large campfire, over which hung a cooking pot. Horses, tethered to stakes and tree stumps, chomped on hay bags. Forming a circle just outside the camp itself, about halfway to where the trees began, Peter saw a series of stakes planted in the ground. From the top of each stake hung a cluster of something white and bulbous. It took a moment for him to realise they were strings of garlic bulbs. Protection.

Now Peter saw someone jump from the low step of one of the caravans, and as he watched the gypsy crossing the circle, something caught his eye. He dropped to a crouch, and crept a little closer.

Sitting against a large birch trunk on the far side of the clearing was Sofia. She was alone, in the snow, with her legs out straight in front of her, and her arms by her sides.

Seeing her there, and puzzled by it, Peter forgot all about what he had come for, and his anger with her. He crept forward nearly to the edge of the trees, then began to circle round towards her.

He was used to moving through the winter forest, and he made no sound as he deepened his arc slightly to approach Sofia from behind. For a while he thought he had lost sight of the tree where she was sitting, but there it was again, ahead of him.

Now he understood.

A series of ropes were tied tightly around the trunk and around Sofia. They had bound her to a tree, and outside the circle of garlic.

'Sofia!' he whispered.

There was no reply, but then, she was on the far side of a thick trunk, unable to move.

As he crept closer, his dexterity deserted him. The head of the axe caught against the trunk of a dead sapling, which cracked loudly. He glanced ahead and saw Sofia's hair flick out – she had turned her head.

Fearing she might call for help, he rushed the last few paces until he was right against her trunk.

'Sofia! It's me! Peter.'

Nothing for a second, but then he heard.

'Peter!' it was no more than a whisper. 'Thank God! Set me free!'

'Why did they do this to you?' he asked.

'Not now! Set me free.'

Peter nodded. He pulled his knife from his pocket and began to saw through the thick hemp binding her. As he did so it crossed his mind that maybe she had been tied to the tree for a good reason, maybe she had even been . . .

No. It was daylight. She couldn't be one of them and out in the daylight, he reminded himself, and kept on sawing.

'Quick!' Sofia called. 'They might come out at any time.'

'There!' Peter called and loosened the rope.

Sofia stayed motionless, waiting to check that she was unobserved, then flung the rope away and spun around the tree into Peter's arms.

'Thank you!' she cried. 'Let's go from here.'

'I can't,' said Peter. 'I've come to stop them from attacking my father. They'll have to listen to me.'

'No!' Sofia cried. 'They'll kill you. Nothing is going to stop them. They tied me to the tree because I tried to stop them from stealing the sword from your father. I told them to leave him alone, and they did this to me! One of their kind!'

'They would have left you out in the night?'

'They threatened to. I think it was just meant to scare me. I think. But you can't stop them.'

'I have to try, Sofia.'

'Peter! Listen to me! My own uncle tied me up. Imagine what they will do to you and your father! Come. Come away.'

She pulled Peter's hands, dragging him deeper into the wood, and he knew she was right.

He shook himself.

'This way,' he said. 'I've got Sultan with me.'

They ran.

The Approach

*I*t didn't take long to reach Sultan, but Sofia was shattered by the time they found him. She had been sitting on the frozen ground all morning and her legs would barely move at first, but Peter urged her on. He had to lift her onto Sultan's back, then swung up behind her. Very soon, with the warmth from horse and boy, Sofia began to feel better.

They trotted through the trees, aiming nowhere until they were convinced that there was no pursuit from the camp. Peter slowed Sultan to a walk, mindful of the double cargo the horse was carrying. As he rode with his arms around Sofia, he felt her leaning back against his chest. But Sofia had other things on her mind.

'It's up to us,' she said.

'What do you mean?'

'This is all going to end badly, Peter.'

Peter grunted.

'My uncle went to talk to the Elders. The woman called Anna?'

'Yes,' Peter said.

'He tried to warn them of the danger, but they ignored

him. She is a difficult woman, and thinks she knows best how to run her village. We know better than her about hostages, but she refused to listen. After hours of talking, they did nothing.'

'But there are other ways of killing the . . . hostages?'

'The hostages, yes. They did not want to become what they are. It is like a disease, it makes them become that way. It is not a question of killing them, but returning them to the ground. For ever. And it can be done without the sword. But the sword is easier. A single cut from it is enough. And they fear it. It is as if the power of the Winter King is inside it. Inside the blade.'

'But what can we do?' Peter cried. 'You and me. A boy and a girl.'

'Peter. There is nothing else now. The villagers are too frightened to know what to do. Your father refuses to help, or even give the sword. My people may kill him for it now, as he has killed one of us.'

'Sofia, I'm sorry. I wasn't there. I might have stopped it.'

'And you might be dead too,' Sofia said. 'Don't worry. I am not surprised it is Georg who is dead. He was always first to anger. I heard he rushed at your father, with his knife. Your father defended himself, and the others fled back to my uncle. But listen Peter, it won't be long. Once they've licked their wounds they'll be back. If you go to stop them you'll be hurt, too. And the epidemic is growing worse. Very soon there will be more hostages in the village; if it spreads, it will become impossible to control.'

Peter thought about what she said, about Tomas, and her

uncle, and about the hostages, but one thing she had said stood out.

'*You might be dead too.*'

She cared about him. And that small spark was enough to kindle something in Peter. He couldn't lie down and die, like the meek shepherd. He was going to fight.

'Sofia. I will help you. What can we do?'

'We are not powerless. We can act. We need to show the village that they must act, despite their fear. And we need to do this before my people hurt your father.'

'How?'

Sofia hesitated. Sultan hesitated too, and came to a standstill. Peter barely noticed. Sofia twisted around so she could see Peter's face. Around them the snow-laden branches of the bare trees hung heavily, pointing their twig fingers towards the couple on horseback. There was total silence across the face of the earth, and the silence centred on this small universe in the trees.

'We have Sultan,' Sofia said, slowly. 'There is an old way of finding hostages in their own ground.'

'You mean, in their graves?'

Peter's mouth twisted with fear as he spoke.

'Yes. We must start there. If a virgin rides a horse over a grave where a hostage lies, the horse will know, and will refuse to cross. We must find the graves of the hostages, all of them, and prevent them from leaving the ground.'

'How?'

'There are ways. We could stake them in. That holds them to the ground. Or we could put nets into the grave. That works like the millet; they have to unpick every knot

162

before they can leave again. But we have no nets.'

'I've heard things like that too,' Peter said. 'My father said they were fireside tales, but now . . . '

'You know it's true. We could put charcoal in the grave. They must write with the charcoal and that keeps them from returning until the charcoal runs out.'

'Or we can use buckthorn,' Peter said. 'That's what they did at Radu's funeral.'

'Yes. The thorns are like little stakes,' Sofia said, nodding. 'They pierce the skin. They cannot move through the thorns. But if that's what they put into Radu's grave, and he still came out . . . '

'What does it mean?'

'My uncle knew about this. It is why we are so afraid. It's never been like this before; it is as if there is something more powerful happening. Something giving them greater power.'

Peter shook his head.

'I don't know. Is there nothing else we can do?'

'Yes. You could sever the head with your axe, and place it at their feet. Only two things work better than that. Fire. And your father's sword.'

Peter stared straight through Sofia.

He knew there was no way he could sever a head, even the head of a corpse.

'If you're too afraid, then give me your horse at least. I'll try on my own.'

'No!' Peter cried. 'I'm not afraid. I'll help you.'

He kicked Sultan into a walk again.

'We'll need a spade,' he said. 'We can steal one from the sexton's shed. I know where that is.'

Sofia laughed.

'Excellent! And we can cut some buckthorn on the way.'

'But . . .'

'What?' asked Sofia.

'You said we need a virgin to ride the horse.'

Sofia twisted in the saddle once more and slapped Peter's cheek.

'That's me, you pig!'

Peter burst out laughing.

'I'm joking,' he cried, rubbing his face in mock pain, and now Sofia laughed too.

'Be careful, Peter,' she said, but with a warm smile on her face.

'Let's go, Sultan!' he said, grinning.

Holding not only the reins, but Sofia too, he spurred the horse into life and they thundered towards the village.

Ordeal

'*R*emember. It is day. We have an hour or so before there is any danger to us. No matter what you see, remember there is no danger.'

Peter nodded.

It was a bitter afternoon. It had begun to snow heavily as they rode around the outskirts of the village, and more than this, the snow was being driven by a nasty wind from the east, straight off the mountains. It had come from nowhere, quite suddenly, and now the storm was at its most furious. On any other day, Peter might have cursed it all, but today was different. They were glad of the appalling weather because it meant no one else was about. They seemed to have the village to themselves, which was as well given what they were about to do. Tomas and Caspar had both been locked up for doing the same.

They had cut buckthorn from a large bush, and just as easily, Peter had broken the lock on the sexton's shed with one swing of his axe.

Now they stood at the edge of the graveyard.

The snow hurled itself out of the sky, tearing around their heads, making it hard to see more than a few feet, never mind to the far side where the wooden church hunkered into the slight hillside, as if trying to escape the storm.

'Ready?' Sofia called.

Peter smiled.

'Go on.'

He made a stirrup with his hands to help Sofia into the saddle. She smiled and allowing him this indulgence, settled herself. She guided Sultan to the gateway, and Peter followed, axe in one hand, spade in the other.

With the back of his wrist he brushed at the snow clogging his eyebrows, and then opened the gate for Sultan and Sofia.

'Where?' he asked.

By way of answer Sofia steered Sultan over to the path that ran down the middle of the graveyard, to the first grave in the first row. That made sense. To start at the beginning.

They exchanged one last look, and Sultan walked forward.

It was slow progress. At first, Sultan seemed unsure of what he was supposed to do, but at last he understood. He stepped over the first grave, passing the wooden cross, and to the other side.

Nothing.

He had moved as calmly as if he had been walking in a summer's hay meadow.

Peter looked up at Sofia, but she didn't look back, urging Sultan to the next grave.

Nothing.

Again he moved happily across the ground.

The third grave approached.

Nothing.

Sofia urged Sultan on.

'Sofia,' Peter called. 'It's not . . . '

He didn't finish what he was saying.

Sultan reared so suddenly and violently that he threw Sofia before she could do anything about it.

Peter ran to her side as Sultan shied into the snow, becoming a grey ghost in the gloom.

'We've found one,' Sofia said.

'Are you . . . ?'

'I'm all right,' Sofia said. 'Hurry. We have to try.'

She got to her feet.

'Come on!'

It was so hard. What they were doing was so hard, and the ferocity of the snow storm only made it harder.

Peter picked the spade up again, his hands numb already, and began to dig. His first efforts cleared the snow, and then he hit the ground. The winter had frozen the soil solid but he didn't give up, driving the spade down with his boot. He prised up a huge sod and flung it to one side and with that achieved, his work became much easier.

In a short time he had dug a hole half way along the grave, going deeper with each blow.

Suddenly the spade tip struck something, something other than soil.

'Wood!' he called to Sofia. 'I've found it.'

She nodded.

'Now what?'

She grabbed the axe and seemed to be about to swing it, when Peter stopped her.

167

'That's my job,' he said, taking the axe from her, 'and anyway, I've got an idea. Go and fetch Sultan back.'

Sofia stalked away into the swirling snow, to Sultan, who had been too scared to come any closer and too scared to leave altogether. She coaxed him back towards the graveside, in time to see Peter swing the axe at the surface of the coffin. He had made two blows already and shattered the lid. He left the axe sticking out of the wood, and came over to Sultan. From the horse's saddle he took a rope and tied it first to the axe, and then to Sultan's saddle.

Immediately Sofia understood his intentions and they both began to walk Sultan away from the grave. He was only too happy to oblige, and pulled.

There was an ear-splitting crack and half the lid of the coffin flew up in to the air to land on the snow beside them.

Now that they had done it, they realised that the worst bit was still to come.

They stood motionless, not even daring to look at each other, but staring at the lip of the hole they had made. Peter couldn't move. Then Sultan whinnied and seemed to goad Sofia into life. She sprang forward, giving herself as little time to think about what she was doing as possible.

Shamed, Peter rushed to her side and saw what she had already seen.

'It's empty!' he cried. 'Sultan was wrong.'

Sofia was silent, as she peered deeper into the coffin.

'Sultan was wrong,' Peter repeated. 'This isn't going to work.'

'No,' she said. 'Sultan wasn't wrong. Look!'

She pulled Peter down beside her.

As they leant into the hole, they were for a moment oblivious to everything else around them. They no longer noticed the snow, and they didn't hear Sultan snorting. They didn't see the snow shifting strangely on top of the graves that lay behind them.

'Look,' Sofia said again.

Peter didn't need telling. He remembered what Sofia had told him about the things you could bury with a hostage to stop them from walking. Charcoal. That was the one. Charcoal.

Peter stared at the inside of the coffin they had uncovered. Every inch of wood was covered in writing, in charcoal. It was scrawled, as if written in a fury, or a great hurry, but nevertheless it was legible. And with every word that Peter read his heart grew colder and his hair became a little whiter.

'What does it say?' Sofia said. 'I can't read. What does it say?'

Peter shook his head. He wished Tomas had never taught him to read, because then he wouldn't have had to read what was written on the inside of the coffin. Words of such anger, and malevolence, and hatred. Towards the living. Descriptions. Statements of intent. Jealous rantings. All the disgusting horror to be perpetrated on those still above ground.

'If I tell you,' Peter said, 'you'll wish I never had.'

Sofia looked away from the writing, and then they both heard something slither behind them.

They turned, and Sofia screamed. Sultan bolted, and this

time nothing was going to keep him in the graveyard. It was all Peter could do to keep from screaming. They watched with a deep and mortal fear as snow slid from the top of graves on every side.

Sofia whirled around.

'Peter!'

He followed her, and saw the same thing happening behind them. What they saw next was even more terrible. All around them, squares of snow lifted bizarrely into the air. The graves were opening. Snow slipped from the squares to reveal coffin lids being pushed upright, being pushed aside.

Then came a hand, grasping for something to hold onto. Desperately Peter and Sofia looked around. Sultan was long gone, and every glance showed them something worse than the last.

They came out.

In front, behind, to the left and right, they came out, and it was clear they knew Peter and Sofia were there.

'This can't be happening!' Peter cried. 'It's daylight!'

'I know,' Sofia shouted.

'Run!'

They ran, heading for the side of the church, aiming for a gap between the hostages. But there were dozens of them now, all running for them, all with a simple, deadly intent.

'Quickly!' Peter shouted, and pulled Sofia onwards.

But she stumbled in the snow, and fell awkwardly against a gravestone. Peter reached to help her, but only got half way when one last grave opened before him. The lid flew off as if blown apart by gunpowder. Snow fountained into the air, then settled, and Peter gasped.

Not one, but two figures rose from the grave hole. The first was Stefan, and with him was a girl. Agnes.

The Sword

*P*eter and Sofia backed away from the menace on all sides. Radu was there, and Willem, who had made Radu a hostage. Stefan and Agnes joined the others. Agnes' mourning dress wafted around her, making her look like a black ghost against the snow.

Instinctively perhaps they had edged backwards to the church until they found themselves pressed up against its northern wall, and they were trapped.

Peter knew what would happen next. He had heard enough stories in his time. His father had told him those stories were nonsense, but now he knew they were not. Very soon they would become hostages too, and rage against those still living like a murderous pestilence.

He felt Sofia beside him, and could hear her breath coming in short, stilted gasps. He put his hand out to his side and found hers, squeezing it tightly.

'If we're going to go, we may as well fight,' he whispered. 'I don't care what the song says.'

In another two paces, dozens of pairs of hands would be on them.

He leapt forward, with a roar, hitting out with his fists,

kicking with his feet, but it was no good. Their strength was beyond human strength, and they brought him to the ground with ease. He heard Sofia scream, and knew they had got her too. Hands held him fast on all sides. Hands with swollen blotched fingers, long, yellowing fingernails; and, like the faces that harried him, the skin was bruised, blue-black and dry. Peter saw the face nearest to his own. It had been a man, once, but from the dried blood crusting its mouth, he was sure there was nothing human left in it.

'Go on, then!' he cried, shutting his eyes.

But nothing happened. He flailed some more, then opened his eyes, and found he was being lifted to his feet.

No killer blow came. No claw-like hand. No savage bite.

He twisted furiously in his captor's grip and saw that Sofia was nearby, likewise held, but unharmed.

'What is it?' he called to her. 'What are they doing?'

'I don't know!' she cried. 'They shouldn't be able to do this. It's still daylight!'

It was true. It was a weak, miserable, grey afternoon, with no sun in sight, but it was still daylight.

Something occurred to Peter.

'Is it the Shadow Queen?'

Sofia didn't answer, but she didn't need to. As Peter mentioned the name of the Shadow Queen, the hostages all around seemed to shiver and some began to wail, wordlessly.

It was true, then. It was her power which was changing things.

The hostages gripped them more tightly, and forced Peter and Sofia to walk. They made their way out of the graveyard.

Peter had been sure they would head for the forest, but he was wrong. In full daylight, they walked into the village square, heedless that they might be seen.

And now they had been seen. An old woman, venturing out to her woodshed, saw the unholy procession. Screaming, she crossed herself, and fled back indoors.

At this other doors and windows opened, and Peter watched aghast as other people saw them, then flung their doors shut, leaving them to their fate.

They were forced on, faster and faster, through the village.

'Where are they taking us?' Sofia called to Peter. 'What do they want?'

It was slowly dawning on Peter what was happening, but he didn't dare voice his fear. They were moving, almost at a running pace, and the edge of the village came in sight.

They moved on, and now Peter was sure. They were being taken to his very own house, and he knew why.

As they passed the village gate, many of the hostages hung back, letting Peter and Sofia be taken by eight, four of them holding each. Stefan was among those holding Peter, and he saw Agnes pushing Sofia along. He tried to pull free once more, but their strength was far too great, and their speed increased still further.

The hostages began to run, and Peter and Sofia found their feet lifted from the ground, as they skimmed along, inches above the snow.

There.

The hut came into view.

'Father!' Peter called out, trying to warn Tomas, but it was useless.

They had arrived.

Peter knew why they had come. The hostages had taken some hostages of their own. There was only one thing they feared, and they had come to barter for it. Peter and Sofia would be held against the surrender of the sword.

Before, when Radu had chased them from Agnes' hut, the river water was enough to stop him from crossing to the island. Under the Shadow Queen's power, Peter wondered if they could now cross the bridge, but then realised they wouldn't need to.

They would draw Tomas out.

'Father!' Peter cried, and before the words had reached the hut, he found himself held high in the air by his throat. Stefan had not been a strong young man when alive, but now he could have snapped Peter's neck at a moment's notice.

One of the other hostages, an older man, with swollen belly and bloodied eyes, stepped forward. His hair was long and filthy, uncut for years. He raised a hand and pointed at the hut.

'Come out!'

Peter shuddered at the sound of the man's voice. He fought to breathe in Stefan's grip, trying to lift himself on Stefan's arm, to find some air.

'Come out!' The voice was quiet, but commanding. It was indeed dead, but it carried across the safety of the water to the hut.

Sickeningly, Peter heard the door on the far side of the hut, hidden from view. There was an awful pause, during which Peter fought to see.

Tomas appeared, and Peter's heart sank.

Tomas was drunk.

He staggered uneasily, swaying from one foot to the other, stopping to try to balance every now and again. In one hand he held a stone bottle of rakia, in the other, the sword, naked and dangerous.

'No!'

Peter tried to cry out to his father, but the warning was crushed by Stefan's grip.

He watched in dismay as Tomas came towards the bridge. He waved the sword around, holding it loosely, heedless of the risk of cutting himself. The bottle he held much more tightly, and pushing it to his lips, tilted his head back for a long swig.

At the sight of the sword, the hostages murmured restlessly. It was this they had come for.

'The sword. For your boy.'

That was it. Peter had guessed rightly. They were the trade off for the sword, and as if to prove the point. Stefan squeezed Peter's throat, choking him, taking his air completely. Peter kicked and struggled, but he might as well have been made of rock.

He knew he didn't have long left, but in his heart he still prayed that his father would stay on his side of the water, perhaps safe. Perhaps.

Tomas stepped forward, and put his foot on the bridge. He staggered over the water, and somehow managed not to fall in. As he reached the other side the hostages began to wail with delight, while their leader withdrew a little, pointing at Peter, warning Tomas to come no nearer.

'The sword.'

Tomas tried to focus. He turned his head one way and the other, as if utterly failing to comprehend what was happening. But it was clear he knew what was expected of him.

He took another half-step away from the safety of the bridge, and then, turning the sword around, threw it onto the snowy ground, just in front of the leader's feet.

There was a shriek of ecstasy from the hostages, and their leader moved to pick up the sword.

Peter had almost passed out, but he had enough life in him yet to be amazed.

Suddenly, Tomas changed.

'Now!' he shouted.

There was a rustle in the sky, and a dozen gypsies dropped from the trees onto the hostages' backs. The surprise was enough to make Stefan let Peter fall to the ground. Peter rolled away, in time to see his father fly forwards, beating the hostage to the sword where it lay. In a single motion, Tomas rolled on his back, picked up the sword, and slid it into the man's chest.

Once the initial surprise was over, the gypsies were no match for the strength of the hostages. They were thrown to the ground. All seemed lost, but Tomas had left his first victim in the snow far behind. He walked steadily into the heart of the fight, and the sword swung around him so fast that Peter could barely see it moving.

Now Peter saw the power of the sword. All it took was a single cut from its blade, and the effect was immediate. Hostage after hostage fell, unmoving. Only three remained,

Agnes and two men.

Peter scrambled over to where Sofia lay in the snow, to see if she was all right.

Sofia cried out and Peter turned to see Agnes right behind them, reaching ice-cold hands towards their throats.

Behind her, Tomas made a mistake. The final two hostages closed on him at the same time, and he hesitated, trying to decide which to attack first. One of them punched him so hard that he was sent spinning to the ground.

In that endless second he recovered himself. With a single sweep of the sword he made an inch deep cut in two necks. They fell to the ground, at rest once more.

Tomas squirmed in the snow, the pain in his stomach enough to prevent him from standing.

Seven. There had been a girl, too, and craning his neck he saw her, with her hands on Peter's throat.

In desperation he threw the sword at her, but it missed, landing short in the snow.

Sofia grabbed Agnes' arms, trying to break her grip, unaware that the sword lay just behind her, but her efforts were meaningless; the hostage was stronger than love, stronger than hate.

Sofia let go of Agnes' arms.

She took a step back.

Then she began to speak. To call it singing would be a lie. She mouthed the words at first, and seeing Agnes look away from Peter for a second, hope rose in her.

She gave the silent words a voice, still not singing, but whispering.

Agnes' hands dropped to her sides, and Peter gasped air back into his lungs. He stared at Sofia, in wonder at what he was seeing.

But now Sofia was singing.

She sang the Miorita, and now, finally, Peter understood the meaning of the song.

He tried to join in, but at first his damaged throat would give no voice.

Sofia sang louder, and Agnes backed away from her, floundering through the snow, yet somehow transfixed by the song. And at last Peter found his voice.

Together they sang the Miorita, and as they reached the end of the song, Agnes lay down in the snow, as still as all those who had been touched by the sword. Sofia fetched Tomas' sword from the snow and handed it to Peter.

He hesitated, but Sofia held his hand.

'A single cut?' he asked, and Sofia nodded.

He moved the tip of the sword towards Agnes, surprised by its weight, then made a mark so small on her neck that it might have been a pin prick.

'Sorry,' he whispered, so faintly that even Sofia, a step behind him, didn't hear.

He gazed at the girl he thought he had once loved lying in the snow, dead.

The Song of the Miorita

*P*eter scrambled to his feet, and rushed to Tomas, who had managed to sit up.

'How did you do that?' Peter cried. 'You were so drunk!'

Tomas smiled.

'Haven't touched a drop all afternoon,' he said. 'But it worked.'

Sofia came over. Her uncle was with her.

'Tomas,' Milosh said. 'Are you hurt?'

Tomas chose not to answer this.

'How are your people?' he said.

'Some are hurt. Some badly, but all are alive. Thanks to you. I am glad you came to your senses at last.'

'I didn't come willingly,' Tomas said.

'What happened?' Peter asked. He turned to Milosh. 'You came to take the sword by force.'

'Yes,' said Milosh, 'but when we got here we found Tomas waiting for us. It seems something had changed his mind. Someone.'

Peter glanced at his father, then looked away at the ground, his heart pounding.

'We knew they would come for the sword, so we waited.

181

We didn't expect them to bring you, but it played into our hands.'

Sofia looked at Peter, smiling, but Peter was looking at his father on the ground.

'Are you hurt? What happened?'

Milosh knelt down beside Tomas, feeling for the wound.

'One of them got a blow in. Here.'

He winced as Milosh pressed his stomach. Pulling back Tomas' clothes, they could see a huge discoloured swelling already forming.

'You're bleeding. We must get you inside.'

'No,' said Tomas.

'No?' said Milosh.

'Peter. What did you see in the village? There are others from the graveyard, aren't there?'

Peter nodded.

'Dozens.'

'That's not possible!' Milosh cried.

'It's true, Uncle. I saw them,' Sofia said. 'And they won't stop now.'

Tomas sat up further.

'We have to act. We have learned a lot today. We have seen hostages walk in daylight. It seems Agnes was among them. There may be others. I have never heard of that before. So, the Shadow Queen's power is growing. Some of them may even have been living among us, biding their time. And the hostages have learned about the sword, and they want it. Well, they will get it, but we have learned something else too.'

Tomas turned to Sofia.

'What you did . . . How did you know?'

'I . . . I didn't,' Sofia said, slowly. 'I just believed.'

'There!' Tomas said. 'And what did you believe?'

'I'm not sure . . . '

She shook her head, puzzled, and Peter laughed.

'I know!' he said. 'I believe it too. I understand the song.'

'And what does the song teach us? Does it teach us to go to our deaths, without fighting? To accept our fate?'

'No,' said Peter. 'No. It teaches us to embrace death while we live, to understand it, that when we do finally come to die we may accept it without fear. And that way we can live free of fear, believing in ourselves.'

'That is it,' said Milosh. 'That is it. Death is part of life. They are inseparable. You cannot have one without the other. The song teaches us that if we accept a wedding with death, we can go to our graves content. It is people's failure to understand this that makes them prey to the Shadow Queen.'

'How?' asked Peter.

'She can feel the discontent of the dead, those who were not content, those who had not understood the Miorita. These people are open to her power, and so she brings them back from the grave.'

'And now we have another weapon!' Peter cried. 'A song!'

Peter could feel this faith within him, as a presence that he had failed to see until now. Belief in the song, and true understanding of its message, that was it. Enough to give power, enough to lay the hostages to rest.

'Yes,' said Tomas. 'And a great confrontation is upon us. Help me to my feet.'

183

'No, father!' Peter cried. 'You must rest. Let someone else take the sword.'

'Your son is right,' Milosh said. 'Give the sword to me. I am not as skilled as you, but I will do my best. You are hurt.'

Seeing no help from anyone, Tomas rolled onto his side, then scrambled to all fours. He raised his head, and trunk, and knelt. He put one foot flat in the snow, and pushed for all he was worth. He stood.

'No, Milosh. I am not hurt,' he said. 'I am dying. But my swordhand is singing. I will take the sword into the village, and put an end to it.'

Milosh dropped his head, unable to meet Tomas' stare.

'Please, Father,' Peter said. 'Please don't.'

Tomas turned to his son, his face pale with pain.

He spoke softly, so that only Peter could hear.

'I have been a bad father to you. Please give me the chance to be a good one.'

Tears welled in Peter's eyes, and he wiped them away with the back of his hand, but he looked his father in the face, and nodded.

'We will help you,' he said.

'The song!' Sofia cried. 'We can help you with the song!'

Tomas nodded.

'Then let's be ready. We have the sword. Milosh. You have six men here. More in your camp. Peter, my son. Sofia. And we have the song! If only I had a horse. Peter, you should have seen me with King Michael! When we rode our warhorses into battle, the ground itself shook with fear!'

'But look!' said Sofia. 'You do have a horse! Sultan!'

They all turned and saw the old white horse walking

serenely through the trees towards them, his head nodding as he came.

Tomas laughed.

'What do you say, Sultan? Can you manage it?'

Sultan snorted.

Resurrection

*T*hey made an extraordinary sight, but there was no one to see them as they made their way through the forest, towards the stricken village.

At their head, a fat, red-cheeked man rode a stocky white horse. The rider and horse formed the point of an arrow, as behind and to each side walked his friends. His son. His dead comrade's brother and daughter. Others of their kind, maybe twenty in all.

They saw no one, and no one saw them.

They reached the village, and they saw no one.

They walked down the long main street that led to the square and still they saw no one. Not a word was spoken, and the silence in the streets was absolute.

They arrived in the square, and stopped.

And now they came.

From every alley and street, they came. Those who the Shadow Queen had brought from the ground.

They did not come slowly. They ran, they hurtled towards the man and his horse.

'Sing!' he shouted.

They sung, twenty voices in unison, with full lungs and loud voices. It worked. The hostages began to falter and hesitate, slowing in their great number. But still they came on. And there were scores of them.

The rider knew the moment had come.

He looked down to his son, and smiled.

He kicked the horse into action.

'Sultan!' he cried. 'Hah!'

Away he rode into the fight. Behind him, the singing voices lifted higher and higher, reaching out to protect him as he darted this way and that through the crowds, the sword flashing in the failing light in the square.

Bodies began to pile all around him, bodies that lay still, that did not wish to leave the ground any more, and as he fought on through the grappling hands and the clawing fingers, he saw that he would die.

There was nothing for Tomas now.

Not the singing.

Not the square.

Not the dead.

Not even Sultan.

Just the sword, that flew so fast that the air itself was cut in two.

But the hands grasped and grappled and there were too many. He was pulled from Sultan's back landing clumsily in the mud.

From a seemingly vast distance, he heard a cry.

'Father!'

Peter. It was his son, Peter, sprinting to be beside him in a moment. Dimly, Tomas saw Peter snatch the sword from the ground and begin to swing it wildly about him. The hostages faltered, shocked by the fluid energy of the boy, by his strength.

Tomas' eyes were closed, but in his mind he could see Peter twisting and stroking the blade from side to side.

'That's it,' he whispered. 'That's it. Feel it.'

In his heart, he heard Peter's reply.

'Yes, Father. My swordhand is singing.'

Tomas found himself staring at nothing but a bright white light that seemed to open in the sky above him, pouring down onto the blade, bathing him in joy.

Joy that he had been good, one last time.

That he had given.

That he was a good father, with a good son. It was the joy of completeness.

Even as Peter swung the sword for the last time, and gave rest to the last of the hostages, and fell to his knees by his father, the joy was irrepressible.

As Tomas died, his heart was singing, and a smile spread across his face.

A Perfect Shade of Green

*D*ays pass, whether you want them to or not. For Peter the days passed slowly, but nonetheless, one day, winter had gone.

The gypsies stayed on through the winter, living in the clearing just as they had before. Every day, Sofia would visit Peter and Sultan on their little island.

Peter seldom spoke on these occasions, his mind drifting, but Sofia would talk to him anyway, tell him of news from the camp, and from the village. She told him that when St George's Day arrived, they would be on their way once more. This was a piece of news that Peter *had* taken in.

One day, as Sofia cooked some soup on the stove in the hut, Peter got to his feet abruptly.

Startled, she looked at him.

'What is it?'

'Come with me,' he said.

He took her by her lovely brown hand, and gently led her out, and round the side of the hut, to the tool shed.

'Look,' he said. 'That was the first thing I found.'

Sofia shook her head, not understanding what he meant.

All she saw was a row of tools. Saws, chisels, hammers, gouges, laid out on a bench in a neat line.

'He was never like that,' Peter said. 'The tools were always a mess. Whenever he finished with something he'd leave it where it fell. If he put things back in here at all, he'd leave them all over the place. But when we came back from the village. That last day. This was the first thing I found. At some point, when he and Milosh and the others were waiting for the hostages' attack, he came out here, and tidied up the tools.'

He hesitated.

'Why did he do that?'

Sofia shrugged.

'He knew,' she said. 'He'd already decided what he was going to do. He did it for you, because you brought him back to himself.'

What happened after Tomas fell from the horse was a blur to Peter. He knew he had rushed to his father, that he had taken his father's sword and fought for him, but he couldn't remember the details.

He knew they had won. He remembered that the villagers came rushing out from their houses, among them Teodor, and Daniel, who fell on their knees in thankfulness before Peter and the gypsies.

And then there was Anna, old Anna, whom everyone feared. Even she came and begged forgiveness from them all.

'What can I do to thank you?' she wailed.

Milosh had told her.

'Stand up,' he said.

She did so, a puzzled look on her face.

'Turn around,' he said, and again the old woman complied.

Before she had turned back, Milosh had snatched the sword from the ground by Tomas, and with a single stroke cut Anna to the ground.

There had been shock and outrage. But only at first, as Milosh gently rolled Anna's body face down.

There, he pointed out what no one else had seen, or at least understood. The old woman's back was covered in sawdust.

'From a coffin,' he explained. 'That was why she didn't want to help us. She was one of them! She was guiding them, infected perhaps by the Shadow Queen herself . . . I would have understood sooner, but we didn't know they could move by daylight.'

Milosh had turned to give the sword to Peter.

'This is yours, now,' he said, but Peter shook his head.

'No,' he said. 'I don't want it. It's what my father didn't want to be. Let me give it to you. You will need it. You can use it.'

Milosh nodded.

They buried Tomas in the very graveyard from which the epidemic had first sprung, now truly a place of final rest, thanks to their efforts.

Finally, St George's Day came, and with it, Sofia came to see Peter for the last time.

It was a beautiful spring morning, full of bursting hope. The trees were heavy with leaves, and flowers had leapt into life in the meadow. Peter sat on a tree stump on his island, thinking how the early green of spring was the most perfect of the year, when into his vision walked Sofia.

'May I come over?' she called.

Peter waved and she crossed the bridge.

Beyond her, Peter saw the gypsy caravan on the path through the trees, and knew the day had come.

'Don't say anything,' he said, as she came close.

The smile softened his words, but Sofia still ignored him.

'Why don't you come with us?' she said.

'I can't,' Peter said. 'You know that, as well as I do. This is my home. I belong here, in the home my father and I built. I want to stay.'

Sofia hung her head.

'Besides, who'd cut their stupid wood for them?'

He nodded towards the village.

Despite herself, Sofia laughed.

'Where are you going?'

'I don't know,' she said. 'Wherever we need to. Wherever we hear of hostages that need to be freed. But first we are going to roll through the forest, and eventually we will find the meadows that lie beneath the mountains. They will be full of flowers, and bees, and the rivers will be full of fish. We'll stop there for a while and rest. We'll sing, and make music.'

'It sounds wonderful,' said Peter.

'It is.'

'God bless you.'

'And you, Peter.'

She stepped forward, and finally closed the gap there had

always been between them. She kissed him, and then they both heard laughter from the caravan.

She pulled away, blushing, and without another word, walked back to her future.

As she went, she sang, and Peter heard the final verse of the Miorita float into the air, where the shepherd marries a princess from the heavens.

He watched as she climbed aboard the cart, next to her uncle, and they disappeared into the trees.

Peter wandered back to the hut, but he found his eyes pricking and his head full of sorrow. Deciding he needed to be busy, he walked round to the tool shed, intending to sharpen the axes. There on the bench, as before, everything lay in neat and tidy rows, but suddenly he saw something he had missed before, a small rag, twisted into a ball. He picked it up and a tiny object inside the cloth fell into the sawdust at his feet.

He bent down and picked it up.

It was a carving, a small wooden carving.

Of a goose.

When his father had carved it, he didn't know, but Peter knew it was for him. Tomas must have left it with the tools as he and Milosh and the others waited.

Peter knew what it meant.

His mind drifted back to the first day when he'd seen Sofia arrive in the square. Something had tugged at his heart that day, but he had not known what it was. Now, suddenly, he knew. It was right in front of him, in Sofia, in his hand, but until this moment he just hadn't seen it.

It was their life, their nomadic life. He thought he was tired of travelling all his life, always on the move with his father. But now he saw that it was the only life he knew. It was the life he wanted. He looked at the carving again, identical to the one his father had made for him on his fifth birthday. He saw it not only as an apology, but as a message, and knew that like the geese, it was time to fly away again.

And just like the shepherd in the song, there was a princess waiting for him.

Gently, he tucked the goose into his pocket.

'Sultan!' he cried, running to the stable, and Sultan came.

He flung himself onto the horse, and they hammered away over the bridge.

'Wait!' he called. 'Wait! I'm coming with you!'

After Chust . . .

BLOODBEARD

*T*hey were at the gates of the city, the others far behind them now, and with a trembling heart Peter raised his hand to bang on the massive wooden doors. Behind him, Sofia sat hunched on Sultan's back, her whole figure shrouded in a thick grey woollen blanket, as if she were a leper hidden from view, as if she were plague-ridden, though there was nothing wrong with her, yet. Nothing physical, perhaps, but Peter knew what ailed her.

He'd felt the same thing many times too since he'd met Sofia, as they'd travelled north across the eager face of the world, and once it got hold of you, it was hard to shake.

It had been easy at first. The day they'd trundled out of Chust the sun was shining, birds were singing in the treetops, calling to each other that spring had returned at last, at long last, and that there were insects to be plucked from the air and shoots to be teased from the soil. Flowers burst open in the meadows, so bright and full of beauty that Peter wondered if he'd spent his life till then with his eyes half closed.

Maybe it had something to do with riding next to Sofia day after day, maybe that had changed the way he looked at things. Maybe it was that Tomas had gone. His father had loved him after all, but Peter also knew that life with Tomas had been hard, and that his father's poisoned view of the world had tainted his own vision.

The days passed and as Peter rode Sultan steadily through the countryside, the cart and the caravans rolled along next to them, and the grass that the cartwheels crushed grew ever more lush.

Peter wondered where they were going, but only vaguely.

'We'll go where the bees hum and the mountain springs tumble into the forest streams,' Sofia had said, as if that were an answer, but in truth Peter didn't care where they went, as long as they were together.

Sofia! It was all Peter could do not to spend all his time staring at her, but she seemed not to mind, and always smiled back when she caught him looking at her. Nevertheless he tried to hold back what he felt for her, frightened that he would scare her away. He didn't know what she felt. Since the kiss she'd given him that day they left, there had been nothing more said or done between them, nothing special, and yet the others, Milosh and the other gypsies, seemed to understand. They sent Peter and Sofia to do various tasks together, they left places for them together around the campfire, they never chided them when they walked half a mile behind the rest of the caravan, dawdling at a brook, gawping at the golden fish skinking under the water.

Spring had rolled under the wheels of the caravan, and they had seen little sign of hostages. Summer had come and Peter had almost forgotten that this was what the gypsies did; hunt for hostages, free them. He'd given his father's sword to Milosh, that day in the square, and had all but forgotten that too, forgotten its lethal beauty and its unworldly power over those who came back.

Sofia had taken it on herself to teach Peter all they knew of the ways and the many guises of the hostage.

'Two years ago . . . or was it three?' Sofia told him, 'we

were in the far south, in Greece, where it's never cold. They call them vrykolak there. Then we travelled north into the mountains. Blautsauger! Ugh!'

She shuddered.

'Kudlak and lampir. We found a forgotten town in the Balkan hills that was crawling with hostages. That was last year. We lost three men.'

She fell silent.

'And that's all you've ever done?' Peter asked. 'Hunt hostages with Milosh.'

'For as long as I can remember.'

'You're very brave,' Peter said.

Sofia looked at him and shook her head.

'I don't know anything else,' she said. 'We ended the winter to the east of here. They call them upyr there. Then we headed west as the cold set in and tried to find a village where we'd be safe for the hardest of the winter.'

'Where was that?'

'Chust, Peter! We didn't find safety; we found your father, and a village full of troubles. And I found you.'

I found you. Peter had noticed what she'd said, not 'we' but 'I'.

When summer came Peter learned something else.

'Well,' Milosh had said one day, 'I've looked at our silver. It's about time we earned some bread, and that includes you, Peter.'

They were sitting round the fire one evening, as usual, the stars twinkling over the forest clearing where they had camped as if they had come out to shine for them alone.

'But what can I do?' Peter asked. 'I can cut wood. That's about all.'

'So can we,' Milosh said, 'but that's not how we earn a living. We might exist to find hostages, but we earn money as any gypsy does.'

'You know,' Sofia said, 'you saw us doing it! We make music.'

Milosh handed Peter a shallow drum and a short drumstick.

'Until you learn the fiddle, you can keep time with this. Be warned! Everyone will make jokes if you stay a drummer. There are four musicians in the band, they will say, and Peter, the drummer! So you had better learn to play something else in time, but for now, do this, and do it well. It's harder than it looks.'

Peter must have looked scornful, because Milosh wagged a finger at him.

'Yes, anyone can hit a drum, but can you hit a drum in perfect time for ten minutes at a go?'

At Peter's first performance he had seen the truth of what Milosh had said, but he got away with it, and thanks to Sofia's beautiful voice they had a cup of coins by the end of their first day.

They rolled on, singing and making music, summer blowing up into a fearsome beast that oppressed them even in their sleep at night. Then, one night, with a tremendous thunderstorm and lightning show, summer evaporated, and autumn arrived.

North, they headed ever farther north.

Then the hostages started to come again, and Peter knew

what it was to feel fear every night, and relief with every day. They fought hard, for the hostages fought hard too, unwilling to be sent back to their grave soil without a struggle, but they had the sword, and it made all the difference.

Milosh seemed not to feel the fear at all, Sofia seemed to cope well enough, but Peter wrestled not to show his fear every single time they heard some villager mutter under their breath, 'strigoii, moroii, nosferatu!'

Milosh laughed.

'But with the sword our work is easy, so much easier than before. You saw it Peter, you saw your father use it. You used it! So easy!'

He swiped the air with an imaginary blade, laughing to himself.

'Shoosh!'

So it had gone, and sometimes Milosh had given the sword to Peter to use, and he *had* used it, twice more, and though full of terror at what he had to do, he'd done it well enough, almost easily, as Milosh said. Almost.

They travelled on, across the mountains, from town to town, from village to village, until the pastures of his homeland were so far away that it made Peter weak to think of it. They left the south behind and headed into the Hansa states, up on the northern coast.

Then, one day, they came to the sea.

The gypsy caravan crested a hill, and there it lay a short gallop away. As the others trundled down the hillside, Peter and Sultan came to a standstill. Sofia noticed they were falling behind and jumped down, running back to Peter.

'What is it?' she called. 'What's wrong?'

'Nothing,' said Peter. 'Nothing. It's just . . . I've never seen the sea before.'

Sofia laughed, then stopped, realising Peter was serious. 'And Sultan?'

Peter stroked the horse's neck.

'Who knows?' he wondered. 'Who knows what he saw with Tomas?'

Peter shook himself, swung Sofia onto Sultan's back, and they trotted down the slope to rejoin the others.

That evening, they came into a village by the shore. They gave a performance in a large hall, that went down well and were handsomely paid. When they finished, Sofia ran to Peter and flung her arms around his neck, laughing.

'Your drumming is getting better!'

'But not perfect?'

'Nothing is perfect, Peter,' Sofia said. 'Not even me!'

She smiled.

'I want to dance,' she cried, 'let's dance before they stop playing.'

The gypsies drank and ate, others kept the music going, and the villagers made them welcome, and then, as Peter and Sofia whirled around each other to the frantic fiddle music, Milosh came over.

'Hey! You two! They have a chovihani here! We're all going. Come on!'

'What?' said Peter.

'No,' said Sofia, who seemed a little drunk, 'no, I just want to dance!'

Milosh pulled her arm.

'What is it?' Peter asked again.

'Chovihani,' Milosh said. 'Well, that would be our word for it. Fortune teller. We have no one with the gift, it's been ages since anyone's been read. Come on, Sofia!'

'I just want . . . '

'. . . to dance,' said Peter. 'I know, but you can dance later! I want to have my fortune told.'

He pulled Sofia's other arm and between them, Milosh and Sofia and Peter staggered after the others, laughing.

One by one, the gypsies went in to the small room at the side of the hall, and each came out again just the same, smiling and laughing, maybe still clutching a mug of beer, maybe a leg of chicken. Milosh went in and seemed to be gone for a long time, but came out smiling.

'I think I told her more about us than she told me about me,' he said, then looked so puzzled that everyone burst out laughing again.

There was just Sofia and Peter left.

'You go first,' said Sofia. 'You've never been before. You should go next.'

'Oh no,' said Peter. 'I'll come back out to find you dancing with someone else! You go next and then I'll go last.'

He dragged Sofia to her feet and pushed her towards the door, but Sofia clung to his wrists.

'Then you come with me! I want you to hear what she says too!'

They stumbled into the little room, and there was the fortune teller, a woman of middle age, large and seemingly a permanent fixture in the room, like the chair and table at which she sat.

She smiled.

'Sit. Please.'

She waved a hand before them at the single chair on their side of the table.

They looked at each other, then Sofia pushed Peter onto the chair and sat herself on his lap.

'So,' said the woman, 'you are in love.'

There was a long awkward silence, then Peter whispered in Sofia's ear.

'That's very impressive.'

Then they both burst out laughing again.

The woman bristled.

'Which of you am I reading?' she snapped.

'Me,' said Sofia, 'Me. Please ignore my friend. He's been dancing too much.'

'Give me your hand.'

The woman stretched out her hands and Sofia put her left hand into their reach. She was startled at their roughness for a moment, then glanced at Peter, smiling still.

The woman began to speak.

'You are a fighter,' she said. 'You are another fighter. So many of them tonight! You are a singer, too.'

Peter sighed and looked up at the ceiling, hoping they weren't paying too much for this obvious nonsense.

Sofia nudged him, but the woman seemed oblivious now.

'A singer. You are. A fighter. A lover? You have not been a lover, yet. Your father is gone, yes?'

Now Peter began to listen, he felt Sofia's figure tense on

his lap as she strained to listen to the woman's whisperings.

'You had a father, but he died when you were very young. Some kind of soldier. Your mother died so early, too. Poor child! So much for the past. What of the future? What of the things that are yet to be? Wait.'

The woman closed her eyes for no more than a moment, then they shot open again. She stifled a shriek and pushed Sofia's hand away from her as if it were red hot.

'What?' Sofia said, staring at her hand uneasily.

The woman shook her head, looking sideways, refusing to meet Sofia's eyes.

'Nothing. Go. I have said enough.'

'What? What is it?' Peter asked.

Sofia pushed her hand across the table towards the woman again, palm open and facing up.

'Look at it!' she cried. 'What is it? You have to tell me!'

'Please,' said Peter. 'What did you see? The future? Did you see her future?'

The woman looked at them now, and spoke very quietly.

'Yes, the future.'

Then she took Sofia's hand and closed its fingers, gently pushing her closed fist back away from her.

'Go.'

Sofia sat motionless, and Peter stared at the fortune teller.

'What did you see?' he said. 'By the Forest, tell us or I will do you harm.'

The woman smiled at him, as if challenging him, then she rose.

'Do not dare to threaten me, boy,' she said, then scowled at Sofia. 'And you. You are unclean. Or you will become so.'

207

She walked to the door. Sofia stood too, and Peter followed her.

'What can I do? Is there anything I can do?'

The woman seemed about to walk out, but then hesitated.

'Go to the city. Reval. Look there for a man called Jola. He is wise in my arts, far wiser than me. He may know what to do. Or he may simply tell you more than I can.'

'Thank you,' said Peter. 'Thank you. We'll go, Sofia, everything will be right.'

'Perhaps,' said the woman, 'perhaps.'

She left, but as she did, she muttered under her breath a single word, and Peter knew that she was talking about what she had seen for Sofia; what she saw her becoming. Peter heard it, and prayed that Sofia had not, but as the following day came, and they sat brooding in the camp, it was clear to him that she had heard.

'Nosferatu.'

They left the next day for Reval, all of them. They were a family, Milosh said, and what affected one of them affected all of them. There was little to discuss, it was something that could happen to any of them at any time, living the lives they led. One skirmish too many with a hostage and any of them might suffer the fate of becoming one, despite all their protections and safeguards, despite all their knowledge of those who walk after death. So there was nothing to do but go and find the man the fortune teller had spoken of, Jola, the wise man.

They moved up the coast, always in sight of the sea, still heading north, and though at first they made good progress, the weather finally turned, and the cold swept against their faces, a cold as vicious as anything any of them had ever felt.

Their mood sank, and as Sofia's fear began to take hold of her, her joy slipped away. She seemed to have become infected by it, as if she was truly ill. They trudged slowly into the chilling wind, and then the snows came. After three days of snow, none of them spoke, until one day Peter turned to Sofia.

'Look!' he said. 'Look at the sea. There's something wrong with it. It's slowed down.'

Sofia looked and saw what he meant, the sea had become thick and moved sluggishly, like a gelatinous soup.

'It's freezing,' Sofia said.

'Is that possible?' Peter asked, but it was. A few more days and the sea had frozen solid. The silence that came with it after weeks of hearing the crash of the waves on the shore was eerie, and reinforced the silence of the caravan.

With each passing day, and Reval still not in sight, the snow piled higher. Twice they dug the caravans out of snow drifts, then twice more. Then they were stuck for good.

For hours they tried to free the vehicles, but as fast as they did, more snow fell and was blown to hem them in again.

'I'm sorry,' said Milosh. 'We'll have to camp here, find some shelter.'

'But we can't stop,' cried Peter. 'We have to get Sofia to the city!'

Sofia said nothing.

'I'm sorry. There's nothing we can do.'

'But there's something I can do,' Peter said. 'We can go on, with Sultan. He can walk through the snow.'

'Very well,' Milosh said.

With that it was settled, and taking an extra blanket, the three of them, Peter, Sofia and Sultan set out by themselves. As they went, Milosh called.

'Wait! Peter!'

He climbed up into his caravan and in a moment re-appeared clutching a leather bundle, long and narrow. Peter knew what it was immediately.

'No,' he said. 'You need it.'

But Milosh tied the bundle to Sultan's saddle bag.

'And you may need it more, and there are only two of you. Come back as soon as you can. We'll wait for you here.'

Peter nodded at Milosh, his heart as full of thanks as fear.

He turned away, and lifting Sofia up onto the saddle, whispered into his horse's ear.

'Come on Sultan, it's time for you to work again.'

They came to the gates of Reval the following day. It was barely past noon, but already the sun was low in the sky, lurking behind a thick bank of cloud, slinking back down towards the grey horizon as if exhausted by its meagre journey. Peter and Sofia were exhausted too, and Peter barely had the strength to bang on the wooden doors of the gate they had come to, but very soon a small door within the larger one swung open. A gatekeeper, a young man not much older than Peter, greeted them.

'What brings you to Reval?'

Peter smiled.

'Please let us in,' he said, waving a hand at Sofia's huddled form on Sultan's back. 'We've come to see a man who can help my friend. She's sick.'

210

It wasn't so far from the truth, Peter thought, and something stopped him from talking about the fortune teller's prophecy. He knew it could often be a mistake to mention hostages.

'I see,' said the gatekeeper. 'And where have you come from?'

'From the south. We've been travelling for a long time. We were told that a man called Jola might help her.'

The man's mood seemed to change. He waved them in. Peter lifted Sofia from Sultan so the horse could walk through the doorway, bowing his head.

'Jola? The wise man? Yes, we know him. He's a good man. He lives over by the other gate of the city, by the water. There's a tower called Fat Margaret. Find that and then turn inside by the city wall, to the west. Take the stone stairs that climb along the wall. He lives in a house that you'll find at the end of the first run of the wall.'

Peter helped Sofia back onto Sultan's saddle.

'Thank you,' he said. 'That's very kind of you.'

'It's nothing. We are not unfriendly people here. We take a little time to judge someone, and then you are our friend.'

He hesitated.

'One thing. It's getting dark. This is a friendly city, but . . .'

'What?'

'We have been cursed. You should take care. The city is suffering from a terror. Beware night time. Don't go out after dark, for that is when it strikes you down.'

'What? What does?'

The gatekeeper whispered fiercely.

'The veripard. The bloodbeard!'

Peter clutched the bundle at Sultan's saddle tightly as they made their way into the city's heart, and as they walked he thanked Milosh again and again for his kindness.

The city's streets were finely cobbled, and they made their way up a street that led away from the city's walls. Fine houses, three storeys tall, lined the street on either side. Here and there smaller alleyways ducked out of sight between the taller buildings, and Peter avoided those, preferring instead to follow a line of torches set in the walls that led them up into the city's market square. A high walled cloth hall with a copper roof and fantastic carved dragons sprouting from its sides formed the centrepiece to the square, but the other buildings were no less impressive. Peter had never seen anything like it. He longed to talk to Sofia, would have loved to have laughed and joked with her, loved to have idled away an hour looking at all the things for sale on the market stalls, but he could not. Sofia had become a mute. She almost seemed to have become a hostage already; her skin was as pale as death, the light in her eyes had vanished long ago. But Peter shook himself, it wasn't true. She was still alive and it was up to him to make sure she stayed that way.

'Please,' he said to the nearest stallholder, 'I'm looking for Fat Margaret.'

The woman nodded and without saying a word pointed at a street that led away from the corner of the square.

'Thank you.'

Once more Peter asked his way, but then the way was clear. A single long street led away, running slightly upwards once more, twisting gently like a snake, but pointing

212

inevitably to where at the far end, maybe a mile away, he could already see a squat round gate tower set in the city wall. Fat Margaret.

Sultan's hooves clipped on the cobbles and the noise echoed loudly in the streets. Peter realised how empty of people the city was, and then he knew why. It was getting dark, dusk would come soon, and he already knew enough about frightened people, and how they behaved, to know he would shortly be alone in the streets.

He doubled their pace.

Another door, another threshold to cross.

Sultan stamped his feet impatiently in the street below, as Peter half carried Sofia up the stone stairs, and hurried along to Jola's door.

It had to be the one. Small and unassuming, yes, but solid and well built, with an air of importance, the house clung to the inside of the gigantic stone wall that ran like a ring round the whole city.

The door opened and a man's face appeared.

'Yes?'

Peter felt relief the moment he saw him. In his mind he'd painted Jola as an intimidating figure, but he knew his fears were unfounded. A small man with a little frizzy hair and twinkling eyes stood before them.

Jola smiled.

'Yes? How can I help?'

Peter stirred himself.

'It's my friend,' he said, 'Sofia. She's ill. In a way. We were told you could help.'

213

'But I'm no doctor,' Jola said. 'The doctor lives a couple of streets away. I can take you there.'

'No!' said Peter. 'No, you see, it's not a normal sickness. It's about her . . . Her future, what will happen to her. We were told you could help us.'

Jola opened the door fully.

'I see,' he said, gravely. 'Well, in that case, you'd better come in.'

Jola led them into his house, which, on this floor at least, seemed to be a single room, mostly kitchen, but with chairs and bookcases and even some kind of bed in the corner.

The old man busied himself while Peter and Sofia sat by the fire, and for the first time in weeks, they felt warm.

'Don't sit too close,' Jola called over to them. 'It's not good after being so cold. I'll get you something to eat. I have some soup. Would you like some soup? Yes. I'll get some for you.'

'Peter?' Sofia spoke so softly that at first Peter wasn't sure he'd heard anything at all.

'Peter? Where are we?'

It was the first thing she'd said in days.

Sofia pulled the blanket from her head and looked about her. Jola came over with steaming bowls of soup and some thick black bread.

'Safe,' Peter said. 'For a little while. This is the man we've come to see. Jola.'

At the mention of his name, Sofia seemed to shudder, and Peter regretted talking about the curse just when she'd started to relax a little. Jola smiled.

'I think it best we leave your friend for a while before we

214

tackle your problem. Daylight is the time for that. We'll talk tomorrow.'

'But we can't leave without your help!' Peter said. 'We have nowhere to go . . .'

'No, I understand. You can stay here. It's nearly dark now, and . . .'

He stopped, briefly, then forced a smile.

'There is a . . . thing . . . in our streets, at night.'

'We were warned,' Peter said. 'The veripard?'

The man shuddered.

'An ugly name. Bloodbeard. He wears a huge beard of his victim's blood, from the mess of his feasting. I have little room, but there is a stable underneath this room. You can stay there.'

'Oh!' Peter said, standing up. 'Sultan! I forgot Sultan. Can we put our horse in your stable? He's outside in the street, and he'll be freezing.'

'Leave it to me, young man,' Jola said. 'You finish your soup and I'll get your horse inside.'

'Peter. My name's Peter. And thank you.'

'Would you like some beer?' Jola asked, and Peter nodded furiously.

'Very much so,' he said, and Sofia laughed.

Peter smiled.

'I keep it in the stable. It's best served cold. It has a strange taste but it's a delicacy of the region. I'll bring some back up.'

Peter and Sofia could not stop thanking Jola, but when they were downstairs in the stable, getting ready to sleep, Sofia couldn't help but wonder what, if anything, the old man could do for her.

It was on Peter's mind too.

'Maybe,' he said, 'Maybe what the fortune teller said . . . It doesn't have to come true, does it?'

Sofia shook her head.

'Our people,' she said. 'We take these matters very seriously. We believe in them. Not everyone has the skill to see into people's future, and when you meet one who does . . . She knew everything about me, Peter. My father, my mother.'

'Maybe,' said Peter, 'maybe she just worked it out. Everyone else had gone first, you heard what Milosh said. He might have mentioned something about you.'

Sofia came over to him, and gently put her arms around him.

'Thank you,' she said, her head on his shoulder.

'Come on,' Peter said. 'It's cold in here. Eh, Sultan?'

Away in the stalls of the stable, Sultan whinnied softly. Peter threw a blanket over him.

'Sleep well, good horse.'

'That only leaves two blankets for us,' Peter said, 'and the straw.'

'Then we need as much straw as possible.'

They set about piling up a small hill of the stuff, and then putting one blanket on top, they lay down beside each other and covered themselves with the other.

'We need to keep each other warm,' Peter said, slightly awkwardly.

'Yes,' said Sofia, 'yes. But I'm so cold. And stiff. I ache all over.'

'It's the journey,' said Peter, 'I feel it too. It's because of the journey, and the cold.'

'Yes,' said Sofia, yawning. 'Yes. Good night, Peter.'

But Peter didn't answer, because he was already asleep. What woke Peter wasn't the smell, it wasn't the sound of Sultan pulling madly at his tether, it was the feel of the blood dripping on his face.

He opened his eyes and saw a shape crouched over them where they lay in the straw, and another drop fell onto his lips.

He tried to wipe his mouth, and couldn't. He tried to move, to sit up, to hit out at the figure. He couldn't.

He tried to scream, and he couldn't even do that. All it seemed he could do was move the muscles of his eyes enough to look up at the dark shape inches above them, and then he understood.

The bloodbeard was on them.

It was pitifully dark in the stable, but as the figure of the monster leant down towards them, Peter saw who it was. Jola.

It was Jola, and the lower part of his face was smeared with fresh blood. Not a real beard at all, just one painted on with blood that dripped onto Peter's face.

Peter tried to scream again, and managed to make a small gurgling sound. He strained his eyes to his left and saw with a mixture of horror and relief that Sofia was awake too. Her eyes bulged, wide and staring. Her chest moved with short heaving gasps, as she too tried to scream but could not.

Jola leant right down over them.

217

'Now,' he whispered, as another drop of blood fell from his chin, 'which of you is going to be first?'

Peter was so close he tried to butt his head into the blood-beard's face, but there wasn't enough movement in his muscles to reach.

Jola smiled at Peter.

'Did my beer make you sleepy?' he sneered. 'It can have that affect on some people.'

Peter struggled again as Jola smiled at Sofia.

'Oh yes,' he whispered. 'So beautiful. So very lovely. I cannot imagine how I can wait any more.'

He bent in to Sofia's body, pulling the blanket from her neck and chest, and then finally Sofia did scream. Peter realised that if she could scream, it meant she could move a little more, and frantically began to try to move himself, wriggling his fingers, and lifting his head. They moved, stiffly at first, but they moved.

He managed to lift an arm, but it clumsily fell back by his side.

Jola seemed unaware, and was licking Sofia's neck. Peter saw blood but didn't know if it was hers or just what was on his face already, but it was enough to stir the paralysis from him.

He kicked out hard and sent Jola flying from Sofia's body, who now managed to sit up herself.

Sultan stamped his feet madly, and Jola curled into a ball from the fall and then got to his feet. Somehow he seemed to grow in size in the darkness of the stable, and glared at Peter with appalling menace.

'I will kill you, little man,' he said, spitting every word.

Peter said nothing, and tried to run towards Sultan, but his legs failed as the drug still curdled his blood. He ducked into a tumble and landed underneath Sultan's saddle.

The bloodbeard ran at him, and in a moment Peter reached up, pulled the long bundle from the saddle bag, slid out the sword and threw it like a spear at the onrushing Jola, who slid with a deafening hiss into the straw at Peter's feet. He twitched for a moment, and then was still.

Sofia crawled over to Peter.

'He drugged us!'

'Yes,' Peter said, 'but there's something else.'

'What?'

'Don't you see?' Peter said, laughing bitterly. 'She sent us here. The fortune teller sent us here. Right into the house of the bloodbeard. She knew what he was. She must have been in league with him.'

'So she made it up? She pretended to see something, just to send us here? Which means . . . '

'You're safe,' Peter said. 'Yes, you're safe.'

Sofia got to her feet, pulled Peter up onto his.

'I told you it was all nonsense,' Peter said, smiling.

'Maybe so, but that wasn't,' Sofia said, looking at the horrible body on the floor of the stable.

'I thought it was your blood.'

'No,' Sofia said. She wiped her neck with some straw. 'Must have been some other poor victim before he came home for us.'

'To give time for the drug to work.'

Sofia shuddered.

'Well,' Peter said. 'Let's find somewhere warmer to sleep. And then tomorrow, we'll find the others. We need to pay a certain fortune teller a visit, don't you think?'

Sofia nodded.

'Yes, Peter,' she said. 'Oh. And you know I said no one's perfect?'

'Yes?'

'Well I was wrong.'

She stood on tiptoe, kissed Peter gently on the lips, and led him upstairs to the warmth of the fireside.

THE KISS
OF DEATH

Marcus
Sedgwick

For Ellie and Bob

I have only one wish now, one . . . desire.

I want to be near you. I want, and I need, to reach out to you across this dark water that divides us and touch you. I want to be close to you, once again. Surely you can let me get close to you one last time? You owe me that, and you can't be afraid of me, so why not let me come and see you?

And then, when I have you in my arms, I know you will lean in towards me, so your lips will brush mine, but I will hold you a little tighter, and then I will put my hands up to your neck, and I will begin to squeeze. I will hold you until your feet have stopped shuffling on the wet paving stones, and your hands have stopped scrabbling against my arms and my face, and I will go on squeezing until your lips have stopped twitching and you are no more.

I will drop you into the water, where, for all you have done, you can rot.

Then, and only then, my friend, will I let you go. Then we will be done with each other, you and I.

Then we will be done.

I'm coming for you,

A.

ONE

1

*D*eath can come in many forms, but in Venice, death comes by water.

The boy held the letter lightly between his fingers, and read the words written there, as he had read them twenty times a day for twenty days.

Marko stared at the handwriting. It was his father's elegant script, and he knew it was genuine. He could almost smell his father's scent on the paper. Smell the medicines from his surgery. Smell his mother's fear as he'd left the house, six months before.

Grimly Marko folded the letter back into nine and slipped it inside his coat. His eyes lifted to the dark horizon, and only now did his senses return to the heave of the boat, the swaying of the cordage around him.

Water slapped at the windward side of the caravel as it turned the headland and made for the islands. It was January, the air was icy and seething with damp. He was cold. Cold and tired, but he had not even begun to think about these things yet.

One page of a letter, and a strange one at that. It was not addressed to anyone, did not begin with any formal introductions, and yet it ended as a letter should. Everything not quite as it should be, and then there were the words themselves; words etched in thick rich splattering ink; words that spoke of hatred and bile, and the threat to kill. Marko did not recognise his father in among that violence, it spoke of a man so very different from the gentle doctor everyone knew him to be. But he knew the writing so well, as it was the writing he read everyday as he assisted in his father's surgery, mixing powders and dispensing potions for the sick of Piran.

The letter had arrived one day, almost three weeks ago, at their house in the hills. Marko had been wrestling with his eight younger brothers and sisters, trying to get at least one of them to wash, when his mother had come in clutching the letter. She'd broken the seal and was holding it out to Marko, a mixture of fear and curiosity on her face. It made no sense. Someone else, in a different hand, had written their address on the back of the paper, folded and sealed it to make it its own envelope, and sent it on its way.

There was another thing. A scrap of paper fell to the floor. Marko picked it up and read a few words, written hastily in the same hand as the address:

The doctor, Alessandro, has gone missing.
We fear he may be dead. Come quickly.
I will wait at the Leon Bianco.
S. Bellini

That was all.

Now Marko's heart began to sound the time of his arrival, and it was a late one.

'Hour till landfall!' called the ship's captain from the low deck behind where Marko clutched the rail.

'So long?' he asked a sailor who stood pulling on a rope near at hand.

The deckhand didn't bother to look round.

Marko tried again.

'So long as an hour? It looks so close.'

'But it's not,' spat the sailor in reply, too busy with his work to pay Marko much attention.

Marko looked out across the rail towards the horizon again. Dusk had fallen and all that remained of daylight was a faint green glow over the mountains way beyond the lagoon. He struggled to even make out the vague shape of the island city in the gloom. He didn't know much about the place, even though it was where his father had been born, where he'd grown up, trained as a physician, and practised medical arts for many years. Marko suddenly felt a stab of regret. Why had he never known more about his father? Should he have asked more questions, listened more? Perhaps, but perhaps the fault did not lie with him, but with his father.

So Marko only knew what his father had told him before he left, and the little he'd managed to glean from the letters he'd sent. Then the letters had stopped, for months on end, until the one arrived that had brought Marko here now, across the water in the gathering night, to Venice.

2

*W*ords are not enough.

Marko could clearly remember his father telling him about this strange city, and, as usual, his father had been right.

Marko had often travelled with his father, especially as the years had started to slow him down. Once a month they made the journey on horseback, over the hills from their little port of Piran, to the great massing sprawl that was Trieste. There, Marko would idle away a few hours in the square while his father concluded his business. Then, their saddle-bags full of herbs, spices, stones and dried animal parts, Marko would tear his eyes away from the long-legged girl who worked in the tavern and they'd set off home, arriving well into the dark hours of the morning. Marko, therefore, thought he knew what a city was like, and that all cities in the world must be more or less the same, but when the boat slipped like a wet ghost into the Venetian lagoon, he knew how wrong he'd been.

'Yes, Father,' he muttered to himself, as the caravel drifted silently alongside the first buildings. 'Words are not enough.'

Someone slapped him on the back, and he turned to see Captain grinning at him.

'Think you're dreaming?'

Marko shook his head.

'I don't know. How does it . . . ? Why doesn't it . . . ? Who thought . . . ?'

Captain laughed.

'Of course, it's not the place it once was,' he said, mock serious. He was a decent man, Marko had decided. A spice trader, come to buy and sell in the city at the centre of the world, as he called it. He had a handsome face, but one that had fought the sun and salt for too long, and lost. Their journey had been three days from Trieste, and Marko had grown to like him, and like all the ship's hands, called him Captain. He'd been at sea so long he had no other name.

'Once they ruled the world, these people,' Captain said. 'Well, the seas, at least. If you wanted to trade anywhere from Barbary to Turkey you had to ask here first. Those days are gone, happily for me, but it's still enough to make most men weep.'

He sighed.

'What do you mean?' Marko asked.

'It's too much, this place. Too strong. It does for most people in the end. I wouldn't live here for all the salt in the sea. It's too beautiful, the wine's too potent, the stories are too frightening. The women are too friendly, the men too vicious. This city will suck you in and spit you back, inside out. I'm telling you this because you were a good passenger and earned our respect.'

'Telling me what?' Marko asked. The small ship drew closer to the walls of houses that seemed to stand right in the green-black water, thrusting up from the mud with elegance and indifference. In the half-light, Marko could see the outline of the rooftops, towers and domes of the skyline. Torches flickered in windows and archways, and their redness danced across the dark mirror of the water towards him.

'What are you telling me?' he repeated.

'Just to be careful. That's all. Be careful.'

Marko smiled.

'I will. I can look after myself.'

'Sure of it? I hope. You're strong enough, for your age. But some things aren't about strength, are they? I don't know what you're doing here, but if I were you I wouldn't stay too long.'

'How long is too long?' Marko asked, grinning.

Captain laughed.

'That's for you to find out,' he said, as he left, heading aft to mind the steering into harbour.

Marko had said nothing about the reason for his journey. He had money to buy his way across the sea, and that was all anyone cared about. No one on the ship had asked him what he was doing.

It had been one evening, after days of indecision, that he'd finally convinced his mother to let him go and find his father. It hadn't been easy.

'What if you never come back too, Marko?'

She must have said it a thousand times in those days before he left. And he knew she was right. Supposing he never did come back, and left her with the eight little ones to look after? Tomas, the oldest boy, was only eight, and Irina and Elena, the twins were twelve. The others were just babes really, and none of them earning a living.

But in the end, Marko had won.

'You'd have us give him up? Never even try to find him?'

Five days ago, he'd got up earlier than normal, dressed in his best clothes and stoutest boots, and then joined his mother at the big table in the kitchen. They counted out all the money they had left from his father's safe keeping.

'We'll halve it,' his mother had said, making two piles. 'You'll need more than we will here. It's expensive to travel and to eat.'

'No, mother,' he said. 'There are nine of you and one of me. And the children need feeding.'

So they counted half of one half back into the pile of money that was to stay in the house in the hills above the port of Piran, and Marko had put the rest in a bag round his neck.

'You bring him back, Marko,' his mother said. 'Bring him back so I can wring his silly old neck.'

She tried to smile.

He kissed her, and she began to cry, then he waved at his brothers and sisters, who were fighting among themselves, and barely noticed him go.

3

*M*arko sat at a table in a gallery that ran round the high walls of the large open ground floor of the place he now knew to be the Leon Bianco. Below he watched the comings and goings of the hotel, and for the first time on his journey, he felt alone. Not only that, but a single seed of doubt germinated in his mind. What on earth was he doing here? There was no chance that he could find his father in this teeming, writhing city. He didn't even know his father's friend, the one he'd come to Venice to help. The letter had been from him, S. Bellini, the glass-maker. It occurred to Marko that the man could walk right past him and he wouldn't know him. All he knew was that he was in the right place, the White Lion, the Leon Bianco.

Captain had brought Marko as far as the hotel. He seemed to have taken pity on the boy.

While the deck hands had unloaded their cargo onto the quayside, Captain stood with Marko. He scratched his head.

'The Leon Bianco, eh?' He glanced around at his men, then back at Marko. 'Give me five minutes to sort this lot out.'

Half an hour later, well into the evening, Marko and Captain had jumped aboard a long narrow boat, shaped like a sliver of fingernail, but painted black. They joined three other passengers, who each pressed a coin into the boatman's rough hand, and set off and out of the harbour. Marko noticed that one of these passengers, a tall man in a black cape, wore a plain white mask. Some disfigurement to conceal, presumably. The pox, or maybe a duelling scar.

The Captain chatted away single-handedly, and Marko took little notice. He stared as the boatman leaped up onto the covered stern of the boat and facing forwards, began to push on an oar held in some kind of ornate rowlock at his feet. In this way, he deftly flicked the boat from its mooring and into open water.

Captain caught his eye.

'He's a gondolier,' he explained. 'This is called a gondola.'

Marko nodded.

'See how he only rows on one side? So why aren't we going round in circles?'

Marko shook his head, then stared at the boat a little harder.

'It's not even,' he said. 'It's shaped like . . . '

'Like a banana!' Captain chuckled. He stopped. 'You do know what a banana is, don't you?'

But Marko shook his head again.

'Well, it's a type of fruit. And it's yellow, and it's shaped like a gondola!'

Briefly, Captain was pleased enough to stop talking, but then he was off again, uttering more words than Marko had heard him speak on their entire journey across the sea, and Marko realised the veteran sailor was excited by his return to Venice.

A few more strokes and the gondolier was propelling them towards the mouth of a river that seemed to cut into the heart of the city itself. All around them were countless other boats;

hundreds of the tiny gondolas, some slightly larger versions with two oarsmen, and large ships, as large as Captain's caravel, which glided through the water as if guided by a magical hand.

People were everywhere, in boats, standing in windows and doorways, but something bothered Marko.

'Where are the streets?'

'You're on the main one right now,' Captain said.

'This river is a road?'

'It's not a river. It's a canal, the Canale Grande.'

'It's artificial?'

'This whole city is artificial. They say it was built on marshes, over a thousand years ago. They were just simple fisher folk who lived on the mainland, until the Mongols began to rampage and murder along the coast. The fishermen went out into marshes and built some little huts on legs, and they never came back. Look! They're still here!'

He pointed at the extraordinarily magnificent buildings that stretched out of the water, five and six storeys high, and away down the length of the Canal.

'They built these houses onto the highest clumps of mud, building up, up, up, and they diverted the course of the rivers that flowed into the lagoon so it wouldn't silt up. That made the water deeper. Now look at them. The fishermen. The richest fishermen on earth.'

Marko nodded.

'You were right,' he said. 'What you said on the boat. I am dreaming. It can't be real. But aren't there any streets at all?'

'Small ones mostly. What you're looking at is a series of tiny islands, joined by bridges. On each island, there are streets just like anywhere, but they're very small, because they used as much ground as they could for building the palazzi. The houses.'

Marko returned to his reverie, while Captain talked and talked.

'Of course, we don't usually stop at the Leon Bianco. Bit grand for us. We usually put up at a little albergo by the harbour. But it's been a good trip and I am the captain, so when you said you were headed for the Leon, I thought to myself, why not? You deserve it, I thought. Do the men good to be out of my clutches for a while, eh?'

He went on in this way, until the gondola put in right beside the front of the Leon Bianco, and they stepped onto a wooden landing stage, then straight into the chaos of the tavern.

Almost immediately, Marko was on his own. The captain met a woman who he seemed to know very well, as they disappeared somewhere upstairs within seconds. Marko heard him talking to the woman as they went.

'Why not, I said to myself. You deserve it.'

A girl whisked by with a tray of glasses and a large wine jug held high above her head. Nearly bumping into her, Marko stepped back and fell over someone's boot. He landed flat on his back and lay winded for a moment. He stared up into the face of the owner of the boot. A very tall, very old man, dressed in black, with a black cape, pure white hair, and a deeply lined face towered over him. As Marko's breath returned, the man stooped and with one hand took Marko's arm and pulled him to his feet. Somehow, before he knew it, the old man had with unlikely strength set him upright again.

He spoke quietly.

'Take care how you fall.'

It was a strange thing to say, and he spoke too with a strange accent to his Italian, an accent that reminded Marko of his mother's home tongue far away in the mountains to the east. Then he was gone, and Marko decided to stop drawing attention to himself. He found a table up above the noise, in the gallery, and clutched the wine he'd bought from a serving girl, a girl who was actually a woman twice his age.

'You want to watch it,' she said, as he fished in the bag at his neck for a coin.

Marko glanced up at her, and saw she meant well. She smiled.

'You shouldn't flash all that around. Not if you want to keep it. Hide it.'

Marko groaned to himself, as he pushed the money into her hand. His first night in the city and he was behaving like a fool from the countryside. He knew better than that. This place couldn't be any worse than Trieste, he told himself.

He watched the life of the Leon Bianco hustle by. The whole ground floor opened into one large tavern, with plenty of drinking, tables for eating, but also tables for doing business. Even at this late hour, he saw money changing hands between all sorts of different people. Something else struck him. He'd assumed the masked man in the gondola was hiding some deformity, but now he saw that almost one of every three people in the hotel wore a mask of some kind. He could remember his father telling him about Venice suffering from the pestilence. Marko had asked him if that was why he'd left Venice, but he'd simply shaken his head and changed the subject. Could all these people bear the ravages of plague?

No, he saw now that many of them removed their masks to drink, eat, or just to chat, and held them by the ribbons which secured them to the face. He watched as people came and went – some taking masks off, some putting them on. Some never removing them at all.

The whole place reeked of seedy affairs, of bad business, of violence, sex and money, and Marko wondered, if this was supposed to be a stylish place to stay, what the Captain's place by the harbour was like.

People drifted to the first floor and to the rooms of the hotel above and behind the waterfront, and almost hypnotised by the flow, Marko suddenly realised that he was tired.

His eyes grew heavy, his head fell forward onto his crossed arms, and he began to doze.

He woke to the sounds of laughter and shouting. People were jeering and sniggering. Marko looked down over the balcony and saw a rowdy group pushing someone around. He could see the figure in the centre now. He was clearly drunk, reeling around the circle of people, swinging his fists wildly and ineffectually. He shouted incoherently, and then someone pulled the hood of his cape from his head. With a shock Marko recognised the old man he'd bumped into earlier. It was hard to reconcile his powerful calm with the drunken creature swaying on the tavern floor. The laughter rose and rose, and then as the old man landed a punch on someone, more by accident than skill, the laughter turned to ugly taunts.

Marko looked around the room. He felt sorry for the old man, but it was none of his affair, after all. He couldn't afford to get involved. Across the room, at the bar, he saw someone pointing straight at him, leaning over and talking to a girl dressed in black.

He felt uneasy, slightly sick from his broken sleep. Standing up, he began to push past the other tables in the gallery. The ruckus below grew louder and he heard two young men discussing the entertainment.

'What did he say?'

'Same as before. His Italian is dreadful, but he keeps shouting about vampires. Vampires in Venice!'

They broke into fits of laughter and Marko doubled his pace for the exit. He was too late. The girl from the bar stood at the head of the stairs blocking his way.

'Who are you?' she said. She was young, but not *so* young, Marko saw immediately, and was finely dressed; a black cape over a black silk dress, with long sleeves. She wore a hood to cover her head, but underneath he saw her black hair was braided in elaborate patterns.

'No one,' he said. 'I'm just leaving.'

He pushed past her, not caring this time that he was being rude, and set off down the stairs, but she called after him.

'Do you know Alessandro Foscari?'

That stopped Marko dead. He turned and made his way slowly back up the stairs towards her.

The noise from the fight downstairs was reaching a climax, and there were shouts from the street now too.

'Do you know Alessandro Foscari?' the girl repeated. 'Answer me quickly. We don't want to be here when the police arrive. They'll arrest anyone they don't like the look of.'

From her stare, she clearly meant Marko.

'Yes,' said Marko, 'I know Alessandro. He's my father.'

4

*T*he girl was thrown, confused. Angry.

'They sent *you*? I've been coming here every night for two weeks, for *you*?'

She said something, obviously some curse, but Marko didn't understand. Her Italian was odd, he thought.

She sighed, looked at the fight, and made up her mind.

'Come on,' she said. 'We'd better be going. No, not that way.'

The girl grabbed Marko's arm, and they hurried deeper into the palazzo, down a steep flight of stairs, through a low doorway, and out into a courtyard. A fine mist had risen from the lagoon, hanging like a ghost over their heads as they rushed diagonally across the yard and into an alleyway so narrow they had to turn sideways to enter it. The girl led, twisting this way and that, and then they were in a wider paved street, but only for a second, as she turned another corner and headed back towards the water. Marko could smell it coming, and then they were at a flimsy landing stage on a small waterway.

The girl jumped into a gondola, and pulled Marko in after her. They sat opposite each other, Marko facing forwards, with the gondolier behind him.

'Don't we have to pay him?' he asked, nodding his head at the oarsman.

'No,' the girl said. 'He's ours.'

They pushed out of the narrow water and Marko saw they were back in the Canale Grande, but a few houses further down from the Leon Bianco.

'That was a neat trick,' he said, looking back at the hotel.

'Look,' she said, and Marko saw the fight spilling out into the doorway of the palazzo. Someone fell into the water and then there were more screams and angry shouts.

'The police have arrived.'

Marko turned back to her.

'I'm Marko.'

The girl said nothing, so he tried again.

'Who are you? How do you know my father? How did you know where to find me?'

'I wrote to you, to your mother,' the girl said. 'Remember?'

'The note was signed, yes. S. Bellini. Simono Bellini, my father's friend.'

'The note was from me, I assure you. My name is Sorrel Bellini, his daughter.'

'Sorrel? That doesn't sound very Italian.'

'No, and it's not Venetian either. It's an English name. I was born in London when my father worked for the King of England. My mother was English.'

'Was?' Marko asked, but regretted it. The answer was obvious enough.

'She's dead. She died years ago, when I was small. Then we came back to Venice.'

'I'm sorry,' Marko said.

'Why?' Sorrel said bluntly. 'Everyone dies in the end, don't they?'

Marko could think of no answer to that and they fell silent, as the gondolier pushed them out across the Canal, heading for a slender gap in the buildings in the far bank.

Marko stole glances at Sorrel. There was something so peculiar about her, he could see that already. His first glance had told him she was ugly, but his first glance had been wrong. He now realised that she was indeed very pretty, but what hid this was two things; her manner, and her make-up. Thick black rings of kohl circled her eyes, eyes which were actually a delightful green. That, and the scowl on her face, lent her the air of misery which had fooled Marko at first.

Around them, the water lifted and fell, gently, sucking at the flat bottom of the gondola; a real beast, but in elemental form. Cries of night-time in the city reached across to them, torches cast eerie shifting shadows on every side, and as the boat reached the far bank, they were eaten up whole by the massive palazzi of brick and stone that dwarfed the tiny waterway.

Barely wide enough for the gondola to pass, their speed dropped to a crawl.

'Where are we going?' Marko asked.

'Home,' Sorrel said.

Something in her voice again stopped Marko from saying anything more. After a moment, she spoke again.

'Home. To the House that Kills.'

Marko leaned forwards.

'What did you say?' he whispered.

Sorrel leaned towards him, and spoke in an exaggerated whisper.

'They say there is a curse on my home,' she said, her eyes dancing with sick joy. 'There is a curse, and so they call it the "House that Kills". And that's where we're going.'

'You're joking.'

'Do you think so? I'm only telling you what they say. I don't believe in the curse.'

She stopped, then added, 'At least, I didn't.'

5

*S*queezing between the buildings reminded Marko somehow of the forests behind their home in Piran. There was the same sense of entrapment, of being surrounded, hemmed in on all sides, unable to see more than a few yards, though here the trees were made of stone and the forest floor was made of water. But at last the little gondola was spewed out of the maze and emerged in open water.

The mist was thicker here and Marko suddenly doubted his sense.

'Where are we going? I've come to find my father. Why are we leaving the city?'

'We're not,' Sorrel said.

'But we're heading back into the lagoon.'

'No, we're not. Just watch the mist.'

Sorrel said something hurriedly to the gondolier, who chuckled strangely, but Marko didn't understand what she said.

'What language were you speaking? Italian?'

'We speak our own language here. It's Italian, sort of, but we have our own way with most things.'

'What did you say?'

'To Francesco? I told him to hurry up so the little boy didn't get scared.'

Sorrel looked him right in the eye, holding his gaze, daring him to be angry. He looked away, and over her shoulder, cursing her bitterness, cursing his ignorance and indecision.

'Where's my father?' he blurted out. 'What do you know about him?'

Sorrel put her head on one side as she answered him.

'I don't know where he is. That's why I sent for help. And they sent you!'

She fell silent again, staring moodily at the water. Marko opened his mouth to answer her back, but thought better of it.

She'd been right. Looming out of the mist was another island, which might have been a mirror of the one they'd just left.

'This is where we live. Giudecca. It's the shark that swims alongside the whale that is the rest of the city. Our palazzo is on the far side. We'll be there in minutes.'

Again the boat dove into the buildings, cutting through the heart of the island, but Marko soon saw what she meant about Giudecca – it was thin, its ends were out of sight in the mist. Within moments they were on the far side and there, finally, lay the lagoon itself. Marko could smell the cold wet wind from across the marshes, and knew the sea proper lay beyond all that.

'Our house,' Sorrel said, pointing over her shoulder without turning.

'Which one? The one with all those people? Where the boats are?'

Sorrel stared at him, then spun round. She jumped to her feet and began to shout.

'Hey! What are you doing? Hey!'

Marko craned to see past her as their boat drew up to the house. There were four people, two men and two women, and

247

three row-boats with oarsmen waiting. Luggage and parcels were being carried from the house and now the last were being piled up in the larger of the boats.

'Hey!' Sorrel called. 'What are you doing?'

One of the older men called back to her.

'We're leaving, Signorina. I'm sorry.'

'What do you mean, you're sorry? You can't leave. You just can't!'

'We're very sorry, but we won't stay another night.'

Sorrel jumped from the boat onto the thin strip of pavement at the water's edge and ran to them, pleading.

'Carlo, no! Maria, please. You can't leave us! Carlo, stop, talk to me, talk to me.'

But no one would even look her in the eyes as they climbed aboard and began to row away.

'Wait! Please. Come back!'

They didn't, and as Marko came to stand by her, she lost her temper entirely.

'You swine! You dogs! You . . .'

She let out a stream of curses and insults in Venetian dialect, whose meaning was clear, even if the words themselves were unknown to him.

Francesco had tied the boat to an iron ring set in the paving of the quayside, and gently put a hand on Sorrel's shoulder.

She looked up at him and waved her hands at the departing boats.

'How *could* they? How could they?'

The tall boatman said nothing, but gently guided Sorrel to the front door of the palazzo.

'Who were they? Why are they leaving?' Marko asked, as she stood watching the boats disappear into the mist. The creak of the oars in the rowlocks drifted back across the water, even after they were out of sight.

'Well,' said Sorrel, still breathing heavily from her anger, 'That was our cook, her husband, the maid and the cook's boy. And they left because they are terrible, terrible people!'

She flung the last words into the mist where they fell dead on the water.

'What's the use?' she said, more to herself than Marko. She closed her eyes, then turned to look at Marko again. 'Come on, it's getting late. Have you eaten?'

'No, no. I'm starving, but . . . '

'But what? What! You want to know what's going on, you want to know what you're doing here. You want to know what's happened to your father. Well, so do I, and I want to know why they sent you and no one more useful, but I'm hungry, so let's eat first and talk later, yes? Especially as we'll have to get the food for ourselves now that the cook has run away!'

They went inside. Marko stood a step behind Sorrel in the huge entrance hall to the Ca' Bellini.

'Our family have lived here for centuries,' Sorrel said. 'Apart from my father's time in London. But then we came back. To this.'

Like a ghost she waved her hand in the faltering light shed by a vast candelabra suspended in the middle of the hall. It hung from a chain that stretched high up to the ceiling at the level of the second floor. What it illuminated was, Marko thought, like a dying animal. Some noble beast, like a wonderful stallion, but now on its last legs. What he saw spoke to him of years of wealth and grandeur, of commerce and opulence, exotic riches and domestic luxury, but which had all fled the scene, as mourners flee a funeral. That wealth and splendour was a thing of the past, what was left was a spectre of its former self; faded, rent, and sunken.

'It's incredible,' Marko said, though he knew that Sorrel knew he lied.

He stared at discoloured paintings, tattered rugs and tapestries, chipped chairs, the rotting staircase to the first floor, the grimy window glass. Wax from the candles had dripped to the floor, forming a series of small mountains of bizarre shapes that grew out of the Turkish carpet covering most of the hall. Marko had trouble pulling his eyes away from their grotesque deformities.

'And your father?' he asked. 'Is he here? When can I meet him?'

Sorrel's voice was as thin as the wind outside in the lagoon.

'You can't,' she said. 'That would not be . . . a very good idea.'

6

'Why did you come?'
'You wrote to me.'
'I wrote to your family, to your mother.'
'She couldn't come. She has the children to look after.'
'So she sent another child instead?' Sorrel said viciously.
'You're no older than I am,' Marko replied defensively.
Sorrel ignored him.

They sat in the dining room on the first floor, a room that spanned the whole width of the house. They'd chosen a small table by a window at the front of the house overlooking the lagoon, rather than the views across the roofs of other houses on Giudecca onto the city itself. Far away in the distance fires burned on some remote speck of mud, some excuse for an island.

'The mist must have lifted. In that direction at least.'
He pointed at the distant firelight.
Sorrel nodded vaguely.

They had not had to prepare their food after all; almost before they'd left the entrance hall Francesco had brought plates of cheese and bread and they'd followed him upstairs to the dining room.

'So,' Sorrel said. 'You're our cook as well as our boatman now?'
Francesco had nodded, and smiled.

251

'Won't you join us?' she added, but he bowed solemnly, and left them.

'Thank you, Francesco,' Sorrel called after him, so earnestly that Marko realised she was thanking him for more than fetching food.

Marko had no idea how old Francesco was. Not young like Sorrel, not old like his father, or that man in the Leon Bianco. He was somewhere in the middle. He had brown skin, presumably his birth colour and not a tan, given the dank and sunless winter in the lagoon. His face was only lined at the corners of his eyes, wrinkling when he smiled, which he seemed to do often.

'He doesn't say much,' Marko said once he'd left them to eat.

'He doesn't say anything,' Sorrel replied in her most withering voice. 'He's mute.'

'Oh?'

'He can't talk. He was a sailor, he fought with the Venetian navy, but they were captured by the Turks one day. He escaped, but without his tongue.'

She said it all calmly, as a matter of simple fact.

'That's awful.'

'Yes, it's awful,' she agreed, but again there was no emotion in her voice. She might have been speaking about the day's weather. Marko was reminded of what she'd said in the gondola, about everyone dying in the end. She seemed so . . . what was it exactly? Disinterested?

'It all happened a long time ago,' Sorrel explained. 'He was little older than you. Or me.'

She forced a faltering smile, and Marko knew it was an apology of sorts.

'Doesn't it cause trouble? Having a servant who can't speak.'

'If anything, it makes life easier. He never gets involved with the others, with their arguments. Got involved, I should say. It's just me and him, now.'

'And your father?'

'Yes, and my father.'

There was another silence, and Marko was again left to wonder what the mystery about Simono was.

'And what about me?'

Sorrel put down her knife.

'I told you. You're no use to me. I'm sorry, I don't mean to be rude, but there it is.'

Marko restrained himself, but it was hard. He was still tired and the food had not worked any magic on him yet.

'And why,' he said, 'am I no use?'

'I meant for them to send someone, someone to investigate. Men. And they sent you, when what I need is a policeman.'

'They wouldn't send police across the sea to look for a missing doctor!' Marko said. 'What were you thinking? There was no one else who could come but me. If you wanted police why don't you get help from the authorities here?'

Sorrel laughed, and picked up an apple.

'This is Venice. The last people you want to turn to for help here are the police. Far too dangerous a strategy. You don't understand, you're not from here. Things are different here. No, I needed help from someone who knew your father, from someone who I could trust.'

'And you don't think you can trust me? His own son?'

Sorrel stopped eating and looked hard at Marko.

'Your father was from Venice originally, wasn't he?'

'Yes, he left when my mother was heavy with me. We came to live in her homeland, across the sea.'

'So, you're half Venetian. Well, that may count for

253

something. I suppose I have that much. But what can you do? Are you strong? Are you clever? Are you brave?'

Marko waited a moment before answering. He looked at the strange girl in front of him, with her woven hair and dark circles around her moody eyes. Her quick lips and sharp tongue.

'Sorrel, I don't know if I'm any of those things, but I'm something more useful than any of those. I'm angry, Sorrel. I'm angry. My father has gone missing. Without him my family, my mother, my three brothers and five sisters, will become destitute. You say he has gone missing. You even told us he might be dead. Someone is responsible for this, and I intend to find out who. And I'm angry enough to do it.'

He nearly added, so don't take me for a fool, but he could see he'd made his point, for Sorrel had turned to the window, trying to hide a tear that had formed in the corner of her eye.

7

*W*hat little joy there is in the girl, Marko thought. What little joy in this whole miserable place.

After they'd eaten, Sorrel had gone to bed.

'I can't talk any more tonight,' she'd said to Marko's protests. 'Please, let me be. I'm too tired.'

He'd relented, and she'd shown him a choice of bedrooms. After he'd seen six, he'd stopped her.

'This will do fine,' he said. They were all more or less the same. Each felt as though it had not been used in a hundred years, and there was little to distinguish between the mouldering state of one over another.

'Where's your room?' he added. 'In case I need anything?'

She looked curiously at him.

'But I thought you were brave, Marko,' she said, teasing. 'Very well. My room is that one, at the end of the corridor. And I'm going there now.'

She left him in his doorway and Marko watched as she shut her bedroom door behind her.

What little joy.

He undressed, then pulled the sheets from the bed and wrapped the coverlet around him like a cloak. His room was at the corner of the building, with windows to the front and side. He opened the shutters at the front for a few minutes. There, across the bay, he could still see that flickering firelight, and tried to work out which island it was coming from, then the cold got too much too bear, and he shut himself in again and lay on the bed, waiting for sleep to come.

It came swiftly and easily, like death comes in the night, and then he was gone far, far into the underworld of dreams.

Of nightmares.

8

*T*he line between dream and nightmare is a fine one, and is easily crossed. Marko's mind replayed events in broken and disjointed segments. The arrival of the letter was mixed with his father's departure six months earlier, his journey on the caravel from Trieste became his gondola ride with Captain. He wondered where Captain was now, whether he was snoring soundly at the Leon Bianco, or had gone back to join his loving crew.

Sounds swished into range and out again. The lapping of the lagoon at the foot of the house. A footstep above his head, maybe, creeping in the corridor outside. The hoot of some night bird.

More visions muddled themselves in his drifting mind. Francesco became the old drunk from the tavern and they danced a minuet down the passageway outside his room, until the old man suddenly attacked Francesco brutally.

Marko saw a doorway, and it was Captain's doorway, and it was his own, right at the foot of his bed. He saw a crack in the old wooden panels, weakened by rot and worm, and through this crack a wild white eye glared into the room. It scanned this way and that, lids spun far back into the socket, as the eye flicked here and there, as if trying to soak the room up from beyond the door.

Somehow he knew in his dream that the owner of the eye

was a woman, some ancient crone, withered with dry, pale, almost white skin, cold to the touch. He could tell all this from the eye alone. She was some sort of, yes, oh God! Some sort of witch. He moaned softly in his sleep, turned over, and drifted again.

Then there was screaming, and it was real screaming, which sank deep into the sleeping heart of Marko's brain, and was flung across the early morning waters of the lagoon, where it would hang for hours before finally evaporating.

Marko dived out of bed, winding a sheet around his waist. He staggered into the corridor. It was obvious where the screaming was coming from, it was a woman's screaming. There was only one voice in the house that high, and anyway, Sorrel's door stood open.

He rushed into the room, and found Sorrel with her back to him. In her hands she clutched a hand mirror.

'Sorrel! Sorrel! What's wrong?'

Sorrel turned and Marko's eyes widened with the shock.

Sorrel's face was an appalling sight. Her whole face was painted white, death white. The black circles she wore round her eyes had been worked outwards, enlarged into the hollow sockets of a skull, and her lips were hidden beneath a black patch the size of her fist that looked like the toothless gawp of a death mask.

She had stopped screaming now and began to wail uncontrollably.

'What have you done? Sorrel! What's the matter?'

She tried to hold back her cries, but still great heaving sobs dragged out of her mouth.

'Why did you do this?' Marko said, but all Sorrel did was point. At first he thought she was pointing at him, but then he realised she was pointing over his shoulder, behind him.

He was suddenly aware of someone standing behind him. Slowly, still moving as if in a nightmare, he turned, then leaped backwards, falling against the bed.

He swore.

There, no more than a hand's breadth away, was a man. An old man, his face painted with the same mocking death mask that Sorrel wore. His dreadful bloodshot eyes were wide open, and did not blink, nor did they focus, but stared straight across the room at the dull wall opposite. He wore a frightful white powdered wig, that might have been elegant once, but which now surrounded his head like the hair in a child's drawing, crazed and tangled. On his lips was fixed a rictus of a smile, thin and frozen.

In one hand he held a black stick of paint, in the other, a white one.

'Holy Mother!' Marko spluttered. His lips twitched with revulsion. 'Who the hell is that?'

Sorrel could only sob, and as Francesco's footsteps sounded in the corridor outside, Marko just had time to hear her choked reply.

'My father. It's my father.'

9

After Francesco had taken Simono back to his room, Sorrel began to calm down. Marko sat with her, still wrapped in his sheet, until he began to shiver so badly that even Sorrel noticed.

'You can get into the bed,' she said, 'but stay down that end.'

She pointed to the foot of the bed and Marko gratefully climbed underneath the covers, pulling them around his shoulders as he did so.

'Are you all right, now?' he asked, but Sorrel didn't reply. She got out of bed properly, and lifting the hem of her long nightdress slightly so she didn't trip, she went to the washstand in the corner of the room, then returned carefully carrying a bowl of water and a bundle of flannel rags.

'Hold this, would you?' she said, and got back into bed. 'Thank you.'

Slowly, she began to dab and rub at the face paint. Her efforts only made it worse; the paint smeared into a worse vision than the death-mask her father had painted on her. Her face looked like a skull left out in the rain, that had somehow begun to dissolve.

'Let me do it,' Marko said, moving towards her.

'Stay where you are,' she said. 'Why aren't you dressed anyway?'

'I don't sleep in my clothes. It's cleaner not to. Especially when I've been wearing them for three days.'

She grunted.

'We'll get them washed.'

'Why did he do it?' Marko asked gently.

'What?'

'Why did your father do that to you?'

'He's done it before,' she said.

'That's not what I asked.'

Again she didn't answer his question directly, but at least she was talking.

'I was asleep, and dreaming that a spider was walking over my face. I brushed it off twice but it made no difference. Then I woke up and my father was leaning over me. He was looking right at me, but as if he couldn't see me. Does that make sense? Anyway, I knew what he'd done before so I grabbed a mirror. I don't know why it upset me so much.'

'Why does he do it?'

'To make me look like I'm dead.'

'But why would he do that?'

Now Sorrel became angry.

'Because he's mad, of course. My father is insane! Do you understand?'

Marko waited for Sorrel's anger to dissipate. She sat heaving in great sobbing breaths, but after a while she began to dab at her face again.

In the silence, Marko heard the sound of singing. A woman's voice, quite a decent voice, and though it missed a note here and there, there was an indescribable beauty about it.

'Who's that?' Marko asked. 'Someone here?'

'No, no. It's the lady who lives in the palazzo next door.

Venetia. She arrived a couple of weeks ago to take part in the carnival.'

'What's the carnival?'

'You're so full of questions,' Sorrel said irritably.

'It's the best way to learn.'

'Maybe,' Sorrel said.

She picked up the mirror.

'Oh, I'm only making it worse.'

'It's greasepaint,' Marko said. 'You need cold cream, not water.'

Sorrel stopped what she was doing and looked at him.

'Yes, you're right, but how does a boy know that?'

She went to her dressing table and rummaged in a drawer, then returned with a small brown pot.

'I'm not only a doctor's son,' Marko said, 'but his assistant. I'm used to preparing creams and powders. You learn things, doing that.'

He stopped, something suddenly occurring to him.

'So, this is why my father came to Venice? To help your father?'

She nodded.

'He hasn't always been like this. This bad. Just the last few weeks. He knew he was getting ill, but he was still in his right mind. He wrote to your father and asked him to come, begged him to.'

'But they hadn't seen each other in almost twenty years, my father said. We couldn't understand why he'd leave us and cross the sea to help someone he didn't know any more.'

'There was a powerful connection between them. There is, I mean. That's all I know.'

'But why didn't you consult the doctors here? When your father got ill?'

262

'I told you. This is Venice. You no more want to consult a doctor here, than you would rely on the police. Oh, of course, they came, but my father dismissed them all, one by one. They were quacks and charlatans. They'd row up to the house, holding their hands out for their fee before they'd even come ashore. Then they'd swarm around him, diagnosing diseases no one's ever heard of, prescribing treatments that could possibly do more harm than good. One told him to eat sheep dung every morning, and seaweed every night. Another told him to swim across the Canalazzo every day, then climb the campanile in San Marco.'

'What's the Canalazzo?'

'Sorry, the Canale Grande, that's what strangers call it.'

'And the campanile?'

'The bell tower in San Marco. San Marco is the heart of the city, the main square by the cathedral. Hah! I just realised. You are Marko, too. Is that why your father called you that? To remind him of the city he'd left?'

'I don't know,' Marko said, as if surprised. 'I've never been told.'

Sorrel smiled, then sighed and went on with her story.

'A third took one look at him and screamed that he had the plague. Then he ran back to his boat. It's not a good thing to say that word in this city. We've had too much of it. Anyone who knows anything knows my father doesn't have the plague.'

'So what *is* wrong with him? His physical symptoms, I mean.'

Sorrel looked at herself in the mirror, then looked at Marko.

'How do I look now?' she asked.

Beautiful, lovely, happy, sad, were the words that came to

his mind, but what he said was, 'Fine.'

That seemed to be enough for her, and putting the things on the dresser, she came back to the bed. She stood, hesitating.

'What is it, Sorrel?' Marko asked. He sensed her unease. 'What is it?'

'I think the best way you can understand what's going on, is this.'

She removed her pillow and then felt down behind and underneath the mattress by the head of the bed. For a moment she appeared to panic, then her hands found what they'd been searching for, and she pulled out a bound book, covered in soft hide, and tied shut with a taut leather cord.

She opened it, and leafed through the pages to about halfway, then held it out to Marko.

'I'm going to get dressed,' she said. 'And while I do, you take this back to your room and read. From this page. Then you'll understand. You want to know where your father is, and so do I, but you need to know this first.'

She passed the book to him.

'You can read, can't you?'

'Yes, of course I can,' Marko said. 'I am a doctor's assistant. I have to be able to read. Is it in Italian?'

'Venetian. But you'll get the idea. Take it away. I'll come for you when I'm dressed. Read, and then you'll understand.'

10

5th May 1682

The doctor has left and that is the last I will see of his kind. They are at a loss, I know that now, though I have not wanted to believe it so. The more they fail to understand what is happening to me, the more desperate and extreme their proclamations become. I will go forwards alone from here.

9th May 1682

After a few days respite from my condition, it returned last night and gave me no peace whatsoever. This morning I am pale, a haunted reflection of my normal self.

12th May 1682

Still nothing will work for me. And I have tried everything. My dear Aurora says I am trying too hard, but I cannot stop myself. My heart pounds in my chest and the blood beats in my brain, and the more I crave them to stop, the harder their rhythm becomes.
Four nights now.

13th May 1682

Five nights, and still nothing. Whatever I do fails.

15th May 1682

My hair is growing thin, I think. Possibly. Certainly, my eyes are pink and their veins shot through with blood. My skin is feverish, my heart beats wildly, and the pressure of blood in my body is giving me fierce headaches. I look in the glass as I write, and I see my pupils have shrunk to tiny pinpricks. Yesterday I spent two hours reeling round the dining room like a drunkard. Aurora thought me so, and would not believe I had not drunk a single drop of wine. And indeed I had not, though I love its taste so much.

16th May 1682

Eight nights now, eight days and nights, without a single solitary moment.

I can bear it no more. I am ashamed to confess even to these private pages that I have contemplated ending my own torment, but I know I will not be able to do it. Oh! How I wish I had that strength, and then I could give myself what I crave, what is denied me.

17th May 1682

Sleep. Even the word, writing it, seeing it is torture to me now. I cannot sleep. Ever. How is it possible? I am dead, though I still stand on my feet. I am a ghost, a spectre, a wraith. I am the mist that walks on the water; I am the water itself. I am the foul lagoon, and I am death's feather-wing that floats on high and descends to sweep mortals into their graves. I am death.

But I am not sleep. Not sleep.

4th June 1682

The miraculous change in the weather from that ill-starred May to the beautiful sunshine of June has marked a turning point for me, a wonderful thing! I slept for four whole hours. That was four days ago. I was so terrified it wouldn't happen again that I didn't dare record it here, but last night, o joy! I slept for nearly seven hours. Am I cured? Is it possible? With the sunshine I see new hope. Aurora is so beautiful in the sunshine, and this morning I was able to show her how beautiful she is, for the first time in months. She laughed as we kissed. And I think, o God, that you have released me from my punishment. Praise be to God.

16th June 1682

How hateful I am! I cannot read the bitter words above without a knife stabbing my pounding heart. I spoke too rashly, indeed, and now I am four nights without a moment's rest. I have become a slave to this, an automaton, going through the actions of living as a real person does, but without the thinking and the feeling to make it real. At some moments Aurora tells me that I fall into a sort of stupor, with my eyes open and yet I appear to sense nothing, but these times give me no peace, no rest, and I know now that I will die for want of sleep. It is only a matter of when. My heart beats harder every day, the blood hurtles round my brain, but my soul is as grey and limp as the unseasonable mists that have returned to cling to the city day in, and day out.

17th June 1682

Though he is only seven years old, today I formally transferred ownership of the Ca' Bellini and the Bellini glass-shops to my only dear son, Simono. I have done all I can do for Aurora, and for my son, for the future, and I will be leaving soon.

19th June 1682

Yes. Swans. Or geese. Feathers anyway.

20th June 1682

How my cursed blood hurts me! Surges through the temple and the gut. My legs are iron, my eyes are hot coals. The sweats are bad. Bad.

21st June 1682

Every thing has death. All is very clear to me this evening. Every thing has death. The ancients believed that only man had death. That a stone is immortal, that a mountain, a river, the sun, are immortal. Even the trees and the animals, the plants and the birds are immortal. One bird may die, but there is another! One plant may be eaten, but its seed gives rise to another. Immortal. Only man has death, the ancients thought, because only man knows that he is going to die. That is the difference, I see that now. Only man knows that he is going to die, and so that must affect everything he does in life.

True? Or not?

That question, I cannot yet answer, but whether a thing knows it or not, there is an end to every thing. Even the stone, the flower, the river, the mountain. All will be gone one day. Even this miserable misty city will disappear one day, back to whence it came. Back to the dark water.

Only man knows he is going to die, and I know my death will be soon.

3rd July 1682

Sunshine. Glass. Aurora. Wine. Simono.

11

*T*here, the diary ended.

Marko lifted his eyes from the book, his head still ringing with those mysterious last five words. The awful implication, left by half a diary of blank pages, was that death had come soon after. Marko hoped it was sooner, rather than later. Later would have meant more days of that torturous madness.

Holy God, Marko thought. What a way to die. Could there be anything worse in Death's arsenal than to die from lack of sleep? A total absence of rest that led inevitably to a massive failure of the heart, or a seizure of the brain. Sorrel said he would understand, but the book raised more questions than it answered. So, he knew his father had come to the city to try and help Simono, and he knew that Simono had the same disease that had killed his father, but it still didn't tell him anything about where his own father had gone. He had to get Sorrel to tell him more, if only she was more forthcoming. Whenever he asked her a direct question she would retreat into herself like a timid kitten hiding under a bed. He thought about his father, about the way he would deal with difficult patients.

'Get their confidence first,' he would say, 'Get them to like you. Then they'll tell you anything.'

That was what Marko had to do.

He got up, dimly aware of the singing from the

neighbouring building again. He threw open all the shutters, then pulled the windows closed to keep out the cold. It was a foul morning, even hard to tell whether the sun had lifted itself into the sky, or not. A thick fog blanketed the whole city, a shroud of forgetting, Marko thought. Anything that had happened last night was gone today. Good, or evil.

The singing seemed close now, and a shutter opened in the building opposite. Only a small canal divided the two properties, and the window was on the same floor as Marko's room, so as he ducked back into the darkness of his room, he was able to see Venetia from very close range. She was so beautiful his heart nearly stopped its beating.

There was a knock at his door, and without waiting for an answer Sorrel came in.

'We found you these clothes. I think they'll fit, you can . . . '

She stopped, catching him spying from his window.

'Yes,' she said, an edge to her voice. 'She's beautiful. Everyone agrees.'

'No, I . . . ' Marko said, feeling guilty, but vaguely wondering why that mattered.

'Yes, she's beautiful, but she's also a prize bitch. Just so you know.'

'Sorrel,' Marko said.

'What?'

He held up the diary.

'Your grandfather's?'

She nodded.

'Gentile Bellini. He was a great man.'

'He was a glass-maker, like your father?'

'He was the greatest glass-maker in Venice, which is to say he was the greatest glass-maker in the world. He died before my father was old enough to learn anything from him, and yet my father trained with one of Gentile's men, and went on to achieve things that surpassed even those of my grandfather. His work took him across Europe, and eventually to London, where he worked for the King of England.'

'But he came back here. What happened?'

'The King had been a generous patron, but things change. Later, my father told me the King had got into some problems with investments in the South Seas. Many aristocrats were ruined. The King himself was immune of course, but could no longer be seen to spend vast sums on matters and objects deemed frivolous.'

'Your father's glass?'

'And so we came back here.'

'But I don't understand. The house. You believe this illness that befell your grandfather is the same one that is afflicting your father now?'

'Yes. And there have been other cases in the family. You read about Aurora?'

Marko nodded, but already had an awful premonition of what she was going to say.

'It took her not long afterwards. My father grew up an orphan. The richest orphan in the city. When he was old enough he took control of the glass factories on Murano. And there were others, even longer ago.'

'So if the house is doing this, why not move? Why do you stay here?'

'Believe me, we've tried. When we had to leave England, we lived in several places, but my father seemed broken by his experience with the King. He could get no work. We came back here, the family home. And there was something else. Despite what he said, my father seemed almost to want to come back here. As if he could go nowhere else.'

'Why not sell it and move somewhere else, somewhere smaller?'

'And tell me, who would buy the House that Kills? People shun this place, like a plague house. You saw for yourself last night. Even our servants have finally had enough.'

'But the curse . . . '

'So you believe in the curse already, do you? Hah! And you a doctor's son! And having got to know your father, you should be ashamed. Your father is a rational scientist, not some quack like the ones here. I give you this much, Marko, your father was the only man who seemed able to help my father at all. And that's why I want him back. We have to find him, find him before . . . '

Marko knew what she had been about to say, and the thought of her grandfather's end came back to him, but his pulse quickened at the mention of his father. He couldn't play this game of cat and mouse any longer.

'Where is he, Sorrel? When did you last see him?'

'About a month ago. They went somewhere. They wouldn't tell me where. That was the last time. My father was found the following day wandering round San Marco. They arrested him for drunkenness, and locked him up for the night. Then someone recognised him and brought him home.'

'And my father?'

'He never came back, at all,' Sorrel said bluntly. Then, almost as an afterthought, she added, 'I'm sorry.'

12

*A*t the far end of a dead-end alleyway, a calle that led only to a short drop into a canal, a tall figure sat hunched under his black cape. He had pulled the hood over his face, and at a casual glance, even from a few paces away, looked like a bundle of cloth left out to rot. Maybe just a foot away you would see two eyes burning from under the black robes, eyes that seemed to sear the morning mist, through the stones and through Time itself, seeing happenings from long ago, and far, far away.

His eyes blinked shut as he thought about the night he'd passed, crouched in this stinking alley since the small hours, after endlessly wandering the city. He thought of the tavern and realised that even at his age he could still make stupid mistakes. He felt angry with himself. Surely he hadn't spent all these years travelling only to find he had learned nothing?

One mistake could still be his undoing, and he'd come too far and lost too much, to let it come to that. He thought about what he'd come for. What he was doing in this dreamlike place, and it gave him little satisfaction. Still, it had to be done. He'd spent his whole adult life for this, to find her. Find her and kill her.

His head twinged slightly from the drink, but he ignored it. To give it any welcome would to be to admit that he had drunk too much, though deep down he knew he had. Why else would he have made such a fool of himself, and been thrown out, to spend the night like a beggar? He'd walked for hours through the deserted streets, crossing tiny canals by bridges without railings, getting himself thoroughly lost as if in a maze. He'd never known a place like it in all his years of travelling. Such a fantastical city, and that was something given the extraordinary places he'd been in his life, and the extraordinary things he'd seen.

He cursed. But it was the shame of losing his self control, not the damp cold that bothered him. He'd known cold all his life, and yes, this was a nasty wet coldness that sank into his bones, but it was nothing like the cold he'd known as a boy, the cold that he'd grown up with every winter, in the deep, deep forests.

He opened his eyes again, but he didn't see the dull red of the plaster wall across from where he sat. Instead, his vision was filled with a thousand memories, and every one of them was white, for they were memories of snow.

The Queen of the Shadows

A Fairy Tale

There is a story as old as the moon and as dark as the night, a story from an ancient kingdom in the heart of a forest. It is just a story, but it is a terrible tale of love and death, and after all, what else is there? For these are the two pillars upon which life balances.

The King of this forest land was a good and just ruler, feared and respected, and it had been his blessing to have three daughters. In the course of the years, these little girls grew up to be fine young women, more beautiful than any other in the land; more elegant, more beautifully dressed, more refined. And yet, perhaps, more vain than any other girls in the kingdom, too.

Now the time came for the daughters to be married, and so the King held an enormous celebration, a festival that would last for thirty days and nights, during which time, all the suitable princes and noblemen from a thousand leagues around might come and ask for the hand of one or other of the princesses.

The festival began, with great pomp and great joy, as the King's subjects enjoyed day after day of feasting and dancing and happiness, and all at his expense. The suitors came from every kingdom, and a fine young bunch of men they were, and within ten days, the eldest daughter had found a man to match her, and consented to his proposal. They held the wedding that very night, and the festivities were greater than ever.

Within another ten days, the middle daughter had also met her match, and that night another wonderful wedding feast was given.

But another ten days passed, and still the youngest daughter, who was perhaps the vainest of all three, was satisfied with no one. Many proud princes had ridden for days to come to the feast, and all but two had gone away empty-hearted. The King despaired, but on the last day of the celebrations, seven young princes arrived to seek the hand of the youngest, and some said most beautiful, of the three princesses.

One by one, the princes paraded before the princess, who sat on her throne, occasionally glancing away from her looking glass, to cast a bored eye over her suitors, and one by one, she turned them down.

The King was furious.

'I have thrown the most magnificent celebrations the world has ever seen. They have lasted for thirty days and thirty nights! You have seen as many potential husbands in that time, and each and every one a rich and handsome fellow, and still you are not satisfied!'

The King stormed about the hall, and everyone grew afraid, all but the princess herself, and then the King made a decision.

'Very well!' he roared. 'Since you cannot decide for yourself who is to be your husband, the fates will do it for you!'

He pointed to the back of the hall, to the great archway that led outside.

'Your husband will be the very next man to walk through that door!'

The hall was all astir, and every head and pair of eyes within them, turned to peer towards the door.

Now, it just so happened that at that moment, a wandering

tramp had been passing the castle, and hearing the festivities, had ambled in to see if he could beg for some food. Finding the castle grounds deserted, he made his way through the courtyard and towards the doors to the hall, and as he made his way inside, he was very surprised to see a hundred faces turning and facing him, as if they had all been waiting for him.

'There!' cried the King. 'Your husband!'

'Father!' the girl cried. 'No!'

TWO

*V*enice, the city that bears the name La Serenissima, 'the Most Serene', is a liar. For yes, she has a great beauty. From a distance, her reputation is great, her architecture is noble, and her people famed for the same quality. Get a little closer and much of this beauty remains intact, and unblemished. A rich couple stroll across San Marco, their expensive clothes gently whisking across the masegni, the paving stones of the city, their ornate masks sitting under even more ornate wigs. They are walking to a masked ball in a fabulous palazzo where they will dance and drink with other Venetian aristocrats. But come closer, look under the masks, take off the wigs. The woman is an old hag with thinning hair, too stupid to know she's not beautiful any more. Her face is gaudily painted. The ugly-intentioned man is her husband, but they ceased to be married in any real sense two decades ago. They prowl the night streets as foul and lecherous animals, throwing their money around casually in the hope it will attract some foolish and starry-eyed young beauty. Even the magnificent house they dance in is a fraud. It is a mere façade of elegance, and like the old couple, its face is cracked and lined. There is dirt and squalor in the dark corners of each room. The building is damp and rotting, and perilously weakened by it. It sits on a thousand soggy piles of Russian timber, all shoved down into the lagoon's black mud waters, where the waste from every water closet in the city now flows. It is a city floating in its own sewage, but it believes that it remains serene.

The Most Serene.

That is Venice.

2

*T*he morning struggled to arrive, but finally a little light permeated the gloom of the lagoon mist. The city woke up. In the Doge's palace all was chaos. The newly elected Doge was to make his triumphant procession in two days' time, and there was so much still to be done. Shipwrights tumbled out of their houses in the Arsenale to get back to work. There were the final repairs to make to the Bucintoro, the ceremonial barge, which would carry the Doge in full glory along the Canalazzo. On the island of Murano, away from the hubbub of the city itself, glass-makers were stoking their furnaces, coaxing white heat from glowing embers, happy that they would be warm today; probably the only citizens of Venice who would be. At the Leon Bianco, Captain staggered blinking into the sunlight, rubbing his head, cursing his stupidity at leaving his crew alone all night, and thinking of what he might have done the night before, apologised to his mother, even though she'd been dead for eight years. Upstairs in the inn, the ladies counted their money and brushed their hair, sighing over their lot, and pushed any sad thoughts away with fresh dreams of the luxury that might one day be theirs.

In the cluttered corner of a forgotten campo, yet another body lay still, half hidden by rubbish. The only thing that moved was a slow pool of blood oozing from beneath it. Another random murder in Venice, though, had anyone known, this particular death was more sinister than a mere mugging, or some love-rivals' duel.

On Giudecca, a small boat tied up alongside the gondolas, and there was an argument over nothing between the gondoliers. In the house next door, across the tiny canal, Venetia stroked her long golden hair with an ivory and hog's bristle hairbrush, admiring her long neck in the looking glass by her bed.

And in the House that Kills, Marko sat with Sorrel in her room, as she talked about her father, and he realised suddenly that his life had changed. Whatever happened now, things would never be the same. His own father might be dead. He was miles from home, far across the water, with a girl he'd only met the night before, whose father, the sole link he had to his own father's disappearance, was a madman.

Things will happen that I won't want to happen, he thought. I will see things I don't want to see, and know things I don't want to know, before this is over. And what then? What will 'over' mean?

He shook himself. It's her, he told himself. Sorrel was affecting him. *Infecting* him, with her own special brand of misery. And this city with its clinging fogs, that was infecting him too. He shuddered.

'How long?' he asked her, interrupting her.

'What?'

'How long have you been like this?'

She stiffened.

'Like what?'

'So . . . black. So miserable, so full of . . . '

'Of what? Pain?'

'Yes, I suppose so . . . '

'Maybe since my mother died. When I watched her die. Or

284

maybe when I had to come back and live in this rotting pile. Or maybe when I knew my father was going to die, slowly, right in front of my eyes. Which of those do you think it was? You decide. I don't care.'

She was full of anger and bile, and Marko regretted his words. He felt stupid, like an idiotic child, for having broken her reverie. At least she'd been talking. Now she was just fighting.

He got up, took a deep breath, and walked around her room, peering through grimy glass over the lagoon. His mind drifted out with the tide and back again, and his attention was caught by a bottle on the windowsill. It was small and blue, and some habit from his father made him pick it up and remove the stopper. He sniffed it, his nose wrinkled, then he saw Sorrel staring; he pushed the stopper back and returned the bottle to the windowsill.

Marko turned away and idly gazed at the bookshelf next to the window. His eyes skipped across the titles and he began to slide out the largest and oldest looking book, a leather bound tome without words on cover or spine.

'Put that back,' Sorrel said, but without anger.

'Why . . . ?'

He hesitated, the book half drawn from the shelf.

'Just put it back.'

Marko did as he was told, sliding it back into position among the others, and Sorrel came and stood by him, seeming to want to explain herself.

'My father gave it to me, before he was . . . like this.'

'What is it?'

'The Pentameron. It's full of stories. They were written a hundred years ago by a man called Giambattista Basile. My father loves them. He gave me that book for my last birthday.'

She turned, moving back to the bed. Marko saw that she

was trying not to cry. He walked over to her and sat by her on the bed. She was dressed in black again, another black dress, with a lower neck than the previous one, but with black lace cuffs to the long sleeves. Again, she'd woven her hair into extraordinary ropes of plaits, which she had pinned into wonderful patterns. Tentatively he put a hand on her shoulder. She sprang up from the bed, shaking her head.

'No!' she said. 'Don't do that. This isn't good enough. We have to start doing something, not just sit around here.'

'I thought I was no use to you,' Marko said.

Sorrel opened her mouth to say something, then stopped.

'Do you think my father is still alive?' Marko asked.

'I don't know. I hope so.'

'Because you think he can save your father?'

'He was so much better when Alessandro was here. He hadn't been out of the house for days. It had been awful, Marko. You have no idea. He would stagger around like a drunkard. He was sweating all the time, despite the cold weather. We brought him clean shirts five, six, seven times a day. They said it was the plague, they said it was a fever, but they were wrong. He'd fall into a kind of stupor, but with his eyes open, or he'd walk about with his eyes shut. Then, when Alessandro came, he started to get better. I'm sure of it. He even slept for half an hour one morning, and the change in him from just that was wonderful. Then one day Alessandro said he was going to take my father out, that they had to go somewhere. And then . . . '

'Your father went mad, and mine went missing.'

Sorrel nodded.

'Where did they go?'

'I don't know.'

'Didn't they say?'

'They wouldn't tell me, but I know it had something to do with business.'

'Glass-making?'

'Yes. We have the house, but we need money to live on. My father hadn't worked in weeks. He has a workshop on Murano, that's where all the glass is made. Your father said he had an order to complete, and that anyway it would be good for him to stir from the house for a while.'

'So they went to Murano? To see a customer?'

'Not necessarily. That's where my father makes his glass, but the customer could have been anywhere in the city. Or beyond the city.'

'But haven't you been to Murano? To ask about? Maybe someone saw them.'

Sorrel shook her head.

'I was waiting. I was waiting for help. I sent the letter so someone would come.'

Marko bit his tongue.

'Why,' he said as softly as he could, 'did you wait? Why didn't you go yourself?'

She lifted her gaze from the floor and held his eye briefly.

'Because I'm scared, Marko. I'm so scared.'

She looked away again and something in her manner sent a shiver up Marko's spine, making the hairs stand up on the back of his neck.

A little while later, they left the room, closing the door on Sorrel's small world of pain. On the shelf by the window, the books sat waiting for someone to open them, and in their midst lurked the Pentameron, and neither Marko nor Sorrel knew that sticking out of the pages, hidden from view against the wall, was a sheet of paper which had gone astray, and on which their destiny was written.

3

*M*arko and Sorrel stood on the fondamente, at the water's edge, outside the Ca' Bellini, waiting for a boat to the city to come by.

'Why don't you ask Francesco to take us?' Marko asked.

'Not in a gondola. Murano's too far. And anyway, someone must stay with Father. We can't leave him alone for that long.'

'Yes, of course,' Marko agreed. 'My God, it's so cold this morning.'

'It's the damp air. It chills your bones.'

Marko was about to say something in reply when he became aware of someone sliding past him and squaring up to Sorrel.

'I want to see your father.'

It was Venetia. Marko stepped back a pace; she'd stepped between them as if he wasn't there, and he was thrown by her sudden presence.

'Your father took my money weeks ago. I shall have what I've paid for.'

Her voice was surprising; bitter and sharp and not what Marko expected to hear from such a lovely form.

'I'm sorry,' Sorrel was saying. 'I know he's been working on your tiara. He's spoken about it often. I'm sure it won't be long.'

'The procession is the day after tomorrow. I must have it for the procession.'

288

'Of course. I'm sorry. It's just taken a little longer. It's such a fine piece after all. It will be worth the wait.'

'It had better be,' Venetia snapped. 'Because if I don't have it by tomorrow night, and if I am not absolutely satisfied with it, then I will report your father to the Ten. Or the Three! And your father will be locked up as a fraud and a criminal.'

Venetia paused. Her lovely oval eyes narrowed to slits.

'Is your father – here?'

Sorrel hesitated.

'He's at his workshop.'

'Really? I haven't seen him leave the house for days. Are you sure he isn't here? I want to speak to him.'

'No!' said Sorrel.

'Why not?'

'Because he's not here,' Marko said, stepping in. 'You heard Sorrel. He's busy at his workshop.'

Venetia turned, as if only now aware of Marko. She looked him up and down, once, then again, very slowly. Her lip curled.

'And why,' she said, 'do you think this is any of your business?'

'This is my cousin, Marko,' Sorrel said. 'Father's on Murano, working on your tiara. We're going there now. We'll see how it's going. And there's a boat coming, we must hurry. I promise it will be ready for you. I promise.'

She dragged Marko along the quay and they almost threw themselves aboard the traghetto that would take them across the water.

Venetia spun on her heels and walked back to her house.

They watched her go as they bobbed across the water towards the city.

'I see what you mean,' Marko said, and Sorrel laughed

despite her mood.

'What was she asking about, anyway?'

'She commissioned a tiara from Father, the very day she arrived in Venice. It's one of his specialties. He makes fantastic glass tiaras for ladies to wear at special occasions. They're so amazing, and so sought after, that they're worth as much as something made with diamonds or pearls. She paid him on the spot, there and then. And then his illness came back worse again.'

Her face fell.

'Now it will never be ready and she'll have him arrested. Even if we find your father, that tiara will never be ready for Venetia.'

'What's happening, what's so important?'

'It's the Doge,' she said. 'The new one. He's the ruler of the city. Sort of. He doesn't actually do very much. There's the Great Council, and the Council of Ten. And the Three.'

'Who are the Three?'

'Shush!' Sorrel hissed, then whispered to him, glancing towards the other passengers.

'The Inquisitors. They have spies everywhere. They're best avoided.'

Marko nodded.

'So what about the Doge?'

'They've elected a new one. It's taken months. Anyway, he's declared there will be three days of festivities to mark his election, and a parade around San Marco. All the rich ladies will try to outdo each other, try and look the best, wear the best clothes. It's even more serious for the young, unmarried ones. That's why Venetia wants the tiara.'

'To attract a husband?'

'To attract a rich husband.'

'But she seems to be very rich anyway.'

'That's the thing about rich people. They always want to be richer.'

They fell silent for a while until the boat started to put in to the jetty at San Marco.

'Aren't we going to the island? Murano?'

'Yes,' Sorrel said. 'But it's away on the other side of the city, quite a long way into the lagoon. We'll walk across the city and take a bigger boat from there.'

They stepped up onto the stones of the piazzetta, the smaller of the two squares that approached the church of San Marco itself.

'This is where it will all happen,' Sorrel said. 'The procession of the Doge. That's his palace there. On the corner.'

She pointed, but Marko was already staring at the incredible building, intricate and ornate, dozens of slender columns holding up a façade of delicate brickwork, magnificent windows and little turrets.

The piazzetta was alive with activity; hundreds, if not thousands of people in throngs, shouting, laughing, trading, jeering, walking, staring and hurrying about their business. Nearby, a group stood around a low stage, from which two men addressed the crowd. They seemed to be both selling something, and acting out some kind of performance, but around them on a pair of trestle tables was a scene that Marko was very familiar with. Dozens of pots, jars, dishes and mixing instruments lay scattered on the tables. There was an elaborate set of scales, and one of the men was holding up a series of jars, extracting bids from the onlookers for their purchase.

'Teriaca!' the man cried. 'What will you give me for this wonder of the gods? It's the mystical medicine, the Venetian

Panacea. Cures all ills! Protects against poisoning! Brings an easy sleep! Teriaca. There is nothing else on earth that can compete with its health-giving properties. You sir! Yes, you, you look like you could do with a little pepper in your pipe!'

The crowd laughed and cheered, and Sorrel pulled Marko away.

The teriaca merchant handed a green bottle with a cork and waxed stopper to a woman in the crowd, taking a jingle of coins into his hand from her. She hurried away, nursing the bottle as if it was a small injured animal.

Sorrel led the way past the palace, and Marko followed, his head spinning as he craned his neck to stare to the top of an enormous bell tower on his left. Some workmen were hanging about at its foot, and shouting up to the men near the summit of the tower. Various ropes and pulleys hung underneath where they clung to the tower.

As he passed, an elderly man clapped his hands in delight, and addressed Marko as if they were old friends.

'The Flight of the Turk!' he cried. 'Oh yes!'

He went gleefully on his way, and Marko saw him accost the next person with the very same exclamation.

'The Flight of the Turk!'

Sorrel was leaving him behind. He felt stupid again, an ignorant country boy, and he determined to stop acting like it. He hurried after her as she slipped out of the far corner of the piazza near a large and particularly hideous looking cathedral.

The square had been busy, with people coming and going, workmen going about their business, and street vendors shouting their wares, but now, a few steps away, the city seemed deserted.

In a few further steps, Marko realised he was utterly lost, or would have been without Sorrel. She flitted ahead, taking a turning here on the left, another to the right. It seemed impossible to walk in a straight line for more than ten yards, before the narrow streets ran into seeming dead ends, forcing them into alleys and over bridges, or sidling through some dark passageway that might suddenly open into a campo, a small square, a field of stones.

The sky was a grey blanket, glimpsed occasionally beyond the high walls of the labyrinth that surrounded them.

'Are you sure you know where you're going?' Marko asked, but Sorrel clearly did, and she either hadn't heard, or simply didn't bother to reply. She seemed desperate to get through the city as fast as possible, and now their route took them over a small footbridge with no hand rails. The water beneath was foul and still. It made Marko think of some monster or snake, lurking, and he quickened his pace over the wooden arch, ignoring the danger of slipping on its smooth worn and wet surface. They entered a series of claustrophobic alleys, each of which ran for no more than a few yards, before turning at right angles into the next. The walls of the houses pressed in on them from either side, windowless and bare, and suddenly as Marko turned a corner, hurrying after Sorrel, she was gone.

He'd only been a few feet behind, but there were two options open to him, a turning ahead and to the left, and one to the right. He panicked, knowing he had to choose quickly, or even the correct choice might leave him stranded as Sorrel left him far behind.

'Sorrel?'

He called out. Nothing.

'Sorrel?'

Still nothing. For a moment he thought he heard footsteps, but if anything, they seemed to be coming from behind him. He held his breath and the sound disappeared.

Quickly, he stuck his head round the right hand opening, and saw nothing but a long passageway ahead, so he tried the left hand one. Again there was no one in sight, but he reasoned that Sorrel couldn't have got out of sight in the long right hand corridor so quickly. He took the turning to his left and began to run, as fast as the narrow bends would allow, and then, with relief he saw Sorrel waiting for him at the next corner.

He began to smile, but she cut him dead.

'I told you you're no use to me. You can't even keep up.'

'That's not fair. This place is crazy. And I'm used to having a sun in the sky to navigate by.'

She shrugged and set off again, turning more corners, and Marko was suddenly struck with the ridiculous notion that it was the city guiding them, rather than Sorrel knowing the way. He stirred himself as she entered a long alley, amazingly straight after the twisting maze they had just been through. It led away, and at the end Marko could see daylight, but once again the walls leaned in on them from above, so close that three storeys up they nearly brushed against each other. Ahead, the alley pinched to the width of a narrow waist, and then they squeezed through onto the wide pavement on the northern banks of the city.

Out in the lagoon, Marko saw a small island.

'Is that it?'

'No, that's San Cristoforo and San Michele. Two islands, one behind the other. Murano is twice as far.'

She pointed.

'Come here. Look. There.'

Marko followed her outstretched arm.

'Murano.'

Through the mist that hovered a few feet above the water,

through the murk, it was just possible to make out the grey shape of another, larger island. But he might have been imagining it, it was so indistinct.

Marko thought he heard something behind them, and turned, but there was no one there, nothing but the mouth of the tiny alley from which they'd emerged.

A large lagoon boat was making ready to put out to Murano, and they hurried on board with the last of the passengers.

'Have you got money?' Marko asked, thinking that they'd already paid for one boat journey, mindful of his own dwindling supply of coins.

'I've brought all I could find in the house,' Sorrel whispered. 'It's enough.'

The boat heaved away from the fondamente, its nose drifting slowly round to point to the islands. As it went, a tall figure stepped from the end of the alleyway, and watched them go, then retreated into the darkness once more.

*T*he boat appeared to make hardly any progress at all, and yet imperceptibly, Marko could tell that the city was moving further away. The smudge of Murano had disappeared altogether now, and they seemed to be heading for oblivion.

They sat opposite each other on low wooden boards that served as seats. The boat was almost empty.

Marko watched Sorrel for a long while. She gazed forward intently, as if her salvation lay there, though there was nothing at all to see.

'You can't see forward,' Marko said. 'You can't see the future.'

She turned away from the future to look at him.

'What do you mean?'

'Nothing. Nothing much. About what I said before. In your bedroom. I'm sorry I upset you.'

Sorrel nodded, but didn't give him the satisfaction of accepting his apology.

'I'm sorry,' he went on, 'but you're so sad. You hide behind your black eyes, but I can see past the make-up.'

'What of it?' she asked cautiously.

'I can't explain this exactly,' he said. 'But suppose things don't end up as badly as you think they might? Maybe we can find my father, and he can make your father well again. Things wouldn't be so bad.'

She nodded again, but didn't seem prepared to speak.

'And then, if that happens, things will be all right. So what I mean is, why spend time now, thinking that the worst is going to happen, when it might not? It won't change what happens, but you're killing yourself simply with the fear of what might be. You can't change the world, but perhaps you can change how you feel about it.'

Marko stopped, wondering if Sorrel understood anything he was saying, whether she agreed with any of it. She looked out to the mist again, and then turned back to him. She spoke softly, but her words were full of crawling pain.

'The world is a vampire,' she said, 'sent to drain us of our souls. Our spirits, our joys, our happiness. And when it has finished, it leaves us gasping against the horror it has replaced those things with. We struggle, but we choke on that bile, and then we go spluttering to our grave. That is the world.'

She turned back to the sea again, and now, at last, Marko knew there was no point trying to reach out to her. He knew it was in his nature, since it was in his father's nature, to try and help people, to make them better. If they could not be made better, then at least their suffering could be eased while they waited for the end.

But with Sorrel there was no point, no hope. She didn't want to be helped.

'Very well,' Marko said aloud, but so quietly that she didn't hear.

There was no point helping this miserable girl, but he might be able to use her to find his father, and sail away from this rotting carcass of a city, back to their home in the hills, in the glorious, warming, forgiving, healing sunshine.

5

'So where do we go?'

'I don't know. It was your idea to come here. We don't know this is where they came.'

'We have no other path to follow,' Marko said. 'Where's your father's workshop? Is there someone there we can talk to?'

'It's at the far end of the fondamente. There's the foreman. Pietro. I don't like him.'

'Do you like anyone?' Marko said flippantly.

'Not especially,' Sorrel said, with a withering look.

Marko rolled his eyes, and despite her venom, he smiled. 'Come on, then.'

It was hard to believe Murano had anything to do with Venice. Here, the buildings were all single storey, simple houses, very like the houses in Piran that Marko was familiar with. They were painted bright colours, reds, yellows and blues, so the fisherman who lived in them could see them from a distance through the frequent winter mists. Marko couldn't see that it would help much, but it certainly gave the town a more easy-going, informal atmosphere than the imposing nature of Venice.

As they passed various open doorways, Marko caught glimpses of roaring furnaces belching fire in the dark interiors of workshops.

'There,' Sorrel said, pointing to an archway that led away

from the canal which bisected the island. They hurried down an alleyway and from the painted sign above the door, Marko knew they'd walked into the workshop of Simono Bellini.

'What do you want?' barked a voice.

They turned to see a squat, ugly man glaring at them. He stood by the open doors of the furnace, naked from the waist up, seemingly unaware of the enormous heat pouring from inside. His body was brown and greatly scarred, and though he was short, he had tough muscles on his chest and arms. In one hand he held a pair of forceps still glowing from having been in the jaws of the furnace.

'What do you want? Clear off!'

'Pietro,' Sorrel said, coming a little closer. 'It's me, Sorrel.'

The man squinted through the gloom and heat haze.

'Sorrel? Where's your father, then? Tell me that.'

He was either angry, or rude, or both. It was hard to tell.

'He's not well,' Marko said. 'But we've come to see you instead.'

'And who's this?' Pietro asked Sorrel, waving the forceps aggressively towards Marko.

'My cousin,' she said. It was as good a lie as any to keep using, and they both sensed that there was no reason to explain everything to everyone.

Pietro grunted.

'Where's your father? We want paying.'

'We told you. He's ill. I'm sorry you and the men haven't been paid in a while. I'll talk to Father when . . . '

'Well, there's only me left now, so don't worry about anyone else. All the others left. Men and boys. Gone to work for people who'll pay them. So just tell your father I want paying. And if not, then I'm going to go to the Council and have this place made mine. I've worked without pay for two months now. I'm owed something, and the only reason I'm still here is to see I get it.'

'Please,' Marko said, daring to step a little closer. 'I promise we'll get you your money, if you can just help us. We're trying to find someone.'

Pietro squinted some more.

'What of it?' he said.

'Can you tell us, when did you last see Simono? Did he come here, about a month ago? We think he might have come here, to see a customer, perhaps.'

Pietro shook his head.

'No,' he said. 'There was no customer. But he did come. With another man. He wasn't a customer. I'd not seen him before.'

Marko's hopes began to lift.

'Describe him. This other man.'

'Tall, old. Old like Simono. Strong face.'

'Did you hear his name?'

Pietro shook his head.

'No, no. Unless, it was something like . . . oh. It could have been Sandro.'

'Yes!' cried Marko, turning to Sorrel. 'That's him. Alessandro.'

'So they came here,' Sorrel said. 'Did they talk about what they were doing, where they were going to next?'

Pietro shook his head.

'They went into the office. In five minutes they were out again. Then they left.'

'So why did they come?'

'Not to pay me, I can tell you that,' Pietro spat.

'We'll get your money.'

'I want it now,' Pietro said, and took a step towards them.

He still held the forceps in one hand, and his body was running with sweat from the incredible heat. In the furnace light he looked like a cross between a dwarf and a devil, and they backed away slowly until he cornered them.

'I want paying now, Signorina,' he said.

Sorrel swallowed hard, Marko didn't dare take his eyes off Pietro, off the iron tool in his hand.

'Very well,' she said.

Bravely, she turned her back on Pietro and fished around inside the neck of her dress. She counted out a few coins from a bag, and then, putting the bag away, she held them out to her father's foreman of works.

'It's all I can manage,' she said, trying to sound confident.

'Is it?' he said. 'Is it?'

He took the money, and slid it quickly into his pocket.

'But you must tell us what you know,' Marko said. 'What they did here.'

Pietro glared at Marko, who expected the forceps to come swinging towards his head at any second. But Pietro stepped back, smiling.

'Yes. Fair enough. Since you've paid me some of what I'm owed. But you tell your father I want the rest soon, or I'll take this place for my own.'

'All right. All right. But please tell us.'

'I said. They came and they went. It was all very quick. But they left with a box. Not too big. I think it was something Simono had been working on for a while. You know what he's like. Often works in secret on his special pieces. We never see them.'

Marko looked at Sorrel, and could see the same thought had crossed her mind, too. Could it be Venetia's tiara? If so, then one small problem might be solved.

'But where did they take it?' Sorrel persisted.

Pietro paused.

'Maybe they took it . . . ' he said uncertainly. 'That is, I think perhaps they took it to San Michele. I heard them talking, when they were in the office.'

He looked furtive, he had obviously been eavesdropping.

'And they went to San Michele?'

'I'm not sure. But I heard them mention the church of San Michele. There's a priest who lives there. We've done work for him before.'

'For a priest?' Marko asked.

Sorrel ignored him.

'You think that's where they went?'

Pietro nodded.

'Yes, now I think of it, it must be. You should try the priest.'

'What's his name?'

'Father Fei. His house is behind the church.'

With that Pietro turned back to work, pumping at the bellows to the furnace, sending a blast of sparks and heat roaring into the workshop.

Sorrel was only too eager to leave.

'Come on,' she said. 'I've had enough of him.'

They scurried back out into the dank morning, but they had found a small rag of hope to hold onto.

'I'm coming, Father,' Marko said to himself. 'I'm coming.'

6

They had to wait a long time for a boat to San Michele. They could see it across the water, halfway back to the city, tantalisingly out of reach. The mist had lifted slightly and weak sunlight shone down on them from time to time, before disappearing behind thicker cloud again.

'If this box they left with had Venetia's tiara in it, why did they take it to San Michele?'

'I don't know,' Sorrel said. 'Maybe it had something else in it. We're just guessing it was the tiara.'

'What else had he been working on?'

Sorrel sighed.

'He'd done no work for months. Not that I know of, anyway. We didn't even know what was wrong to start with. One day I thought Father seemed to be holding his head strangely, as if he had a stiff neck, you know? But when I offered to rub some balm into it, he got angry and said it was nothing. Next day it was worse, and he started knocking into things. He became very clumsy. I thought he was drunk. So did the first doctor who came. And the third, and the fifth. Then he started to sweat, his eyes shrank into their sockets; his pupils were like little black dots. He told me about the curse on our house, though in truth I suppose I had known it all along somehow.

'And then I knew he was dying.'

303

Marko threw a pebble into the water. They sat on a stone bench by the quay, waiting for someone to leave for San Michele. Had it been Sunday, there might have been a steady stream of traffic for the church, but with little else on the tiny island, and its twin, San Cristoforo, no one was hurrying to get there. Eventually someone would take a boat out, and they could beg a ride, maybe for free, maybe for a song. The only other option was to hire a boatman, and that would cost.

Both Sorrel and Marko were aware that their money was all too exhaustible.

'It must be awful,' Marko said, thinking of Sorrel's father. It was hard to associate her with the black-eyed madman looming behind him in Sorrel's room that morning. Something occurred to him.

'Didn't you try that stuff we saw, that they were selling in the city?'

'Teriaca?' Sorrel said, 'Yes, we tried it. And all the idiots who came to the house tried it too. It made no difference. It's supposed to be an antidote to any poison, and yes, it's supposed to bring an easy sleep, and deep. But it never helped my father. You tried it. Well, you smelled it, at least.'

Marko looked at her, a question on his lips, but then he remembered the small blue bottle in her room.

'It's not the worst of it,' she said grimly. 'You read my grandfather's diary. That was while he could still write. Just about. They say the end stages of the death are the worst. It takes for ever. You get more and more desperate for sleep, but it doesn't come. Your heart starts to race, and your eyes shrink to nothing. Then you become paralysed, unable even to speak, but all the time you can still think clearly. Finally your heart gives out. And then you die.'

Marko threw another stone. He had no idea what to say to

the sad strange girl whose awful story he had walked into. He wondered whether he'd even chosen to be part of it. Hadn't it been thrust upon him? An unwilling participant. But then, he'd had no choice. He'd wanted to come and find his father, he had to. And his father had had to come and help his old friend. And he'd done that because of some bond of friendship that went back many years, long before Marko was born. It all seemed part of an unbroken chain that probably went back through the pages of time, in which Marko's ancestors lived and died.

From there, to here. And now, with Sorrel, waiting for a boat.

'Or maybe they didn't go to San Michele at all.'

'Yes,' Marko said. 'That's possible. But as I said before, we have no other path to follow. If we talk to the priest and he knows nothing, we'll be at a dead end, but at least we've explored the possibility.'

'You're very clever,' Sorrel said suddenly. 'Like your father. Just like him. He would talk like that, explain things. You know?'

'Yes,' said Marko. 'I know.'

And he took some comfort from the fact that though Sorrel might not like him very much, she seemed to have a great respect for his father.

'The diary was very strange in places,' Marko said. 'Do you remember that bit about birds, about geese and feathers? And the last five words. What did that mean?'

'You have to understand that by then he was probably mad half the time. He wouldn't have known what he was writing.'

'Yes,' said Marko. 'I suppose you're right. But it's strange. Odd.'

'I know what strange means.'

I bet you do, thought Marko, but he smiled.

'Yes, I just can't explain myself very well.'

Frustratingly other boats rowed and sailed across the lagoon, and they even saw one land at San Michele, though it had come from another direction. Eventually, they managed to convince a kind fisherman who'd just returned from the lagoon to put out briefly once more to take them the short distance to the island. He rowed steadily across, not asking what they were doing, and paused alongside the jetty just long enough for them to leap ashore. Then he left them.

'How will we get back?' Marko asked.

'Someone will be leaving sooner or later,' Sorrel said. 'That's how it works.'

She didn't sound too certain.

*I*t was late afternoon. They had travelled such a short way in truth, but it had taken so long. Marko found that his legs were slightly wobbly from the three boat trips they'd made that day. Sorrel seemed fine and Marko reflected that she, like any other inhabitant of the city, must be used to the constant movement between land and water; an amphibian existence, like that of frogs.

Their destination was obvious.

There was little on the island apart from the church itself. A few single storey houses, some no more than huts, some sturdy enough brick buildings, and a few walls that seemed to denote the boundaries of non-existent properties. The church was out of all proportion to these humble houses, and dwarfed them all, a massive white marble construction, squatting on the island; a leviathan of stone. It seemed likely that the island would at any moment sink under its weight, down into the water.

'Shall we?' Sorrel said, and Marko was already on the way. The place seemed deserted. A small mangy dog ran past them, but otherwise the only life they'd seen was an old woman shrouded from head to foot, working a bucket at a well.

They tried the front of the church, but the door was either stuck, or locked, or simply too heavy for them to move.

'He said round the side, didn't he?' Sorrel said, thinking

about the awful Pietro. Why her father had employed him was beyond her, though she knew he'd had little choice.

Around, away from the lagoon-side of the church, they came upon a cluster of buildings that huddled into its protection. They tried the doors, knocking on each, and calling.

'Who's there?' came a voice from inside, and then a black door opened in a whitewashed wall, and a head stuck out. It was obviously the priest.

'Father? Father Fei?' Sorrel asked.

The man nodded. He was middle-aged, very tall, and quite gaunt, with a balding head. His lips were pale, and his skin sallow, but he smiled at them in a friendly way.

'Yes? How can I help you children? Come inside, come inside.'

He ducked back through the doorway and Sorrel and Marko followed. They were in a simple room. A door led off in the direction of the church, and another to rooms leading towards the rest of the village, such as it was. There were two tables in the room. The smaller table was bare but for a couple of dishes and some tiny bottles. Their eyes were drawn to the larger table, which was spread with a decent looking meal, and at the sight of it they both realised how hungry they were.

'How can I help you?' Father Fei repeated.

'We're looking for someone. Two people, really,' Marko said. 'We think they may have come here. About three weeks ago. One of them was Simono Bellini, the glass-maker.'

As he spoke Simono's name, Marko watched the priest's face, hoping for some kind of recognition, but he saw none. Disappointed, he continued.

'He was with another man, about the same age, but taller. Did anyone like that come here? Or to the island itself?'

'I'm sorry, but I don't know. I mean, people come here all

the time. Especially on Sundays. Was it a Sunday? I'm afraid then there are many people here.'

'But you'd know a stranger, wouldn't you? Your whole congregation can't be so big you wouldn't spot a stranger.'

The priest considered this.

'Yes, you're right. I know everyone.'

'So you don't think you know the men we're looking for?'

The priest smiled.

'No, I don't think I do. Is it important?'

'Very,' Sorrel said, trying to suppress the desperation in her voice.

'I'm sorry,' Father Fei said. 'I hope you find them. Maybe someone else on the island can help. Have you asked anyone else? No? Then you should! But I can see where your eyes are leading you. Would you like some?'

They both tore their eyes from the food on the table, and nodded.

'Yes. Yes please.'

'Excellent. You are always welcome in God's house.' He turned to Marko. 'My friend, would you fetch another chair for yourself, while I help the young lady to some sustenance. There's a spare chair in the bedroom at the end of the corridor.'

Marko did as he was bid, anxious to return before Sorrel had eaten everything. He opened the door to the corridor, and found himself in the dark. He fumbled down and along the passageway until his fingers closed on a door handle, then went in.

This room was slightly lighter, and he saw the chair beside what must be the priest's bed. He entered the room and as he did, smelled a subtle scent that he recognised. He turned in time to flinch as a massive metal hammer swung towards his head. On the other end of the hammer was the swarthy violence of Pietro, his mouth grinning madly with the effort of swinging the weapon.

Marko lifted an arm as he ducked and deflected the full force of the blow, but still the hammer glanced off his head. It seemed like a lifetime went by as he staggered a step forwards, stunned at what had happened, then closed his eyes and sank to the floor. As he blacked out, as if from a great distance, he heard Pietro mutter.

'Now for the pretty one.'

8

Sorrel barely knew what happened.

She had just raised a tumbler of water to her lips when the door to the corridor burst open. Expecting to see Marko, she was horrified as Pietro stormed in, wielding a heavy mallet.

'Now I want the rest of my money!' he yelled at her.

She jumped from the chair and stumbled backwards, turning to Father Fei for help, then felt her hope die as she saw him laughing.

'You stupid innocent little girl,' he sneered. 'You'll pay us both twice over for your stupidity.'

She knew she was going to die. Frantically, she made a lunge towards the door, but the priest grabbed her arms and pulled her back against him. She could smell his awful odour, feel his rough hands on her arms, his stubble digging through her hair into her scalp.

'Your boyfriend's dead already, pretty one,' Pietro snarled. 'So there won't be any help from him. Just play nicely, and give us the money and then we'll think what to do with you.'

She knew what they would do with her. And then they would kill her.

She struggled again, harder, and tried to stamp on Fei's foot, but he only held her tighter and bent her arms back so she thought she would faint from the pain.

The door crashed behind her, and she saw the snarl on

Pietro's face turn into a mask of surprise.

He pushed past Fei and Sorrel, lifting his hammer. Fei whirled round, throwing Sorrel from him. She fell to the floor, catching her head on the table as she went down, and sank into blackness.

She heard a thin slicing sound, twice, like the wind in the tops of poplar trees, and then nothing else. All was silence, and her eyes closed.

9

*T*he small mangy dog, with wiry black and grey hair, trotted round the island from house to house, as usual, begging for scraps of food. In a couple of places he was given a morcel of old bread, and in the depths of his dog-mind he could dimly remember the day when someone had given him a huge bone to chew, but today he was hungry. He stopped and drank from a puddle, then trotted on. The night was closing in over the lagoon, and the dog could smell it coming. He lifted his head and waited, and then realised there was something else in the air, another smell. A sweet smell. His nose twitched and pulled him towards the door of the church, which unusually, stood open. That in itself would have been enough of an incentive for him, since he was a curious dog, but it was also where the sweet smell was coming from.

A chill gust of wind slipped across the water and the island, and the dog. He scampered over and squeezed through the narrow gap in the church door. He'd been inside the church once or twice before, but he was nervous. He knew there was a tall man in black who always chased him out, with a kick and a curse, so he went cautiously along the nave, sniffing. The sweet smell seemed to have disappeared, or rather, been masked by the other scents in the church, incense and the tallow of the candles. Then, as he passed a small side door, he picked it up again, and moments later he found a room with

313

a table spread with food. He hopped from chair to table, and began to gnaw at half a cold chicken sitting there.

He was so busy doing this, so hungry, that he didn't stop to think about the girl lying still on the floor, or the two men beside her, or the pooling blood in which they all lay.

10

Sorrel opened her eyes and didn't understand what she saw.

She blinked a couple of times, but the world was definitely wrong. The room she was standing in had turned sideways, and half of it was red. She blinked again and some of the redness got into her eye.

Then she lifted her head slightly, and saw what was next to her, and she screamed.

In the bedroom at the end of the corridor, her screaming found its way slowly into Marko's ears, but from there it was a much longer journey into his mind, clouded and befuddled as it was. Nevertheless, it gradually found its way and woke him from his stupor. He sat up suddenly, bent over and retched from the pain in his head. Gingerly he put a hand up to his left temple, and found a massive lump growing there. He sat for a moment longer, remembered the screaming and lurched down the corridor. As he stood in the doorway, he saw an appalling sight. Sorrel flinched as he came in, then saw who it was, and at least her screaming stopped. She jumped up from where she was and ran to him, burying her head into his side, shaking. Marko stared over her head at where she'd been lying on the floor. On one side of her lay the body of Pietro, a little closer lay the body of the priest. But not quite all of them lay on the floor, for both their heads were missing. The amount of blood covering the floor was both shocking and horrifying, and yet somehow horrendously fascinating. Marko stared at the scene for ages, half in shock, half wondering what had happened. Only after a long while did he realise there was a dog standing on the table, happily eating the food that was supposed to have been for them.

Suddenly, Marko felt he was going to start screaming too, and if he did, he would never stop. He pulled Sorrel down the corridor, still unable to take his eyes off the scene, though as he backed away it shrank in size like a genie in a dream. He got into the priest's bedroom, and pulled Sorrel onto the bed, where they both immediately passed out.

11

*W*hen Marko woke again, it was to the sensation of the dog licking his hand. He sat up, and looked at the dog angrily for a moment, then changed his mind. It had nothing to do with any of this. It was lost and hungry, and Marko could do nothing but sympathise. He was half lying on Sorrel, and he got up now, and looked at her. She was an awful mess. The half of her that had been lying on the floor was covered in blood, from head to foot, and that blood was now thickening and drying. She still slept deeply, and Marko was grateful for that.

He looked around the room. It was a simple room, as a priest's room should be, but then, Marko knew that this had been no decent man of God. Who knows what else he was hiding behind the cloth? There was the bed they lay on, the chair he'd been sent to find, a wooden coffer at the foot of the bed, and a large chest of drawers, on the top of which sat a basin and a blue jug. Carefully, he lifted himself off the bed and walked over to the jug. The dog followed eagerly, and as Marko looked inside the jug and saw it was full of water, he felt pity for the animal. He set the basin on the floor and poured a little water into it.

'That's all you can have,' he said. 'We need the rest. So make it last.'

The dog ignored him and began lapping it up furiously.

Marko sat down on the bed beside Sorrel and began to rip small strips from the sheet. These he dipped into the water jug, and then carefully began to wipe the blood away from Sorrel's face.

She stirred gently, but still didn't wake, so he grew bolder and wiped a little harder. For a while he just seemed to make the mess worse, and the blood mixed with her habitual black eye-paint at first, but then he started to see the girl underneath the mess again, and smiled. He looked at her hair and sighed. That would be harder.

He glanced over to the dog and saw it had finished drinking, and was now sitting happily on the floor, its tongue lolling as it gazed at Marko from under comical bushy eyebrows. He took the basin and filled it with water, setting it on the seat of the chair by the bed. Then he lifted Sorrel's shoulders so her hair hung into the bowl, and began to wash it. The clean water was soon pink and then red, but as darkness began to grow in the room, he could no longer see clearly, and he no longer cared.

In the gloom, gazing at her face, gently wiping the water from her brow and neck, he had as much to imagine as to see her face, but he found he could bring it to his mind's eye with ease. His fingers slowed in their task, and he had a rare privilege, to be close to beauty and to be allowed to stare at it without shame. He felt the weight of her head and shoulders in his arms, and sensed her breathing, shallow and disturbed now, and he knew that at that instant, his heart had gone out to her.

She whimpered, like a dreaming dog, and he whispered to her gently.

'It's all right. I'm here.'

At last he thought he had done enough, and he began to lift

Sorrel back fully onto the bed. He felt her stirring, and she opened her eyes suddenly, full of panic, and the quietness of moments before evaporated in an instant.

'What are you doing?' she cried. 'Get off me!'

'Sorrel! Sorrel! It's me. Marko. You're all right. We're all right.'

She struggled to sit up and felt her hair.

'What are you doing to me?'

'It's all right now,' he said, trying to soothe her. 'It's all right.'

'Marko!' she said, as if surprised. 'Oh . . . '

She moaned, and he knew she was remembering everything.

'It's all right,' he said. 'I was just cleaning you up. I . . . '

'They're dead, aren't they?' Sorrel said, interrupting.

He paused.

'Very.'

'What happened?' she cried. 'I thought you were dead. I thought they were going to kill me. And then . . . '

'I don't know. Pietro hit me on the head. When I woke up I came in and found you. And . . . them. And him.'

He turned to point at the dog, and realised it was drinking from the basin.

'Oh, that's disgusting,' he said, 'Stop it!'

He grabbed the basin from the chair and crossing the room, opened a window and threw the water out. The daylight had almost totally gone now and it was hard to see anything in the room itself.

'What are you doing?' Sorrel asked. 'He's just thirsty.'

'The water wasn't . . . clean.'

Sorrel felt her hair again and decided not to ask any more.

'I didn't know what to do about your dress,' Marko said.

'What do you mean?'

'It's . . . not clean, either. I don't think it will wash out, and we don't have much water left.'

Sorrel felt her dress and shuddered, then jumped to her feet and began to drag it off, her fingers scrabbling desperately at the hooks and laces.

'Sorrel . . . '

'I'm not staying in it,' she cried, her voice shrill with fear. 'Thank God it's dark in here. God! Take it from me. I don't want it!'

She threw it across the room. Marko could make out her thin arms and legs, and the slightly paler colour of her underclothes. As far as he could see, her thick dress had prevented the blood from staining them.

He stood, and felt like crying at the pitiful mess they were in, but he found that he could not cry, and that it wouldn't help them, so he spoke to Sorrel instead, in what he hoped was a calm voice.

'Get under the blankets. I'm going to have a look around, try and find a light. Then we'll decide what to do.'

He fumbled his way to the chest of drawers. He'd seen there were two shallow drawers at the top, and guessed rightly that one of them must contain candles or a tinderbox.

His hand fell on something even better. There were candles, yes, but he whistled as he took out the strange object from the drawer. He'd only seen one once before, in the house of a rich merchant in Trieste.

'This priest seems to have forgotten the simple life,' he said.

'Why?'

'He owns a tinder pistol. Give me a minute. I've never used one before.'

He set the little hand gun on the top of the chest of drawers and put a candle next to it, ready. He opened the lid of the tinder chamber, a small metal pot where the barrel of the gun should have been. The rest of the gun was still as it had been designed, with a flintlock mechanism. He cocked the pistol, and fired it. There was a flash of sparks, flickering like fireflies in the darkness, and then was gone.

Sorrel shrieked, then sighed.

'You need powder, too.'

'Yes, of course,' said Marko.

He hunted in the drawer, and felt for any secret chambers in the handle of the body of the pistol, but he could find no powder.

'Just have to try without, there may be enough left in the tinder. If we're lucky.'

Five more times he cocked the pistol and fired it. Each time a shower of sparks illuminated the room, then disappeared, plunging them into darkness again. Then, on the sixth attempt, the tinder caught, and a tiny flame licked up into the room long after the sparks had flown.

'Quick!' Sorrel called.

Marko didn't dare answer for fear he'd blow the feeble flame out, but soon had lowered the wick of the candle into its path and the darkness in the room receded a little.

'There's another one. Let me light that too. There.'

With two candles, the room seemed almost cosy.

With more light in the room, Marko suddenly realised that he had missed another chest that stood by the wall. Something about it drew his attention, and he took a candle and went to inspect it. It was a heavy square-topped chest, with a latch, but which appeared to be unlocked. Lifting the lid, his eyes narrowed. Inside was a collection of bottles and phials, which made him remember the others on the table in the dreadful room along the corridor. They were of different sizes and shapes, and contained various liquids and powders. The dishes seemed to have been used for mixing and heating of various contents. He whistled, puzzled now, and turned to find Sorrel next to him.

'What is it?' she asked.

'I . . . don't know,' he said. 'Strange things for a priest to have in his bedroom.'

He picked up one of the bottles and sniffed the stopper, then thrust it away from him in disgust at the horrible odour. He coughed.

'Who knows?' Sorrel said. She shivered.

Marko began to rummage through the rest of the chest of drawers.

'What are you looking for?'

'Something you can wear. You shouldn't get cold.'

'What? Of his?'

'We can't stay here. It's a miracle no one's found us already. Or them. It's our good fortune that this is a miserable little island and no one seems to know, or like the priest. We must have been asleep for hours. But someone will come sooner or later, and then . . . '

'But we didn't do anything.'

'Like you told me . . . '

'Yes, you're right. The last thing we need is any more trouble. But how are we going to get away?'

'Pietro must have come in a boat. The island's not that big. We'll find it and leave while it's dark. But you need something to wear. There's more blankets in here. A bible! I wonder if he ever opened it . . . Wait a minute. What's this?'

Marko's knuckles smarted as they struck something hard in the deep bottom drawer. It was a box, made of wood, about three hands wide and one deep.

'Look,' he said, and brought it over to the candlelight where Sorrel sat shivering under her blanket.

'What is it?' he asked. 'Do you think there's money?'

'Open it and see!'

'It won't. It's locked.'

'Isn't there a key?'

Marko went back to the drawer to look for the key, but found nothing.

'I suppose . . . ' he said.

'What?'

'The key might be . . . '

He thought about the body in the other room, and whether he could face going through its pockets.

'Marko!' Sorrel cried. 'Look!'

She held one of the candles right up to the box, and now he saw what he'd missed before. It was a small paper label, pasted in the top left hand corner of the lid. There was a handwritten address on the label, Canareggio 6506, and a name, Nicolo Bruno.

'So?' Marko asked. 'That's where it's going.'

'No, you don't understand. This is my father's writing. This is one of his boxes. It must be the piece they came to collect. And this must be the customer it's for.'

'Then that's where we're going next,' Marko said.

'Yes,' Sorrel said excitedly, 'Yes, but . . . '

The same thought had just crossed Marko's mind.

What was the box doing here, in the possession of the foul priest, when it should have been delivered by their two fathers to its new owner? Did that mean it had been taken from them, taken by force? And what if it did?

Marko pushed those thoughts away, and took the box from

Sorrel. He shook it gently, and a soft rattling came from inside.

'Careful!'

'Yes,' Marko said.

'What's is in there?'

Marko swallowed hard.

'I'll see if I can find the key,' he said.

12

*T*he city prepared itself for sleep, as night drifted down from the hills and brushed everyone and everything with a touch of the eternal rest that would one day be theirs for good.

All across Venice that weird change that happens once every day was taking place, as somewhere perhaps familiar by daylight becomes foreign, an alien cityscape, of mysterious sights, improbable liaisons and unfulfilled promises. Small boats and larger ones made their way to and fro across the waterways, and as the events of the day made way for the events of the night, many people set out for Giudecca, an infamous place of debauchery and pleasure. Others closed their shutters tight against such wickedness, and prepared to make the long journey through another January night.

In a forgotten corner of the city, an old woman shuffled slowly along. The people she passed paid her no attention, and she both loved and hated this. Oh! She knew what they thought, if they thought of her at all. There goes a senile old hag, no use for anything anymore, too old, too old. She had no strength left, she was weak, and powerless. And how wrong they were! How very wrong they were. Somewhere in an alley behind her lay the body of a strong young man, a body that lay twisted and spent; his death mask a mixture of horror and surprise that recorded the moment of his passing.

Elsewhere, a hopeless gambler strapped on his belt, threw

his coat around his shoulders and headed for the Ridotto where he knew his luck was due to change.

A prisoner in the Piombi, the lead-roofed cells in the Doge's palace, scratched at what he thought might be flea bites, then froze as he thought for a moment he heard another scratching from nearby, beyond the wall, as if in answer to his own.

The proprietor of the latest animal attraction to stir the city, a small black rhinoceros, swept away the latest offering of dung, threw fresh straw down for the beast, wondered if it really was looking more ill than the day before, then shrugged and went to count his day's takings.

In the house of the priest at San Michele, nothing happened at all, as the two headless corpses lay in a thick black-red pool of their own making. Even the dog had left now, having sensed the badness of what had happened there.

It trotted out into the night, a misty, damp and cold night, and decided that life could be better than it was. It sniffed the air and picked up a scent, and the scent told him that it was the best thing that had happened to him in a very long while.

He followed it.

Marko and Sorrel hunted around the banks of the island of San Michele, looking for Pietro's boat, and Marko thought to himself for the tenth time how it would probably be best not to make any comment about the makeshift clothes Sorrel was wearing. They'd found some trousers and a nightshirt that must have belonged to Fei, and deciding that he no longer needed them, Sorrel had tried them on. The trousers were ridiculously long; the priest had been a tall man, and even rolling them up had helped little. In the end Marko had used a knife to hack the bottoms from them, and Sorrel had pulled the huge nightshirt over her head and tied it around the waist with a belt made from a strip of cloth. The linen was old and stiff, and Sorrel looked terrible, but there was nothing else to do. Still, she refused to leave her dress, which she carried rolled up under one arm.

As they were hunting for the boat in the darkness, edging their way with a candle as light, daring to use no more, they suddenly heard a scuffling noise. They both stopped instinctively, and scanned the mist for the source of the sound. Sorrel laughed. The little stray trotted into view and right up to Marko, where he sat, looking up expectantly at what he had decided was his new master.

Sorrel laughed again.

In a short skiff in the middle of the Northern lagoon, the tall old man in black bent over his oars and drifted for a while. He was as far from land as he'd be for the whole journey, and bending under the thwart he pulled out something long and thin. In the lightless gloom of night on the lagoon, what he held was indistinct, a harmless looking object about three feet long, like a stick, or a baton of some sort. But the old man, who had nearly forgotten that his name was Peter, knew exactly what it was. He rummaged around by his feet once again and found a scrap of rag. Then, very, very carefully, almost lovingly, he wiped the drying blood from the curved blade of the Turkish sword, as if wiping a baby's mouth after a messy feed.

When he was done, he threw the rag overboard, and slid the sword back into its leather scabbard. Once upon a time there had been no scabbard, just a long wooden box, but as the distances he travelled had become greater, and the need to travel light had grown greater too, he'd had a tanner in Reval make the sheath for him. It was perfect in its own way, though even this scabbard was very old now, and showed signs of the years and the miles it had covered. Peter had had the tanner emboss the faces of the leather with various patterns and markings, and had been insistent as he'd instructed the man to inscribe a name at the scabbard's mouth. The leather was old and worn now, and the name had been rubbed countless times by Peter's hand as he grasped the sheath in his left hand, pulling the sword itself with his right. It was hard to read anymore, and Peter himself had nearly forgotten it, but a close inspection might have yielded the name, a girl's name.

It might have been Sophia.

The Queen of the Shadows

A Fairy Tale

It was no use.

Though everyone tried to persuade the King to change his mind, he would not be swayed.

'If I don't stick to the rules that I make,' he said, 'how can I expect my subjects to obey them?'

And with that, the pair, the princess and the beggar, were married, and more than that, the King was so angry with the girl that he sent them away that very night, banishing her from the castle for ever.

The beggar was very pleased with his good fortune, and though he was poor, he was not so old, and even a little handsome. He thanked Fate for steering his course. The princess's sisters took pity on her, and begged their new husbands for a little money to give the poor couple before they left, but though the men were rich, they were jealous of their wealth, and would only spare a few coins to send the princess and the beggar on their way.

The princess was distraught, but the beggar was happier than ever. It was more money than he'd ever had in his life, and with it he bought a small hovel, deep in the woods, and an axe.

The couple set up house, and for a while, things were miserable for the princess, and wonderful for the beggar. He used the axe to cut down trees, and began to make money selling the firewood. His wife was young and beautiful, and life was good, and amazingly enough, as the years rolled by, the haughty princess cried so many tears, that she washed all the pain out of her heart. She looked up one spring day to see her husband coming home with a bag of coins in one hand, and a rabbit for the pot in the other, and she realised with a shock that she loved him.

THREE

1

*I*n a deathly hush she moved on the water.

There was no stopping her, for she was the air one moment, water the next, fire if that was what was needed. She approached without warning, as she had done so many times, moving here, moving there, bringing with her her own variety of evil.

She was death. She could be life too, but only rarely. Her face was the face of abject horror, of abandonment, of defeat, of resignation to the inevitable. One breath from her could take all breath from her victim, and she looked forward to doing that again, and again and again.

She felt all her years gathered about her like an army, countless centuries of the evil she'd done sweeping round her like plague rats on a doomed ship.

She'd been so many places, lived in so many hearts turned bad, and won so many victories, and she didn't intend for it to end. Ever.

A smile appeared on her face, her wide thin mouth like a slit in a bag of white flour, opening and closing like a trap for beetles to stray into, her nose like an eagle's beak jutting over it, her black eyes, in truth quite elegant, radiating all manner of devilment and destruction.

She thought of all the names, everything that anyone had ever cursed her with, had ever whispered in horror, and yet, in all the years, there was still one that suited her best, the one they used in the forests in the east.

The Shadow Queen.

She laughed, and as she did so, small creatures withered and died.

2

Now, Marko and Sorrel, and their new companion, drifted in open water, bobbing slightly on the swell, though it was a lifeless night on the lagoon.

It had not been easy to find Pietro's boat. They'd started their search close to the church where it stood by the water's edge, but in the end hunted right round the small island's banks and shores without success. Finally, as they approached the church again after making a complete circuit of San Michele, Marko saw a tiny cut in the bank they'd not seen before. It was almost invisible from the direction they'd started from, and even in daylight would have been hard to see. On their way round the island they'd tiptoed past houses with candlelight inside, and the muffled sounds of domestic life. Once a door had opened, and they'd frozen like statues until it closed again, Marko's heart in his mouth as the dog had cocked its head towards the sound, perhaps imagining it was a sign of the arrival of food. But the dog had remained quiet enough, and had not given them away.

'Is this the sort of company you usually keep?' Sorrel had asked, teasing Marko about the dog. He'd ignored her, though he was pleased to hear her say something. She'd barely spoken a word since she'd donned the terrible clothes. It wasn't just that they were a man's clothes, ill-fitting and dirty. There was something awful knowing they belonged to a dead man, and one who'd tried to kill them at that. Marko shuddered at the thought of it, and determined to get Sorrel back into her own dress as soon as it was possible.

They sat in the boat, exhausted, their thoughts mixed and troubled. Even the dog seemed to sense the mood, and lay in the bottom of the craft, his chin resting on Marko's foot.

Between them sat the box. Marko had not been able to find the key, though it was possible he'd missed it. It had not been a pleasant job. In his work for his father, he was used to seeing wounds and sores, festering cuts and disfiguring illnesses, and even the occasional basic surgical exploration inside a human body, but nothing could have prepared him for his second visit to the room where Fei and Pietro, or what was left of them, lay. Without heads, without their faces, it was hard to think of them as men at all, just grotesque lumps of meat, bone and fat. That was all they were now, he decided, and tried to detach himself from what he had to do. If only there hadn't been quite so much blood. He'd approached the bodies cautiously, as if they might leap back to life at any moment. He'd tried Fei's robes first, feeling inside the priest's habit for any pockets, chains or purses. He'd found nothing, and almost with relief had moved onto Pietro. Unlike Fei, who'd been lying on his back, the glass-maker's man was prone, chest to the floor, and Marko realised he would have to turn him over to reach into his pockets.

He swallowed hard, put a hand on Pietro's shoulder, and began to pull. There was an awful sweet smell and a sucking sound and then Marko noticed something else, a mark on the back of the glass-man's neck, beneath the frighteningly smooth cut which had severed his life from his body. That was enough for Marko, and suppressing the urge to be sick, he dropped the shoulder back to the floor. As he left, however, a desire for knowledge, stronger than his disgust, overcame him. Something nagged at him, and making his way back to Fei, he'd lifted and rolled him with a foot, so that he too lay chest down. There on his neck, was the same mark.

Marko had fled as if the devil was behind him.

3

'*W*hat do we think happened?'

Marko lifted his head and the dog stirred. He vaguely noticed that Sorrel had said 'we', not 'you', and for some reason he couldn't quite place it gave him a little hope. They'd brought some blankets from the priest's room, and huddled under them in the small boat.

'Do you mean . . . to those two? Who killed them? Why we weren't killed too?'

Sorrel nodded. 'No. Well. Yes, that too. It's an extraordinary thing.'

Marko smiled to himself. That's not the way he would have described it, but then Sorrel always seemed to have an unusual view of things.

'I meant what happened to our fathers. What really happened out there. On Murano, on San Michele.'

Marko thought for a while, and though he'd been running all sorts of ideas back and forth through his mind all night, the cold was affecting him so badly that he struggled to put these thoughts in any kind of order.

'Your father made . . . something. For someone. And it's whatever's in that box. Agreed?'

Sorrel nodded, too tired and cold to tell Marko how obvious he was being.

'We don't know what it is. Maybe it's Venetia's tiara. But

then why would it be addressed to this man, Nicolo Bruno? And you're sure it's your father's writing?'

Sorrel nodded again.

'Yes, I think so.'

'You think so?'

'I know so. It's just a bit shaky. Uneven.'

Marko thought to himself that it was amazing that Simono Bellini could write at all, given the mad wretch of a man he'd met the night before. But on the day that he and Alessandro had made the trip, Bellini had been better. Maybe not utterly well, but much, much better than he had been.

'All right. So let's assume it's not Venetia's tiara, but something for someone else. Something for Nicolo Bruno. My father and your father went to collect it from the workshop, to take it to Bruno, to sell it to him. But it never got there. Somewhere it went missing, Pietro or Fei, or both of them, must have stolen it from them.'

'In which case . . .'

Sorrel stopped. The conclusion was obvious. In all likelihood, Marko's father had never left Murano. Not alive, at least. Maybe he was already drifting towards the bottom of the lagoon somewhere.

Marko shook his head.

'But listen. Where was your father found? Not on Murano?'

Sorrel understood.

'No. No, he was found wandering around San Marco. Back in the city. Then they brought him home.'

'So if he got back as far as the city, that means that my father probably did too. That whatever happened to them happened there, and not on Murano, or San Michele.'

Sorrel hesitated, but she could not stop herself from expressing her fears.

'Does it?'

Marko ignored this. It was something he could not afford to ponder too deeply.

'Assume they made it back to the city, but they never made it to Bruno. Fei and Pietro follow them, and fight them, steal the box, take it out to San Michele. Pietro only sent us there as a trap, I don't think our fathers were ever there at all.'

'No,' Sorrel agreed. 'Maybe not. In fact, I think you're right. But where does that get us? Where do we go now?'

'We go to Bruno. We deliver the goods to him, as arranged.'

'And why do we do that?'

'Two reasons. We could use the money. And more importantly, he might just know something. When they were supposed to come. Who they spoke to. Something.'

Sorrel didn't reply but her silence was enough to anger Marko.

'What else are we going to do, Sorrel?' he asked bitterly. 'What else?'

She hung her head and Marko knew that was as much agreement as he'd get.

He looked away from her and across the water to the light of the city.

Somewhere, in some room of some house in the city, his father was still alive. He couldn't let himself think otherwise.

4

*T*hey spent the rest of the night moored to a huge wooden post that reared from the lagoon some way off shore, and only as day broke did they head in for the banks of the city. It was another grey and cloudy day, and as they drew into the fondamente the buildings seemed more ghostly than ever, rising out of the water like painted drops in a theatre, flat and pale.

They were frozen stiff after their night in the boat, but as Marko began to row, he started to feel his blood warm him again. He looked across at Sorrel. Without her eye paint, in the early morning light, she no longer looked angry and bitter-tongued. She looked tired and lonely, but lovely too, as she tickled Dog under his chin, feeling his warmth on her fingertips.

'Head up that way,' she suggested. 'It will be quieter there, past that basin. It's a little harbour. Beyond are fishing houses and washing houses.'

Marko bent to the oars and did as he was told, and very soon they chose an obscure jetty to moor alongside.

'What about the boat?' Marko asked.

'We're not stopping here,' Sorrel said. 'We'll go on to Bruno's house in it, as far as we can. But I want to try something first.'

Marko watched as Sorrel walked quickly away across the

pavement that led to the first houses, lower and much more modest affairs than the grand palazzo in the heart of the city by the Canalazzo. Even though it was only just light, Sorrel had seen that the washerwomen were already at their work, scrubbing clothes in the great stone basins designed for the purpose, hanging them out on lines to dry. The washing lines were strung from building to building like sails, Marko thought, making them look like huge sea-faring vessels. Sorrel was talking to a washerwoman who stood pinning wet clothes over the washing lines. Marko doubted that they would dry quickly, if at all, in the damp cold weather, but while he was thinking about this he saw Sorrel pointing and the woman nodding back at her. She disappeared inside a house for a while but came back out with some things bundled in her arms. Sorrel picked at the bundles, then seemed to agree something, and then Marko saw her hand her blood-stained dress to the washerwoman. Then both of them vanished inside the house, and a minute later Sorrel reappeared wearing a simple red dress, close to a perfect fit. She came back to the boat, and smiled.

'It's not great, but it will have to do.'

'What did you say?'

'I swapped my dress for this. Mine's worth much more, even in the state it's in. She was happy to give me this one for it.'

Marko looked at her, and couldn't see the problem. It was a deep red colour, not silk, but linen, and in his eyes suited her well. It just swept the ground, and had a high waist that pulled in tight, making her look as shapely as a woman ten years older.

'I don't see what's wrong with it,' he said, genuinely.

Sorrel pulled a face.

'Well, it's not black, for a start,' she said, but she smiled.

Marko laughed.

'We can always dye it later,' he said. 'Come on. How do we find this house?'

'In the boat. The house numbers are sometimes a little hard to follow, and I don't know this area of the city very well.'

They climbed back into the boat, and Sorrel inspected the label on the box.

'5696,' she said. I think that's more likely to be back towards the centre, towards the Canalazzo. We'll try this canal here.'

She pointed to a canal that led straight into the heart of the city. It was reasonably wide, wide enough for two large boats to pass each other comfortably, and travelled dead straight until the mist hid it from view.

'We can ask as we go. If we find any houses between 5000 and 6000 we'll know we're getting near. It usually works.'

'Usually?'

'Usually.'

Marko untied the rope from the jetty, and was starting to pull away when Sorrel laughed.

'Aren't you forgetting someone?'

Marko looked and saw the dog was still on the pavement, ferreting around for a scent. Suddenly it heard a squeak of an oar, saw that they were leaving, and ran for the jetty, hopping into the boat with a spring that didn't seem to trouble it at all.

Immediately, it took up its position at Marko's feet, but with its head raised and looking eagerly over the side, trying to see where they were going.

'Don't you think it's about time you introduced us?' Sorrel said, smiling.

Marko didn't smile, but bent his back to the rowing.

'I don't know what he's called,' he said.

'Then perhaps he needs a new name. To start his new life.'

'His new life?'

'With you.'

'Maybe. But I still don't know his name.'

'Then you should give him a name, Marko. You owe him that at least.'

'I do?' Marko said. 'All right. I'll give him a name. I'll call him Dog.'

'Dog? You can't call him Dog!'

'Why not?'

'I could have given him a better name than that.'

'But you said it was up to me to name him, so there you are. His name's Dog. Dog, this is Sorrel. Sorrel, this is Dog.'

'Well!' Sorrel snorted. She glared at Marko, then stared over the side of the boat into the mist. 'What sort of a name is that?'

Marko pulled on the oars and grinned to himself, then grinned down at Dog, who looked back at him, panting, apparently very happy with his new name.

5

They left the boat far behind, and Marko was glad of it. He resisted the temptation to say 'back on firm ground' because to him nowhere in Venice felt like firm ground. It was impossible to forget for a moment that the whole city rested on the unstable muds of a marshy lagoon, even the pavements frequently rang hollow under their feet, witness to the drains and other hidden channels that lurked beneath.

He found himself swaying as they set off on foot, his body having spent so long trying to accustom itself to the swaying of life on the water that it refused to behave now they were on dry land.

Sorrel had no such problems, but Marko reasoned that she would have grown used to this amphibious routine, switching from water to land a dozen times a day.

'6105,' Sorrel said, and pointed to a number on a house nearby. Not every house had one, but most seemed to; one brick was painted white and edged with black; the number elegantly but boldly painted in black inside.

They came to a sort of crossroads, one arm of which led over a small wooden bridge, the others led straight into more alleyways.

'There,' Sorrel said. '6072. We'll try that way.'

She seemed to be right, as the numbers began to fall consistently.

Marko, who was carrying the box, checked the number again. 5696.

The sun poked its feeble face out from the grey sky, and things seemed to be going well, but then Sorrel stopped. The numbers continued to fall as they crossed a couple of small alleys, but then began to climb again.

'We'll have to go back,' she said, but didn't sound concerned, though Marko began to wonder how anyone found their way anywhere in this labyrinth.

'Here?' Marko suggested.

'Here,' Sorrel said, and set off again, with Marko and Dog obediently following. Marko knew there was no sense in interfering; this was her territory. Sure enough, the numbers began to fall again, until they found themselves at 5712.

Sorrel stopped again.

'Now what?' Marko asked, looking ahead. 'Look. There's 5710.'

'I know,' Sorrel said sharply. 'But we're not going that way.'

'Why not?'

'Because I know where we are, and I won't go that way.'

She nodded ahead, refusing even, it seemed, to lift her hand towards the route ahead.

Marko began to feel frustration rising up in him.

'And why won't you go that way? It looks easy enough.'

'Because there are stories about this place,' she said. 'And I won't go there.'

Marko put the box down and turned Sorrel by the shoulders to face him.

'Stories?' he said. '*Stories?* I didn't think you were supposed to believe in stories and superstitions.'

Sorrel pulled back out of his grasp angrily.

'This is Venice,' she whispered, almost as if the houses

346

might overhear her, 'and you don't know anything. You see that house there?'

She pointed, but said nothing.

'Yes,' said Marko, following her brief gesture with puzzlement, wondering what was so special about a house that seemed more or less like all the others in the row.

'Oh!' she said. 'Never mind.'

With that, she picked up the box, and set off the way they had come, then turned the corner of the street.

'Sorrel! Wait!'

Marko rounded the corner and found Sorrel waiting for him impatiently.

'What?' he said. 'I didn't say anything!'

'You didn't need to. I know what you're thinking.'

'Do you?' Marko asked. 'Why not try me? Listen. Tell me what's wrong. I promise I'm listening. If something is so bad that it's scaring you then I'm more than happy to go another way. But please let's just do it quickly.'

Sorrel's shoulders dropped and she sighed.

'I'm just being foolish, I suppose,' she said. 'I'm sorry. I shouldn't be scared, but there are all sorts of stories from that house, that street.'

'What sort of stories?'

'Lots of them. But that house. They say a magician used to live there. My father told me, too, so it must be true. He was an awful man, so the stories say. A brutal, terrible man with no fear of life or death or anyone or anything. They say he'd made a pact with the devil, more than once.'

She paused and Marko could see she was truly frightened by her own story. He let her continue.

'He was coming home late one night, past the cemetery, and suddenly a thick mist fell around him, and he couldn't see to put one foot in front of the other. So he called out to the devil. "Lucifer! Lucifer!" he said. "Throw me a torch to light my way." And immediately a burning torch appeared in his hand and with it he made his way home. It was only when he got there that he saw what he'd been holding. It was the hand of a dead man, and each of the fingers was alight.'

Marko swallowed.

'What did he do?'

'He laughed! This wasn't the first time the devil had played a trick on him in some way or other. He blew the torch out, put it in his log basket, and went to sleep. The next night, when there was no mist, he took it back to the cemetery and gave it back to the dead man who it belonged to, who thanked him and went back into his grave.'

She stopped, and despite the strengthening sunlight, Marko shivered. Something reminded him of the markings he'd seen on the back of Fei and Pietro's necks, marks that he had since realised were tattoos. He wondered whether to tell Sorrel what he'd seen, but decided against it. Suddenly, the certainties of life in his father's surgery in Piran seemed very far away. He'd been brought up to trust only what his eyes saw; his father spent hours when Marko was a child, teaching him, showing him the way the world seemed to him. He could clearly remember his father letting a bee sting his own hand, and hold it under a microscope so Marko could watch the action of the sting as it pumped its poison into the skin. His father had ignored the pain, just so he could explain what was happening to the little Marko. Marko had watched wide-eyed, half in wonder, half in fear for his father, until with the back of his nail Alessandro had scraped the sting away, then set about mixing a small concoction.

'Vinegar and a little *saleratus*,' he'd told Marko. 'That will destroy the poison. The pain will subside soon.'

His father was a remarkable man, who had even confided to Marko that he thought there was no such thing as God, though swearing him to secrecy on the matter.

'Only trust what your eyes tell you, Marko,' he'd told him, adding hastily. 'But tell no one I told you this. I would be in a lot of trouble. The church would try and execute me. And what your mother would do would be worse.'

But in Venice, things didn't seem to follow the same rules, and Marko had begun to doubt that he could always know what was right and what was false. Maybe it wasn't always possible to trust what your eyes told you.

He looked around the empty streets, and finally back at Sorrel.

'Let's go another way, shall we?' he said.

'**A**re you hungry?' Sorrel said.

'Are you joking?'

She shook her head. They'd taken a detour as Sorrel had demanded but it was taking a long time. Once or twice Marko even suspected they were lost, but he didn't say so to Sorrel. It was mid-morning and the day was as bright as it was probably going to get.

'I'm ravenous,' Sorrel said. 'We'll be there soon, but there's a water-shop around the corner. We can buy something to eat. Have some coffee. Do you like coffee?'

'A little,' Marko lied. He'd never drunk coffee in his life. He knew it was a sophisticated drink from the city, and that his father often moaned about not getting any in Piran, but that was all. But he wasn't going to let Sorrel know that.

'Well, come on then.'

Dog trotted after them as they turned the corner and ducked under the low doorway of the water-shop. There were no other customers, and it was dim and cosy, a pleasant change from the chill day outside. The shop sold a lot more than water, Marko soon saw. Drinks of all sorts; lemon water, juice from oranges, chocolate, various kinds of coffee, and wine from all over the Veneto.

'What kind of coffee do you like?' Sorrel asked, approaching the counter. A kind-looking old woman stood waiting for them to order.

'I'll have what you're having,' Marko said quickly. 'And can we get some water for Dog?'

Sorrel laughed.

'He can drink at the fountain in the street like any other cur. We passed one just outside.'

Marko took Dog by the black fur at his neck and shoved his nose towards the small fountain that poured a continuous stream of water out of a small carved lion's mouth set into the wall of the street. Dog however, was having none of it and as soon as he went back inside, he immediately followed.

'There's no getting rid of you, is there?' Marko sighed. 'Well, if you go thirsty it's your own fault.'

He was ducking under the doorway when his attention was caught by three figures coming down the street. He guessed from their clothes and their gait that they were all men, but the masks they wore completely covered their faces. The three were loud and raucous and something about them made Marko step back inside the shop quickly. They went past, shouting and pushing at one another; if it hadn't been so early Marko would have guessed they were drunk. Their masks were unlike any he'd seen so far; many people wore either a mask with a huge bird's beak, or a plain white mask that more or less copied the human face, but which jutted out from the top lip, to enable the wearer to sip at a drink without removing it. The masks that these three wore were altogether different; they were painted red and black, scowling, fiendish things that made the men look like devils.

'Why do people wear those?' Marko asked, sitting down next to Sorrel. Dog curled up at his feet and the woman trudged over with two cups and a steaming pot of coffee.

'It's Carnival,' Sorrel said. 'Anyone can wear a mask during the carnival.'

'But why?'

Sorrel shrugged.

'It's what we do. Just because we can. Maybe to hide, or to pretend you're someone else. Anyone can wear a mask, rich or poor, nobleman or peasant. Under the mask, people become more or less the same. You could have affairs with your lovers and go unrecognised. Eavesdrop, find out what is being said about you, to spy on others . . . The Three, the Inquisitors, make much use of them, I'm sure. But only during Carnival. To wear a mask outside of Carnival is a terrible crime. It is punishable. With whipping, and prison.'

'They send you to prison for wearing a mask?'

'For two years, if you're a woman. Longer for a man.'

Marko shook his head.

'That's crazy.'

'There's a saying here; "Respect Venice". It's not wise to ignore it.'

'I won't forget.'

'Good. Drink your coffee.'

Marko gingerly lifted the cup to his mouth. It smelled bitter, but quite nice, he thought, though too hot to drink. He put the cup down. Sorrel sipped at hers, unconcerned.

'And the carnival? What happens then?'

'Everything happens then. By night mostly, but there's going to be the procession of the new Doge. That's tomorrow afternoon, but it'll go on late. Very late. That's what Venetia wants her tiara for . . . '

'Don't worry about her,' Marko said.

'I won't. We've more important things to worry about. But it's the high point of the carnival. The whole city will don masks, more or less. And there'll be the Flight of the Turk, too. That's wonderful. It's my favourite thing. I can remember the very first time I saw it after we'd moved from London. You won't believe it.'

Sorrel stopped, realising she'd got carried away, and had for a moment, forgotten the predicament they were in. The truth that her father was mad and dying, that Marko's father was missing. But Marko saw that for a moment, she'd been happy. Really happy, he'd seen her whole face change, relax, become lighter, and prettier, like she'd looked the previous night as he'd washed her hair while she slept. He encouraged her to go on.

'Tell me about it,' he said. 'It sounds fun. Who's the Turk?'

'Well, he's not a Turk. Not any more. It can be anyone, someone different every year, sometimes more than one man. They fix a rope, right up in the sky, from the bell tower of San Marco to the balcony of the Doge's palace. Sometimes they even run the rope out to sea to a ship anchored in the lagoon. Then a man will walk the rope, like at the circus. Have you ever been to a circus, Marko?'

'They come to our town sometimes,' Marko said. 'You mean the man who walks on a rope? He walks right across the square and out to sea? That's impossible!'

'It's dangerous, but not impossible. Many men have died trying it. That's why people come. Like an execution.'

Marko sensed she was sailing back into gloomy waters and tried to steer her out.

'But the rope, it must swing about.'

'Yes, terribly. But it's a very thick rope, about half as wide as your foot, very heavy. So they just swing with it. And most of the time they make it. You're not drinking your coffee and we should pay and get going.'

Marko knew she was right, and picked up his cup, nervously.

'Lovely,' he said, and took a long drink.

Immediately he felt terrible. It felt as if thick black acid was pouring down inside him, and almost straight away his heart began to thump in his chest. Trying to hide it, he couldn't help but pull a face. He opened his mouth to speak but couldn't.

'Yes,' Sorrel said, standing up to leave. 'You're right, it's not very good. But they don't always get the best stuff.'

She made her way to the counter to pay, and Marko let his forehead sink onto the table, panting for breath. Dog looked up at him, cocked his head to one side, and then began to lick his hand.

'It's all right, Dog,' Marko gasped. 'I really think I'll be all right.'

7

*C*anareggio 5696.

They stood in front of the door, listening to the tinkling of a bell die away.

Marko let his hand fall from the bell pull, and turned to Sorrel. 'Trust what your eyes tell you,' his father would say, but why was it that he was filled with a terrible sense of dread about this place? It was still the only choice they had, the only path to follow, but now that they were actually here, something seemed wrong.

It was hard to explain. They were back in the heart of the city, and the buildings were fine and grand. 5696 was perhaps not the largest house, but it looked a well kept merchant's house, or similar, and generally prosperous, from the varnished front door to the shiny brass bell pull, cold to Marko's touch.

He opened his mouth to say something, but Sorrel beat him to it.

'I know. But what else are we going to do? I'm sure Bruno is a reasonable man if he's one of my father's customers.'

Marko nodded, trying to look confident. He held the mysterious box tightly, tighter than he needed to.

'How shall we do this?' he asked, but Sorrel never answered, because a face appeared in a tiny window by the door. It glanced at them, then disappeared. There was a muffled call and the door swung open.

A short, thin man, with a miserable look stood before them. He kept one hand on the door as if he might slam it shut in an instant. His eyes were as thin as his fingers, and not only was he short, he stooped terribly from age. Behind him another indistinct figure scurried away into the bowels of the house.

'Yes?'

Marko tried to sound more composed than he was.

'We've come to deliver this to Signor Bruno,' he said, and indicated the box.

The man said nothing. He seemed unimpressed.

'Very well. You'd better come in. I'll see if the master is free to receive you.'

They followed the old servant into the house, and he shut the door behind them. It closed with a heavy thud and both Marko and Sorrel felt their fears flutter inside them.

'Wait in there,' the man said, pointing to a room straight ahead of them, while he turned and made his way up a broad staircase that wound out of sight to the first floor.

They did as they were told and found themselves in a formal reception room, which spanned the width of the house. It was dimly lit, but they could see well enough that it was an imposing room. The floors were polished wood, and the walls were hung with an ornate printed paper, luscious red-gold foliage on a midnight blue backdrop. There were paintings, mostly scenes from the Bible; a Madonna and child, the martyrdom of San Sebastian with his arrows holding him to a withered tree, Lazarus rising from his grave. There was little else in the room but at one end was a dais, a small raised platform, and on this stood a large and heavy chair, practically a throne given its size and magnificence. Marko and Sorrel both had the same thought at once. Whoever sat in this chair was used to being obeyed. Dog whimpered slightly and hung close to Marko's legs.

A voice cut towards them through the darkness.

'Who comes?'

A man entered the room, a creature. A thing. He walked slowly, but steadily he made his entrance. He was enormously fat. Marko had never seen anyone so large in all his life, and he had to struggle not to stare as the man dragged one foot after the other in his approach to the chair on the platform. He was finely dressed, in a rich coat and wig, and well-made shoes of red leather. He had reached the dais and Marko and Sorrel could do nothing but watch this vast figure lift one foot then the other the few inches up onto the platform. It required vast effort and for a while it looked touch and go as to whether he would make it at all, but he won this battle and took four more tiny steps before turning and collapsing on the throne.

He closed his eyes. No one spoke. Then his eyes flicked open again, Sorrel wished they had stayed shut. They were hideous slimy yellow things that poured hate out into the room, yellow like a weeping sore, with black dots for pupils, and the only mercy was that they were largely hidden by the drooping folds of eyelid. His whole face drooped in the same way, like some bag of flesh from the butcher's market, it sagged, quivered and twitched at the slightest movement, as if there were rats moving beneath the bloated, blotched skin.

He spoke. His voice was thick and cluttered, and for some reason Marko was reminded of the corpses he'd occasionally seen on his father's surgery table.

'I think, that that is for me.'

His eyes speared the box.

'But who are you?'

The voice roared and the flesh quivered; the rats scurried around inside the face.

'I am Nicolo Bruno!'

Sorrel faltered.

'I'm sorry.'

'Sorry?' he roared, but then lost interest. His eyes crawled back to the box once more.

'I think I asked you a question. Doesn't that belong to me?'

Sorrel felt her fear grow even wilder. She felt there was something not being said, and it was something bad.

Bruno laughed.

'Do you not know who I am? I am Nicolo Bruno, and I am one of the Three Inquisitors of Venice. And you are in a lot of trouble.'

He laughed again, and Dog began to whimper.

8

'Why have you come here?'
Bruno leaned forward slightly in his chair, peering at them through slits.

'We've brought this for you,' Marko stammered. 'We have come to collect payment for it.'

Sorrel spoke hurriedly.

'My father made it for you but it was never delivered. We want to know if you have seen my father.'

Bruno ignored her.

'Is that it?' he drawled.

'Yes,' said Marko. The box felt like lead in his hands.

'Come closer,' Bruno ordered. 'I want to see it.'

Unwillingly, Sorrel and Marko stepped closer to the platform.

Bruno sneered.

'Your father is Simono Bellini, yes?'

Sorrel nodded quickly.

'Simono Bellini,' Bruno said, his voice sprawling over the name with such distain and distaste that Sorrel would never forget it. He spoke her father's name as though it was an insult.

'And you want to deliver this to me? Yes?'

'That's right,' Marko said.

'You would swear to that in a court?'

359

Sorrel hesitated, Marko opened his mouth but closed it again.

'You would *swear* it?' Bruno roared and Marko was so startled he stammered back an answer.

'Yes. We want to be paid for it.'

'So,' Bruno said, and here, he slowly and deliberately pulled himself to his feet, pointing a short fat finger at them. 'You want to deliver this to me, and you expect to be paid for it. But tell me, why would I want to pay for something that has already been delivered to me once, and for which I have already paid?'

His words floated into the silence of the room and died. Marko cursed quietly. It was worse than they might have thought, much worse.

'So, it seems I have a pair of thieves before me. A pair of urchins who dare to sell back to me what is already mine. Such stupidity! Such gall! But that is what you are! Thieves!'

'No!' Marko cried, 'It's not like that. We found the box, and we thought it hadn't been given to you yet . . . '

Bruno shouted over their heads.

'Beppe! Call the men!'

'No! Wait! We found it. We'll give it back to you. We'll just give it back and go.'

'And where did you "just find" the box?' Bruno sneered.

'We found it on San Michele,' Sorrel spluttered. 'There were two men.'

'Who?'

'A priest and a glass-maker.'

'And they gave you the box?'

'No, not exactly.'

'Beppe!' Bruno screamed, his whole face wobbling from side to side with the effort. He stepped off the platform towards Marko and Sorrel, who stepped backwards defensively. Dog scrabbled to his feet and began to circle Marko's legs. Bruno heaved himself towards them.

'And these men can vouch for what you are saying?'

'No, no they can't,' Marko said uneasily.

'Why not?'

'Because they're dead.'

'What! Dead!'

'Someone killed them,' Sorrel explained.

'Not you?' Bruno sneered. 'Someone?'

Marko and Sorrel started to back away to the door, and then Dog snarled and they turned to see what he was snarling at.

There in the door were the three masked figures they'd seen pass the water-shop.

'At last!' roared Bruno. 'Take these two away and lock them in the strong room.'

'Run, Sorrel!' Marko yelled. 'Run!'

She'd already had the same idea, and they both sprinted towards the door, trying to dodge past the three men. Sorrel managed to miss the first hand that grasped for her, and made it to the hallway with Dog running at her heels, but Marko, still clinging onto the box, was caught straight away by the largest figure. He felt arms tighten around his waist and saw the third man coming towards him. He wrestled his arms free and threw the box at this man as hard as he could manage.

As he did so, two things happened simultaneously; Nicolo let out an ugly cry of despair, and the man Marko had thrown the box at deftly caught it, and then gently put it on the floor, before turning back to Marko with a snarl loud enough to hear from under his mask.

'Well done!' cried Nicolo.

Sorrel turned as she ran, and saw Marko was caught.

361

'Run!' he gasped at her, and as she turned back towards the door, she ran straight into the withered old man who'd let them in. They both went flying to the floor, and moments later the first of the men was on her, yanking her by her hair onto her back, standing over her. He reached down and slapped her across the face.

Marko yelled something, but it was too late. The man who'd caught the box leered at him, and while his partner held Marko tight, he swung a hard fist into his stomach.

Marko slumped over, and in his daze saw Dog running madly around the hall, unsure what to do. Marko mustered all his energy to scream at him.

'Run!'

Dog did as he was told. It was pointless, but somehow there was a tiny sense of delight in the fact that Dog skipped through the hall, right through the old man's legs, who swung at him with a boot. Dog took one leap onto a chair that stood by the wall, and then scrambled through the open window next to the front door.

Marko lifted his head, trying to see Sorrel, and his skin crawled. Her assailant stood over her, dragging her to her feet, but as he did so, Marko caught a glimpse of the back of his neck. There it was again. That strange tattoo.

Subdued, and beaten, Marko and Sorrel were hauled back in front of Bruno. His chest heaved as if he'd exerted himself in the fight, when all he'd done was watch happily as his men got the better of the two.

'As I said.'

He paused for breath, then his slug of a voice crawled over their faces again.

'As I said. Take these two and lock them up. As it happens I have already today received an accusation from the Mouth of

Truth, denouncing the girl's father. It seems they are as thick as thieves. I will decide what is to be done with them later, but they are to be arrested on the suspicion of having committed grievous crimes, foremost of which are robbery, fraud, and murder.'

*T*he worst of it was the silence.

The hunger was bad, and the worry and fear. The dark too, but the long and endless silence made all those things feel ten times worse than they otherwise would have.

Their money had been taken from them, and then they'd been thrown into a room at the back of the house, on the ground floor. They assumed it had been a store room of some kind, but it could not have been better designed as a prison. The stone walls were solid, cold and damp, so thick that sound would not escape. There were no windows save a slot at the top of the wall by the low ceiling, but even this was recessed deep into the thickness of the wall. It was like a small tunnel, longer than an arm, no wider than a hand. It shed sparse light and there was no thought of getting through it at all.

Their hands had been trussed behind them, and they'd been thrown into different corners, but they'd struggled to crawl over to each other, and had found a way of sitting back to back that took some of the strain off their aching arms and legs.

As they sat like this, Marko suddenly felt Sorrel's fingers touching his, and he made to move them away, but then felt her reach again and hold his fingers tight.

'Please,' he heard her whisper, and he was only too happy to do so. He held her fingers in his own, as firmly as he could manage. It was their only comfort.

They talked for a while, but it was hard. Neither of them had the strength, the will to find much hope, and could only dread what might come.

'We'll appeal to whatever court they take us to,' Marko said, with little conviction. 'They have to know that we've done nothing wrong.'

Sorrel didn't answer, and Marko remembered what she'd said about Venetian justice. Worse than that, the man they'd crossed had turned out to be one of the Three. Their chances of success looked very, very slight.

'What did he mean?' Marko asked. 'What he said about mouths?'

'Oh, that,' Sorrel said, sighing. 'Yes. The Mouths. We have a system here, for anyone who wants to make an accusation against any other person. All across the city are stone carvings, mostly lions' heads, but other faces too, of men and animals. The mouths are open, and behind is a letter box. You write down your accusation and post the letter. All the letters are read by the Council of Three, and they will then decide what to do.' She stopped.

Yes, Marko had seen one of these mouths on their journey across the city the day before. He had never guessed their purpose – they'd seemed nothing more than ornaments. Sorrel explained how, in order to try and to prevent people from making false accusations, the punishment for doing so was very severe.

'If you make a false accusation, and are discovered, then you're punished as if you had committed the crime you spoke of. If you accuse someone of fraud, you're tried as a fraud. If you speak of murder, you'll be tried as a murderer.'

'And someone has accused your father through the Mouths.'

'One guess who that is,' Sorrel said.

'Venetia.'

He hesitated to ask his next question, but he had to know. 'And then?'

'Then, we will be tried by the Three. We'll be put in the cells in the Doge's palace. Maybe in the Piombi, in the attics, but more likely in the Pozzi in the basement. The Piombi are for prisoners of high status, rich men, politicians. That kind of thing. And then? Who knows?'

As they sat in the deepening silence, the light dwindled, and they knew that night was coming on again. They tried to move nearer a wall where some old sacking lay on the floor, so that perhaps they could sleep for a while. But sleep would not come, and as the darkness grew in their little prison, Sorrel felt an awful new fear creep into her.

She thought about her father, her mad father. She knew Francesco would be looking after him as well as he could, but that ultimately there was nothing he could do, if . . . if the worst were to come. Why only Marko's father Alessandro had been able to help Simono was a mystery to her, but she prayed they found him soon. Without him, her father would continue the long slide into sleeplessness, a nightmare journey that would end with a hideous death. And already she missed him, longed to see him smiling down at her again, to have him hold her hands and dance. What if he were to go for ever?

Sleep.

As the night wore on, Sorrel felt Marko's body slump against hers, and knew he was sleeping, and yet, as long as she waited, she knew that sleep was not going to come for her tonight.

She felt exhausted, but somehow with every passing minute she felt sleep was getting farther from her. Her fear grew worse still, her heart began to thump, and her mind raced.

What if . . . ?

It had happened to her father. It had happened to many people who had lived in the Ca' Bellini. What if it was happening to her?

The death of no sleep.

She began to panic and struggled with the bonds round her wrists. She whimpered to herself and could bear it no longer.

'Marko! Please. Marko. Please wake up.'

Marko grunted and struggled, moaning at the stiffness in his arms and shoulders.

'Marko! Please. Oh, God.'

'What is it, Sorrel?' Marko opened his eyes in the darkness. He could see almost nothing. He felt disorientated, his senses dulled by tiredness and pain. 'What's wrong?'

'Marko! Oh God. I think it's happening to me.'

'What? What's wrong?'

He twisted, managing to shuffle round so that he was facing her, even though he could barely see her. He could sense that she was panicking, desperately frightened.

'What is it? Tell me what's wrong.'

'I think it's happening to me. I can't sleep, Marko. I can't sleep. I think it might be starting to happen to me, too.'

'No,' Marko said. 'No, you don't know that.'

'But I can't sleep! I'm so tired, but I can't. I just can't. What if it's happening to me, too?'

She began to cry, gently at first, but once she'd started, the tears seemed to take hold of her, and her cries grew worse. He felt a surge of pity for this poor strange girl, with a life so young, and yet so troubled.

Marko thought frantically. What would his father do? He tried to keep calm, though the urge to panic himself was strong. What would his father do? He thought hard and remembered a time when a local woman's child had died. She'd been hysterical from the shock. His father had given her medicine. And brandy. He had neither, but his father had spoken to the woman too. He'd talked calmly, but what had he said? Marko remembered very clearly that he hadn't tried to tell her anything she didn't want to hear, he hadn't tried to tell her everything would be all right, he'd simply spoken to her calmly until that calm had rubbed off on the poor woman.

'Sorrel,' he said, trying to think what to say. 'Sorrel. I'm here. I'm going to be here. For you. I don't think you're ill. I think you're very worried. Your body is exhausted, but your mind won't let you sleep, because you're too worried. It's only natural. It's a terrible thing that's happening to your father. To you.'

He would have liked to have added, 'to me', but bit his lip. He had to concentrate on Sorrel.

'I'm here. Whatever happens to us, I won't leave you alone. I promise. I promise.'

So he kept on talking, and gradually Sorrel grew less agitated. He leaned right in to her, and though he couldn't touch her with his hands tied, he brushed her cheek with his and spoke quietly and gently until her tears had stopped altogether.

Suddenly, Marko was aware of a small whimpering sound, and at first thought it was coming from Sorrel, but quickly he realised that the noise was coming from behind him. He turned, and saw the faint slot of grey in the blackness of the room that showed where the window recess was.

The whimpering was coming from outside, and something

told Marko what was making the sound. Dog. Somehow, the little black hound had heard, or smelled, or sensed where they were, and was waiting outside.

'Dog?' Marko called softly, and the whimpering grew louder. He knew he was right. 'Dog! It's all right. We're here. Sorrel. It's Dog. He's outside.'

He didn't know why it mattered or helped, but it was a small crumb of comfort to Marko.

Dog began to whimper louder, and Marko was wondering what to say to keep him quiet, when all of a sudden the noise stopped. Did he imagine it, or had the pale grey slot just darkened completely? He turned his eyes sideways, using the more sensitive vision to be found there in the dark, something else his father had taught him.

It was hard to tell, but maybe there was someone else out there with Dog, someone blocking the pathetic grey light that filtered into their cell.

For the next five minutes, there was total silence, a silence so profound that though they strained their ears, all they could hear was the pounding of Sorrel's heart.

'What's happening?' Sorrel whispered. She sensed, as Marko had, that something had changed. Not outside, but in the house.

'I don't . . . '

Marko was cut off as the door swung suddenly open. The light coming from behind was weak, but still enough to blind them.

All Marko could see as he blinked and squinted was a figure framed in the doorway.

10

'**W**ell,' said a voice. 'Are you staying in here? Oh. I see. Your hands.'

The figure swept around and about them like a bat flitting through the evening air, and with two sharp tugs the ropes fell from their wrists.

'I think now it is time,' said the voice, and Marko began to recognise it. There was something familiar about the strange intonation, the order of the words.

Marko struggled to his feet. Sorrel stumbled as the numbness in her legs took hold, but the tall figure lifted her up in his arms as easily as if she was made of straw.

'Come then,' he said, and now Marko had it. It was the man from the Leon Bianco, the old man who'd plucked him from the floor when they'd collided, the old drunkard who started the fight raving some silly nonsense about vampires.

He didn't care, it could have been the devil himself in the room, as long as he was going to get them out, and that seemed to be exactly what the old man had in mind. He stooped under the low doorway with Sorrel in his arms, and Marko hurried.

The main body of the house was not in darkness, torches burned from the high walls, and suddenly, in the most awful fashion, Marko had the answer to the question uppermost in his mind. How on earth had the old man simply walked into the house?

Here was the answer. They were back in the large hallway that led to the street. The old man had not messed around. Beppe, the doorman, lay sprawled on the floor, a vast cut opening his belly from side to side. Sorrel shrieked and the old man reached up from under her with his left hand and clamped it over her mouth.

'Ssssh,' he hissed. 'There may be others to come.'

They reached the door, which stood ajar, but as they went, Marko turned to see three more bodies in the large reception room where they'd met Bruno. At least three, each of them still and bloody.

Terror grabbed Marko by the throat, and began to squeeze tight. They were through the door and out in the street, and there, Dog was waiting for them. He leaped up at the sight of Marko, who stopped to ruffle his ears, but the man was striding quickly away down a narrow calle, towards the canal, and Marko followed hurriedly. They were free, but my God, he thought, was this the devil who'd come to free them? He tried to keep up, but the man moved fast, even with Sorrel in his arms.

He turned to Marko briefly.

'Hurry. We must go now,' his voice urgent, and strong.

How old was he?

Marko dimly wondered how a man who looked at least seventy could be so powerful, and move so fast. They climbed down into a small burchiello that was moored to the jetty. The boat bobbed and heaved in the sucking black water, torchlight flickered all around them, sparkling like jewels on the endlessly moving surface of the canal, and then they were gone, as the man pushed them out into the stream and away from number 5696, Canareggio.

11

*T*hey were back on the Grand Canal, at night, just as they had been the evening Marko had arrived, only a couple of days before. So much had changed in that short time, so much had happened, that it seemed to Marko a lifetime had passed.

It was well into late evening, yet there was life on the canal, and in the palazzo overlooking it. Marko watched idly for a while, but Sorrel seemed to be in shock. She sat mute in the covered section in the middle of the boat. Marko sat next to her, but faced the back of the boat, where the old man skulled the single oar through the water, like a natural born gondolier. Only now did Marko see the point of a long scabbard poking from the man's robes. The same weapon which had saved them on San Michele, he knew.

Dog lay in his usual place, keeping Marko's toes warm. Marko wondered which question to ask first.

Who are you?

What are you doing here?

Why did you help us?

But he said nothing, and instead put an arm around Sorrel, who turned and smiled.

'Are we free?'

Marko nodded.

'But what about him?' she whispered. 'Dear God! Those bodies . . . '

She fell silent.

'Here!' the man called to them. 'I put you down here. You will be safe now.'

He began to pull into the far bank of the Canal, and Marko realised with a mixture of relief and fear that he was going to let them go. The relief he could understand. The man killed without compunction. He was obviously some sort of madman, a lunatic. That would explain his extraordinary strength. His father had told him of such things, and now Marko had seen it for himself, but the fear? Why fear? Because there was something about the man that was so . . . comforting. That was the word. Marko realised he felt safe being near him. He'd just marched into a strange house guarded by some very ruthless men, swept them aside, and pulled Marko and Sorrel to safety.

'Wait!' he said. 'It was you. On San Michele. You saved us there, too, didn't you?'

At first the old man appeared not to hear Marko, intent as he was on putting into a quiet little landing stage, quite deserted, but then he looked at Marko.

'You were there?' he said, casually. 'I thought I recognised your girl. I thought she was dead. I am pleased she is not. If you were there, then . . . '

He shrugged, as if to say, what of it?

'I was in another room. But you saved us there and you saved us again tonight.'

'You are not happy?'

'No, no, it's just . . . '

'You killed those people,' Sorrel said, finding her voice. 'You killed all those people.'

'Yes,' the old man nodded. 'Yes, I did.'

373

'You can't do that. No matter who they are. You cannot just kill people so easily.'

There was a long and awful silence, which seemed to be the old man's way of saying, *But I can.*

'You can go, and be safe now.'

He pointed to the bank, but Marko and Sorrel didn't move.

'Wait,' Marko said. 'You have helped us twice, but there's more going on here. We're in trouble. My father is missing somewhere in the city, we have to find him. Sorrel's father is ill and only my father can help. We both need him.'

'What of it?'

He reached with one hand now to grasp a post that jutted from the water by the landing stage, and kept the heavy craft moored alongside the jetty. There was something truly unsettling about it.

'It can't be chance that you've turned up twice just when we needed your help. It's like a miracle, like something supernatural.'

Marko waited for an answer. He didn't get one, but the old man's air of disinterest had gone.

'Why did you kill those men? Why are you helping us?' Marko threw his hands in the air. 'Who *are* you?'

The old man let go of the post he'd been holding and let the burchiello drift into the canal again.

'Yes,' he said thoughtfully, as if changing his mind. 'You are right. I see it all now. I see it all.'

He swished the oar into the water once again, and the boat nosed south.

'I know a safer place,' he said. 'Rest now. Be still, and then we will talk. Sometimes life is like this, that these things happen, and they happen for a reason. It may be that you can help me, and that I can help you.'

So they went, and as they did so, Marko had the strangest feeling that neither his relief nor his fear had vanished, but that they had simply switched places with each other.

12

From high above Venice a pair of black eyes watched the city, seeing her plans unfold. She saw her disciples everywhere, in all the sestieres, and a deep and true knowledge of what she was going to do welled up inside her shrunken white chest.

She smiled in satisfaction.

From her vantage point, nearly touching the stars, her keen vision spotted one of her newest recruits staggering like a drunkard into the gambling house, just as she'd whispered in his ear two nights ago in the forsaken little calle where she'd found him. He'd responded easily to her suggestions, and now she saw three others greet him, and take him upstairs. They pulled off the man's shirt and sat him in a chair, pushing his head down onto a table on which were placed a bowl of blue black ink and various dirty-looking needles.

One of the men wiped a filthy cloth across the newcomer's neck, in a vain attempt to clean it, and then set to, etching out the first letter. A small, neat 'V'.

The man twitched against the pain and the tattooist jolted away, in frustration. He shouted something to the other two who grabbed their victim's arms and shoulders, then got to work again.

Yes, it hurt. But they'd all had it done, and lived.

This one would be no different.

The Queen of the Shadows

A Fairy Tale

Then, one day in the autumn, the peasant girl who had been a princess, had a baby, a beautiful baby boy, and the couple were so happy that the girl almost forgot where she had come from and who she really was.

Winter came early that year, and stayed for a long time, and things grew hard for everyone. The young couple struggled to keep themselves warm, and they struggled to feed themselves, and their baby. The young man tried to sell as much wood as he could cut, but everyone was starving, and no one had food to spare. Door after door was closed against them, until one day, the one-time princess had no choice but to swallow her pride, knock on the great doors of the castle, and ask her father for help. The King had changed, and had become a bitter and vicious ruler. All his people were starving in the grip of the terrible winter, and he either would not, or could not help them.

'Who?' he asked, when they told him his daughter was at the gates. 'Who? I have but two daughters, now queens, and they are far from here in warmer kingdoms, with their good husbands. Whoever the girl is, send her away! She is no queen!'

With that, the girl stumbled away in the snow, back towards her hovel, and her husband and child.

'Oh God! Is there no one to help us?' she wailed, and when no answer came, she cried out again. 'Not even God will help me. The devil would be kinder!'

With that, she collapsed in the snow.

A little time later, she felt a hand at her elbow, and found herself looking into the face of a wizened old man of the woods, helping her to her feet. She was startled, and shrank away from him, for there was something about him that she did not like, but he merely smiled back.

'My dear,' he said. 'I heard you call out. I think you are in a predicament, and I think I may be able to help. I can grant you one wish, and you have my word that whatever you wish for will come true.'

'Is it true?' asked the girl, too frightened to think.

'It is true,' said the old man, nodding. 'Just one wish.'

'Then,' said the girl, 'I wish that my baby and my husband will never go hungry again!'

The man smiled.

'But that,' he said, 'is so easy. Nevertheless, it is done! Go home now, and be warm.'

He walked away into the snow, and the girl was so excited that she never even saw that where the man had walked, he left behind not foot prints, but hoof prints.

She ran the rest of the way home, and burst in through the door to tell her husband the incredible promise she had been given, and she saw that her wish had been granted, for there lay her husband on the floor, and her baby in the cot, with not a breath of life between them.

They would never go hungry again.

FOUR

1

*S*o, tell me. What do you know of the world?

It seemed a strange sort of question, but then this was turning out to be a very strange night.

The old man had rowed them through the narrowest canals in the heart of the city, heading east, and even Sorrel had lost her sense of direction. Somehow though, their dreadful saviour seemed to know exactly where he was going. At last they emerged in more open water, and Sorrel recognised the walls of the Arsenale ahead.

Even though it was the middle of the night the sounds of work drifted over the high protective walls of the military harbour of the city. Inside, carpenters and shipwrights were still working on the Bucintoro for the Doge's procession. Each dreaming of the rewards if they finished in time, and dreading the punishments if they did not.

The boat turned again, and then the old man moored up, leading the way under a low archway, down a stinking alley, and into the abandoned log store in which they now sat.

To their immense discomfort, it appeared that he had been living in this slum for some time. Even Dog circled more than usual, trying to find somewhere clean to rest his belly.

Nevertheless, that was where they now sitting, and while Marko and Sorrel chewed on some dried ham he'd given them, the old man made a small fire round which they warmed themselves, though choking on the smoke, with no chimney. Dog lay on the ground, eyeing the ham enviously. The old man laughed and found a piece for him, too.

'Yes,' he said, talking to Dog. 'You deserve something. You saved your master tonight, did you not? Showed me where they were.'

'Were you looking for us?' Marko said with wonder. 'Were you following us?'

'Not you.'

'Then who?'

'What do you know of the world?' he said. 'What have you seen?'

Marko refused to answer, he had plenty of questions of his own.

'Why did you change your mind? About leaving us just now? You know something, don't you? What do you know? What have you done? Tell us your name, at least.'

The old man swung his gaze from Marko to the fire, to Sorrel and back to the fire.

'I am called Peter,' he said eventually, as though it had been a struggle. 'I am called Peter, but no one has called me anything for a long time. It is not important. Not anymore. And you.'

He turned to Sorrel.

'You are the daughter of Simono Bellini. You are the English girl, but I forget your name.'

'Sorrel. And I'm half Venetian,' she said. Marko smiled at her, she seemed at last to be feeling herself again.

'Yes, yes, we are all mongrels here. Do not be ashamed.'

'Mongrels!' Sorrel spluttered. 'Who do you . . . '

'We are all mongrels. You are half English, half Venetian. I am a mongrel. My father was city born, my mother was a gypsy.

And you?'

He looked at Marko.

'You. You are like me too. Your father is Venetian, but your skin tells me your mother is from somewhere to the east of here. Yes.'

'You know my father?' Marko exclaimed, but Peter ignored him.

'And our friend on the floor. He is the last of us four mongrels.'

Marko grew angry.

'Tell me what you know about my father. For God's sake!'

'Yes. I know your father,' Peter said. 'I know both your fathers, though they do not know me. And I only realised I know who you are in the boat. Something you said about San Michele. Then I recognised this pretty girl!

'My poor children, I must tell you things that are not very good. But your fathers are alive, yes, both of them. The doctor Alessandro, is in prison. In the Doge's palace. He has been accused of witchcraft, of heresy, and will be tried very soon. This is difficult, because I want to talk to him very much.'

Marko's spirits leaped at the news of his father. He had forced himself to believe that he was still alive, but until now, he had not really known. The relief made him want to laugh and cry.

Peter was not finished.

'Yes, this is very difficult. To free him from there I think is impossible, even for me. And I need to talk to him. He can help me, I think, just as he was helping Simono.'

At her father's name, Sorrel began to tremble. Somehow she could not keep her eyes from straying to the long scabbard inside which she knew was the terrible weapon which had taken the men's lives away.

'Please,' she said quietly. 'What do you know about my father? Do you know what's wrong with him?'

Peter shook his head.

'I do not. Though I think I know what has broken his mind.'

This statement seemed to make Sorrel angry, but Marko spoke before she could.

'What? Who?'

Peter turned to Marko.

'You are a clever boy. I think you have listened to your father. He has taught you how to think. It was something that took me many more years to learn. I only used to know how to feel, and that is something quite different. And that is why I ask of you, what do you know of the world? Of hidden things?'

Sorrel nodded.

'But who?' she asked. 'Do you mean the Council of Ten? The Three? The Inquisitors?'

'No. It is much more serious than that.'

'How can it be worse than that?'

Peter raised a hand as if making an oath.

'This is why I say to you; what do you know of life? What have you seen? What do you believe? Because you will need to think again about these things. Do you understand?'

Marko shook his head. It was all too much to take in, let alone understand.

Sorrel whispered quietly, 'I don't understand anything.'

'Then it would be best to tell you a story. It is not a happy story, but it may help you to understand. It will explain things to you, so that you can see that everything is connected, everything.'

2

'*I* am not from Venice,' Peter said, as if it were not obvious. 'I am from a long way away, from a land beyond the forests. Closer to where your mother is from, I think, Marko. I grew up there with my father. My mother, I never knew. My father and I moved about. We did all sorts of things, but most of the time we worked as woodcutters in the deep forests, moving from place to place, until one day we came to a small village. And there I knew that I had known nothing of the world, that I had only seen a small fraction of its joys, and yes, its horrors too. Because there, I fell in love, and there I discovered the true nature of the evil in the world.

'I fell in love with a wonderful girl, a gypsy.' He smiled now, and his eyes twinkled with some distant fondness. 'I know her name, better than I know mine. Sophia.'

He breathed her name, a sigh, and for a while, said nothing more. Then he snapped himself from his thoughts.

'She taught me much. She helped me to understand my father, but in the end, no one could save him. He died trying to save us all. From them.'

His voice had dropped to a whisper, and Marko's followed suit.

'Who?'

'Those who live after death. Those people who are hostages to her great evil, those who come back to take others with

385

them. You would call them, I think, vampyri.'

'Vampires!' Sorrel shouted. 'That's ridiculous.'

Peter said nothing, but slammed one hand into the other in a gesture of anger.

'No, please,' cried Marko. 'Don't listen to her. Please tell us. Please?'

'Marko, don't tell me you believe this. Vampires! What would your father say about thinking something like that? Come on. Let's stop wasting time.'

She began to make for the low door, when Peter swung back towards them.

'Yes!' he roared. 'What would your father say? Now that he is locked in the Piombi? Or your father? Now that he is out of his mind!'

Marko turned to Sorrel.

'Listen to me. Listen. I saw something. Twice. On those men, the ones . . . '

He looked nervously up at Peter.

'The ones I killed?'

Marko nodded.

'What?' asked Sorrel.

'There were marks, on the backs of their necks. All of them. It was a tattoo. There was a skull, and above it, the word vampyri . . . '

'That doesn't mean they're really vampires,' Sorrel said. 'There are all sorts of secret societies in Venice, they often brand themselves with some mark or other. What you saw was probably just that. Not real vampires.'

'You are both right,' Peter said before Marko could answer. 'Yes, Sorrel, there are really such creatures as vampires, but no, Marko, I don't think these men with tattoos are such things. I would know, trust me, I would know. I think they are playing a deadly game of vampires, and yet, there is someone here who is controlling them, someone I have been hunting all my life, ever since that village in the forest. She is an ancient being now, but her intent is terrible, she will never rest. She goes by various names, but I call her by the one I first heard. The Shadow Queen. I have followed her for years, ages it seems to me, and I have found her at last.

'She is here, in Venice.'

3

*T*he fire began to fade as they spoke, and by the time it had died completely, Marko believed every word that Peter told them. There was something in his voice, something about his manner, that compelled him to believe, and so believe he did.

He told them of the years of travelling, fighting the creatures he called hostages.

'Because, you see, it is not their fault that they are what they are. They are taken prisoner, their very souls become hostage to the thing that makes them into these monsters. Over time they have changed, they have become more sophisticated creatures, they have changed their habits, become harder to see, harder to kill, and yet, I have changed too. For when I started, I was only full of horror and hate for these things, but as the years passed I began to understand the old name for them, "hostages", and I came even to pity them. Though that is not to say that I had to stop what I was doing. I could no more stop killing them, than the farmer who kills the sheep with the broken back. It is pity that makes us do so.

'And with every one I set free, there is one fewer to create more. My life has been very long, and I have been very successful. I believe there are very few of them left now, very few indeed. I think I have taken something from the Shadow Queen, over the years, that her powers are growing weaker.'

Sorrel gazed at the old man.

388

'How long have you been doing this?' she asked gently.

'Oh,' said Peter, and his old face cracked into a smile. 'Oh, since I was his age.'

He waved a hand at Marko.

'And when was that?'

'When? The year you mean?'

Sorrel nodded.

'I think I remember that in that following winter we went to a place called Reval. It was sixteen hundred and twenty five.'

Sorrel sat up.

'No,' she said, but kindly. 'You must be mistaken. That would make you well over a hundred years old.'

Peter stood up from the fire.

'No,' he said simply, and picked up the scabbard and the sword within it. 'I know the year, because I had the man put Sophia's name on one side, and the date on the other. That was the year we were married.'

He tipped the end of the scabbard towards Sorrel, as if he was suggesting she pulled the sword from the sheath, but instead he jabbed an old finger towards the date. There it was, embossed in the leather.

1625.

Peter sat down again, and stroked Dog's head, who snuffled contentedly.

Sorrel looked at Marko, her eyes wide with wonder and fear at this strange old man who had saved their skins twice.

Marko opened his mouth, shut it again, and shook his head, thinking just the same as Sorrel. He had to be mad, or deluded, which was the same thing, and yet . . . There was something about him which made them doubt their doubt.

Peter was still, and the fire went out.

4

*T*he old man seemed to be asleep; his head rested on some sacking, his eyes closed.

Marko and Sorrel whispered to each other in the darkness. Dog snored and whimpered alternately. Occasionally his paws flicked and Marko hoped he was dreaming of rabbit chases in sunny meadows, rather than being hunted by foul men through the streets of Venice.

'What should we do?' Sorrel asked.

'God, Sorrel. I don't know. I can't think straight. I'm so tired.'

'I know,' she said. 'But listen, do you think we can trust him?'

'Peter?' Marko lowered his voice even further. 'That depends on what you mean. He could have killed us twice over, and instead he saved us twice over. He didn't have to do that.'

'I know, but he did it as if we were of no importance to him. As if we don't matter.'

'I don't think we do,' Marko said, 'to him. But he's at least a good enough man to save us, since he could. I think we're safe with him. The question is rather . . . '

' . . . whether he's going to help us.' Sorrel finished Marko's sentence, and added, 'And we don't have much time. The procession is tomorrow afternoon; if we don't make peace with Venetia somehow by then . . . '

'Venetia's the least of our problems, I keep telling you.'

'I know. I know.'

'But he said he wants my father's help. At least he's alive.'

'And we know where he is, but . . . '

'What?' Marko asked.

'I'm afraid he's right. No one escapes from the Piombi. They might let you go, once enough years have passed, but Marko, you should know there's usually only one way people leave that place.'

She didn't need to explain what she meant, and Marko's head fell.

'Maybe he *can* help us,' Sorrel said quickly. 'Maybe . . . '

'Maybe,' Marko said, 'he's just an old madman, a murderous old lunatic, and we're just lucky he seems not to feel about us the way he feels about everyone else he meets.'

'I thought you believed what he was saying?'

'I don't know,' Marko said. 'But I tell you this, I'm not sitting here any longer. We're going.'

He sat up, and began to stoop towards the door.

'Where?'

'Yes. Where?'

They turned and saw Peter sitting upright, wide awake.

'Where are you going? To the Piombi? And what would you do there? Against the guards of the Ducal palace? But yes, it is time to go, and if you will trust an old lunatic, then you will come with me.'

After an awkward moment of silence in which Marko and Sorrel realised they'd been overheard, Sorrel found her voice.

'Where? Where are we going?'

'To Giudecca,' Peter said, and jabbed a finger at Sorrel. 'To your house.'

5

The three, Peter, Marko and Sorrel, and the ever present shadow of Dog, crossed the water to the tip of Giudecca. Away to their right, torchlight on the waterfront lit the Doge's palace with a luminous red glow. Marko's heart wrenched, burned with it, burned with the knowledge that just across the water, in the attic cells of that very building, his father lay mouldering in some windowless cell.

Every stroke took them farther away. Peter stood at the back of the burchiello, and this time, on the open water, Sorrel helped from the front with another oar. Marko had tried at first, but couldn't manage the strange standing rowing position that it demanded. Sorrel, to his surprise, was much stronger than she looked.

'Francesco taught me,' she explained. 'Though Father doesn't like me doing it.'

Dog stood on the prow of the boat, sniffing the air, and soon the island approached through the night, which was clear and free from mist for once.

Sorrel stared forwards as she tried to pick out the Ca' Bellini. As they made the headland they ought to be able to see it, taller as it was than most other houses on Giudecca.

At the back of the boat, out of earshot of Sorrel, Marko asked Peter, 'Why are we going here?'

'I have been slow to think tonight, Marko,' the old man

said. 'I have been as slow as my years are long. I have been foolish. I think Bruno or his men will come for her father.'

'Bruno? Didn't . . . ? I mean, didn't you . . . ?'

'No, I did not kill him. He was not in the house when I came for you. Rest assured, I would kill him if he was there. He is the cause of much of this I think. He is deep in all this.'

'How?'

'I do not know that. I have been watching, for many months. I have moved from here to here in the city, watching, listening. I knew that something was spreading through the city like the plagues of old. And all the time, the paths that I followed led me back to this man. Nicolo Bruno. Then I discovered that he is a powerful man, and I began to fear. This is often the way, evil finds its root in the great and powerful; those who cannot be accused, who cannot be deposed so easily. It is another layer of protection for them, you understand?'

'But you think his men will come for Simono. Why? He's just a crazy old man.'

'Perhaps. I was foolish. I have not seen the patterns here. There are still some patterns I do not understand, but I fear for Simono now. His daughter is clever, but she is not with him. We ought to be there. He has only the servants to defend him should they come.'

'No,' said Marko, shaking his head. 'They all left. There's only one, Francesco.'

Peter cursed in a language he didn't understand.

'Then we have been even more foolish. We must hurry. They will come tonight if they have not come already.'

At the front of the boat, Sorrel had discovered the source of her fear.

'Look!' she cried back to them. 'There are no lights. There's the house, but there are no lights.'

Marko tried to reassure her.

'It's the middle of the night, they may be sleeping.'

As soon as the words were out of his mouth, he realised what he'd said.

'My father will not be sleeping,' Sorrel said, and Marko held up a hand to apologise.

As they turned into the canal which led to the house, their worst fears were realised. The front door flapped open in the wind that swung in from the south lagoon.

'No!' Sorrel cried.

They put in, but even before the boat had touched the embankment, Sorrel sprang from the prow. Dog sensed the excitement and leaped after her, and the pair were inside the doors of the darkened house before Peter had tied the boat.

'No!' he shouted. 'It may not be safe. There may be . . . '

Marko ran after Sorrel, and felt the creeping dread again as he watched a man of supposedly a hundred years overtake him in two long strides. As he went, Peter pulled the sword from its scabbard in a single fluid motion, brandishing it behind and above him as if ready to swing it down without warning. The sword seemed to give a sighing sound as it emerged into the night, a swish, that almost seemed alive to Marko. It was as if the sword was singing to itself. Pushing this ludicrous notion from his mind, he trailed into the hall and saw Peter bounding up the stairs to the first floor.

He gave chase, and caught up with Dog, as they hunted from room to room.

Suddenly there was a scream from Sorrel.

'Here!'

It was impossible to tell where the call had come from, but he saw Peter hurrying along the second floor landing, towards Simono's bedroom.

He rushed up, and burst into the room to find Sorrel crouched over a figure, Peter striding round, his sword flashing in the darkness, and Dog skittering here and there, unsure of what to do.

Marko knelt by Sorrel who crouched over Francesco.

He was alive, but seemed badly shaken, and a little blood stained the faded carpets beneath him.

Sorrel lifted Francesco's head and felt her hand dampen. She pulled it away.

'What?' she asked frantically. 'What happened? Are you all right?'

Francesco nodded gently.

'Have they taken Father?' she cried.

The mute nodded, closing his eyes to show pain.

'Who? Where?'

'Wait, Sorrel,' Marko said. 'One question at a time.'

He looked at Peter.

'Can you find some water?' he asked, but the old man seemed to have entered some kind of trance, some fighting state, as he prowled around the room. Marko cursed and turned to Francesco.

'Have they taken Simono?'

The mute nodded.

'Where?'

Francesco shook his head. He didn't know.

'Who? Did you recognise them?'

Again he shook his head.

'Was there a fat man? I mean, a really fat man?'

Once more, the shake of his head.

'He wouldn't come himself.'

Peter stared down at the scene on the floor. He spoke in portentous tones, his blood still swimming with the prospect of violence.

'He would not come himself. She has an army of men to do these things, and he is just one part of that army.'

'Did they say anything?' Sorrel asked Francesco, but again he shook his head. 'Are you all right? Are you hurt?'

Francesco managed to sit up, and put a hand to his neck.

'Here, let me see,' Sorrel said, but Francesco pushed her away, and managed to lift himself onto his master's bed, then he pointed, and thrust his finger, jabbing it, until they understood.

'He means we should go. We should go and find Simono.'

Sorrel grabbed Francesco's hand and kissed it.

'We will. We will. But what about you?'

Francesco waved her away, began pointing again. He indicated the bed.

'He'll be all right,' Marko said. 'I'll find him some water.'

'But where? Where are we going to look for him?'

The question fell into the silence of the room, and no one answered it, at least, not at first, then Peter stepped away from the bed and looked out at the city.

'They are massing. I know her. She is massing her armies, but for that they will need space, somewhere they cannot be seen, while they prepare themselves. I believe they need Simono, that his illness and his genius are all connected to this. And that is where they have taken him.'

'But where?' cried Marko. 'He could be anywhere, the city is so large.'

'No, not the city, I think. It is too crowded, too busy. They need somewhere secluded.'

'Like the islands? Sorrel said.

'Yes, perhaps,' said Peter.

'But there are so many of them,' Sorrel cried. 'They could

be anywhere.'

'No.'

Peter and Sorrel turned to Marko, who stood at another window, that looked south across the lagoon.

'No. Not anywhere. I know where they are.'

They followed his gaze, and there, near the horizon, they saw what Marko had seen, what he'd seen on his first night in Venice. Bonfires on a distant island.

'Tell me, Sorrel,' he said. 'What is that place? Does anyone live there?'

'My God,' she whispered. 'You're right. That's Lazaretto. No one lives there. Not any more. No one even goes there, not even fishermen.'

'Why not?'

'Because it's the old the plague island. Everyone shuns it now, but during the plagues it was where the sick were sent. It has awful stories, terrible memories. If you became ill with the plague you were sent there. If you were still alive after thirty days, they let you come back. Very few ever did. Since then it's just been empty. No one goes there.'

'No?' Marko said. 'Well, there's someone there now.'

Peter stooped to look out of the window more easily, and clapped a hand on Marko's shoulder.

'Yes, you are a clever one,' he said. 'Yes.'

And was it their imagination, or even at this great distance, staring at the flickering light of those remote fires, was it possible to see figures leaping and dancing in front of the flames?

They readied themselves to go.

They left Francesco in Simono's bed. He kept pointing, urging them to hurry.

They found some blankets and coats. Sorrel went to her

room, and changed into one of her own dresses.

'That's more like it,' she said.

'Yes,' said Marko. 'Well, it is black.'

Peter went to the kitchen and returned with two long knives for Sorrel and Marko, putting them into their hands as carefully as if they were precious and delicate jewellery.

Dog ran around, and then sensing they were ready to go, stood stock still.

'So,' Peter said. 'She is massing her armies, and in reply, we have ours. Us three.'

Dog gave a single short bark, and Marko laughed.

'I think that means four,' he said.

They left, and as the burchiello slipped away from the bank, a face watched from the first floor window. Francesco had got out of bed the moment he heard the front door close, and now stood far enough back not to be seen.

He rubbed the back of his neck. Yes, there was a little blood, but it was not so bad really. The funny thing was that he could still smell the ink they'd used. That blue-black ink. He wondered if they got it from squids.

He made his way downstairs.

'*H*urry!' Peter whispered through the darkness.

As they passed under the balcony of the beautiful Venetia's house Sorrel cursed silently, and for a moment thought she heard the strains of singing floating down to them, but she knew she had to be imagining it; it was the small hours of the night now, the dog watch.

She spat into the water, and made a promise to herself. If they found Simono, and rescued Alessandro, she would stop Venetia from hurting her family again. No matter what it took.

Sorrel rowed until her arms burned and her shoulders with them, and then she collapsed into the centre of the boat. Marko tried the rowing motion again, and having watched Sorrel made a better go of it, but in truth, their great speed came from Peter, who silently worked at the stern of the boat, repeating the forward and back snake of his arms again and again, with no sign even of breathlessness. Occasionally he flicked his arms a couple of times to the side to correct their steering, but otherwise he powered them as though the devil was behind them, and the black water of the lagoon shushed past on either side like rapids in a fast-flowing river.

Sorrel gazed up at Peter, and moved cautiously down the length of the boat to the covered section towards the stern.

'Who are you?' she said quietly. She did not mean that Peter should hear, or that he should answer, but it seemed his hearing was as powerful as his arms.

'You don't mean that, do you?' he said. His voice sailed easily to her against the slight breeze from their movement forwards. Marko caught his words, and half turned, trying to hear and row at the same time. 'You don't mean that. What you mean, is *what* am I? Yes?'

Sorrel nodded.

'I'm sorry. I don't mean to be rude, but you are . . . impossible. The things you do. I have worked it out. You must be about a hundred and twenty five years old. No one lives that long, and even a thirty-year-old man could not do the things you can do.'

She stopped, and having been asked no question, Peter did not answer. Sorrel swallowed hard.

'Are you,' she said, 'the devil?'

Peter laughed, a thick rasping croak.

'Why not an angel? No? I could be either I suppose, but you choose the bad one. No, I am only a man. It is not me that does these things, or perhaps I should say, I was not born this way. I was a woodcutter's son, as I told you, but . . . it is the sword. The sword has made me this way.'

'What do you mean?'

Peter didn't slow his rowing in the slightest degree, nor did he move his eyes from the firelight dancing ahead of them.

'I think it is the sword that has changed me. I noticed only after a few years. It is very subtle. Every time I used the sword to release the soul of a hostage, I felt something. At first I thought it was the thrill of it, and I felt guilty for this, so I didn't speak of it. I was ashamed that I felt pleasure. A pleasure, of sorts. But then, as I continued to use the sword, I looked at what it was that happened, and I realised that it was not something I was feeling in my heart, but a real, physical thing. Every soul I freed, every life I ended, seemed to give me something. I felt something enter into me, and I found I was stronger.

'At first I thought it was a wonderful thing. This sword, you see, was made in Turkey, years ago. Very many years ago. And it was made to free hostages, to stop this plague of death. It was giving me the strength to do it, and so I was delighted with the power it gave to me, to help me in my fight. But then, one day, as my wife and I travelled through a high mountain pasture, we stopped to make camp for the night. The sound of cowbells drifted up to us from the meadows below, and we were suddenly very, very hungry, and eager to eat, and sleep.

'It was coming on to evening, and though it was late spring, there was still snow on the highest peaks. The sun was setting, and I remember that two larks were circling in the air, calling to each other, some way below us in the valley. It was, I think, the most beautiful moment of my whole life.

'I called to Sophia, and bid her look at the larks. "They are like us, my love," I said, laughing. "Still so much in love." And then I turned to look at Sophia, and I saw something I had not seen before. I saw lines on her face, even through her dark gypsy skin, deep lines around her eyes. "We are getting old, Sophia," I said, and then, she turned to me, and she said, "Yes, Peter. I have been getting old for some time, but no, not you . . . You are still a young man." And then she lifted one of my hands to her face, and put my other hand on my own face. "There," she said.'

Peter stopped for a moment, his mind far away, but still his arms pumped like the devil. Marko had stopped rowing altogether to listen, and his oar trailed in the water, as Peter resumed his story.

'Still I didn't believe it at first, but next time we came to a town, Sophia bought a looking-glass to prove it to me. "How long have you known?" I asked, and she said she'd been watching it for many years. "Haven't you noticed the miles we've travelled, my dear?" she asked. "The summers that have come and gone?" I shook my head. I'd been too busy fighting, too busy doing what I thought I had to do, and I had not seen my wife grow old. My own face, in the mirror, was that of a young man, while Sophia told me that she had spent over forty summers with me, since we'd met.

'And then I knew that what the sword had done to me was a dreadful thing. That it is evil to me, even though it does good for others. That the sword was giving me the lives of everyone it killed, making me stronger, slowing down the rate at which I grew old. It must have done the same to my father too, at first, though then he stopped using it for years, until that final time . . . But still he may have been much older than I thought.

'So I went on fighting, and following wherever I heard word of that hideous and ancient beast, the Shadow Queen. And at last I think I have run her to ground.'

Sorrel's voice trembled, like the water of the lagoon.

'And what about Sophia, what happened to her?'

Peter finally stopped rowing, and let the boat drift for a time.

'She died,' he said simply. 'She died the following year. She was not so old, but not so young either. "The miles have worn me down," she said, and one day she went to sleep and never woke again. I made a pyre and burned her so that she would never be able to become one of my enemies, and then I took her ashes back to that mountainside, where I had first learned the truth. I scattered them from the highest spot I could find, and, do you know, I saw those two larks again, circling in the sunset. And I knew that we were still like those two love birds, even though she had gone ahead of me.

"'Ah,' I said, to the mountain winds. 'Is this, perhaps, death?' And I thought I heard the winds answer me. 'Yes,' they said. 'This is death, but not for you. Not for you.'"

With that, Peter grasped the oar tightly again, and the boat surged forwards.

'It won't be long now,' he said, but neither Marko nor Sorrel knew if he was talking about their arrival at Lazaretto, or something else, entirely.

7

*L*azaretto, the plague island, was suddenly right before them, looming out of the darkness, bathed in a glow as if all the devils of hell were stamping their feet and making bright sparks fly from their heels.

'Silence,' Peter said. 'Be still. Lie down in the boat.'

Marko and Sorrel did as they were bid, and Marko gently stroked Dog's ears to make sure he was happy and calm.

Even Peter knelt by the stern now, in case he cast any kind of silhouette that might be seen from the shore. With one hand he flicked the oar from time to time, just enough to keep the boat moving silently across the water. He turned the nose of the burchiello, so they were moving alongside the bank of the island, a short distance out. They approached the harbour, dozens of small boats and one or two larger ones lay moored to a series of landing platforms sticking out of the black water, but Peter rowed on and left it behind, obviously seeking a more private place to make landfall.

Marko gazed at the vague shapes he could see in the darkness.

'Aren't there any houses at all?' he whispered to Sorrel.

'No, only ruins. It's been a long time since the plague. No one comes here. It's an evil place.'

It took little more to convince Marko of that. As they glided past the dark banks of Lazaretto, they caught the occasional whiff of bonfire, and the comparison to hell was even easier to make. He pictured how it must have been during the plague time. Ten thousand people on this tiny speck of an island, and all dying or dead from the Black Death. He saw it all before him; the crush of the people, the awful sights. The noise of groaning and wailing. The bark of dogs, the circling carrion birds overhead. Some going mad from the horror of it all, running and screaming like the damned, throwing themselves into the lagoon, swimming for the mainland, either to drown, or be drowned by the guards on watch.

Marko was lost in these awful images, when suddenly there was a flash of golden sparks, a shower that chased upwards into the starry sky. Someone had stirred one of the big bonfires into life and sent its seeds skittering into the air, picked out like shimmering stars among the thick plumes of black smoke that were almost invisible in the darkness.

With this tumult of fire, a loud hullabaloo rose from the island, something between a moan and a cheer, and with it, although they could not yet be seen, Marko and Sorrel realised for the first time just how very many people there were at this infernal pageant.

The hair rose on the back of Marko's neck, and Dog gave a low growl.

'Yes, Dog,' Marko whispered. 'I feel it too.'

8

*T*he shower of sparks flared again, throwing wild swirling patterns into the night sky, mixing with the thick smoke, forming a living tower that roared upwards with great and terrible fury.

Marko and Sorrel cowered in the bottom of Peter's boat, as he swished his oar purposefully through the water, propelling them without a sound a little distance off shore. Dog lifted his head from between Marko's arms, sniffing the air. He whimpered quietly, and Marko knew how he felt, because he felt the same; an all-consuming fear was spreading through his bones and his belly. He turned to look at Sorrel in the wavering light thrown from the massive bonfire and saw the same fear reflected on her face too. He watched Peter and on his face he saw nothing. Not one emotion played across the old man's features, not fear, not doubt, not excitement, not even interest. The only thing Marko could read there was a look of concentration, and he knew that Peter was entering that state they'd seen him in at the Ca' Bellini. He was preparing to act, and Marko almost felt sorry for whoever stood in his way.

Another loud cheer rose from the place of the fire, and Marko turned his head back to the island, as Peter started edging the boat closer inshore, looking for a place to land, unseen. The din was lifting up from beyond the ruins that lay near the banks of Lazaretto, a crumbling silhouette of brick, stone and wooden beams, behind which they would be well

406

obscured from view. Peter suddenly made his choice and with a flick of the oar they were heading into shore.

'There's no jetty,' Peter called. 'Marko. Leap ashore and pull our nose onto the mud.'

Marko turned to argue, then saw the look on Peter's face. It told him there would be nothing to be gained by arguing and so, pulling a grim face, he crept to the prow of the burchiello and waited to time his jump ashore. Here the land didn't fall straight into the water like almost everywhere else in Venice, but was a natural shallow beach of mud, weed and gravel, and Marko wanted to avoid the worst of it if he could.

He jumped, and as he did, he heard a low chant begin to sound from the devilish party beyond the ruins. The boat glided into the mud behind him and he turned and gave it an extra tug to get it safely ashore, its nose on the land and its stern gently afloat still. Peter strode down the length of the boat and pulled Sorrel with him, leaping as far over the water as he could.

'Safely done, Marko,' he said, striding past, and without hesitation headed for the ruins nearby.

Sorrel found Marko in the darkness.

'Where's that dog?' he whispered. 'Where is he?'

'He seems nervous.'

Dog stood at the grounded prow, hesitating. He lifted one front foot then the other, dithering, sniffing the air again, the whiskers above his eyes twitching.

'Come on, Dog,' Marko whispered. Then, a little more firmly, 'Come on. You'll be safer with us.'

Dog waited a moment more, then finally leaped from the boat, landing right at Marko's feet.

'We'd better tie it up, just to make sure,' Sorrel said, pulling the painter from the prow, searching in the darkness for somewhere secure to tie the rope.

Marko thought for a moment about being stranded on this

hellish place, and then decided he didn't want to think about it anymore.

'Where's he gone?' he said, meaning Peter.

'He went that way,' Sorrel said, pointing away to the left slightly, to a dark shape that they knew was the outline of the ruins, and they followed. It was hard going, though they only had a short distance to cover. The ground sank beneath each footstep, a sticky, smelly, sucking mud that seemed to want to hold them back, but as much as Marko and Sorrel would have loved nothing more than to run in terror from their destination, they knew that their only path lay ahead.

The chant rose higher and higher with every step they pulled from the mud, and as it did so, another great shriek and wail was thrown into the night. Marko looked up to see a bank of sparks scurry into the night, and watched with fascination as the clouds of swirling and ducking sparks flew in crazy patterns. He thought they seemed to be forming a picture, some kind of definite shape, and then, in a moment of complete madness, he thought he could see a face in the sky, a giant face of orange and white fire, leering down at them all, grinning and laughing.

It was the face of an old woman.

Marko pulled his eyes away from the sky and looked to see if Sorrel had seen, but she had her eyes on the ground, intent on finding an easier way to the ruined buildings.

'Sorrel . . . ?' Marko called.

She stopped and turned, keeping her feet where they were. Marko glanced nervously at the sky again, at the tower of flame, then thought better of it.

'Nothing,' he said. 'Let's find Peter.'

She nodded.

A few more strides brought them into the lee of the buildings, and a voice hissed at them from the shadows.

'Here, you clumsy fools! Here!'

There was no mistaking Peter's thick accent, and with relief they picked their way over to where he stood in the shadow of a crumbling doorway. Dog had already arrived and seemed for the time to have transferred his allegiances to Peter, almost as if he knew his chances of survival might be greater there.

'Let's take a look at our friends, shall we?' Peter said, grinning in a most unnatural way. Marko and Sorrel exchanged a look, but followed obediently enough as Peter led the way into the ruins. He turned and set off up a rickety flights of wooden stairs that still clung to the interior wall of the old place. Peter could not have moved faster up the stairs if he had flown like a bird, but Sorrel, and Marko behind her, picked their way gingerly, testing each dilapidated step as they went. And they were right to, for the fourth step from the top collapsed the moment Sorrel put her toe onto it, falling with a crash into the dark below. She reached for the next and finding it good, practically jumped for the top.

Marko hurried after her and seeing the missing step clearly before him had soon joined Peter too.

They were outside. The upper storey of the building had gone, leaving a low misshapen wall on three of the four sides, and a floor of dubious safety. Peter seemed unconcerned, and strode to the naked edge of the building. Marko and Sorrel again tiptoed after him, and then immediately both shrank back a little as they gazed down at last on the scene that had been waiting for them since they left Giudecca.

It was an orgy, a riot, a party, a festival and carnival all in one. In the centre of an open space between the ruins of what had once been the centre of Lazaretto the bonfire blazed. It was enormous. Its core was a great white and red heart of fire that stood higher than two men. From here the vast flames licked up like the tongues of mad dogs, sending out the billows of sparks that Marko had seen from a distance. The fuel for the fire was wood from the many old buildings; floors, and panels and beams and joists. Marko wondered how many nights they'd been out here, and realised that the devils were slowly burning the place into nothingness.

Around this centre, every conceivable activity was taking place, as well as a few that were inconceivable to Marko. The whole scene reeked of evil, sadism and vile happenings. Figures leaped, dancing round the fire, as well as numerous other smaller fires. They seemed drunk, whether on wine or the intoxication of their badness, Marko could not guess. Elsewhere, other bodies lurched round the open tops of vast wine barrels, almost bathing in the stuff in their eagerness to drink. Other figures groped and grappled shamelessly. Marko counted at least three fistfights, and on the far side of the square from where they looked, a brawl between half a dozen men was reaching some kind of conclusion. Marko watched with appalled terror as one of the men, a huge brute, maybe seven feet tall, picked up a hunk of fallen stone and dropped it onto a figure lying prone beneath his feet.

The dancing continued. Many of the figures were half naked, women whirled and danced in the firelight, their skin gleaming with sweat despite the cold and damp of the winter lagoon. Another fight broke out between two men, one of the dancing women trying in vain to pull them apart. She gave up and went off to join a group round a barrel of wine, while the two fighters drunkenly took it in turns to exchange blows.

Many of the revellers, Marko now saw, were wearing carnival masks, some plain and simple white affairs, others were ornate and splendid, with gold trimmings that flashed in the firelight. And others wore the demonic face of the three who had attacked them at Bruno's house in Canareggio.

From all sides, the chanting continued, rising and falling as more voices joined then gave up the tune. It was a baying, formed of syllables of nonsense. Yet somehow the chant spoke of the baser, more depraved things in life.

410

Marko glanced at the sky, at the tower of sparks, half fearing to see that dreadful leering face again, but with relief he saw only fire, this time.

'What's that?' Sorrel asked. 'What are they saying?'

Marko was about to ask her what she meant but then heard it for himself. The chanting from the rabble had finally taken on a meaningful sound, a single word, broken into three stunted syllables.

'Vam-pi-ri! Vam-pi-ri!'

The chant reached a crescendo as more and more voices joined, all now in perfect unison.

'Vam-pi-ri!'

'My God!' cried Marko. 'Are they all vampires?'

'What do we do?' Sorrel whispered to Peter.

He seemed not to hear, but stood, his toes inches away from the drop to the ground, heedless of everything. He gazed out over the debauchery.

'Is it safe to stand there?' Sorrel asked. 'Anyone could see you.'

'No one will see us here,' Peter replied. 'We are standing in the darkness and their eyes are blinded by the fire. Besides which, their minds are on other things. We could walk right down there and they might not even see us.'

Sorrel noticed he said 'might not'.

'So what do we do? What are we waiting for? Simono must be here somewhere.'

'Indeed,' said Peter. 'But first, we must see. We must see if She is here. Because I might just take on all of these people, but there is only one I want to kill.'

Marko glanced sideways, and stared at Sorrel. His eyes were wide, and he dared not even voice Her name, but instead, he mouthed three words to Sorrel. She stared back at him, reading his lips.

'The Shadow Queen!'

9

'*T*here!'

Peter pointed, and following his stiff rod of an arm, Marko half expected to see the Shadow Queen herself, but far across the square, a group of figures had emerged from a building. They were distinct immediately, merely from their gait. These figures were not swaying drunk or lurching with hungry desires, but sober. It was apparent that they were about some business. There were six of them, but two were instantly recognisable; the first was the mass of flesh they had met the day before, in whose house they had been locked up, Nicolo Bruno. He made his way slowly, waddling into the square, looking about him as he went.

With him was an older man, thin, with a shock of white hair above his pale face.

'Father!' cried Sorrel. 'Oh!'

'Still,' Peter called, harshly. 'You can see for yourself that your father is well enough. He is alive.'

'I know,' Sorrel said, 'but . . .'

'But?' Peter said. 'Do not worry. I want him alive, as you do. Because he will lead me to *her*. Do you understand?'

Neither Sorrel nor Marko were sure they understood anything.

'What are they doing with him?'

'I'm not certain,' Peter said. 'They have something with

412

them. Look! Do you see the man beside Bruno. He is carrying a box.'

'Yes,' Marko. 'It's the same one, I think. The one we found on San Michele.'

'And what is in it?' Peter asked.

'We don't know. It's something that Sorrel's father made for Bruno, but we didn't have a key. We didn't open it.'

'Why didn't you break it open?'

'I don't know,' said Marko, 'but I suppose, we thought we might be able to use it to find out something about our fathers from Bruno. If we had broken it . . . '

'Perhaps, but you should know better than to walk up to a stranger and expect good things to come your way.'

Marko thought about asking Peter if he counted himself as a stranger, but decided not to.

'Look,' he said. 'Something's happening.'

Marko was right. As the small group, with Bruno in its midst, made its way into the square, people fell still and silent. They seemed to be heading towards the great bonfire, and as they went the chanting and dancing, the drinking and the shouting were all gone.

Everything was suddenly quiet; the only noise came from the terrible crackling and roaring of the fire.

Bruno stood, impassive, as a crowd formed around him in a rough semi-circle. Marko began to count the figures now that they were still. He had counted three hands worth before he lost his place, but knew that it would have run into the hundreds. From every dark door and alley, more robed figures stole into the night, every one as silent as the last.

It was an eerie sight.

And then Bruno spoke.

From their bird's nest viewpoint, at such a distance, and

with the noise of the fire to obliterate the sound, the watchers on the roof heard nothing of what Bruno said.

He lifted his short fat arms up, to the sky, as if waiting for something. Then he pointed at Simono.

Simono himself stood, seemingly unaware of everything occurring around him. He made no move to fight or to run, and none of his guards seemed concerned that he would do any such thing.

Now Bruno pointed at the man with the box, and he stepped forward, holding the box high above his head.

There was a low murmur from the crowd, the first sound they'd made since Bruno had walked among them.

Bruno waved his hands, the crowd erupted, and a short but loud roar of pleasure burst out. Then, with great showmanship, Bruno rummaged inside his voluminous robes and pulled out a small object, holding it up for all to see.

'It's a key,' Sorrel whispered.

'They're going to open the box.'

They did open the box, but there was another shock for Marko and Sorrel first.

One of the figures who had followed Bruno into the firelight, swathed and hooded in a sumptuous velvet cloak of dark green, stepped forward. They'd paid this mysterious form no heed, but now, as all eyes turned to the figure, and as Bruno bowed low before it, the figure swept the hood of the cloak back, and Marko and Sorrel were horrified to see Venetia's beautiful blonde hair and face emerge.

10

*I*t took a moment to believe what they were seeing, but there could be no doubt, even at this distance.

'My God!' Sorrel whispered. 'She's caught up in all this too?'

Venetia flicked the clasp at her neck, and the cloak fell to the earth, revealing her in all her glory. She was dressed in a shimmering green gown that swept the ground. Her hair was held up in a high stack, exposing her long white neck, and her delicate ear lobes, from which hung sparkling rings of gold.

'Is she a prisoner too, like Father?'

Marko shook his head slowly.

What followed was a bizarre pantomime, some kind of dumb mime-show that was played out as if for the entertainment of Marko, Sorrel and Peter.

The crowd seemed uneasy, restless. Bruno stood impassive again, resting his hands on his hips, his legs slightly apart. He stared at two men who carried a long narrow table into the arena, and set it down before him. Another man brought a smaller table of the same height, and set it by the head of the first one. Bruno placed the box on this smaller table, slid the key inside the lock, and with a flick of his wrist, unlocked it.

He whipped the lid back and even from their distant viewpoint, the watchers from the ruins could see a gleam and glitter as of jewels.

There was a murmur from the watching crowd, a growl of desire and expectation.

'Money?' Marko wondered aloud. 'Diamonds?'

'I'm not sure,' Sorrel said. 'Look.'

She nodded, and they watched as Bruno lifted something out of the box, and turn towards Venetia.

'The tiara!' Sorrel gasped. 'So he *did* finish it after all!'

'So why did she ask you about it? Outside your house?'

'Playing games with us. Evil games.'

They watched as Bruno took a step towards Venetia, and then, placed the tiara on her head, a vampire's coronation.

It was an awesome moment. Everyone was silent, the only sound the roaring and cracking and spitting from the bonfire. The tiara was spectacular. It shimmered like diamonds through the darkness, and was composed of five rows of glittering glass droplets, one above the other, which danced to the slightest movement Venetia made.

But Bruno wasn't finished. He beckoned a man forward from the crowd, and pointed at the table. The man sat on the table, then swung his legs up onto it and lay down. Bruno turned to Simono, then, who stood without moving, until Bruno took a short angry step towards him. Then Simono, as if sleepwalking, stepped over to Venetia, and reached up to the tiara, and after a moment pulled two of the droplets loose from her beautiful crown.

Expecting Venetia to fly into a rage, Marko was stunned to see her smiling serenely as Simono turned to the man on the table. What happened next perplexed Marko even more. The man opened his mouth and Simono began to fiddle inside, pushing and poking the glass droplets into the man's mouth.

Now Venetia approached, slowly, languidly, and as Simono backed away, she moved in, bent over the man on the table, and kissed him on the neck.

A vampire's kiss. A kiss that hinted of death to come.

She stepped back, and Sorrel gasped as Venetia's face came into view once more. Her mouth dripped with blood. Luscious red blood, which she wiped away gracelessly with the back of a hand.

The man got to his feet, unhurt by the kiss. Ignoring the blood trickling down his neck, he stood up on the table and punched his fists in the air. He roared like a beast from the wild forest, and was answered by a deafening roar from the onlookers. Something twinkled in his mouth.

'What did your father do to him?' Marko asked.

'I have no idea,' Sorrel said, then she grabbed his arm. 'Look! They're doing it again.'

She was right. Another volunteer had stepped forward and was lying down on the table. Again, Simono, in his dreamy way, began to select another pair of droplets from the tiara. He turned to the man, who had already opened his mouth in expectation.

Venetia stood nearby, and even at this distance, Marko and Sorrel could see her eyes wide with passion, her chest heaving with excitement. They watched Simono bend to his task.

'Is he helping them?' Sorrel asked. 'He can't be helping them.'

Peter turned to her.

'He has no choice,' he said. 'Don't be afraid. It is time to act.'

Nothing Peter could have said could have scared them more than those five words. What were they to do? What could they do against these dozens of lunatics and monsters?

'Don't be afraid,' Peter said again. 'I have work for you two to do. Take the dog with you. It is simple work. When you are done, come and meet me at the place where we tied our boat. I will have your father and we will leave.'

'It's that simple?' Marko asked derisively.

'If you do your part well,' Peter answered. 'Yes.'

'How will you get her father out of there?'

'Let me worry about that.'

'And what's to stop them just following us?' Sorrel asked.

'That's your part of the work. Go now, take the dog with you. They will be busy for a while down there, the box holds many of the things. That will give you plenty of time. Go back along the shore to the harbour, where we saw all their boats. You must sink them, every last one. Then come back to our boat, and I will meet you there.'

He clapped a hand on Marko's shoulder, spoke softly.

'Can you do it?'

Marko nodded, but Sorrel began to protest.

'But I want to come with you and help find Father.'

'No,' said Peter. 'You don't want to come with me. Go and do your job well and that will save your father. You understand? You must sink every boat and ship. Yes? Now go!'

11

'*I* don't like it,' Sorrel said.

They hurried as fast as the soggy shoreline would allow, making their way back to the harbour they'd passed on their way in. Night was drawing on, and they were exhausted already. Neither even dared to think about the task ahead, and Sorrel couldn't shift the feeling that she should have gone towards her father, not away from him.

'It's the only way,' Marko said. 'We can't help Peter. We can't fight, or do the things he does. He's like a ghost, a phantom, the way he moves silently and quickly.'

He paused, his eyes straining in the darkness. 'Look, I think there're boats ahead. Come on!'

They ran on, and found firmer land which rose to become a proper embankment from which the old planks of the jetties ran into the water.

'We can't do it,' Sorrel said breathlessly.

'We have to,' Marko said, but their task seemed impossible. Before them lay two dozen small boats, two rascone, large transport boats designed for the lagoon, and, worst of all, a small ship.

'We might be able to sink the boats, given all night,' Sorrel said, 'but we'll never be able to sink that brigantino.'

She pointed at the ship.

'Well, we have to, somehow,' Marko said. 'And we have to

do it fast. It'll soon be dawn.'

Sorrel saw the glimmer of light on the Eastern horizon. It was only a pale gash in the curtain of black, but it was there.

'They won't stay past daylight. We have to work fast.'

So saying, Marko bent to the task. He tried the nearest boat, starting small. It was a burchiello, very much like Peter's in design. Marko tried to lift its nose, to tip the stern under, but couldn't move it more than a few inches. He gave up, and waded back to the shore, then returned, carrying a stone from a ruined building. It was as large as he could carry, and he smashed it down onto the bottom boards, trying to force a hole that would let water in and sink the craft. He didn't even make a scratch.

He tried a different boat, a small skiff, and this time began to push its side down towards the water. He managed to get the lip of the side to touch the water, and a little sloshed in, but then the boat's weight pulled it back upright.

Desperately, he turned to Sorrel.

'I might be able to do it this way, but it's going to take all night just to do one! Look at them all! And I can't even sink one!'

'Wait a minute. Wait,' Sorrel said. 'We have to think. There must be a way.'

But they couldn't see it.

Marko sat on the wooden planks of the jetty, defeated.

'If only my father were here,' he said. 'He'd know how to sink a boat.'

'But how?'

'He always says there is a way to do everything. But you just have to see it in a different way.'

'We need to get water into each boat, and we have probably less than an hour to do it.'

'No, we don't!' Marko said suddenly. 'We don't have to sink them all, we only have to make them useless.'

'But how?'

'The oars! The sails! We just have to get rid of them all.'

'Yes! That's it. That's it. But what about the big one?'

'I've got an idea for that too,' Marko cried. 'Come on! You start with the boats. Get all the oars and bring them to the brigantino. Throw them up on the deck.'

'Wait!' Sorrel said, 'Supposing they left someone aboard it?'

They looked at the small ship that lay at the centre of the flotilla of smaller craft. It was a low decked beast with higher poop and fore decks, and two-masted. There was clearly a cabin at the rear, and hold space to the fore. There were no lights aboard, but they crept up to it slowly.

'We don't have time for this,' Marko called, and taking the plunge, jumped aboard, and disappeared into the cabin at the rear.

Sorrel waited nervously, at any moment expecting to hear the sounds of a struggle, but a minute later, Marko emerged, grinning from ear to ear. In his hands he held aloft two weighty oil lanterns.

'We can do it,' he shouted to Sorrel. 'We can do it!'

Sorrel clapped her hands.

'Yes!' she called. 'Wonderful!'

'You get the oars, and the sails too, if you can. Throw them onto the deck here, and we'll have a bonfire of our own. I'll get started, then come and help you.'

Sorrel turned and waded to the nearest boat. Marko dodged back into the cabin, looking for flint and steel, but Dog stood on the jetty, watching the pinprick of light bobbing in the water, a little way off in the lagoon. He wasn't sure, but he watched it carefully. It seemed to be coming towards him.

12

Marko dragged a chair from the cabin on deck. It had a wooden back, but a small upholstered seat. He kicked the chair into pieces and laid them at the base of the foremast of the brigantino. In a moment more he'd ripped the covering from the seat of the chair and pulled out the wadding inside; a piece of hessian over a mass of horsehair; dry and perfect tinder. He smashed one of the oil lamps over the wreck of the chair, soaking the fabric and the wood alike.

He felt their luck was turning. Not only had he found the two lamps, but also a wonderful little tinder box, well made and ready to use. With his first strike of the steel he sent a shower of sparks onto the oil-soaked mess and within moments the whole thing was alight, dirty oil-fuelled flames licking up against the well-seasoned wood of the mast.

Sorrel appeared beside the ship and threw an oar onto the deck. Marko's plan was a good one; once the deck had caught, everything else she threw there would go up with it.

'Well done!' she called to him.

He laughed, knowing it could work. But he had to make sure, and with great care, he pulled out a burning chair leg from his fire, picked up his other lamp, and skipped back under the low doorway of the cabin. A second fire in here would finish the ship for good.

Outside, Sorrel found new strength as she sped from boat to boat. The oars were heavy though, and very long, so unwieldy once out of the water. She could carry a pair together if she was careful, but wished that Marko would come and help her soon. She made her way back to the brigantino and threw the oars on deck. Marko was still inside the cabin, and she turned and ran down the landing stage. She untied every boat she'd finished with, shoving them with her foot towards the lagoon, wrenching sails from masts, throwing oars into the water, dragging whatever she could towards the fire on the ship.

Then she turned, and screamed.

A man stood behind her, a lamp in his hand.

'Oh!' she said with relief. 'It's you. What are you . . . ?'

Without warning, he swung a fist and caught the side of her head. She reeled, but didn't black out. She sank to her knees and felt Francesco's arms scoop her up from the planks of the jetty, and carry her off.

Dog began to bark furiously, and snap at Francesco's heels. Francesco kicked out viciously, connecting with Dog's ribs, and he backed off, growling fiercely, but too scared to attack.

Francesco strode away with the dazed Sorrel in his arms, heading inland, straight towards the vampire camp.

Dog barked again now, louder and louder, running in circles, madly.

In the cabin, Marko was pleased with his work. He'd made a big pile of furniture and old cloth, and drenched it with the oil from the second lamp. He set it alight and was just backing out of the cabin when he saw Dog going crazy on the jetty.

Panicking, he looked frantically for Sorrel, and then saw the figure of a man, with a girl in his arms. They were a hundred paces inland perhaps, and then they disappeared round the corner of the first building.

'No!' Marko shouted, and without thinking, he and Dog were off in pursuit.

They thundered down the jetty, past the destruction wrought by Sorrel, and within moments rounded the corner of the ruins. A long dark street, lifeless for two hundred years, led away from them. Broken windows and shattered doors gave every house a haunted look. There was not a light to be seen anywhere. But at the far end, Marko saw the glow from the huge bonfire, and there, the silhouette of a man carrying Sorrel at speed, heading for the festivities of the vampire orgy.

He doubled his speed, and knew he was gaining on his quarry, but too late. As Marko put his hand on Francesco's shoulder, they emerged into the uproar of the square. Francesco spun round and recognising him, Marko hesitated.

'What are you doing?' he shouted, but Francesco dropped Sorrel to the floor and swung out at Marko. He parried the blow, but it knocked him off his feet.

The revelry in the square was reaching fever pitch. There was no sign now of Bruno, or Simono, or Venetia. With horror, Marko saw that their little altercation had been noticed. A few men, and a couple of drunken women stood nearby, but broke off from their wild cavorting.

They pointed, laughing as Sorrel and Marko got to their feet, backing away from Francesco, who suddenly pulled the neck of his shirt down, spinning round to show them his tattoo. With shock Marko understood. Francesco had been made one of them, had been called by the Shadow Queen, unable to resist her summons.

Francesco pointed at Marko and Sorrel, trying to get the vampires to understand that they did not belong, but his mute gestures and thrashings only reduced the others to more laughter. He turned back on the two and made a lunge for Sorrel, who dodged. Marko saw his chance and threw his fist, connecting with Francesco under his ear. He staggered, and they saw their chance to run, but now the others understood, and closed in on them. Hands grabbed at them from all sides, and though they fought back, it was in vain.

Suddenly the hands began to falter, and then they saw Dog, leaping and biting, snarling and snapping at those holding them. They tried to grab Dog, but he was too fast and slipped between them all like a twisting eel. They fell back, clutching their bites, still trying to kick at Dog, and missing. Dog had gone wild, and Marko and Sorrel looked about them, desperately weighing their chances.

They were still unnoticed by the mass of the people, but then they saw another flurry among the huge crowd. There was some kind of commotion in the midst of the crowd, and it was heading their way. There were screams, and shouts of terrible anger.

Two figures spilled from the throng. The first was Peter, swinging his sword in deadly arcs with just one hand. People pressed in on all sides, and yet kept their distance, watching the singing point of the sword. Peter's black cape swirled, and Marko had the strangest feeling looking at him. He was almost impossible to see, in the confusion and the darkness, with his black cape and the movement of his sword-arm, he seemed as hard to pin down as a ghost.

His left hand trailed behind pulling the second figure along. It was Simono. Peter held his right hand, and tugged him along like a mother dragging a small child.

'Run!' he shouted, breaking through the edge of the crowd. 'To the boat!'

Marko and Sorrel didn't need to be told twice, and with

Dog's vicious attack aiding them, they wriggled from their assailants' grasp, and broke for the side of the square.

'That way!' called Peter, and they saw a gap nearby, next to the ruined house they'd stood in earlier.

Now the shouts from behind grew more fierce, and they knew that the whole crowd was getting wind of what was happening.

Marko and Sorrel ran ahead, and behind them Peter came with Simono, fending off attackers with great sweeps and thrusts of his sword that threatened to take out five of them in a single swipe.

They rounded a corner and saw the boat, and seconds later Marko and Sorrel had it floating in the shallows.

Peter had lifted Simono in his arms and ran into the water, almost throwing him in.

'Start rowing!' he shouted, and turned to whisk his sword out again, as the first vampires splashed into the lagoon after them.

Marko and Sorrel took up their positions at the stern and prow of the boat rowing as hard as they could. Dog swam through the water and scrambled aboard. Simono lay as if in a trance in the bottom of the boat, while in the shallows, Peter sent several more vampires splashing into the lagoon.

'Help!' screamed Sorrel.

Peter and Marko turned at the same time to see one of the vampires had bypassed Peter and was grappling with Sorrel at the back of the boat.

It was the seven foot monster Marko had seen earlier, and he had Sorrel's arms pinned to her side. He pulled her head to one side, and exposed the long white softness of Sorrel's neck. He leaned in, his mouth opening, and Marko saw something gleaming where his teeth should have been.

Marko took two long leaps down the boat, ducking under the covered section, and emerged with another stride at the stern.

The monster heard him coming, and turned, leering at him, showing a mouthful of teeth, with two long canines that sparkled like jewels. Without thinking, Marko swung his fist straight into the man's mouth and felt something break and shatter. The force of his momentum down the boat was enough to set the vampire reeling, but he rose quickly, and sent Marko tumbling with a single blow to the head. Suddenly Peter was there, and seizing the vampire by his arm, hurled him backwards towards the water. As he fell he lunged forward and sank his teeth uselessly into Peter's arm, where there was the sound of glass cracking; he fell back into the lagoon, as Peter put an end to him with the point of the sword.

He picked up the oar from beside Sorrel, and began to row.

With a few strokes, they were at sea, and though more pursuers tried to wade after them, the water was too deep. Some began to swim, but were soon left behind as Peter resumed the incredible speed he had displayed earlier that night.

By now, the whole bank behind them was filled with the raving mob, wailing and shouting in anger and hate. Then there was a sudden movement among them, and they began to run along the shore.

'They've remembered their boats,' Marko said.

'That is well enough, if you did your task well enough.'

Neither Marko nor Sorrel answered.

'Tell me,' Peter barked. 'Did you do what I told you?'

'Marko set the big one alight. We took care of the rest,' Sorrel said. 'We burned their oars, and sails.'

'All of them?'

There was a brief silence.

'Most of them.'

Peter grunted. He steered them out into the lagoon now, heading back for the city, but they could see the results of Marko and Sorrel's handiwork as they went. The brigantino had caught fire very well, and was a floating inferno, its crazy reflection burning in the water. The fire was so intense that it had set light to the landing stages alongside, and from there the fire had spread to many of the other boats.

'Maybe they're all burned,' said Sorrel. 'Maybe there won't be any to follow us.'

She picked herself up and ran to sit by her father. She put her arms around him and said nothing, but closed her eyes and listened to his breathing. His eyes were open, but whether he was drugged, or in a trance of some other kind, he seemed to take in nothing.

'Maybe,' said Marko, to himself, rubbing his fist. Small bits of whatever had been in the man's mouth sparkled in the bottom of the boat. He picked a sliver up.

It was glass.

He held it up to Peter.

'Look.'

Peter nodded, and then Marko did an extraordinary thing.

He laughed.

Sorrel stared at him, but then smiled with him.

'Glass teeth!'

'Glass!' laughed Sorrel.

'The fools!' Peter said, cursing.

'They've just been playing at being vampires. And Venetia playing too!'

'It was as I thought,' Peter said. 'They are not real vampires, but men making the pretence. And yet, despite this silly game,

428

there is still her presence. They are under the control of the Shadow Queen.'

'Not Bruno? We saw Bruno down there, didn't we?'

'Bruno is her puppet. That is all.'

'But . . . what were they doing?'

Peter didn't answer.

Marko struggled to understand.

'So Sorrel's father made these glass fangs for them? Why?'

'What are they for? To be like the vampire they wish they were. Why did he do this for them? I don't know that yet. But we know that She is behind it.'

'Was . . . she there?' Marko asked. 'On the island?'

'No,' Peter said. 'I did not see her. But she is nearby, I think. Somewhere. Her smell is always in my nostrils these days. And you are wrong to laugh at her. I think perhaps there is a more deadly side to this game. Here, let me see that glass. There.'

He pointed to the bottom of the boat and Marko saw another piece resting in the bilge water. He picked it up and showed it to Peter, who inspected it closely, still without pausing his rowing.

'Look,' Peter said. 'Look carefully.'

Marko examined the broken glass. It had been the form of a canine tooth. The tooth was unnaturally long, or had been, but the tip was broken where it had shattered against Peter's arm.

'Useless,' Marko said. 'It's like you said. They're just playing at being vampires.'

'Perhaps,' Peter said, 'they're playing. But maybe their games are deadly. Look closer at the tooth.'

Marko looked again and saw what Peter meant. The tip of the canine had broken, but inside he now saw a hollow channel, leading to a small reservoir inside the glass. A tiny drop of some thin green liquid still clung to the inside of this bulb.

'Be careful,' Peter said. 'It is poison.'

Marko gasped, and Sorrel turned from nursing her father, hearing the fear in his voice.

'How do you know?'

'Because some of it has entered the wound on my arm.'

Marko leaned forwards and saw a small puncture near Peter's wrist. The point of the glass tooth had entered and snapped off inside. Suddenly Marko remembered that he'd punched the vampire, shattering the teeth under his fist. He hurriedly searched the backs of his hands for cuts, but could see none. But the puncture in Peter's wrist was all too obvious.

'We must have a look at it,' Marko cried. 'It may have left something in you.'

'It did,' Peter said, 'but there is no time to waste. We cannot stop now. We must row to safety.'

He turned and looked back at the island. Daylight was edging its way across the lagoon, casting a hazy light on Lazaretto.

'I think I must ask you to help row, Marko,' he said. 'They have found at least one boat that can sail.'

Marko turned and saw what Peter had seen. First one sail, then another nosed out from the burning harbour, and turned towards them.

'There is a good wind for them,' Peter said calmly, though it was news that terrified Marko. 'There is a good wind, and they can sail faster than I can row. You must help me.'

Marko did was he was told and skipped down the boat to the prow where he tried to match Peter stroke for stroke, but as he did so, he felt his arms turn to aching lead, and he knew that they would be caught.

13

They rowed for another five minutes, as the sun cast a pallid gleam across the dark water of the lagoon. Marko rowed until his arms burned, and Peter kept up his unstinting pace, but there was no doubt, their pursuers were gaining.

Without warning, Peter suddenly fouled a stroke with his oar. He recovered, but a few strokes later, did it again.

Sorrel watched him, fear growing in her.

'Peter,' she called. 'Are you all right?'

He didn't answer, but after a few more strokes, he stopped altogether. He bent double and took a few deep breaths. Marko turned from the prow, feeling their pace drop, and with alarm, saw, for the first time, the signs that Peter was mortal, after all.

'It's the poison, isn't it?' he cried, but Peter did not answer.

'Why don't we sail, too?' Sorrel called to him.

Peter slowly straightened himself, and shrugged.

'I do not know how.'

'But I do,' Sorrel said. 'Marko! Come and help me. If we can get this rigged up we'll outrun them yet.'

She sounded so sure, and yet, even as she began to fumble with the canvas of the sail cloth, she saw a single boat not far behind them.

Marko scrambled down the boat, stepping past Simono, who stared sightlessly into the brightening air. He mumbled

431

something, which Marko didn't catch, too busy with Sorrel and the rigging.

'We have to get the sail out and hoist it with this.'

She put a rope in his hands.

'Wait until I've tied it, then pull when I tell you to.'

Sorrel tugged the sail from its berth along the deck of the burchiello and swung it across the boat. She hitched the gooseneck, and fiddled clumsily with the block, but at last she turned to Marko and almost screamed.

'Pull!'

The sail began to totter up the mast, immediately catching the morning breeze and filling. Marko felt the tug of the boat beneath him as the sail caught the wind, and they began to pick up speed once more.

Sorrel turned to Peter, who'd been watching her with a smile on his face.

'What is it?'

'You remind me of someone. You are clever.'

Sorrel was about to reply, but then saw with horror that the following boat was almost upon them.

'We were too slow!'

They could see the faces in the boat. Three men, all leering and calling to them, two unmasked, but one hidden behind that devil mask Marko had seen before. Dog began snapping and barking, sensing trouble.

'We can still make the island before they reach us,' Sorrel cried.

'Good,' Peter said. 'I prefer to fight on land.'

He didn't seem in any state to fight at all, but he was still their only hope of survival.

'There,' Sorrel cried, pulling the sail in tight, gathering more wind and turning slightly for the shore of Giudecca.

Away to her right, not far, she could see her house, but she headed for the closest point of land, where a jetty pointed into the lagoon to greet them. The following boat was almost on them, and as Peter's burchiello crashed into the jetty, the other boat slammed into their stern.

Marko and Sorrel began to half carry Simono up onto the quayside, and he seemed able enough to follow, still muttering under his breath, while Dog leaped and ran, ran and leaped, trying to be useful and getting in everyone's way.

'What did he say?' Marko asked.

Sorrel held her father tighter.

'Are you all right, Father?' she whispered to him, but all he would do was mutter more of his nonsense.

'What did he say?'

Marko strained to hear what Simono was saying.

'Pentamerone!' Sorrel said. 'He said, Pentamerone.'

Peter turned and backed down the boat, as the three Vampyri clambered aboard and crept towards him. They were unarmed, or so Marko thought, but then, as they dragged Simono to safety, he saw the man with the mask draw a huge curving dagger from behind his back. Suddenly all three came charging at Peter, who moved backwards down the boat, ducking under the awning, pushing his way past the sail and boom. Then he fell, and the man with the knife was on him, but Peter fell with the sword pointing up like a spike, which the man could not avoid. The other two came on more cautiously and Peter took his chance, struggling to his feet, unhurt. He waved at the two, and they edged backwards. Another wave of the sword and they edged back again, falling off the boat and into the water, where they began splashing noisily.

Peter sheathed the sword, and was about to turn to climb

ashore when one of the men in the water managed to grab the side of the boat, and more by chance than design, tipped him into the water beside them.

'Come on!' Marko called to Sorrel, and they hurried to the water's edge to see Peter struggling with the two men.

They were a writhing mass in the water, and unable to do anything to help, Marko and Sorrel watched horrified as all three sank beneath the surface. Ripples and bubbles broke the water for a while and at any moment they expected to see the figures break again, but for a long time, there was nothing. The surface of the water grew still, and then there was Peter, pulling himself up to the light, gasping for air.

He struggled to the jetty where Marko and Sorrel helped him from the water.

'Those men . . . ?' Sorrel began, but one look at the deadly gleam in Peter's eyes told her they wouldn't be coming after them.

Peter rolled onto his back, staring up at the pair of them, then sat up and looked around, still choking from the water.

'But where is your father?' he spluttered.

'Oh no!' Sorrel turned and saw Simono in the distance, heading away down the side of Giudecca.

'Where's he going?'

'He's heading home,' Sorrel said.

'It won't be safe there,' Peter said. 'We have to find somewhere to hide. Somewhere safe.'

But Sorrel was already running away down the embankment.

'Wait! Father! Come back!' she called as she ran.

Marko helped Peter to his feet.

'Are you all right? The poison?'

'I will fight the poison,' Peter said, and began to hobble

after Sorrel, giving Marko no choice but to follow.

As they caught up with Sorrel and Simono, they were a few paces short of the steps to the Ca' Bellini. Sorrel was pulling her father by the arm, trying to get him to stop, but the old man was in a crazy trance, and calling that single word.

'Pentamerone! Pentamerone!'

'Father,' Sorrel cried. 'Please. We have to leave the house. We have to find somewhere to hide. Please. The Shadow Queen will find us if we stay here, her people will find us and take you away again. Please!'

She sobbed and tugged and fought, but Simono would not be stopped. He broke free and ran straight into the house, crying out madly.

All three gave chase, following Simono upstairs, where he disappeared into Sorrel's room. There they found him, lying on the floor, his eyes staring wildly into space, his hand clasped around a book. Sorrel's copy of the Pentameron.

'Pentamarone,' he muttered to himself, almost peacefully now, as if he had found what he had been looking for.

'I don't understand,' Sorrel sobbed. 'What's wrong with him? Why does he keep saying that.'

'Simono,' Peter said, 'We have to leave. The Shadow Queen knows this place now. She will come back for you.'

At that name, Simono stirred slightly. He turned to the three, and for a second, his eyes almost focused to meet theirs. He proffered the book to Peter.

'Pentamarone!' he whispered.

Peter stepped forward and took it.

'Thank you,' he said.

Poking out of the side of the book was a slip of paper, tucked between the pages.

Something about it tickled at Marko's brain, like a face seen in unfamiliar circumstances that takes time to place. He had seen that piece of paper before, or maybe not that one, but another like it.

He reached inside his pocket and fumbled, pulling out the strange letter from his father, that he'd been clutching for weeks. The paper was thick, a dark cream colour, almost yellow, with small brown flecks in it.

Peter turned to face him, letting the book fall open at the page marked by the paper.

'There is a story here,' he said.

He read the title aloud, his eyes wide, his voice low.

'The Queen of the Shadows.'

He put the book down, and held the paper up, showing it to Marko and Sorrel, who was drying her eyes on the corner of her dress.

'My God! Is it true?"

Marko held up his letter, and they saw that they were like identical twins, their colour, their size, even the folds in them were the same. Peter read what his half of the letter said, and then handed it to Marko.

'Here,' he said. 'You had better read this. And then tell me, who is Venetia?'

Marko almost grabbed the letter from Peter's hands, and Sorrel leaned over his shoulder, and with quickly beating hearts, they realised they were looking at the first half of Alessandro's letter. Somehow the two pages of the letter had never been posted, had been separated, and while Sorrel had found the second half, they realised that in his madness Simono had hidden the first in Sorrel's storybook.

Now they held the missing beginning in their hands, and with it, the answer to their nightmare.

THE LETTER

My Dear Lady,

I write to you with a heavy heart, because what I have discovered pains me to my very soul. It has been, I am unafraid to say, a delight and a pleasure to have made your acquaintance over the last months since my arrival here to tend the health of my good friend Simono Bellini. Your obvious concern for his well-being touched me greatly from the start, and I must admit, your great charms have been a comfort to my weary limbs and sad eyes. To gaze upon you is to know the true meaning of beauty, and I am ashamed to allow that those private walks we took around the island on the rare occasions when my patient and his daughter both slept lingered long in my memory.

You are the most beautiful young woman in the world.

Or so I thought! And now, with my heart hanging in my chest like a withered apple on a barren tree, I write to you, Venetia, in the full and true knowledge of who, or rather what, you are.

I know what you are doing to Simono, for I saw you. Yes! I saw you steal across the space between the houses like some awful bird of prey, and suckle the sleep from him. All my own dreams and desires are gone now.

You have killed them, and replaced them only with terror, and fear.

The Queen of the Shadows

A Fairy Tale

From that time on, the girl's heart began to shrink and to shrivel. She left the little hut and walked deep into the woods, hidden from all.

The years passed, and the young woman began to grow old, but still she could not forget her child, and she moaned and wailed to herself as she stole through the forests. And there, she changed. She became old and terrible, and no one ever saw her again.

Still she could not forget, and one winter's day, as she herself approached death, she cried out into the forest once more.

'Oh Devil! I know it was you who took my husband and my child. Come back now! Here! I demand it, and I am not afraid of you! Come back now and I will give you anything you ask for, only give me back my child!'

Then, she fell in the snow, and her eyes closed.

She woke, as she felt a hand at her elbow, and there was the old man again, though not a day older than when she had last seen him.

'Very well, Devil,' she said. 'That was a good trick you played on me. Well, now you can wave your magic again. Give me back my son, and I will do anything you ask. Anything at all. Only give him back to me.'

The old man smiled, the same smile he'd smiled all those years before, and his mouth opened.

'If I am to give you your son,' he said, 'I must have something in return. I must have a soul like his, as pure and noble as his.'

'Very well,' said the old woman. 'I will bring you a soul.'

'No!' said the old man. 'Not just one soul. The soul of your son is worth that of many wicked men, and there are nought but wicked men in the whole of this wide world. For your son, you will have to bring me many, many souls. Will you do it?'

The old woman stared into his eyes.

'I will. But tell me, how many souls do you need?'

'One hundred thousand. Not one less.'

The woman laughed, and as she did so, the snow shook from the treetops and the ground shook.

'Very well. Not one less.'

No one saw her again, but they say that she keeps her bargain to this day, moving in and out of the trees, like a ghost, like a spectre, like a shadow. The Queen of the Shadows.

And they also say, that where she moves, death follows close behind.

But, it's only a story, and an old one at that, an old, old story.

FIVE

1

*T*hrough the tiny streets and alleys of Venice they ran, a motley gang. Two old men, one powerful but wounded, the other tottering along, his eyes wide, his mind stretched beyond the point of reason. With them ran a young man and woman, and at their heels scampered a flea-bitten mongrel, wondering what all the excitement was about.

They had fled the house on Giudecca, knowing it was no longer safe, and rowed across the canal to the main part of the city. Abandoning Peter's boat in the chaos of the moorings, they headed inland, to the very heart of Venice.

Marko's mind was a whirl. Venetia! What was she? Was it possible she was the evil that Peter had come to destroy? Could she really be the Shadow Queen who Peter ranted about?

There were many questions still unanswered, even more than before, but there was no time to consider them.

They hurried on.

'Where are we going?' Marko asked Peter, but the old man did not reply at first. Simono trotted along obediently enough beside Sorrel, too worried to care, as long as they were going somewhere to hide.

'Where are we going?' Marko asked again, tugging at Peter's sleeve. He seemed to be showing few ill effects of the poison, but had become even more taciturn than usual. Marko glanced at Peter's arm. Was he slowing? Was he struggling?

Marko wasn't sure. He grabbed Peter by the elbow, forcing him to stop.

'Please. What are we going to do? Are we going to hide somewhere?'

'Yes,' Peter said, 'but not somewhere quiet. We are going to ground in the very heart of the beast. We will go to the White Lion, and take a room, but first, we need a little local aid.'

Peter turned to go, but Marko pulled him back again.

'Wouldn't it be better if we got Simono to the White Lion first? He needs to rest.'

'There's no time. We need protection. And I . . . '

He stopped, and Marko took his chance.

'Then I will come with you, and Sorrel can take her father to the hotel. We can meet them there. Please. The old man is dying on his feet.'

It was true. Simono was as a ghost walking now, his skin pale, his eyes staring, the pupils reduced to tiny dots.

'If we push him any more, he'll die. You may not care about that, but I do.'

Peter turned and stared at Marko, and for a brief moment Marko thought the terrible old man was going to strike him, but the anger passed.

'Yes,' Peter said quietly. 'I care. Very well. Sorrel, take your father to the White Lion, and get a room. Use a false name. Call yourselves Tomasini. You may have to pay well for a room, they will probably claim they are full. Do you have money?'

Sorrel shook her head.

'Then take this,' Peter said, and fishing inside his cape pulled out a bag of coins.

'It's all I have, so don't lose it.'

With that, Peter stalked on, and Marko was left stranded between him and Sorrel, who stood mystified with her father.

'Hurry!' Marko said. 'We'll find you there by the name of Tomasini.'

'But I want to stay together,' Sorrel said passionately, and nothing she could have said could have given Marko more hope.

'And I want to make sure Peter comes back. That he helps us find my father. Don't worry. Just go, and go quickly. We'll join you soon. And take Dog with you. He'll only get in the way.'

He hurried after the retreating back of the old man from the land beyond the forests.

'Dog,' Sorrel called, 'Come on. Dog! Come here.'

The small mutt dithered between Sorrel and the rapidly vanishing Marko, then looked to Sorrel again.

'Dog. Come here!'

With that, Dog turned and trotted over to Sorrel, who held her father by the hand, while he stared at a wall nearby as if it was the farthest reaches of space.

2

*M*orning had lifted itself over the city's head and it was a fine, if cold, day. A fine day for the Doge's procession and all the other festivities that would begin at noon, and sweep the whole of Venice up in an orgy of excess.

For now, the city held its breath, as behind every door and window people made their final preparations for the carnival.

'Where are we going?' Marko asked Peter as they hurried through crowded streets.

'There!' Peter declared.

They were in a merchants' quarter, and stalls and shops lined the narrow streets. A canal, no wider than a single boat, ran along the side of the alley in which they stood, and people pushed by on either side, while others pressed into the stalls, haggling over everything. Peter nodded his head, so slightly that it was almost imperceptible, but Marko saw what he was looking at.

A few feet away was a workshop selling masks for the carnival. They hung inside the windows and on displays by the doorway, a mask seller ostentatiously flourishing one mask and then another, offering them to a pretty lady to try on, smacking the paw of a small grubby boy who fondled the goods when he thought no one was looking. The shop was surrounded by customers, and Marko understood Peter's plan.

'With the masks we'll . . . '

Peter nodded.

'We'll be invisible, like everyone else.'

'But they're very expensive,' Marko whispered, suddenly remembering that Peter had given all his money to Sorrel.

'We won't need money,' Peter said, and immediately Marko was filled with all sorts of horrible thoughts at what Peter might be about to do, but the old man turned to him and smiled, as if reading his thoughts.

'All I need you to do is fall in that canal. Can you swim?'

'Not very well. I . . . ' Marko began, but Peter was in no mood for discussion.

'Good,' he said, and with that, he took a step towards Marko and without another word sent him flying backwards into the water. Marko went under for a second, and began splashing and clawing his way to the surface.

He broke free and spluttered. The water was freezing, and rank, and he'd swallowed too much of it.

'Help me!' he choked as he went under again, then giving a mighty kick, surfaced. 'Peter! Help me!'

A pair of hands grabbed one of his wrists, and he felt someone trying to pull him out.

'I saw him,' someone cried.

'Saw who?'

Marko called again.

'Help me!'

More hands grasped his wrists and arms, and now at last he began to claw his way up the side of the canal, the pavement a few feet from the water's surface. He landed spluttering and shivering on the stones, and rolled over to see a large crowd gathered around him. He rolled onto his front and choked out the last of the water from his lungs. Peering between the legs of the crowd of would be rescuers, he noticed a tall figure in a black cape striding away down the calle, back towards the Grand Canal.

'Are you all right, my boy?' said a kind old man, his face full of concern. 'That was quite a trick you pulled.'

More than you know, Marko thought.

'Yes, I'm fine. I'm fine.'

He scrambled to his feet.

'I'd best get home and dry out before I freeze.'

And with that he pushed his way through the crowd, making his apologies, offering thanks, and then he broke into a run after Peter, who had already disappeared round a turning in the street.

Sword or no sword, Marko thought, I'm going to kill him.

*S*orrel and Simono sat in their room at the White Lion. A fire roared in the grate and Sorrel felt warmer than she had done for days.

The house had indeed been full, or so the landlord had claimed, but the sight of five whole ducats had made him change his mind. With great grace he had begged Sorrel and the strange man with her to wait ten minutes, and then after the sound of an argument had risen to the level of shouting and banging doors, he had returned and shown them into the best room on the second floor, overlooking the canal. The room had obviously been recently occupied, but whoever had been staying there had clearly lost the argument.

Dog turned circles on the carpet, trying to find the right spot to satisfy him, but every time he settled, he would suddenly leap to his feet again, and start circling once more.

'Dog! Stop it! You'll wear a hole in the floor.'

Dog took no notice. Sorrel sighed. She went and sat by her father, who perched on the edge of a big bed, staring into space.

He had not said a word since she had found him, other than 'Pentamerone'. She held his hand. It was clammy, and feeling his forehead, she knew he was feverish. His pupils were no more than dots, and his breathing fast and shallow. She stared at his face, from a few inches away, and found it hard to see her father there. It was as if he was already dead, already taken from her, and she had forgotten his face, because somehow his face before her looked nothing like her father. It had been the same when her mother had died. A face becomes meaningless once the life behind it has gone.

She buried her own face in his shoulder, throwing her arms around him, and began to cry.

There was a stirring above her head, and she looked up to see her father looking at her with his gimlet eyes. For the first time in months, he seemed to be trying to focus on something, on her.

His mouth opened.

'My child,' he croaked, and with that, his eyes closed and he fell back on the bed.

4

*I*t took Sorrel an awful, long time to realise that her father had not died, but that the most wonderful thing was happening. He was sleeping.

His breathing was so slow as to be almost nothing, but as Sorrel laid her ear against his chest, she could hear the gentle rattle of Simono's lungs. Then the tears came even more quickly, and she rested like that for many minutes, until she was sure she was not imagining it.

In sleep, her father's face began to take on some normality once more, and without those mad eyes to distract her, she could even hear his voice as if he was talking right there and then.

Sleep. The only cure for his disease, and he had found it at last, away from Venetia's influence.

There was a knock on the door, and without warning, two masked men burst into the room.

Sorrel shrieked.

Peter removed his mask and laughed.

'Peace!' he said. 'We were just hiding our faces.'

'And you nearly scared me to death!'

She boxed Marko's ears, who pushed her away as best he could. Suddenly she stopped, and grabbing his wrist pulled him to the bed.

'Look! He's sleeping. Sleeping! Isn't it wonderful?'

Peter joined them.

'This is very good,' he said. 'Very. The rest will do him much good, I think.'

'Oh!' Sorrel said. 'Peter. I bought this with some of your money as we came to the hotel. I thought . . . I thought it might help.'

She hurried to the table where she picked up a small green bottle.

'It's called teriaca,' she said to Peter, who took it from her, a puzzled look on his face.

'It's for the poison,' she explained.

'I thought you didn't think it was any use?' Marko said. 'That it was a charlatan's gimmick?'

Sorrel shrugged.

'It didn't help my father sleep, but maybe it can help counteract the poison in Peter's arm.'

Marko shrugged. He turned to Peter.

'It might be worth trying. But do you drink it, or rub it on?'

'I don't think it will help me,' Peter said, and handed Marko the bottle. Ignoring him, Marko pulled the stopper and sniffed it, as he'd previously done in Sorrel's room.

Again, his nose wrinkled.

'It's got such a smell,' he said. His face creased into a frown, and he took another sniff. 'But there's something about it. I think I've smelled it before.'

'Yes, you did,' Sorrel said.

'No, not then. More recently than that. Wait!'

He dug into his pocket and Sorrel gasped as he pulled something out.

'Do you still have that?' she said, seeing the broken glass teeth in Marko's outstretched palm.

'It's interesting,' he said. 'Father would love something

452

like this.'

He held it up to his nose and tried to smell it.

'It's no good. Thanks to Peter all I can smell on it is canal.'

But Marko wasn't finished, and while Sorrel watched him, and Peter sat down on a chair, muttering, Marko hurried to the window, holding the tooth to the light.

'There's a little left.'

He dried the tooth with the hem of his shirt, then placed it on the table. By the grate, he found a slip of paper spill used to light the fire, and took it to the table. Placing the glass tooth on the paper, he took off his shoe and holding it by the toe, gave the tooth a smart crack with the heel. There was a minute splintering sound, and he quickly lifted his shoe away and smelt the paper.

'Here!' he said, offering it to Sorrel.

'I can't smell anything,' she said. 'Much.'

Marko offered it to Peter, who waved him away with a lazy hand.

'It's teriaca. Only not quite the same.'

'How can you be so sure?' Sorrel asked.

'This is what I do for my father,' Marko said. 'I mix his potions. I know how to tell one from another by smell, and colour, and certain other things. I'm telling you, what was in that tooth, that bit Peter, is teriaca, or something like it. Maybe teriaca with something else added.'

Then finally Marko made the connection.

'That's why it's not the same!' he cried. 'This isn't teriaca. It's something very like it, and we smelled it on San Michele. In the priest's room. This is the smell that was in those bottles.'

Sorrel understood, saw the picture at once.

'So that's why the teeth went from my father's workshop to

Father Fei. He must have known how to mix the poison, and seal it into the fangs.'

Peter sat in an armchair by the window, but listened intently. He too saw the connections spreading out across the city, and began to see the deadly purpose behind all the charades that the Shadow Queen had made.

'But what does it do? Sorrel asked.

'I don't know,' Marko said. He looked at Peter. 'How do you feel?'

Peter shook his head.

'I don't know. I didn't think it was poison. From that tooth.'

'But how do you feel?'

'I feel nothing. I feel . . . tired.'

There was a note in his voice which Marko found hard to recognise, but then he knew what it was. It was surprise.

'I feel tired,' Peter said. 'And that is not something I have felt for a very long time. Not since . . . Not since I used to spend a whole day in the forest, and swing an axe to cut down a tree, and drag the logs home with Sultan, my horse, and get home after dusk, and sit by the fire while my father drank too much. That was tired. That is how I feel, like I am going to go to sleep. Maybe for ever.'

His head hung, and his shoulders slumped. He ran his hands through his hair and if Marko had not known Peter better, he would have thought he was weeping.

Sorrel stared first at Peter, then at Marko.

'And that stuff is in every set of teeth that was in that box?' she whispered. She turned to look at where Simono lay on the bed, softly snoring. 'Oh Father, what have you done?'

5

Sorrel stroked her sleeping father's hair. Marko gazed out of the window at the Grand Canal, watching the fine boats make their way down towards the lagoon. Everywhere people in masks and the finest clothes jostled, a constant stream heading towards San Marco, and the piazzetta, to watch the arrival of the Doge in the Bucintoro, the magnificent ship which would bring him to his palace and to his rightful place at the head of the city.

Peter stirred in the chair.

Suddenly he rose and kicked the chair, sending it tumbling across the floor with a clatter.

'What is wrong with me!' he cried. 'I must act. I am so close!'

Marko rushed to Peter.

'Be still,' he said. 'We don't want to attract attention to ourselves.'

Peter ignored him.

'I must act. But instead we are sitting round nursing our wounds. What is wrong with me?'

'Is it the poison?'

Peter shook himself.

'It does not matter. What is wrong with me? I must act!'

'You mean to kill Venetia?'

'It is something I had not expected,' he said, nodding.

455

'Wherever I have gone, I have been hunting the old woman. She seems frail and pathetic, but she commands great power. She is an awful being. And I have followed her, but always she has been an old woman. I thought her power was weakening, but it seems I have underestimated her. She has found a way to become young again.'

'Venetia is the Shadow Queen?' Marko said. 'That's not possible. She's a young woman.'

'A young and beautiful woman, yes?' Peter said. 'Who has ensnared everyone she has met with her great beauty. Yes? Did you feel it too?'

Marko tried to hold Peter's gaze, but failed, feeling Sorrel's eyes on him.

'Yes,' he said quietly, looking at the floor. 'Yes, I felt it too.'

'Indeed. As did your Simono. And Alessandro too.'

'No!' Marko cried. 'That's not true!'

'You read it for yourself, Marko,' Peter roared. 'You read, in your father's own writing, the delight he took in walking with her. And you had in your own possession, that half of the letter that speaks of her true nature. Your father discovered the truth. He wrote it in a letter, but somehow the two halves were separated and lost. Yes?'

'But how? Sorrel, where did you find that half of the letter? The half you sent to me?'

'In Alessandro's room. He must have written it, but never sent it to her. Then they went missing, and I found it on the floor of his room. My father must have taken the letter, dropped half of it, hidden the other half.'

'Why would he do that?'

'It must have been during one of his worst spells of madness. He didn't know what he was doing, but perhaps he did really: deep down his mind was trying to make me see the connection to the Shadow Queen. To that fairy tale. Maybe even to Venetia.'

'But Venetia only arrived in the city . . . '

'Around the time my father grew ill,' Sorrel said. 'My God! Is it true?'

'It is true. She is the Shadow Queen. She has found a way to make herself young and beautiful again. She has used your father, and in doing so has caused his terrible illness. Sorrel! Do you understand? She stole your father's sleep. And with every night she flew into your house and sucked the sleep from him, she grew a little younger, and a little stronger.'

'But my grandfather died of this! And others of my family!'

'Then she has been coming here for many years, whenever she has needed to free herself of the passage of time. I never knew this. I never knew, but I see it now. It is like I am with the sword. It has extended my life way beyond that which should have been mine. And this foul witch has been doing the same thing with your father, and his father before him, and so on and so on. Now we must find Venetia, and I will destroy her, if I can.'

If, thought Marko. Peter was usually so sure of everything he did. Why was his belief deserting him now?

'She's easy enough to find,' Sorrel said. 'At noon the Grand Procession for the new Doge will start. He arrives at San Marco and is taken to the Ducal Palace, and from there, he will gaze upon the ladies parading before him. The one he judges most beautiful will have the honour of sitting beside him to watch the Flight of the Turk and for the rest of the afternoon. Venetia will be among those ladies. That's why she wanted the tiara from my father, to wear at the procession. To make sure she won.'

'Something tells me she will win anyway,' Marko said,

thinking of those lovely eyes, that delicious skin. Yes, he'd been fooled like every other man who'd met her. Like Nicolo Bruno, like Simono, like his own father.

Peter snorted.

'And then, she'll be in striking range of the Doge, with all her foot soldiers waiting to bite anyone who comes close enough. Pushing this poison into everyone of them.'

He smashed his hand across the mess on the table, sending the fragments of glass teeth spinning to the wall opposite.

'And what then?' Sorrel asked.

Neither Marko nor Peter answered her, for neither of them had an answer to her question, but then another voice spoke into the silence, and Sorrel whirled round to see her father sitting up on the bed, his eyes half open, as after a long and drowsy sleep.

'And then,' he said, 'she will control the whole city.'

6

Sorrel almost flew into her father's arms.

'Gently, my daughter,' he said. 'I don't feel quite myself.'

Sorrel laughed.

'But you're talking,' she said. 'You're actually talking. You slept. You're awake. You're *you!*'

'I feel much better than I have felt for a long time,' he agreed. 'That's true. Oh Sorrel, it has been a terrible thing. I have been in prison; trapped in my body like a prisoner in a cell. All the time I have been aware of what I was doing, what I was being made to do, but unable to stop it. It's been . . .'

He broke off and took a few deep breaths to steady himself.

'And Venetia?' Sorrel whispered.

'It is true. Everything this gentleman says is true.'

He nodded at Peter, who came and bowed graciously in front of Simono.

'At first, I could only wonder.' Simono said. 'I had not been sleeping. My illness had already begun, but I had no idea what was causing it. It was then that I wrote to Marko's father, begging him to come and help. Then one night, I found out what was happening to me. I looked up from my bed to see Venetia standing in the room. "How did you get here?" I asked her, but she did not answer. Then. Oh God! She climbed into bed with me, and she bit me! The last thing I remember was her teeth at my breast, and then I knew nothing more. But I did not sleep. I spent all night awake, and yet in the morning, I had forgotten what had happened. The following night was the same, and so it went on, again and again, but each night I could barely recall what had happened. I grew into myself and became mute, and then Alessandro arrived. By this point I was a prisoner stuck in the living cell of my body, silent and immobile. One night, I do remember, Venetia flew into the room, and was sitting on my chest, when your father came in, hearing some noise, I suppose. He cried out, and Venetia fled by the window, but as she went, he cried out. He had seen the reflection of Venetia in the dressing mirror, and I knew he had seen her true nature, not the young image she had been projecting, but her ancient and horrible reality.'

'But couldn't you get anyone to help?'

'I could do nothing. My voice had gone, my mind was in the control of Venetia, and all I could do was watch from the bars of my prison cell. I have had to watch, as oh God! As she has done all manner of unspeakable and bloody things.'

Marko watched in amazement at the change in Simono. He had only ever known him as a mute madman, now he could see the man who was Sorrel's father, he saw why she loved him. He was a kind, intelligent old man, with a delightful smile, though his eyes were still bloodshot and the pupils shrunken. Nevertheless, he was a different being altogether, and suddenly Marko was overcome by a terrible pang of loneliness and longing for his own father.

'Please,' he said, coming forward and kneeling by Simono. 'Do you know where my father is?'

Simono looked down at Marko, his eyes, puzzled, but with a flicker about them that showed he understood something.

'You are Alessandro's boy,' he said, and it was all Marko could do to nod.

'Then, my son, I have something difficult to tell you. I heard Bruno tell Venetia that your father is to be executed. What day is it? Is it the day?'

'The day of the Grand Procession.'

Simono hesitated.

'I fear we may be too late. Nicolo Bruno is one of the Three but also one of Venetia's servants. He has arranged things for her. To get rid of your father and any help he might have brought me. Alessandro has been accused of blasphemy and witchcraft and is to be hanged at noon, as the opening entertainment in the festivities.'

'My God!' Marko cried. 'It's almost noon.'

'Then hurry!' Simono said, grasping Marko's sleeve. 'Hurry. Save your father, for he is my good friend. Hurry!'

Marko looked at Sorrel, who kissed her father's forehead.

'Will you be all right, Father?'

'Yes! Now go! Hurry!'

Marko and Sorrel rose to their feet, and saw the door flapping wide, as Peter had already bounded away down the corridor towards the stairs.

'Hurry!' Marko called to Sorrel, and Dog scampered out of the room just as the door closed, and they were away into the city's carnival streets.

*I*t was not that it was far from the White Lion to the piazza and piazzetta of San Marco, but the streets were tiny and they were packed with merrymakers, all heading the same way.

Marko and Sorrel had quickly caught up with Peter, slowed by the crowd, but he began to push his way roughly past people. They in turn shoved and fought back, and it was hard going.

Suddenly Marko saw one of the devil masks on a face a few yards away, and he tugged at Peter's sleeve.

'The masks!' he said, and Peter nodded, pulling out three masks from under his cloak. He handed one to Sorrel and one to Marko. Peter had not chosen particularly well, having only had a moment in which everyone had been gazing at the boy splashing noisily in the canal.

Sorrel wore an exquisite green mask with many beautiful feathers, suitable for a young lady, and it looked well enough against her black dress, but Marko's mask was a bird-beaked doctor's mask, with a huge curved proboscis that kept knocking into people's shoulders and wigs, and Peter's was another lady's mask, of pink velvet and looked obviously out of place on the giant man swathed in black.

Nevertheless they felt safer inside them, and Marko was relieved that they pushed past two men in devil masks with no reaction from either.

They tried to hurry, and Peter led, bodily heaving people out of the way, until their complaints and angry cries threatened to turn into a brawl that would have stopped their progress altogether.

'What do we do?' Marko cried, his breath coming hot from under the beak of his mask. 'It's almost midday!'

'Let's try this way,' Sorrel said, and pulled Marko into a small side street.

'Wait!' he cried. 'Where's Peter?'

'Here,' Peter said, joining them. 'Now run.'

'Where's Dog?' Marko called, but he was nowhere in sight.

Sorrel's alley was by no means empty, but she had chosen well, and it was easier to move. They elbowed their way along, and moments later burst into the piazza of San Marco.

As they did, the great clock above their heads began to strike the hours of twelve.

'We're too late!' Marko wailed.

'No! Look! They're late! They won't start without the Doge.'

Away, across the smaller square of San Marco, by the water, they could see the incredible sight of the Bucintoro coming in to its mooring. It was an extraordinary sight, a ship the size of a small palace, entirely covered in gold leaf and red paint. Banks of oars projected from either side, gracefully propelling the Doge's ceremonial barge into harbour. Crowds of people watched, cheering and swaying, as Marko, Sorrel and Peter tried to push their way closer, but here the throng was at its most dense, and it was almost impossible to move.

Sorrel pointed to the far side of the piazzetta where two pillars soared into the sky. On one was a statue of a winged figure holding a spear, on the other a winged lion, the symbol of the city. As if in a nightmare, Marko watched powerless as the Bucintoro docked near the pillars, and a loud cheer rose from the crowd. The new Doge appeared on deck, made his way ashore, and was ushered through the gates of the palace. There was a long pause, and then he emerged again on the balcony of the palace, to the loudest cheer of all.

He lifted a small white handkerchief, then let it drop, and behind them, at the pillars, a drum began to sound. Now, Marko saw the gallows for the first time, and the sight of them spurred him on.

'Come on!' he cried. Peter was making headway at last through the crowd as people tried to move to a new position to get a better view of the Doge. He was dressed in magnificent ceremonial robes of deep red, with a comical little cap squatting on his head, above a hooked nose and wrinkled face.

Then, Marko's heart leaped. There, his hands tied behind his back, his head bowed, unshaven and unkempt, stood his father. Beside him stood the gallows.

'This way!' Marko called to Peter. 'To the pillars!'

'No,' Peter cried, 'There's only one way to stop this. Follow me.'

There was nothing Marko could do to stop him, and despite his urge to head for his father, Peter led them towards the gates of the palace.

'Look!' Sorrel called to Marko as they disappeared under the balcony. 'She's there! Venetia!'

There was no stopping Peter, who seemed to have recovered his strength once more. As he strode towards the guards on the gates of the palace, he unsheathed his sword. The guards lowered their spears, but they were mere ceremonial weapons; clumsy, ornate things with pennants dripping from them. Peter slashed the tips off them, and the guards ran back through the gates, screaming for help.

By the time any help came, Peter was halfway up an internal staircase that led to the first floor balcony, with Marko and Sorrel close behind. A few officials began shouting at them and made to step in their way, but then they saw Peter's sword flashing in front of him and ran for their lives.

They barged into one room and then another, finding them all deserted save for bewildered servants, until they stumbled into a room with a balcony, packed with officials, and other noblemen and women. There were the Council of Ten in their black robes, others in the same style but red, and there, framed by the light from the square stood the Doge himself, flanked by Nicolo Bruno, and Venetia.

Everyone turned at the commotion, and there were shouts from outside, and the sound of running footsteps. The doors on either side burst open and guards, real soldiers this time, poured into the room.

'There!' someone screamed. 'Get him!'

Three men ran towards Peter, but after a sudden singing sound had cut the air, all three lay on the floor clutching bloody wounds. The assembled crowd gasped, as Peter moved away from the bodies, towards the balcony. More men poured into the room, and within four strides Peter was by Venetia.

She was more beautiful than ever, and wore a fine dress of light green silk, low cut and with bare shoulders, clinging tightly to her figure, sweeping down to the floor. Her eyes danced, enchanting everyone, but Peter turned to address the room.

'Stop the execution!' he shouted.

Venetia stared at him, and then a smile spread across her face.

'That is a strange mask for a man,' she said.

Peter pulled the mask off and threw it to the floor.

'Do you know me better now?' he asked her, and lifted the tip of his sword to her throat.

She smiled again.

'I know you, don't I? How old you have become!'

Her voice stroked everyone in the room, like soft silk, reassuring, sensuous and loving. She glowed like amber in sunlight.

'And how young you are,' Peter said.

'And am I not beautiful?'

Peter said nothing, and Venetia screamed at him.

'Am I not beautiful?'

Her voice tore into the room and as it did so, everyone there felt a grave chill enter their bones.

More guards arrived, but no one seemed to know what to do. Several finely dressed noblemen crowded around the Doge, trying to get him off the balcony and out of the room, but the Doge seemed to think he should stay. Bruno was the only one who moved, screaming to the nearest soldiers.

'Kill that man! Kill him!'

Another five men ran towards Peter, who turned, brandishing the sword with such fury that they stopped dead.

'Another step and I'll take her head,' Peter warned and flicked the sword back towards Venetia, who stood motionless, her bare shoulders back, her head erect. Her hair fell in golden tresses around her long white neck, and the thought of her blood being spilled was enough to still the commotion in the room.

Marko and Sorrel edged around the side of room, forgotten in the drama unfolding.

Then Venetia spoke again, clearly and calmly.

'So why don't you?'

Peter turned to look at her.

'So why don't you kill me? You have been hunting me for years. You have wanted nothing else but to kill me, so why not? What is stopping you?'

'Nothing is stopping me,' Peter said, but Marko saw that the tip of the sword had just fallen an inch or two from where it had been before.

'Nothing?' Venetia said, her voice rippling around him, like the water in a limpid pool.

No one in the room spoke a word, all were frozen with fascination at the extraordinary sight of the beautiful young woman and the murderous old swordsman.

'So?' she said, goading him.

Peter tried to lift the sword, but again it lowered steadily more and more.

'Why doesn't he strike?' Sorrel said. 'What's wrong with him?'

Suddenly it dawned on Marko what was happening.

'He can't,' he said. 'It's her poison, it's infecting him like it's infecting everyone else. All he sees is a beautiful woman, not the creature she really is.'

It was true. Peter's sword tip was now resting on the floor, and his strength seemed to have drained from him entirely. As Peter gazed at Venetia, she changed again before his eyes, and took on another form, seeming to Peter to be the lovely olive-skinned girl from the long distant days of his memory.

'My love?' he crooned, as if in a dream. 'Is it you? Sophia?'

Around him, the guards began to close in, and Bruno roared at them to take Peter by force. From outside the sound of the executioner's drum suddenly stopped.

'Quick,' Sorrel said. 'We have to do something.'

Marko looked desperately around the room, and then he saw a glimmer of hope.

'Help me, Sorrel!' he cried. 'Quickly!'

He turned to the wall behind him where a huge mirror hung above a fireplace. Immediately Sorrel saw his plan, and each of them grasped one side of the enormous looking glass and lifted it from its hanging.

'Move!' yelled Marko, and so startled by the sound of his voice, the crowd parted as Marko and Sorrel pushed their way towards Peter and Venetia, shouting as they came.

'Look, Peter! Look!' Marko cried. 'Look in the mirror! Remember what she is! Remember!'

They saw Peter lift his head and turn to the mirror, where he had a perfect view of his own reflection, as well as that of the hideous old creature who stood behind him. A wizened, shrivelled hag, with coffin-white skin and eyes that bled evil.

Seeing her own true form, Venetia shrieked and howled.

'Remember, Peter! Look!' Marko called, and Peter nodded.

It took him a terrible act of will, as in slow motion he lifted the sword once more, and sighed a single word.

'Sophia.'

He swung the sword faster than life passes, but it was not fast enough, and Venetia leaned away from the blow, still hissing at her own ugliness. Peter tilted the blade as it flew, and jerked his sword-arm straight. He struck home, and something gave under the tip of the blade. Venetia was pierced, and screamed in agony, clutching her side where the sword had penetrated. She backed away, and then in a horribly quick motion like a scuttling beetle, she sped to the balcony.

It seemed as if she would jump, standing on the balcony's edge, but instead she stepped out into space, walking through thin air.

Peter hurried after her and Marko and Sorrel followed, as everyone else in the room pushed after them in alarm. In the piazzetta below, the crowd had seen the incredible sight and began shouting and calling to each other to witness this unbelievable thing.

They saw Venetia running across the thick rope suspended between the Doge's Palace and the tower of San Marco for the Flight of the Turk, and more sure-footed than a cat on a wide wall she went, skipping along.

It sent a shiver up Marko's spine just to see it.

Peter climbed onto the balcony, but turned to Marko as he went.

'She must not get away,' he said. 'Go and free your father. She can do no more evil here. You will need this.'

With that he thrust the sword into Marko's hands, and then he stepped out onto the rope to follow Venetia, who had by now already reached the bell tower.

'Peter! No!' Marko cried. 'Don't go!'

But Peter had already gone. His strength returning, his skills on the rope were as unnerving as Venetia's, and he ran, barely bothering to use his arms to balance.

As Venetia made the bell tower, she disappeared inside, then reappeared on the second much longer section of rope, a vast hawser that ran from the tower right out into the bay where it was made fast to the mast of an enormous sea-going galleon.

Peter gave chase, and as he ran, he noticed the blood on the rope. It was black, unlike any blood he had ever seen, but it was blood nonetheless, and for the first time in his long dance with the Shadow Queen, he really believed she could be killed.

As he swung around the bell tower's balcony and set off onto the second rope, he saw that she was over the open water of the lagoon, but he also saw that she was slowing, and long before she reached the galleon he was on her.

Marko strained to see exactly what happened, but, in truth, there was little to see. For a moment the two figures grappled briefly on the rope, and then they fell, tumbling into the water with a splash that could not be heard.

Everyone on the balcony, everyone in San Marco waited, and waited for the two figures who had fallen as one to reappear, but seconds ticked by and became minutes, and then they knew that they were not coming back.

Marko turned round, Sorrel beside him, and saw a room full of Venice's rulers inspecting him. The Doge stepped forward, and Bruno with him.

Marko stared at the sword in his hands, not knowing what to do with it, holding it clumsily and with great fear. And with great fear, he spoke to the assembled room.

He lifted the sword a little higher, and Sorrel saw with a failing heart that its tip was shaking.

'Stop the execution of Alessandro Foscari,' Marko said, in a small voice.

Bruno stepped forward, half a dozen guards flanking him, and then, wiping his hand across his forehead, he answered Marko.

'Yes,' he said, sounding confused. He shook his head as if waking from a long sleep. 'Yes, of course. Yes. We don't execute people in this city any more.'

Marko turned to Sorrel, and, letting the sword clatter to the marble floor, he put his arms around her.

'Thank God,' he said. 'Thank God.'

'No, Marko,' whispered Sorrel into his ear. 'Thank you. You did it. You really did do it.'

Suddenly there was another commotion by the door, a lady shrieked, as Dog bounded through the room, skidding on the marble floor and sliding into Marko's legs.

Marko looked at the ceiling.

'Wonderful,' he said.

'Oh, Dog,' Sorrel laughed, 'Where were you when we needed you?'

*O*f the moment when Marko ran to his father through the throngs of people in San Marco, and threw his arms around him, of the moment when Bruno followed as close behind as his short legs would carry him, and told the guards to release him, of the moment when Alessandro looked down into his brave son's eyes and told him that he was proud of him, Marko remembered little.

Of the moment when he and his father stood at the quayside with Sorrel and Simono, all four united at last, of the moment when Sorrel stepped forward with tears in her eyes and told him that she loved him, that she would miss him, of the moment when they stepped aboard the caravel bound for Piran and sailed away, Marko remembered everything.

He had smiled to see Sorrel and Simono together, as they stood on the quay. Simono had slept again for fourteen hours, and then another twelve the following night, and seemed well on the way to health. He had put a hand on Marko's shoulder.

'Thank you,' he said. 'I have no son, but I would willingly share you with your father.'

Alessandro laughed.

'You're welcome to him,' he said, putting an arm around his son. 'There's eight more like him at home!'

Marko smiled, but there was something troubling him.

'Signor Bellini,' he said. 'May I ask you something?'

'Anything.'

'I read your father's diary. The record of his illness. There is one part that has puzzled me. The last five words. Do you know . . . ?'

'Yes,' Simono said, '"Sunshine. Glass. Aurora. Wine. Simono." Yes, I know them, and they puzzled me for many years too, but now I know what they mean, for when I was trapped in the prison of my illness, I came to see that nothing else matters in life but the things you love. Those were the things my father loved more than anything in the world, and he wrote them down to preserve them for ever.'

Marko nodded, and smiled out of respect for Simono, but could find no words to say. He wondered what would be on his own list of five words, and then he knew one of them, as Sorrel stepped forward and whispered in his ear, and when she'd told him that she loved him, she told him something else.

'You know why you succeeded?'

Marko shook his head.

'Because you are your father's son. He taught you well, and though I thought you couldn't do it; you proved me wrong. And I'm glad.'

She stepped back again, wiping a happy tear from her eye, and then it was time to sail away.

'My son,' Alessandro said to Marko as the city disappeared from the receding horizon. 'What dangers have you faced to find me?'

But all Marko could think of was Sorrel, the girl he'd met who was never happy, but who he'd left smiling as she and her father waved goodbye and shouted their promises to see each other again. All the horrors he'd seen had gone now, all but perhaps one, and it was wrapped in oilcloth in the pile of luggage on top of which Dog lay snoozing.

Marko's thoughts turned to Peter. He struggled to even begin to understand what he was. But he had been there when they needed him, and he had seen his promise to the Shadow Queen through to the bitter end. Marko made his way to the side of the ship and gazed at the water, then began to untie something from their bundle of belongings.

Dog stirred and opened one eye, but shut it again quickly, already feeling very uneasy about sea travel.

'In three days we'll be home,' Alessandro said, coming up beside Marko, but Marko did not answer. He untied the oilcloth package, and took out the sword in its scabbard.

He pulled the blade a few inches clear and they gazed at the burnished metal. Was it evil, or was it good? Perhaps it had done much of both, Marko decided, but he knew what he had to do with it.

'It's beautiful, isn't it?' Alessandro said.

Marko nodded, then slid the sword back into its home, and wrapped it up tightly once more. Then, without ceremony, he turned and dropped it over the side, into the water.

'Yes, Father,' Marko said, 'but it is other things as well. And it doesn't belong with us.'

For a brief second the sword was visible beneath the water's surface, and then it was gone for ever, falling down, down and down to join the dark things lurking at the bottom of the deepest depths of the sea.

Death can come in many forms, but in Venice, death comes by water.

Author's note

Most people are familiar with the whys and wherefores of the vampire, but few realise how far a journey this nightmare figure has made. Today, we can recognise a vampire in film or book by pointed canine teeth, a cape maybe, or an accompanying bat. The suave, sometimes overtly attractive vampire of modern myth is very far from the original revenants of the folklore where these creatures originated. In fact, those first vampires are more like zombies with a bloodlust – being either horrific bloated corpses returned from the earth, or indistinguishable from their former living selves (and what a dangerous thing that would be). Sometimes even the bloodlust is absent; one vampire's preferred sustenance was noted to be milk! In many instances it is impossible to distinguish between what we would know as the werewolf and the vampire.

In writing this book I sought to capture the flavour of the early reports of vampirism, from the well known case of the Shoemaker of Silesia in 1591, to the unnatural dealings of Peter Plogojowitz in 1725, via a myriad of less popular stories collected from various eastern European countries: Pëtr Bogatyrëv's studies of the sub-Carpathian Rus and Alan

Dundes' unsurpassed anthropological collection, *The Vampire: A Casebook* repaid their reading many times over. I also urge you, if interested, to read Paul Barber's *Vampires, Burial and Death* which expounds a well-argued theory using forensic pathology on the possible bio-chemical origin of many of the traits of the vampire.

To make a coherent story I had to pick and choose from among hundreds of stories, many of which flatly contradicted each other – for there are almost as many types of vampire as there are vampire stories. One example would be the vampire's reaction to light – in some stories they may only appear at night, in others they are immune to any potentially destructive power of this force for good. Even giving vampires a name is not a simple thing: here are just a few of them; krvoijac, vukodlak, wilkolak, varcolac, vurvolak, liderc nadaly, liougat, kulkutha, moroii, strigoii, murony, streghoi, vrykolakoi, upir, dschuma, velku dlaka, nachzehrer, zaloznye, nosferatu – this last, quite familiar to us, is the vampire's name in that most unholy of vampire lands – Transylvania, literally the 'Land beyond the Forest'. Transylvania is in fact a beautiful place, with mountains, pastures and forest just as described here. And it is here that the stories of the Miorita, the Wedding of the Dead, and the Shadow Queen would be familiar to local people, though again I have had to take certain liberties for the sake of the story. Nowadays we know all these fabulous stories of the undead to be myth, though it might be wise to remember that there are still some people who do not agree with this conclusion. Even in the first few years of this new century stories have emerged from Romania of modern day belief in vampires; in 2004 the relatives of a Romanian man were prosecuted for exhuming his corpse, burning his heart and drinking the ashes in water, because they believed he had been visiting them in the night . . .

Marcus Sedgwick

London, 2006.

Revolver

Shortlisted for the Carnegie Medal

It's 1910. In a cabin north of the Arctic Circle, in a place murderously cold and desolate, Sig Andersson is alone ... alone except for the corpse of his father, frozen to death that morning when he fell through the ice on the lake.

The cabin is silent – until there's a knock at the door.

It's a stranger, and as his extraordinary story of gold dust and gold lust unwinds, Sig's thoughts turn more and more to his father's prized possession, a Colt revolver, hidden in the storeroom.

A revolver just waiting to be used...

'a punchily written, first-rate action story.' *Telegraph Review*

'an elegant, brilliantly executed tale'

Amanda Craig, *The Times*

White Crow

'Supposing you wanted to prove something, something important. Supposing you wanted to prove, for argument's sake,
that there is life after death.'

1798. 10mo. 6d. I believe he intends to practice some unholy rite, a summoning, a conjuration. A thing of magic.'

Two lives, two centuries apart. But they walked the same paths, lived in the same house, became obsessed by the same question.

When city girl Rebecca steps into the quiet streets of Winterfold that relentlessly hot summer her uneasy friendship with strange, elfin Ferelith sets in motion a shocking chain of events.

'an original and exceptional novel' *The Bookseller*

'an ingenious story full of tension, twists and horror. Reading it is like agreeing to a dare, compelling you to keep going into a frightening unknown.' *Sunday Times*